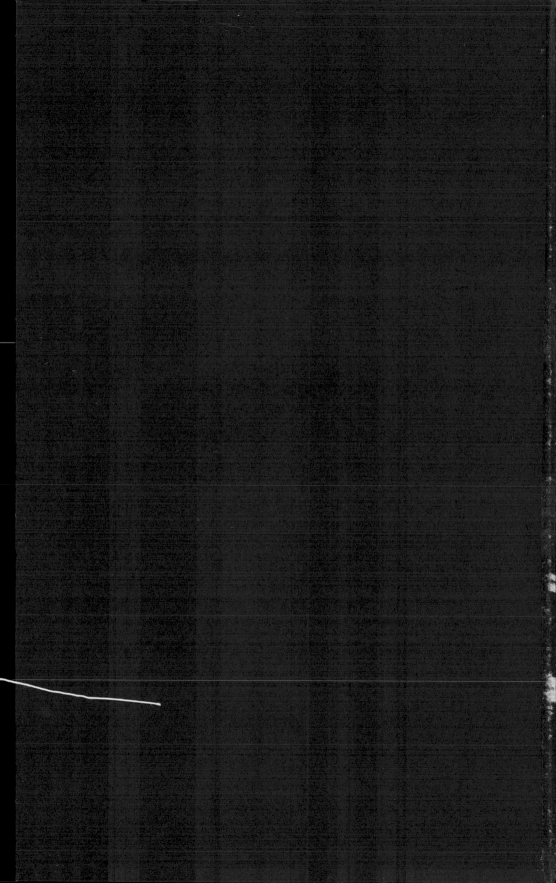

IN THE
FOOTSTEPS
OF
ADAM

ALSO BY THOR HEYERDAHL

The Kon-Tiki Expedition
Aku-Aku: The Secret of Easter Island
Viking America: The Norse Crossings and Their Legacy
The Ra Expeditions
Fatu-Hiva: Back to Nature
The Tigris Expedition: In Search of Our Beginnings
The Maldive Mystery
Easter Island: The Mystery Solved
Pyramids of Túcume: The Quest for Peru's Forgotten City
Green Was the Earth on the Seventh Day

In the FOOTSTEPS of ADAM

An Autobiography

Thor Heyerdahl

Translated by Ann Zwick

LITTLE, BROWN AND COMPANY

A *Little, Brown* Book

First published in Great Britain in 2000
by Little, Brown and Company

Copyright © 1998 by Thor Heyerdahl/J. M. Stenersens Forlag

Originally published in Norwegian under the title
I Adams Fotspor: En Erindringsreise

PICTURE CREDITS
All pictures are from the author's collection except:
7, 17, 30, 34, 38, 39, 43, 44, 47: Kon-Tiki Museum;
27, 28: Forsvarsmuseet; 26, 37: Jan Høst; 10, 12, 15, 22:
National Geographic; 29, 32: *Life*; 13: *MacLeans*.

A CIP catalogue record for this book
is available from the British Library.

ISBN: 0 316 85320 8

Typeset in Horley OS by M Rules
Printed and bound in Great Britain
by Clays Ltd, St Ives plc

Little, Brown and Company (UK)
Brettenham House
Lancaster Place
London WC2E 7EN

Contents

1

The Beginning

– Creation or evolution?

– Adam or apes?

– Do you believe in God or Darwin?

I'll pass these questions on. I have been asked them so many times – even by my own silent *aku-aku* in solitary moments of conversation with myself.

I progressed no further in my attempt to relax over my latest manuscript. I was waiting nervously for my bride-to-be to come out of the bathroom, dressed and ready to go to church.

Church? Was this me? Who in my youth could have sworn that one marriage would last a lifetime?

I had not lived up to my youthful ideals. Here I was, sitting in a hotel room in a desert town in the Western Sahara, waiting to get married for the third time. This time the venue was a Catholic cathedral in El Aaiún, the disputed former capital, where everyone today – except for the priest – was a Muslim.

My first wedding was in Norway, in the bride's own home in Brevik, where a young Lutheran minister from the state Church married us in the presence of two student friends and our parents. We left the next day and travelled to Fatu-Hiva in the Pacific Ocean to spend a year living as Adam and Eve in the primal forest, far from the comforts of civilization. Her name was Liv. An exceptional person. No one else I've met would have had the courage or strength to endure that, equipped as we were with our bare hands in the struggle for survival, isolated from everything and everyone in the rest of the world, and without radio, medicines or matches.

My second wedding was in New Mexico, where the sheriff in Santa Fe married us, in the presence of his pistol, conspicuous on the shelf beside him, and Bill, who was called in from the room next door as a witness. That was Yvonne. She was in a league of her own. I know of no one else with the stamina and courage to stand by my side through those long years of struggle against such merciless adversaries. Scholars were lashing out from all corners of academia, hostile to new knowledge and clinging to old dogmas.

And now the third wedding, when I came no further than writing the first sentences for an introduction to a new book before Jacqueline swept open the bathroom door and I threw down my paper and pencil to follow her down the stairs to the hotel lobby. In my trouser pocket I had a box with the two small wooden rings that I had carved from a small dried branch in the garden. I don't like jewellery on men – or on women for that matter – and I have never owned a ring, but this time it was part of the procedure. Protestant birth, death and divorce certificates from Norway and the United States were also required, all translated into Spanish and certified by both a priest and a bishop on the Canary Islands. These were necessary before I, born a Norwegian Protestant, could marry a woman born a French Catholic in Paris in a cathedral in Muslim, formerly Spanish, Western Sahara.

We flew down the stairs because the priests were waiting. Outside we were met by a world of desert sand, Berbers in long white robes and UN soldiers from sixty nations with blue berets and flags on their sleeves. This was the country where King Hassan II of Morocco had sent 250,000 countrymen armed with red flags in the 'green peace march' to prevent a referendum on the independence of Western Sahara. The situation had not changed since Jacqueline and I had been there five years earlier to study rock carvings in the desert. The only significant difference was that the UN had quietly reduced its troop presence to 500 men.

Outdoors, the morning sun was scorching.

'The bridal bouquet,' said Jacqueline, looking around a world devoid of florists or even green grass. She slipped into the back garden of the hotel and found a cluster of date palms and a lonely hibiscus bearing one large red flower, then we wound our way past Muslims and military personnel toward the large Catholic cathedral that had been left behind in this Islamic desert town by the Spaniards before their retreat from the country after the Second World War. She with the huge red flower, me with the wooden rings in my pocket.

As I was wondering how this was going to work out, avoiding looking at my watch, we caught sight of the cathedral. Two Catholic priests clad in white were waiting for us, one outside and the other inside the door. I am not a churchgoer, so this was unusual for me, but I had no prejudice against the indoor rituals others might observe in searching for their god.

As could be expected in this part of the world, which had once again become Islamic, the cathedral was empty, but on this occasion two of the priest's personal friends had come as witnesses. Only one, Don Enrique, was a Christian. He was the sole remaining representative of Spanish interests in Western Sahara. The embassy had been closed and the UN had unsuccessfully tried to bring about free elections on the matter of whether the country should be annexed to Morocco or declare itself a sovereign state. Coincidentally he had been born and raised on the Canary Islands, where we were also living; he came from Galdar on Gran Canaria, where Spanish archaeologists had recently uncovered thousand-year-old housing foundations similar to ones in Iceland from the Viking era. They had even found remnants of a Nordic-type sword. The other witness was a highly intellectual Arab doctor, Abdel Hafid. He explained, with a smile, that after experimenting with Christianity during his university years, personal conviction had brought him back to Islam.

I looked around. The pews were as empty as the naked white concrete walls, which lacked any depictions of religious figures. Where was Jesus, whose lifeless form was usually shown on the cross? He was not even represented on the altarpiece. Was this in consideration of any Jewish visitors who, lacking a synagogue, might be tempted to venture in for a quiet moment? This church was, after all, dedicated to the god of Abraham. Could this explain the lack of statues of Christian saints along the side walls. There was only one small chocolate-coloured statue of the Virgin Mary standing with her hands folded in humble prayer beside the pulpit.

Neither gold nor any other form of grandeur was on the altarpiece, but one could detect the very simple outlines of the Almighty Creator looming symbolically from his throne on the seventh day, the day of rest. He sat barefoot in a simple armchair, positioned above the heads of four humble evangelists who were depicted in the same simple sketches. A single dove of peace crowned the symbolism.

No one could be offended by such neutral motifs, where only the Almighty himself was dominant. The god up there on the wall was the common god of three religions that were still fighting bloody battles among themselves in the space age.

What are they fighting for?

I was torn away from my unreligious or cross-religious contemplations when a voice started singing in the vestry. Then the two priests appeared in a small procession, clothed in their beautiful white robes. The congregation, all four of us, rose, the two witnesses over by the long wall, and we – the bride and groom – with the two Catholic priests between us, facing the altar and the Lord on the wall. Now I could see there was no face on the painting. They've done it on purpose, I thought. To avoid offending Muslims, who forbid the representation of faces, especially of the Creator God who is described in both the Bible and the Koran as invisible. But then it dawned on me that the face was missing because a leak in the roof had worn away the paint, though only where the face should have been. I ached to ask the priests about it. Later it was confirmed that it was a leak. A coincidence. Sometimes one wonders if coincidences really exist.

Now I had to concentrate on the words being said in French and Spanish by the two priests, and the echo over the empty pews behind us. I suspected that the topic would be Adam and Eve, because the thin little priest, Father Loig, had asked me about creation when we came over on the plane from the Canary Islands the day before. Father Loig was interested in all sorts of things, but mostly in archaeology. It was he who had corresponded with Jacqueline and had enticed us with descriptions of rock carvings in the Sahara, when we went to El Aaiún five years ago. Now Jacqueline had lured him all the way back from Nouadhibou in Mauritania, where he had been relocated. Because of the lack of road connections he had flown via the Canary Islands. As he placed himself two steps above us, next to his superior, Father Acacio, and beneath the large bare feet etched on the wall above, he seemed to be rejoicing just as much as we were, even though this was something he himself had chosen to abstain from. The echoing atmosphere in the cathedral was charged. What would the two of them say and ask us to do? They both faced us with friendly smiles, and with the dove of peace above us the turmoil in Africa was a distant past. Next to his large and seemingly more formal Spanish colleague, who was like a giant protective teddy bear at his side, our small French friend in his long white clerical gown almost seemed like a child waiting for baptism. We knew little about the Spanish priest, except that he was responsible for this cathedral, which was Christianity's last fortress in the

UN-controlled Western Sahara and faced extremist Muslim terrorists just across the border with Algeria. Father Acacio was aware of
the explosive situation in this part of the Sahara because he had just
attended a congregation of bishops in Morocco with his friend the
Archbishop of Oran.

The hatred among different worshippers of the god of love
became a distant problem as the two white-robed priests stood in
front of us below the dove of peace. Father Loig's face lit up and
seemed to replace the one that had dissolved on the wall. He began
to speak about love. The origin of love. The creation of the world.

'The world was created when the Big Bang put the whole universe
into motion,' he said, looking down at me with a smile.

I stole a look at the other priest. With his calmly folded hands, he
seemed to be perfectly happy and unconcerned.

'The story of Adam and Eve and the creation of the world in six
days is not to be taken literally,' we were informed. It is written that
for God, a thousand years is one day and one day is a thousand
years. The whole Bible is filled with parables. Jesus himself almost
always spoke in pictorial language. Adam and Eve are symbols of
love, a self-portrait of the invisible god. An Adam and an Eve were
necessary to create a visible picture of the god of love.

Yes, I almost called out several times. I was in such agreement that
it was difficult to wait for him to ask me if I wanted to marry
Jacqueline. We had in fact spoken about the Big Bang when we were
on the plane from the Canary Islands the previous day. I had admitted that although science had found that the universe came into
existence by a powerful explosion, there still had to be superhuman
and supernatural powers to trigger such a conflagration, not least to
create order out of the ensuing chaos.

'The groom, who is a biologist,' he continued, 'has also said that
the heat from the Big Bang would have been so extreme that an act
of creation would have been required to make life on earth after-
ward.'

I had said that. And I quietly thought that if science could nick-name the creative powers 'Big Bang', then early cultures had an equal right to refer to the Great Spirit in place of what antiquity's founders of religions called Allah and God. I had to admit to myself that believing that a Big Bang could create swarms of stars was more in tune with the philosophy of the atomic age than imagining that a holy spirit hovering quietly over the waters could manage the same thing. The priest did not say so, but I thought it. And I wondered how a man who walked about gently in his white robe and lived in celibacy could speak with such warmth about love. To him it was not carnal love; it had to exist freely like a bird within him. Big Bangs can create hatred in living spirits, but they cannot create love in dead atoms and swarms of stars. We cannot find love with a microscope or remove it with a surgical knife, but we can carry it within us, whether we are striptease dancers or wearing the robe of a priest.

Glancing toward one of the witnesses by the wall, Father Loig had quoted a few passages from the Koran to demonstrate that the prophet Mohammed also had made use of the old parable about Adam and Eve. The invisible Allah created the world in the course of six *yawm*, and a *yawm* is not only one day but also a period of indefinite length. Christians started to depict the Creator God on church walls in the Middle Ages, but Muslims did not allow these in their mosques. The priests, one in French and the other in Spanish, were depicting a Creator God in accordance with the ancient scrip-tures. They were not talking about an old man with wrinkles and a beard, not of a man at all, not even a virgin. The symbolic self-por-trait of Our Lord was a man and a woman together as a couple, the visible symbol of a creative love. It was the primal power behind all matter, behind time and space, that set the universe in motion and spent six of its own days placing human beings on a sterile planet and giving them the ability to create new generations in a matter of nine months.

I was bursting. I wanted to say yes to everything, and when at last

I was asked if I wanted Jacqueline, I answered *Yes!* with such force that when the bride answered afterwards it sounded like an echo in the empty cathedral. Then all six of us embraced, and when Jacqueline and I left, our large wooden rings temporarily set on our fingers, we felt there was still hope for peace and understanding among all of us who followed in Adam's footsteps, even though the peace in Western Sahara for the time being was guarded by UN soldiers.

The same day, just a few hours later, there was an explosion in Algeria at the border with Morocco. The Archbishop of Oran, Father Acacio's friend, was killed by a bomb planted by extremist Muslim terrorists.

Small terrorist groups and great military powers believe in both God and Satan. And in big bangs.

Science looks up at a field of stars with telescopes and inspects atoms with microscopes, and finds no hiding place for heaven or hell. Science cannot help us sort out the difference between good and evil.

2

Time for Reflection

Our Lord did not have to wait for the next day's papers to receive news about the murder of the Archbishop of Oran. One of his most loyal servants had sent him his last greeting as he fell to his death under the sign of the cross, while another person had prostrated himself toward Mecca and given thanks for the success of the deed. The two shared a belief in the god of love who had breathed life into their mutual forefather, Adam.

This time a Muslim had killed a Christian in Africa. According to the same paper, things were rough in Europe too. In the former Yugoslavia, where Tito had secured peace between religions, Christians and Muslims were now slaughtering one another by the thousands. On the emerald isle on the other side of Europe, where there were few if any Muslims, Christians were beating one another to death because some said their evening prayers to Our Lord directly, while others went through the Virgin Mary. Christians and Muslims and Jews all agree that we have a common heritage. Adam and Eve had two sons, Cain and Abel, and as soon as they were two contenders, one beat the other to death because the smoke from his sacrificial fire to Our Lord did not rise in a straight column.

Up in the Nordic countries we were no longer as passionate about questions of religion. We were finished with the worst, had got rage out of our systems in the Viking era. But around the year 1000, when the gospel spread up to us from the Middle East, it didn't take us long to find our long ships and sail down to Jerusalem to behead Muslims. As a good Norwegian schoolboy I had heard, admired and read Snorri and the *Sagas of the Kings*, which told how our forefathers took off on pilgrimages to the Holy Land in the eleventh and twelfth centuries, and how in the course of their journey they slaughtered Muslim infidels along the coasts of Portugal, Spain and North Africa. Some of them might have sought shelter in the good harbour of Oran in Algeria, and taken revenge in advance for what had been taking place while we were hearing about Adam and Eve behind the closed doors of the cathedral. It was under the sign of the cross that the mighty King Sigurd Jorsalfar went on a Viking voyage to the Holy Land and raided towns along the coast of Africa before clearing the way for Christian crusaders to Jerusalem. He gave all the gold that his men robbed from the followers of Allah to the Patriarch of the Holy City and to the Pope in Constantinople and contributed his whole fleet of Viking ships and most of his warriors in the Mediterranean to fight for the Pope against the followers of Mohammed. He himself, and the rest of his party, rode home through Europe on horseback. His predecessor on Norway's throne, St Olav, had already been canonized by the Pope because he Christianized Norway by beheading any countrymen who refused to believe in Jesus. History shows that Christians are not always concerned about living by the rules of their faith as long as they believe in them.

Jacqueline and I were to return to our new home on the Canary Islands the day after the wedding. Father Loig was returning to his post further south in Africa on the same flight. By a misunderstanding we were informed that there was only one seat available on the plane from Casablanca, so Jacqueline went with the two priests to the airport to see one of them safely onboard. Father Loig was already on board the aeroplane when news of the murder in Oran reached El Aaiún. We did not hear about it until that evening from Father Acacio. He remained calm, showing no signs of hatred or vengeance, and even less anxiety for himself. He was left to himself in a cathedral in a country where he alone prayed to God, and everyone else prayed to Allah. The Church has always had martyrs, he said. Martyrdom did not start with the Arab Mohammed who was born when Christianity had already fought for its existence for over 500 years. The Church had been losing martyrs for almost 2,000 years. And there was a new Christian ready to replace his friend, Archbishop Claverie in Oran.

My happiness was no less complete when Jacqueline left for the desert airport. The light from the morning sun shone peacefully over the Sahara's eternally young sand dunes, which concealed so much history and human speculation. I suddenly realized that I had no work to complete and that I was as free as a bird. No duties and no schedule. Although this had not been planned, it was an unexpected and greatly appreciated treat.

I found a deck-chair in a corner of the hotel's roof terrace, where I could flee from the ever present noise of transistor radios and enjoy a rare silence beneath a blue sky. Only the fringed tops of the garden's date palms and the soundless birds in the sky were high enough to enter my range of vision. Time vanished as it does on a raft on the ocean. No mail. No telephone. Just a perfect silence that invited me to let my thoughts wander.

'Now, for once, you can relax,' Jacqueline had said when she left me at the hotel. She claimed that I hadn't had one week without some project or other on the go during the five years we had known each other. She was probably right, but it was because my plan of action was just as much a hobby as it was work.

People might have the impression that I'm a stubborn adventurer who jumps from one raft to the other, from one academic battle to the next. In reality I am a very peaceful person, who is primarily interested in finding solutions to problems, in getting to the bottom of unanswered questions. The more I do and the more I see, the more I realize the shocking extent of ignorance existing among the scholarly circles that call themselves authorities and pretend to have a monopoly on all knowledge. This has to be dealt with.

I have to admit that if I had been unsuccessful every time I gave my all to a new expedition or a new enquiry, I would probably have given up and found something else to do. But every time I make a discovery that I thought I could and should be able to make, I become even more interested in continuing and have fun. During those times, it is not only about scientific curiosity, it's also about joy.

Nevertheless, Jacqueline was right. I had barely completed an expedition or a book before I started on a new one. There were never any breaks between travels, mail and manuscripts. Crazy, I thought.

Crazy.

I thought I suddenly heard an echo inside me. Maybe it's my aku-aku, I said jokingly to myself. I remembered drowsily that the inhabitants of Easter Island had told me that I had an aku-aku. All of their forefathers, and many who were still living, had an aku-aku, an invisible companion who offered good advice whenever necessary. No one else but a capable aku-aku could have told me to come to them on their deserted island and start excavating in the right places in order to find statues that no one knew about.

I thought with pleasure about the joyous months working with the first archaeological excavations on Easter Island. At that time it had neither a harbour nor an airport. It was the loneliest island in the world, the population was barely 1,000 and the island was visited only once a year, when a navy ship from Chile came on a two- or three-day visit at Christmas, bringing provisions for the descendants of the people who had raised the hundreds of gigantic stone statues that were strewn about the terrain. Today there is both a harbour and an airport on Easter Island, but when we arrived in the 1950s and anchored the expedition's ship outside Anakena Bay, each and every family survived solely on the sweet potatoes they could dig up from the earth, and the fish that the ocean offered.

Just like this unexpected opportunity, it had been a time when I could let my thoughts run free. I could relax and think about the seafarers and former bearers of tradition while we excavated their works of art or drowsed during the breaks up in the quarry. Timeless days and nights. In my thoughts I floated back there, with the same blue sky over me. Soon I was neither here nor there, and allowed myself to fabulize. I thought I could hear the voice of the aku-aku.

Ia-ora-na. Kaoha-nui. Good day. It's been a long time.

I had to smile to myself. We were obviously both in a good mood and ready for a joke. I haven't heard from you for a long time, I thought. Has it been difficult for you to keep up after I left that peaceful Easter Island?

I have been with you the whole time; you are the one who has been absent. First you brought me from Polynesia to the jungles of South America, then on timber logs and reed rafts over three oceans, and now you have parked me on a roof in a desert town in the Sahara? What is the meaning of all this? Are you an adventurer or a scientist?

With the exception of four years as a volunteer in the struggle against the Nazis during the war, I have done nothing but scientific research my whole life, ever since I started studying biology at the age of eighteen. The adventures have simply been added attractions. I never seek adventure, but I gladly accept it as an additional pleasure when experimenting with the tools of antiquity or searching for unknown cultures by disproving former dogmas about prehistoric vessels.

People say you've been lucky.

It isn't as much a question of being lucky as it is a question of avoiding being unlucky.

At this moment Jacqueline came back. It was true, I was lucky. It would have been unlucky not to have met her.

We lay and dozed in our reclining chairs on the roof overlooking the Sahara and I could not keep the aku-aku away.

Isn't this a little too much? First you go on a honeymoon to Fatu-Hiva, then you go to Easter Island with another bride, and now you are arranging a wedding in the Sahara – as if you had become a Muslim. The third time! This has to be enough.

Yes, this was definitely enough. Nine lives and three marriages; there have to be limits. And no, I had not become a Muslim. It was here that Jacqueline and I had truly become acquainted, thanks to the priest who showed us the stone carvings.

Do you believe in Allah?

Allah has different names in different languages. I think that the Christian God is the Jewish Jehovah and the Muslim Allah.

The issue is not about believing in the Bible or the Koran. It is about believing in the god that the authors of these books believed in, and both books are about exactly the same god. I learned an evening prayer from my father. He was Norwegian and he never mentioned Allah, but neither did he use the word 'God'. It was simply 'Our Lord'.

At school we had a priest who taught religion. I was fascinated by Adam and Eve, as well as Noah, with all the animals. And I also paid attention when it came to Jesus, who understood nature and said something like, 'Look at the birds on the field, no prince is more spectacularly clad than them.' But when the minister began telling us how Jesus went to a wedding and turned water into wine, I figured he was mistaken and raised my hand.

'Thor,' he said happily, 'what have you got to say?'

My father was the director of the town brewery, so I ached to come with a correction. 'I don't think it was wine,' I said. 'I think it was beer, because it tastes better and is healthier!'

The priest did not like that. Furious, he sent me out into the hall where I had to stand alone, freezing in the winter cold, while my classmates heard about all the strange things Jesus had done.

Ever since ancient times we have honoured the same god that Abraham brought from Ur. That we shouldn't lie, steal or kill is something we've heard ever since Moses came down from the mountain with the stone tablets. But we still argue about whether we should pray to Abraham's god under the star of David, under the sign of the cross, or under Mohammed's half-moon; whether we should honour Our Lord's creation on Friday, Saturday, or Sunday; whether it is a sin to eat pork and drink alcohol, right or wrong to consume the flesh and blood of Jesus. Things like this, which are not mentioned in the laws of Moses, we continue to argue and debate. And by doing so, we show our disdain for everything that Moses, Jesus and Abraham represented.

On the raft voyages, while apparently hovering motionless in the centre of a circle of blue sky and blue ocean, without television or hearing the drone of aeroplanes, you find the time to do some old-fashioned thinking. In 1947, when we set out with the balsa raft, *Kon-Tiki*, on our journey across the Pacific Ocean to Polynesia, the American ambassador in Peru gave me a Bible to keep on board. His equally well-meaning military attaché wagered a case of whisky that we would never return. Although the Bible had remained undisturbed in a box beneath me, the good Lord helped us safely ashore on the Raroia atoll 101 days later. The attaché was relocated, so we never received the whisky, but the Bible came in handy later.

Kon-Tiki's crew consisted of five Norwegians and a Swede, all Protestants, and when the ocean swelled over us as we hit the atoll, I heard Torstein yell to Knut, 'All you believers had better pray now.' I think half of those aboard prayed.

Twenty-two years later, when we launched the reed ship *Ra* in Morocco in an attempt to cross the Atlantic Ocean, we were seven men aboard with totally different backgrounds. I wanted to show that it was possible to live peacefully together in cramped quarters and under stress, even though we didn't have the same skin colour, political views or beliefs. For almost two months, Arab and Jew lay shoulder to shoulder in the small bamboo hut, and the navigator from the United States lay with his face against the feet of the doctor from the Soviet Union. The Arab from Egypt was not a Muslim, but a Copt, from the world's oldest Christian congregation. Abdullah, a Buduma from Central Africa, was black as coal and not an Arab but a Muslim. This time, in his honour we were given a copy of the Koran as a gift from the Pasha in Safi, but Abdullah was illiterate, so it stayed with my Bible until we brought it along again on our next journey, when we had a Muslim aboard who could read. He was a Berber from Morocco who used the Koran every day.

Both the Bible and the Koran that accompanied us over the ocean ended peacefully side by side in the bookshelf behind my desk, in the company of other primary sources about the development of the civilizations of the world. I wasn't done with any of them.

Many wondered why I chose Abdullah, from the interior of Africa, to join us on the first Atlantic journey with a prehistoric reed ship. One doesn't normally venture that far inland to hire sailors, and Abdullah had never been closer to the ocean than the point at which the Sahara meets the jungle, right in the heart of the continent. But in Egypt papyrus reeds had become extinct until the Papyrus Institute in Cairo reintroduced it after the *Ra* journeys, and boat builders who worked with papyrus reeds were found only in the inland seas of Ethiopia and in the Central African republic of Chad.

I have often found the preparations for an expedition more problematic than the journey itself. Sometimes they are also more dangerous. There was political unrest in Chad when I arrived with a

French photographer to look for reed-boat builders. In Fort Lamy, the capital, I rented a jeep in order to follow the long caravan route to Lake Chad, where the Buduma lived, many on floating reed islands out in the lake. We were warned against risking the journey and told that heads from decapitated nurses had recently been found along the roadside. Dusk had already fallen when we arrived at the village of Bol on the bank of Lake Chad. The village consisted of beautiful dome-shaped huts made from papyrus reeds, and at the end of the road there was a shed where wayfarers could spend the night for free. Three walls, a floor and a roof, all of cement.

We were sleeping on the cement floor when I woke up to the low sound of distant music, rhythmic drums and tunes from a wind instrument. The village had seemed lifeless and deserted, and my curiosity was aroused as I stepped quietly out into the dark of night. I stumbled on a camel who responded with a hoarse scream, and stood still for a long time before I felt safe again and fumbled on between the hut walls.

The rhythms from the drums grew louder as I rounded a corner and saw an open square. I could make out the shadows of figures in flowing robes dancing around a solitary kerosene lantern. They moved to the music in a staccato rhythm. As my night vision improved, I also caught a glimpse of the two musicians. Standing in the impenetrable African darkness, leaning against the wall of a hut, I was convinced that I was invisible in the night.

To my astonishment I saw that one of the figures slowly separated himself from the circle and came dancing in my direction. I was hoping that he wouldn't come close enough to discover me when I saw that he had drawn a short sword and was approaching me, fencing in my direction without losing the rhythm. An icy shiver ran through me when I realized that not only had I been seen but that my white body was the target he was dancing toward.

Around the kerosene lamp the others continued unaffected with their dance. The threatening figure had come so close that the sword could be thrust into me at any time. I was unarmed and couldn't escape. I saw no way out, but instinctively I started moving my feet to the beat of the drums, and before I knew it I was standing there dancing with the man who held the tip of his sword against my chest. He seemed to be under the influence of a drug. Slowly he started to dance backward while I followed closely after him, right up against his sword. When we reached the circle it opened and made room for us. The sword was put back into the sheath, and we danced on, behind one another and with the others.

In the glow from the kerosene lamp I caught sight of a generously proportioned female standing with the musicians, and to my amazement I saw that the dancers seemed to be growing tired. One after the other they stepped out of the circle, sweaty and panting, each one offering up a little coin. Toward the end there were only two of us left, and finally I was dancing alone. I had obviously won some kind of competition, and to feel totally safe I put a bill into the bowl where the others had dropped coins. The winner's trophy was the lush beauty, and everyone wondered why I didn't bring her along when I fumbled back to the cement floor.

The next morning it was clear that I had won great status in the village, and amongst my many new friends I met the reed-boat builder Abdullah.

Abdullah had much to learn on his first journey out of the heart of Africa, and we had much to learn from him. He was the only one who had ever seen papyrus, and he knew how to build a reed boat, with lifted curves in the bow and stern so it could dance over and between the waves. Abdullah had never seen any other expanse of water nor any bigger waves than those on Lake Chad at the southern end of the Sahara. On board, Abdullah trusted Allah more than he trusted us, who had never seen a papyrus boat before, but to be on the safe side he also tied a small leather pouch containing magical rocks and leopard claws around his waist. Thus equipped, he scared the senses out of the rest of us by balancing recklessly and fearlessly and without a rope, on the slippery edge of the reed boat. If he slipped into the water, he would simply grab laughingly on to a bundle of reeds and pull himself back on board.

Allah had brought Abdullah into the world in a part of Africa that had seen better days. The Sahara was receding southwards at the speed of a couple of kilometres a year. Some 5,000 years ago, aboriginal inhabitants further north in the desert had decorated reed boats with paintings of people hunting hippopotamus on the cliff walls in the Tassili Mountains. About 2,000 years ago, North Africa was still the wheat basin of the Roman Empire. When Abdullah came into the world, endless sand dunes from the north had already passed Lake Chad in Central Africa and we were slowly pressing on further into the tropical jungle. Not a bush to be seen around the lake, just sand and lush green papyrus reed at the water's edge and on floating islands that drifted about carrying people and livestock as passengers.

While the rest of us live in a world of skyscrapers and astronauts, Abdullah and his two countrymen whom I brought to Egypt to build an ancient vessel had never walked up a flight of stairs before I got them onto the aeroplane in the capital, Fort Lamy. They had grown up in beautiful dome-shaped reed houses with earth floors, and when we were on our way up to the third floor of a hotel in Khartoum they lifted their legs as if they were climbing the side of a mountain. Flown out of a world where a mat on the floor was the only furnishing, one of them put his head underneath the bed until Abdullah, who spoke French, explained that they were to sleep on top. And having seen the toilet filled with clean water, it was with deep suspicion that they let themselves be told about its use. Abdullah reacted to everything with a stoic calm, and before we reached Cairo no one could tell by looking at my three Buduma companions that they had made the leap into the atomic age in less than a week. That is all the time it took. But both their teeth and their eyes glowed in the reflection of the moon when at night we arrived at our camp by the pyramid of Cheops. I had chosen this site in order to build the papyrus ship according to the old Egyptian illustrations. They stared stiffly at the pyramid.

'Who lives there?' Abdullah asked, noticing the difference in dimension from the tents next to him, where we were going to live.

'No one,' I explained. 'It's a grave.'

'How many are buried there?'

'Just one.'

That was too much for Abdullah. 'Those Egyptians,' he said with disbelief. His scepticism did not change when he learned that the Egyptians had built this more than 3,500 years before the birth of Mohammed.

According to the Koran, as a Muslim Abdullah could have four wives. The financial responsibility for the beautiful Buduma woman he left at Lake Chad fell on me. But not many days had gone by at our camp in Egypt before Abdullah invited all of us to Cairo for an Arabian wedding with belly dancing and all sorts of wind and string instruments. I was trusted with the task of stuffing banknotes down between the bride's breasts, and now, before our arrival at the launch site in Morocco, I had to provide for two of Abdullah's women in different parts of Africa. He was already heading rapidly toward his third marriage with a veiled Berber woman in the port city of Safi when we managed to get him on board the reed ship and postpone the wedding until the voyage was finished.

This was in the spring of 1969, at the same time that American astronauts were in the final preparations for the first journey to the moon. NASA had offered to install some equipment on our reed ship so that we could talk directly to the astronauts when they landed up there while our journey was still underway down here. To experiment with a papyrus ship named after the sun god Ra and launch it studded with antennas in order to talk to people on the moon seemed too much of a parody, so I declined regretfully but firmly. To my great consternation, the day before we were scheduled to leave, a representative from NASA appeared on the pier in Safi with a box of moon equipment. My refusal had not been taken seriously. I remained firm, and we left the friendly man with the box. He would be flying home over the Atlantic while we started our journey across the same ocean in our reed ship.

On board, Abdullah proved to be an intelligent man, and he had a quicker mind than most. We had barely left Safi before he learned the use of the compass so that he could pray in the direction of Mecca. Wind and currents gave us the same steady course westward that Columbus had followed, so Mecca remained more or less in the same position. On the other hand, an unexpected problem arose at sunrise the first morning out on the Atlantic. Abdullah reported that someone had spilled salt in the water around us. He stretched overboard and according to procedure washed his face and arms up to his elbows in honour of Allah. Then we heard a scream. Not only was the water salty, it was dirty as well! Black clots were floating in a thin layer of oil on the surface, more visible out in the water than on the dark black face of Abdullah. Abdullah's religious cleansing ceremonies required clean water. Out of everyone's respect for Allah, the problem was first solved by giving Abdullah a small extra portion of drinking water from our clay mugs. In extreme conditions, the Koran permitted a traveller to clean oneself with sand, but the Sahara was already far behind us and quickly disappearing from our sight.

We assured Abdullah that we would soon be sailing in the same crystal clear water I had seen from *Kon-Tiki* twelve years before. At that time we had crossed 8,000 kilometres of the Pacific Ocean without noticing a single lump of oil or any sign that there were other people on this planet than the six of us.

It was Abdullah who came with the first terrible warning: the ocean was in the process of being polluted! And there is only one ocean, because the Atlantic Ocean is connected to all the others.

Thor Heyerdahl

The continents lie like islands in one interconnected world ocean. Day after day Abdullah and the rest of us scooped up lumps of oil, some as small as grains of rice, others as large as potatoes and oranges and often overgrown with barnacles or carrying tiny crabs as passengers. Having looked forward to showing my new friends the wonderful crystal-clear world ocean we had grown to know intimately from the balsa raft, I became so alarmed that I sent the first report about the mounting pollution of the world ocean to the United Nations Secretary-General U-Thant. He had allowed us to sail under the UN flag because we wanted to represent a microcosm of some of what the UN stood for. One world in one ocean.

Abdullah had no other complaints during his first encounter with the ocean. To the contrary he cheered knowingly when he caught sight of the first whale, shouting: 'Hippopotamus on the port side!'

We could not complete our crossing in our first papyrus boat. We were just amateurs. In the twentieth century the world's leading experts were the scientists in Cairo, who had shown us the ancient Egyptian illustrations and wall paintings of reed ships with detailed rigs, and the Buduma from Lake Chad, who carried on the ancient papyrus boat-building tradition but who had not constructed them to resist ocean waves.

None of them understood why the pharaohs had sickle-shaped ships, often with a tall and inwardly bent stern. Everyone was convinced that the elegant inward curl on the stern was there for aesthetic reasons, and since it was structurally independent, the boat builders from Chad removed an important rope, which was strung like a bowstring down to the deck. Little did we know that this would be the Achilles heel of the reed ship *Ra*. The ship lost its elasticity and could not ride the ocean waves, and the reed bundles began tearing loose. When we approached Barbados, it was no longer possible to keep the papyrus bundles together.

*

Exactly one year after *Ra* was launched in Safi, the construction of *Ra II* was completed in the same harbour in Morocco. We were ready for another go at the Atlantic.

Everyone who had been on the first *Ra* voyage volunteered again: Abdullah from Chad, Norman from the United States, Yuri from the Soviet Union, Carlo from Italy, George from Egypt, Santiago from Mexico and myself from Norway. But this time I had increased the number to eight by squeezing Kei from Japan in the small bamboo hut on the reed deck.

Abdullah had waited at his bride's home in Egypt during the year that had passed. Now he was set on marrying the Berber woman whom he had left at the dockside the last time. Then, out of the blue, a telegram arrived from the Norwegian embassy in Cairo: Abdullah had become a father. To a son! Allah had awarded him a gift that no new trip to America could match. Abdullah was back in Cairo faster than an American rocket could reach the moon. When we stood on the reed deck and waved farewell to him, a new crew member was with us waving to the crowd of people on the pier, a Berber from the Atlas Mountains. The day before, this soon-to-be seafarer had been a porter at our hotel in Safi. He had never seen the ocean before he came down from the Atlas Mountains, but he too was a Muslim and almost as black as Abdullah from the desert winds and the high mountain sun.

Madami could read, and in his sack he brought his swimming trunks, his bathing mat and the Koran in Arabic. Abdullah had been the first to cry out about the pollution in the ocean, and now Madami was given the task of keeping daily records of the pollution we saw, scooping up the oil lumps we passed with a net. Once again we were sailing under the UN flag, and this time the Secretary-General had asked us for a pollution report as well as samples of the black clumps we had seen. We complied and collected large and small lumps of oil for forty-three of the fifty-seven days of our journey across the Atlantic. This time we made it all the way to Barbados. U-Thant enclosed our report as 'Appendix A' in his *Report on the State of the Oceans* at the first UN Environmental Conference in Stockholm that same year, 1970.

I got along well with Neil Armstrong, without the NASA antennas, when we later met to confirm before a World Wildlife Fund congress in London that man lives on a very small planet that we can easily destroy. There is so little land and so much ocean on earth that Neil said it looked like a small blue planet from the moon. And the world ocean was in itself so small that you could drift across it on a reed boat without a motor in the matter of a few weeks. Just a little faster than the lumps of oil.

3

In Too Deep

Still drowsy with sleep, I woke up on the roof of the hotel and looked out over the desert. Jacqueline was reprimanding me for having dozed off in the sun.

'Remember the hole in the ozone layer,' she said. 'It's no longer like when you were a boy.'

When we went to lunch, I told her how once in my youth I had made a futuristic caricature of what bathing would be like when people had destroyed the thin atmosphere of the planet. Back then there were no green movements, but some scientist had pointed out something that made me think that the human battle against nature could ruin the perfect balance in the composition of the air, a balance that ocean plankton and virgin forests had created before the birth of humans.

'How in the world could you be thinking about that rather than the team who might win the Norwegian soccer championship?' Jacqueline asked. During the five years she had known me she had thought I was relatively normal.

How had I started thinking along those lines? Not an easy question. When we returned to the roof, we moved our chairs so that our

heads would be in the shade and Jacqueline fell asleep before she was
given an answer.

I was so rested that I had no need for my usual ten-minute afternoon siesta. Instead I lay wide awake and watched the birds fly
beneath the blue mantle of sky, reminding me of my boyhood days,
when the world was eternal and without limitations. We had plenty
of time then. No one rushed for anything, except myself perhaps,
when I was late for school. And I almost had to run to keep up with
my father on the rare occasions I was allowed to go along with him to
his office at the brewery. But, swinging his cane, he walked briskly to
get exercise and to look active and fit to those he met and tipped his
hat to in passing. Not because he was in a hurry.

Pollution? Not in the small town of Larvik. Its white wooden
houses were built on steep slopes, and clean air blew in from the
backdrop of forests. Thousands of Larvik's windows looked over the
fjord, which in turn opened to the great ocean. The town thrived on
the sea and the forest, including extensive shipping across all the
oceans beyond the horizon and whaling in Antarctica. Norway's
only beech forest lay behind the town, and endless pine forests
stretched along the Farris Lake and far into the inland mountains of
Norway. The only industries were Treschow's large pulp mill, Alfred
Andersen's ship yard and the brewery with its pleasant fragrance by
the town square. The streets of the town were swept with brooms,
and a soot-black chimney sweep kept the chimneys clean. In my
earliest childhood they swept horse manure from the streets. A discarded orange peel, a piece of paper or a rusty tin can thrown by the
side of the trails in the woods caused annoyance. We could drink
from any running stream.

These were ideal surroundings for children. Almost everyone had
back gardens to play in, and there were orchards with wooden fences
to climb on and, where the town's cobblestone streets ended, unlimited playgrounds in the woods and on the beaches.

My parents had moved there from what they considered to be

Norway's major cities; my father from the capital, Oslo, which was then still called Kristiania, and my mother from Trondheim. They must have caused quite a few small-town eyebrows to be raised at a time when divorce was seen as exclusive to the theatrical world. My free-thinking mother had already been through two divorces when my conservative father divorced his first wife to marry her.

A competent businessman, my father had started his own brewery. When he began to bottle the local mineral water he received King Haakon's permission to name the spring water after him. Later he went into business with a colleague and they ran what became the town's only brewery. The other one was abandoned and became an exciting playground for us boys, with its large darkened halls, vaulted cellars, empty stables and huge yard behind tall wooden fences. The property reached right up to our own back garden.

It was here that I discovered myself as an individual, separate from my mother's warm body. It was an autumn night at the outbreak of the First World War. I believe I even recall the wail of the autumn storms, accompanied by whip-like cracks from the flagpole rope in the garden. I was afraid of the dark and quite cowardly as a boy.

You, who were so overprotected?

Perhaps for that very reason. I had old parents. They were so afraid of something happening to their only child that I was given the impression that everything was dangerous. Other children in the neighbourhood were allowed to go to the docks alone and to play outside after dark, but not me. Other boys were allowed to use an axe to make a bat or a sharp knife to make a bow and arrow, but not me.

If there was anything that my parents agreed upon – except for having produced and spoiled me – it was a belief in progress, my father because both his own father and his uncle had been pioneers in bringing electricity and farming machinery to the country, and my mother because she was a Darwinist and believed that all progress led in the direction of something even better. In his family album, my father had shown me that his forefathers came from the large forests bordering Sweden, and that they could be traced back twelve generations as landowners until his father and uncle had moved to the capital and established Heyerdahl & Co. They set up the first telephone system in the country between their office and their warehouse. My father had saved a newspaper clipping from Oslo in 1880, describing the first time an electric light bulb was demonstrated to the city's inhabitants: 'And from as far up Karl Johan's Gate as could be seen from the fire house, the light glowed like a shining star, in contrast to the gas lamps that shone with a red glow, like an oil lamp compared to a gas flame.'

Two years later they crowned their work when my grandfather, a major in the civilian national guard, led a royal procession up to the palace while his brothers lit two light bulbs in front of the building. The newspaper *Aftenposten* wrote: 'The facade of the palace emerged from the dark as if by a stroke of magic, and shone in a bright light as if the rays from the sun had fallen upon it. The audience greeted this sudden and unexpected revelation from the world of light with shouts of appreciation.'

And then you turn up two generations later, without matches, in an attempt to return to nature?

I've probably inherited a little from my mother as well. Her family leaned toward a different path, away from the city. Her oldest brother studied theology and wanted to be a country minister. He was very absent-minded. This was during Norway's union with Sweden, and when he folded his hands to begin his first sermon, he said, 'Our Father, who art in Sweden . . .' A statement like that did not sit very well with Norwegian farmers at the time, and his father brought him back to the city. Two of my mother's other brothers studied philosophy in Germany. When they returned to Norway, under the influence of Rousseau, they each bought land and built farmhouses out in the wilderness under the Sylene Mountains. One gave up, but not the other. Mother told me that she received letters from him describing how he was sitting on top of a manure wagon reading Schopenhauer. His children built a road for cars in order to bring civilization into the Tydalen valley.

At an early age I began wondering whether the word 'progress' was leading us astray. It was first used to designate something that moved forward toward something better, but the word had barely passed the lips of our forefathers before it grew out of hand, encompassing everything that implied taking a few more steps away from nature. We have reached the point at which we forget our indebtedness to nature, which brought us into this world. We are a part of nature, and we have it in us and around us, whether we believe that we are created in it or developed by it.

It is not easy to explain why, at such an early stage, I began to suspect that we had to be careful not to damage ourselves by damaging nature. It may be that ever since childhood I had seen the world around me as being somewhat unstable, constantly changing. My mother always spoke about Darwin, about evolution from animals to humans. To me nothing was unchangeable.

My mother had problems with Jesus after he took her mother away while she was still a little girl; her mother had been sickly and spoke incessantly about how she longed to return to Jesus. As a young girl my mother had been sent to England for her education, and she returned influenced by the teachings of Darwin: everything, including human beings, was constantly becoming better and smarter. My father was not a free thinker like my mother. He had been sent to Germany to study brewing and he returned with Martin Luther's belief that Our Lord had created the world and that it was impossible for human beings to improve it. He enjoyed life for what it was and spent no time speculating unnecessarily over problems that could not be solved. He never used words like 'God' and 'Jesus' but directed his Lord's Prayer to the proper address in heaven and seemed to be on good terms with both of them.

'We're making progress,' my mother said, pointing to the vacuum cleaner and the electric stove. To her generation it was still a miracle that someone could boil water for tea without flames from wood or gas but just by way of some wires. My father was not as convinced that mankind was improving. Newspapers described inventions of lethal new weapons, political unrest and rearmament in many countries despite the fact that a horrific world war, with mustard gas and explosives in the trenches and mines and submarines in the ocean, had barely come to an end. Norway had been neutral, but many innocent Norwegian sailors had gone down with their ships. The ocean had become a graveyard and appeared to me as something sinister.

One of my first memories is of being outdoors and crawling up an old and worn stone step on a small hill. It was my first personal experience of something that I would always remember. I had ventured away from my blanket and my nanny, and tried to climb up a step so high that I chose to crawl around it. And there, in the grass, I discovered small ants that were striving just as much as I was. One of them tried to climb up a straw. Even smaller bugs moved like red dots on a leaf, causing a green caterpillar to become a huge dragon standing erect on its tail and swaying in all its length to get a view of the landscape. And then suddenly Laura was there lifting me high up and away from my newly discovered world.

I was a little older when I was led past a small mound of golden sea sand. I pulled away in order to dig my fingers into the fine, loose sand and discovered that, when I was close, the mound disappeared and I was staring into a wonderful world of tiny toys. They were so small that the grown-ups couldn't see them, and my fingers were much too large to grab hold of them. Some looked like doll's dishes, some like trumpets or other amusing things, and others had shapes like real seashells and snail shells, only much, much smaller. I cried in frustration when I was pulled away. How could I explain my discovery to the grown-ups who were so large that they failed to see the small fantastic things that lay hidden in a plain old mound of sand? For the first time in my life I realized that there were things in the world that neither the largest nor those who knew the most could see.

But then I came to experience the world below the surface of the water. I was five years old, and discovered nothing that made it worth the visit. I was not even wearing a swimming suit. It was in the middle of winter and my mother had dressed me in warm winter clothing with heavy boots and a cap pulled down over my ears. I was standing on thick ice, so thick that my father had assured my mother that it would support elephants. It supported at least the weight of a huge brewery horse with a sled that stood next to me. Two men in winter clothing were working at the edge of the white ice, drawing a huge saw up and down in the black open water, sawing large blocks of glassy ice and loading them onto a sled.

My father had bought this dam, which lay within the town's boundaries. During the long Danish occupation of Norway it had belonged to the upper part of Count Gyldenløve's estate. Now the manor had become a town museum and my mother was the chairwoman of the museum society, but father was more interested in the dam that provided the brewery with ice.

I was waiting for the grown-ups to drive away. Boys, big and small, hung with their noses over the wire fence, waiting for the same thing. The two men with the saw were workers from the brewery and they would be driving the load to the ice house. Year round blocks of ice were delivered to customers along with beer and soda from the factory. There were no freezers or electric refrigerators then, but those who had iceboxes had a huge block of ice delivered every week from an enormous warehouse at the brewery. The ice was stored there under a thick layer of sawdust.

The two men drove off, the bells on the horses jingling through town, and when we could no longer hear the bells I ran to the gate with the key.

The next thing I remember is watching some of the boys in wonder. The oldest of them ran and jumped one after another from the edge on to a loosened patch of ice. In the same leap they were back on solid ice. They were so nimble that they landed before the patch tipped over.

This looked like fun. I wanted to show what I was good for. I got ready, ran and jumped onto the ice floe, but I was too slow to turn around before it tipped over and my foothold turned upside-down. With this, I fell into a totally foreign world.

I struggled madly to get back up to the others, but the hole I had fallen through had disappeared. I bumped my head and nose against a solid dark ceiling where I thought the black opening had been. I wasn't aware that while a hole in the ice is dark and the ice is bright when seen from above, everything is reversed when you are beneath it. From this vantage point, the opening in the ice lets in light while the layer of ice is dark. I became totally confused and disoriented, and that is all I remember from my swim. One of the boys must have grabbed hold of a wriggling boot and pulled me up by my feet. I awoke to the sound of my own screaming when I heard someone suggest that I was dead, which scared me so much that I managed to convince the others that they were mistaken. Freezing and soaking wet both inside and out, I ran straight home to our front door, a warm bed and the motherly care that convinced me that I had indeed survived.

I didn't however feel completely safe until my father returned from the office and asked me to sit up and say the Lord's Prayer. This was a secret we had and it provided a pleasant feeling of calmness and warmth. My mother never joined us in prayer. Sometimes when we heard a squeak at the bottom of the stairs, I lay down quickly and my father quietly left the bedroom. Once they met just outside my door and I heard my mother say with a friendly, reproachful voice, 'What *is* it that you are teaching the boy?'

My father never took me to church. He never went himself. He was not that kind of a Christian. His faith was not to be shared with strangers. Just with me. For the two of us, faith and morality were a matter between ourselves and the Lord. Father may well have had a special deal for himself: if he behaved perfectly well in all other respects, he would be permitted to appreciate beautiful women.

Being an atheist, mother believed in Darwin rather than in Jesus, but she adhered strictly to Christian morals. When she came home from England as a young woman with modern silk underwear and a deck of cards in her suitcase, her Lutheran aunts had thrown the underwear and the cards into the stove. Saying the word 'underwear' was not allowed; the term was 'unmentionables'.

How could two such different people stay together?

They probably did it for my sake. But I never heard them argue. I tried to listen through the floor in our old wooden house after they said good night and went downstairs, but all I heard was the old gramophone playing classical music.

After my adventure under the ice, I thought a great deal about life and death. I was more interested in animals and plants than in who had created them and kept everything that moved alive. I guess I never doubted that there was something beyond the visible world, and on this point I was on the same wavelength as my father. However I was more involved in what I could actually see on earth than in the invisible angels of an abstract world beyond the skies that the minister referred to in our religion classes without any special conviction.

Laura, my slender nanny, had pictures of chubby little angels framed in glass over her bed, and the heavy-set cook, Helga, sang about angels when she and her girlfriends met for coffee and played string instruments in her room. Once, as quite a young boy, I crept out of bed and peeped through a keyhole. I got quite a shock. I saw the sizeable Helga trying to lower herself into our bathtub one evening when my parents were out at a party. I stormed back to bed in horror and pulled the quilt over my head. I had never even seen my mother in her underwear, and now I had had a revelation. It was unbearably exciting and educational, but for the life of me I didn't dare take another look. She was just as naked as the angels, but had difficulty pressing her body into the tub. What would happen when she, with her beautiful voice, went to heaven and flew around with wings?

Helga cannot be said to have aroused my interest in the opposite sex, but the water that cascaded on to the bathroom floor stimulated a new version of my daydreams. They were a constant part of my private world after I was left alone in my room at night. If it was summer, I tiptoed silently out of bed and climbed up to the large open window with its view of the Larvik Fjord. We lived on a steep hill, on the side facing the sea; three storeys up I could see over the red-tiled roof-tops all the way down to the long quay and beyond that to the open sea. The voyage continued from there when I was back in bed. If I was lucky, I continued dreaming in my sleep, about native peoples and strange animals in Africa. But now it was winter and too cold to crawl out of bed, since my mother insisted that I sleep with the window open in all kinds of weather. On these nights I pictured myself in the bathroom without Helga, opening both faucets until the water cascaded on to the floor and into the bedroom. It would take the bed with me in it down the hill and out of the fjord, on and on until I could get out of bed in a land of palm trees and playmates who seemed much more exciting than those in the neighbourhood.

In another version, I didn't have to travel at all. I just built a huge glass dome over the old abandoned brewery, turning it into a hothouse where I could plant tropical vegetation and invite Indian, African and Arab children, two by two, just like Noah on his Ark. And the animals, of course.

A boy pretty much removed from reality?

It was during puberty that I became shy. I didn't know my classmates at my new school. In our neighbourhood most children left school after the first seven years. Until then I had been the centre of attention in the gang on our hill. I had the key to the dam, unlimited amounts of orange and cherry pop in the icebox, and everyone thought it was fun to go on my expeditions into the forest.

I was probably inspired by my mother's books about great explorations, wild animals and foreign peoples. Maybe foreign peoples most of all. But you couldn't find any of them in the vicinity of Larvik in those days. I remember a circus arriving in town and everyone running to see a live black man. The disappointment was great when one of the boys discovered that the palms of his hands were white. We agreed that he was just a fake.

There was a lot of wildlife in the forest on the edge of town, pine forest mixed with all sorts of deciduous forests to the east, and a beech forest along Farris Lake to the west. We put away our pop guns and bows and arrows and went on expeditions with buckets and nets to capture wild animals. At that time, except for the great mammals, no species were threatened. There were no toxic pesticides, and pollution did not exist in our part of the world. There were fish in all our streams.

We caught tadpoles in small lakes and ponds, colourful salamanders and big black water beetles. On the ground we caught porcupines, mice, beetles, grasshoppers and snakes. In the air we caught everything from bats to butterflies. And if there were enough eggs in a bird's nest to permit the taking of one, it too would be added to the collection. My father had given me my own newly panelled room in the old brewery stable, and we hung a sign on the door: *Museum of Zoology*.

In everyday life I was definitely a scaredy-cat, but when it came to procuring a new species for the collection, I pulled myself together. My mother almost fainted once when I came home with the flock of boys at my heels. When I rang the doorbell and she opened the door, I presented her with a live viper that I held by the tip of its tail with an outstretched arm. It writhed in evil coils trying to bite me, but every time it curved up I shook it until its head fell. My mother ran to get a glass jar filled with alcohol, and the viper hissed when it was dropped in, head first. Then it relaxed and fell asleep in a coil at the bottom, looking like a precious treasure. I had managed to capture it with a Y-shaped stick pinched over its neck without smashing its head.

You, the shyest and quietest boy in class?

At least that's what Arnold Jacoby wrote. He was my best friend at the new school. Without him I would have risked having a reputation of being a nerd. At least that is how I picture myself in retrospect. I had no interest in sports, like the others in class, I was the last one to be chosen for football teams, and I disliked jumping on the springboard in gym. I preferred leaning over small insects pinned on needles and framed in glass.

My father despaired. He couldn't even get me to try swimming, certainly not beyond a spot where I could touch the bottom with my feet. As a last resort he tried a trick. He brought a beautiful young lady who was carrying a long pole with a rope coil attached. I was meant to hang in it and swim like a frog in deep water outside the dock. My humiliation has never been greater than when I bid him a curt goodbye and left him to swim with the young lady. I couldn't take one more humiliation like that.

By this time I had some school friends who were crazy about sports and who knew to the second how fast Nurmi ran a 1,500-metre race and to the centimetre how far Rustadstuen had jumped in the Holmenkollen ski jump. When they started cross-country running in the nearby forest, I joined in, even though I always finished last. If I saw something beautiful in the woods on the way, I would stop to examine it. Once, however, when three sweet young girls came to watch the start of a race, I thought about the lady with the fishing pole and ran so fast that I passed everyone and reached the finish line first.

That one day I would come to be surrounded by 40,000 sports

fans, welcoming everyone to the Winter Olympics in my home country with a movie star was as inconceivable to me as the possibility of meeting someone who had just been walking on the moon.

My running in the woods gave my father new hope, in spite of the fact that he never managed to lure me into deep water. He noticed that I devoured books about Tarzan, the king of the jungle, and had a bright idea. He had the carpenters at the brewery raise two very high masts in the back yard, and connected them with a cross beam at the top. We fastened a thick climbing rope and two gymnastic rings to the beam, and I could play Tarzan and swing high over the ground in the jungle vines. I used the rope and rings every afternoon, and became so strong in both arms that I could let go with the one and hang by a finger with the other, my elbow at a right angle.

But at school I was just as hopeless as ever at jumping over the wooden horse in gym, and my interest in football declined even further when my father bribed me into attending the Norwegian championship finals. I was promised a new fishing rod if Larvik Turn won. They lost.

Running in the forest, climbing the rope and camping outdoors with a tent and a sleeping bag restored some of the fitness my mother had worked into me during the first years of my life. She was fantastic when it came to a healthy diet and fresh air. The maid had to be taught how to milk two goats that we kept in the backyard in the middle of town so that I could be fattened up on goats' milk. I had to go out in the fresh air and play alone, even if it was raining. I was not allowed to come down the stairs in the mornings before I could prove that my digestion was in order, which was so embarrassing that once I put a scarf and a hat in the potty, emptied it into the water closet, and pulled the chain.

A lasting memory from that time was my family's reaction when the post office at the bottom of the hill caught on fire. The whole town consisted of white wooden houses, and half of Larvik had burned to the ground before I was born. This fire started at night while we were sleeping and the flames soared above the fjord. A rain of sparks reached all the way up to us. My father declared that if the fire spread we should seek refuge under the old brewery's cellar vault. At this my mother ordered me to the potty so that I wouldn't need to go if we were locked underground. Fortunately the fire wagons came with bells and horses before I was finished, and I survived childhood without the fear of fires.

On the other hand, my life almost came to an end for the second time under water.

Beyond the graveyard there was a deep and wide crevice in the hillside that separated an island cliff and its bath houses from the mainland. There was a constant undertow here from the Larvik Fjord that flowed into the crevice and pulled out again with the rhythmic waves of the ocean. The son of the janitor at the brewery had drowned here. There were also some horrible rumours about an unmarried woman who had thrown her stillborn baby into the crevice. The bath houses were empty in the autumn, and a small wooden bridge without a railing tempted me to follow a flock of boys out to play catch on the island. Proud of my ability to run, I attempted to escape a pursuer by jumping diagonally on to the wooden bridge, but I lost my footing and tumbled into the deep crevice. Not even a good swimmer could climb up the steep walls, which were slippery with seaweed. I twisted with the undertow and flailed wildly and helplessly with my arms and legs in cascading masses of water, and can only remember that I sank deep twice – and then the world was gone. A diffident little boy nicknamed 'the American' sped over to the bath houses and grabbed a life-saving ring with a rope and threw it into the witches' brew. How I grabbed hold of the ring is a mystery, but it was the boys' joint effort that dragged me up. My father saw to it that the insecure 'American' became the class hero, because from then on he always showed up at school with a silver knife in his belt.

After this no one could convince me that I too could float by just rhythmically moving my arms and legs. I had tried, and I never would again. My father had to accept that I was growing up with a dread of water. Until he shook my hand, many years later, after the *Kon-Tiki* expedition. By then I had learned how to swim.

4

Head Above Water

The days of reminiscing about the world of my childhood suddenly disappeared in a flood of blinding sunlight.

'Last day. Time to pack! The plane leaves today.'

I woke up and my aku-aku fell asleep as Jacqueline stirred in the chair next to me.

So long for now, I whispered to myself. No more silence and laziness. I pictured the waiting piles of unsorted mail. Metres and metres of unanswered faxes covering the floor of my new home in the Canary Islands. But I was well prepared. I had found ideal working conditions far away from the tourists on an old, secluded and abandoned compound. The property, with large trees and remnants of the finca's former avocado plantation, was uncultivated. Its buildings were preserved because of their old age and thanks to a renowned local poet who had once lived in seclusion behind huge trees and high walls.

I still had to get up at six o'clock in the morning to squeeze enough hours into the day. This was an abrupt transition for Jacqueline, who had changed her breakfast routine by six hours for the sake of her husband. In return, she received the sunrise over the ocean as a symbolic wedding gift. During her years in front of the cameras in Hollywood, she may never have seen a sunrise. Now, with her strong interest in painting and archaeology, she could sit by her window and watch the sun – the first creative artist – kindle the daylight, brushing the ocean, the sky and the tall mountains behind us with a harmonious array of colours that shifted and played silent music. If she hadn't been standing by my side, the aku-aku would probably have made his presence known. It may have been there, quiet as a mouse, just as enraptured as we were.

On other parts of the island, whole towns of skyscrapers had been built for the enjoyment of modern sun-worshippers who paid a lot of money to spend a few days under a clear, blue sky. However, it was the ancient sun-worshippers who had brought Jacqueline and I to this island and this valley, and it was the genuine and uncorrupted symbol of their god that passed over our heads on its daily journey westward from Africa to the jungles of America.

Deeper in the valley there were a few step pyramids that had been there since time immemorial. They had been there for so long that no one knew who had built them. Old people had heard from their grandparents that they had always been there. Younger newcomers to the island were uninterested and simply thought they were beautiful but meaningless stone piles, left behind by the first Spanish conquistadors who had cleared the fields. Up until now the local population had respectfully protected the whole pyramid area, and the town had developed around the old, mystical structures. Tight rows of houses formed a protective screen from the streets that were built to circumvent the area. Schoolchildren had taken paths and shortcuts across the site without moving one single stone from the perfectly constructed pyramid walls. Consciously or subconsciously, the walls were preserved with respect, and the only ones who had paid them any special attention were groups of individuals with esoteric interests who sought out this place in order to meditate on Atlantis or visitors from other planets. The city council had now summarily decided to open the area to new development, and to allow streets to cross it in a manner that would put an end to both superstition and science.

I was just in time to save the pyramids. A white spot on the Güimar map marked the 'Pirámides de Chacona'. However pyramids of unknown origin and on distant islands were not covered by Spanish preservation legislation. The city's plan had been approved by the Spanish authorities long ago. The only structure other than mine to be preserved as a national monument was in ruins, one of the valley's oldest houses. Its many small rooms led to the assumption that it had once been a cloister that had been placed on the highest point among the pyramids. All the woodwork in this magnificent building was charred after arsonists recently had set it afire, professing that the roof was haunted. Wicked tongues construed this to mean that what was actually haunted was the plan to preserve the building. This was the situation when I arrived as an outsider and wanted to add the huge pyramids around the charred building to the list of national monuments.

It was on top of one of these step pyramids that I met Jacqueline for the first time. A newspaper article had reported that I had come to the island in an attempt to save the pyramids, and that I claimed they were similar to the ones in Mexico and Peru. Jacqueline's curiosity was aroused, and she was the first to come over from the other side of the island to take a look. This meeting marked an abrupt turning point in our lives. The valley of the pyramids would come to be our mutual home.

When Jacqueline halted my conversation with the aku-aku on the roof in El Aaiún, we were about to return to this valley. We had decided to venture everything to rescue the pyramid complex and the remnants of the burned cloister-like building that could easily house a museum or special exhibits. We could also restore the old finca in the large garden and make it our home. A long time ago, I had convinced my old friend Fred Olsen to buy the whole pyramid area. He had been fond of the Canary Islands ever since his childhood. Jacqueline immediately introduced me to the responsible authorities, who have long since set the wheels in motion for the preservation of the pyramids and the designation of the whole area as a cultural park. 'Las Piramides de Chacona' was to become a centre of research, connected to the Internet and dedicated to the studies of the origins of cultures and pre-European sea route communication.

The wedding trip to Western Sahara had only been meant as an outing, but it lasted for a week because of the problem of getting a reservation. Now that we were finally on board, Jacqueline was sleeping and I was enjoying the sight of Africa's golden coast line and the Sahara desert gradually disappearing as we flew out over the blue Atlantic. I was on the verge of dropping off myself when an invisible companion came to life.

Do you recognize this?

I looked out and saw only the blue Atlantic Ocean. We must have reached the halfway point between Africa and the Canary Islands. We had sailed over these depths with both *Ra* and *Ra II*, making the crossing between the mainland and the islands before reaching the open ocean. The vitality of the ocean was reduced to a motionless expanse of blue. We could not even see the white caps cresting the waves breaking in the direction of the trade winds toward America. To get a proper impression of the planet, it must be seen at very close range or from the moon.

Do you believe in the lost city of Atlantis?

Just then the landing gear hit the runway and I forgot the whole question in the noise and commotion that followed. At home in the pyramid valley, a fax was waiting and the wheels were in full motion with the new project FERCO – Foundation for Exploration on Cultural Origins. I had so much else to think about that, even if my aku-aku tried to get my attention, I didn't notice.

'You have to go to a barber,' said Jacqueline one day when I was standing with shaving cream on my face, ready to shave in the old-fashioned way. My head has a modest amount of hair, but on my neck it grows incredibly fast. In the afternoon she drove me in to the island capital, where I reclined into the barber's deep chair and made myself comfortable. My companion was there at once.

You didn't answer my question. Are you afraid of science, or are you afraid of being labelled as one of those who seek out the pyramids to meditate on supernatural visitors from outer space or from the depths of the sea?

I am afraid of both. But mostly I am afraid of the kind of authorities who try to make people believe the pyramids are only heaps of stones. The other ones are not taken very seriously. Personally I believe that the pyramids were built by ordinary people who came from Africa with goats and seed aboard simple vessels, long before any Europeans. The legend about Atlantis should not be discarded by science or abused by New Age dreamers. It is far too easy to put on our reading glasses and believe that we can discover everything about the past by researching the printed material in our books, letting ourselves believe that the ancient authors were only trying to record myths and free fantasy.

Like the legend about Noah and the Deluge?

Now it was growing more difficult. The barber wanted to know whether he should trim the hair in my nose, and the aku-aku wanted to direct me toward Noah and the Deluge.

'Both in my ears and in my nose,' I answered. For believers and non-believers, the subject of the Deluge and Atlantis were so delicate that it would have to wait until we had more time.

The next afternoon Jacqueline wondered why I didn't take my usual ten-minute siesta with her after lunch. Instead I stretched out with a notepad and a pencil in the garden hammock, well concealed behind the close foliage of the avocado trees.

The aku-aku didn't wait for long.

How can it be that you who feared water in childhood have, as a grown-up, taken to sea on antiquated vessels that no one believed in?

I agreed that it didn't make much sense. What was it that had gradually given me self-confidence in my youth? I recalled how I spoke to myself then, such a long, long time ago.

As a young student, I had hiked with determination right into a snowstorm in the mountain wilderness. Alone with a Greenland dog, I kept going in defiance of the weather. Snow whipped against my face like sand, and I kept telling myself: This will make the boy a man!

I had grown tired of myself. Tired of being far too timid and shy. Awkward with girls and a loser in competitions and games. I wanted to find myself. Force myself out of an inner hiding place. I consciously attempted to liberate myself from my inner bondage, and it actually felt as if the snowstorm beat me out of my own hide.

After I was saved from drowning the second time, I developed the same feeling for deep water that I had for cemeteries and dentists. All of my friends became expert swimmers and had fun in the Larvik Fjord all summer. Their parents either had a sailing boat or motor boat. Fortunately we did not, and I thanked providence for the fact that my parents were newcomers to Larvik and that they each had a cabin in the mountains. My father preferred his, located over the tree line at Ustaoset, where there was a railway station and a number of holiday cabins. It offered a lot of fun. My mother's cabin in eastern Norway was just as far from the sea, far above the tree line between the Gudbrandsdalen and Østerdalen valleys. There were no roads to Hornsjø that a car could drive on then, but there was a hotel, a primitive one surrounded by a dozen low grass-roofed log cabins, which rarely had guests and was abandoned and half buried by snow in the winter. Half of the buildings were small summer farms that tended goats and produced cheese and were full of life in the summertime. The rest were occupied by city people on their summer holidays. They kept to themselves and fished trout in the mountain lake from their own rowing boats, or took long walks in the wilderness just under and often far above the tree line.

Hornsjø became my second home, the place where my mother gathered my adult step-siblings and her closest family members during holidays. It lacked the Gulf Stream influence and warm swimming water of the fjord in Larvik. After brave dips in water edged by mountain flowers and shrubs, everyone else came shooting out of the water just as fast as I did.

Perhaps subconsciously, it was my mother who steered me on to the track my father had tried to show me when he appeared with the woman with the fishing rod. I had gained a little strength in my arms from training with gymnastic rings and from rowing while trout fishing in the mountain lake.

Then one summer something totally unexpected happened. Right out of the uninhabited enchanted forest behind Hornsjø Lake, a lone man appeared. Dressed in an old-fashioned and threadbare hunting outfit, he knocked on the cabin door with a sack on his back and offered us the largest mountain trout we'd ever seen. My mother suspected that this folk-tale figure might be hungry and invited him in for a meal. How this fellow could tell stories. He had the most marvellous animal tales I'd ever heard or read, about animals that we only caught a glimpse of on a lucky day in the pine forest or above the tree line. Moose, wild reindeer, wolverine, marten, hare – even ermine, snow mice, lemming, wood grouse, cranes and everything else that plays and dances in the forest without letting the rest of us see it. They were all part of Ola Bjørneby's world. He lived with it all, night and day, and it showed itself in his happy state of mind and easy-going sense of humour.

He earned a few extra shillings by chopping wood for us. My mother didn't even protest when he showed me how to make my own bat. And then something incredible happened. One time when he came up from the valley with some supplies to take back to his home in the wilderness, in a small deserted mountain valley, I was allowed to go along to help him carry his parcels. I was worn out when I returned at the agreed time, but I was so infatuated with what I'd seen and experienced that one day my mother, to my incomprehensible joy, let me go into the Åsta valley with Ola for a few days to help out. The valley was cut off from the rest of the world. Only a small path led from Hornsjø to some dilapidated and abandoned mountain farm buildings that were called 'Hynna'.

A magical new world revealed itself to me when we jumped on the rocks where the river ran out into Lake Hornsjø and took off head over heel through the pine forest that closed tightly around us on the way down in Ola's valley. He lived in a small building that once housed sheep. It had an earth floor and old log walls that were so far off the ground that a sheep could crawl beneath them. He cooked his food on an open hearth under a hole in the ceiling that let out most of the smoke. The furniture was the same inside as it was outside: stubs, stones and pine branches. The end of the longest log was drawn all the way on to the hearth, and it became shorter day by day without my having to chop anything other than kindling wood.

In Ola's world, I realized for the first time how simple life really is. People have made it more complicated because we've grown accustomed to it. From the time we learn to sit and stand, we are taught that in order to sleep we need a bed and in order to eat we need a chair and table. I discovered after my first day in Ola's world that without having used any furniture I was still alive.

Ola was a willing speaker, but he never talked about himself. In a roundabout way my mother discovered that he had seen what might be called better days. He was the son of a wealthy man from a family of forest landowners who had fallen on bad times because the father lost his fortune to drink. Refusing the humiliation of any forms of charity, Ola took off to the mountains with his father's hunting and fishing equipment. When he found the simple hut at Hynna, he decided to stay there.

Ola lived with one foot on either side of the law by following the

area's fishing and hunting rules as closely as possible. He was a popular man in the area, even among the hunting and fishing police, and
the long arm of the law rarely reached into the Åsta valley. In this
way, Ola Bjørneby usually managed to get his daily ration of food, in
peace and on his own terms, without having to rely on any assistance,
like a Robinson Crusoe.

One time he appeared in front of the valley's storekeeper with
such a large mountain trout that jealous souls sent the fish and game
warden on a long trip to Lake Lyng, high up in the Østerdal
Mountains. The guardian of the law had placed himself and his
binoculars behind some rough shrubbery when Ola and I came
trekking past in full sight. We set a small boat into the lake, and Ola
grabbed the oars so that I, for the first time, could try fishing with an
otter, which was a piece of wood at the end of a long fishing line with
a lot of fishing flies connected to it; when we rowed fast enough, the
wood cut into the water and pulled the fishing line with the flies dan-
gling side by side out into the lake. This way we could catch a
number of fish at the same time. This method was reserved for the
local population, and strictly forbidden for city-dwellers or any other
visitors.

Ola scouted eagle-eyed in all directions while he was rowing and
suddenly caught sight of the warden's binoculars in the distance. He
immediately let go of the oars and took over the otter board, while I
took over the rowing. It was perfectly legal for me to row, but even
though Ola could claim permanent residence in the community he
would be arrested if he allowed me to hold the otter. I braved it out,
and rowed as if my life was at stake. 'No,' I answered every time Ola
asked if I was getting tired. I was finally so weary that I could only
shake my head when he asked. That damned guy with the binoculars
was able to take it easy! Blisters were forming and bursting on my
palms, and I was becoming so intimate with the hard board I was sitting on that I had to make a cushion out of reindeer lichen and
heather. As the hours went on I found I had less skin but more

nerves to sit on. Not until evening approached and we rowed into land could we see that the warden was preparing to leave. We were leaving Lake Lyng in opposite directions. The man of the law hurried to reach civilization in Gudbrandsdalen before night-time, while we tried to reach the cabin in Hynna.

We had won the battle on the lake, but it was a far from triumphant march through the wilderness when I climbed out of the boat and started walking. My backside stung as if I were being whipped with every step, and with a small portion of Ola's fifty kilos of fish on my back I struggled to keep up. 'No problem, we'll sleep here and get up early tomorrow,' Ola said as he lay down on his back in the heather before falling asleep. We used to crawl beneath the branches of a pine tree when we slept in the forest. Stars twinkling through the fringes of branches are so beautiful. There is still nothing like lying on your back beneath the open sky and having the entire star-studded universe above you every time you open your eyes. This time, however, I missed that view. I must have been on my stomach when I fell asleep on a huge stone slab.

My summer vacations with Ola taught me much that has become integral to my being. But maybe what I learned most was that I am a part of nature, no matter how I dress. Once you've experienced that, you will feel at home no matter how far you are from the closest house, whether in a forest, on a mountain, in a desert or on an ocean. In the forest with Ola, we not only saw wildlife but also saw where the animals had been and what they had done. We saw where the moose bull had swept with his antlers, where a mother had passed with her calf, a hare had torn off a strip of succulent bark, or a fox had hunted a black chicken. There wasn't much left to find out about nature when I returned to school and studied from textbooks.

When autumn approached and the cloudberry bogs turned red, it was with a heavy heart that I left the mountain wilderness to start middle school in Larvik.

*

I was now fifteen and although I had reached the age of confirmation, this ceremony was not for me. The others at school had been confirmed, but only because of the presents they would be given. I didn't like the minister, and I didn't want him to put his hand on my head.

When Arnold and I were philosophizing, much of it was about the girls we liked best in the class and about the mystery of love. Nevertheless, no matter how interesting our female classmates were, they remained – in our inexperienced minds – totally unapproachable. At that time sexual education was unknown in schools, and almost unimaginable at home. Our knowledge was limited to what we had seen in the animal kingdom, and what the larger boys had doodled on the walls of public toilets. I remember once when I was young and a slightly older boy had attempted to give me my first lesson in the hieroglyphics of sex. With a piece of chalk he drew a round circle with a slit in the middle and rays around it on the wall, and then he asked, 'What is it?'

'A sun,' I answered innocently.

He sighed. 'It's something ugly,' he whispered in my ear.

'The devil?' I whispered carefully.

For my own part I was so naive when it came to this matter, that I looked upon girls and grown-up women as a different species from us regular people, as something so incredibly exciting that it was hard to find anything to say to them. One of my friends at school had arranged to meet a girl one evening. He carefully read the sports section in order to have something to talk about.

Arnold and I were certain that love was something divine. It was at this time that my parents decided to separate. They were never divorced: my father simply sold his part of the brewery and all his other business interests and moved to an inn in Oslo until my mother and I moved from Larvik to Oslo, where I started university in 1933. I swore to myself that I'd never divorce the one I chose to be my bride.

And then you were divorced twice, but have never been confirmed?

I was divorced, but not from the belief in love. I was baptized when I was small, but I didn't want to state by being confirmed that I believed in the Larvik minister's vengeful doomsday god. Contrary to the minister, I believed that the god of love would be compassionate to that poor unwed mother who had thrown her stillborn child into the crevice at Kirkebukta, where I almost drowned, because she had not been allowed to bury it in consecrated soil.

Arnold and I often discussed religion and morals when we were out walking and trying to figure out the mysteries of life in the small quiet streets of our town, which were virtually empty when evening approached. The church had lost its hold on the young people, and was attended only when someone was being confirmed and receiving gifts like a watch, cuff links and a first pair of long trousers. Arnold had been confirmed, like everyone else, and he was on good terms with the minister because of his fine bass singing and his piano playing. Both of us enjoyed music, even though I sang off key. My only contribution was the huge gramophone from home.

My form of religion gradually became a belief in an all-encompassing creative power, a force behind the development of nature and everything that grew and moved on the earth. As the son of a gardener, Arnold was fond of flowers and listened to my theories about civilization being on the wrong track. When I told other people that I disliked machines and motors and that in the long run this form of progress would not improve human existence, they thought I was a fool.

What made you think that?

Maybe it was an instinctive belief in nature as the progenitor and master of human beings. If there was a god whose invisible powers extended into everything that had sprung up from the ocean and the earth, then why hadn't he himself invented machines to please humans? I was afraid that machines at some point would get the upper hand and take the place of the natural world that Our Lord had given us.

You didn't believe in progress?

Yes I did, but not that any old step that led us further away from nature could be called progress. I began to feel that we, as human beings, were experimenting with our own way of life. Clearing the forests. Assuming that moving from a farm to a factory is progress. When I was younger, drawing was one of my hobbies. My motif was often a yellow sun shining over round native huts, palm trees and monkeys. Later I exchanged my crayons for pencils, erasers and felt-tipped pens, and I sketched cartoons about the foibles of civilization. I liked travelling by train, and was just as impressed as everyone else the first time a classmate brought something he called a radio to school. With earphones wired to some kind of a battery, we confirmed, one by one and with wonder in our eyes, that we could hear distant music.

I also became more interested in fitness after having tasted the wilderness with Ola Bjørneby. I became especially good friends with a huge fellow called Eric, who ran the cross-country races in the forest with us. He was a jovial oddball, totally different from Arnold. They never became close friends, because Eric had decided to go to sea instead of attending high school with us. They were both large fellows, but since Arnold only liked music and poetry we had only philosophical conversations. Eric was a practical outdoors man, and in my last years at high school, passing my wilderness apprenticeship with Ola Bjørneby and starting to spend all my vacations outdoors in Norway's wildest mountains, it was Eric who came with me.

We weren't ready for each other the first time we met. I was with my own gang of friends, equipped with buckets and nets to catch salamanders in the local forest when we met Eric, who led a group of boys bearing cap pistols and wooden swords. They had built a pirate ship in the forest. Later, when we started cross-country running, I would go home with him. At first I was startled by a fearsome pirate aiming at me from a huge drawing in his room, but later I greatly enjoyed his humorous drawings.

When Eric shipped out to sea we lost contact, but many years later, it was Eric Hesselberg whom I invited to be navigator on the *Kon-Tiki* expedition.

Like myself, Arnold moved to Oslo after high school. While I chose to study biology and geography at university, he went to art school and became a professional illustrator and author. His book *It Also Concerns You* was a great success. It tells the story of Larvik's only Jewish family. They had twelve children and, except for the youngest, all of them died in the Nazi gas chambers during the occupation. We who were Samuel's classmates had no idea that he was Jewish, but only knew that he never came to school on Saturdays. It doesn't take much for faith in the god of love to create hatred. Although friends and foes can believe in the same god of creation, they can also disagree about which day of the week he chose to rest.

I was completely convinced that what we called civilization had become a dangerous thing, that the machines of war that were in full alert all over the world would drag all civilized societies into a new and dreadful war. Alfred Nobel had believed in progress and perpetual peace when he invented dynamite. Dynamite took more lives than gas masks saved during the First World War, and when we were in high school we heard about the invention of gigantic war vehicles that could move over all sorts of terrain without wheels and would make a new war impossible. Eric and I wanted to flee from Europe before all of the new horrific inventions of war were put to use. Eric dreamed about starting an ideal society in Central Africa, far away from the dangers of civilization. There were many blank spots on the map at that time.

I've often been asked what great explorer names like Roald Amundsen and Fridtjof Nansen meant to me in my youth, but it is not an easy question to answer. Both were, of course, great heroes to all of us boys, and they were still alive then. Amundsen had reached the South Pole before we were born, and was way ahead in the contest to get to the North Pole first. I'll never forget when I was at a Boy Scout camp in Åndalsnes in 1928. The Italian, Nobile, had gone down with his airship over the polar region, and in a brave attempt to rescue his competitor Amundsen had crashed in a small plane somewhere above the icy ocean. Our camp heard that Amundsen had been found alive, and everyone stormed out of their tents and danced and cheered, but even greater was our sorrow when we discovered that the news was wrong.

I was only eight years old when Nansen received the Nobel Peace Prize for his great work with refugees after the First World War. We admired him most, because we had heard that he had once let the polar ship *Fram* freeze into the drift ice and come closer to the North Pole than any other human being, except for Johanson, who was with him. We all knew that he had crossed Greenland alone on skis in 1888. When I was a boy no one else had ventured far enough over the inland ice on Greenland to be able to tell geographers whether or not this huge polar island consisted of wild mountain ranges or of a flat glacier.

Then something happened that had a bearing on my own life. In 1931 two daring Norwegian students had skied right across the widest section of Greenland with a dog team and written a book about it. One of them, Martin Mehren, brought some of the Greenland dogs to Oslo.

My mother was crazy about dogs. In one of her previous marriages she had owned twenty white Samoyeds, a slightly more refined relative of the muscular dogs that led Greenland Eskimo sleds. Since the time when I drank the milk from the only back-yard goats in Larvik, I had grown up with a peaceful chow-chow to take the sting out of the loneliness of living in a house with two elderly parents. When school came to an end I had moved to Oslo with my mother. The loneliness did not diminish when my father, to make room for all of my mother's antiques, bought her an apartment on the top floor of a building on Camilla Collett Street, with a large living room that extended from one end of the house to the other and a narrow balcony on each side. Here, in the middle of town, she emerged triumphantly from the elevator one day with a Greenland puppy that she had bought from Martin Mehren. I was overwhelmed with joy, but as soon as she set the dog free and closed the front door behind her our new housemate ran like a wild animal into the living room, jumping like a leopard over sofas and tables. It ran back and forth and out on both balconies, where it kept jumping up, finally coming to its senses as, with its well-grown paws on the brick railing, it looked down six floors with bewilderment.

My life was never the same after Kazan came into our house. I stayed home from the university for three days and used all my strength to force Kazan down on to the rug every time I said, 'Lie down,' holding it down by force until I said, 'Up.' My mother excused the beast by saying that its mother, according to Mehren, had been cross-bred with a wolf. The miracle happened: Kazan became the most obedient dog I have seen, clean and peaceful and able to understand everything I tried to teach it, and much more.

Kazan was so quiet when it was with me that I allowed it to accompany me to lectures at the university, and on my rare visits to a restaurant it lay so peacefully beneath the table that no one noticed. This dog learned to pull fifty kilos on a sled in uneven terrain during the winter, and in the summer could carry fifty kilos on its back. While I was studying in Oslo we were inseparable both in the city and on hikes in the countryside. Both the dog and I were happiest when we could get away from everything, as far as possible from the city and as high as possible in to the mountains. The dog became so attached to my backpack and my thick mountain boots that it gave a clear warning to anyone who tried to touch them in my absence. If the warning did not work, sometimes I had to resort to sticking plasters and bandages.

Eric came along on more mountain hikes than anyone else; old friends have always meant a lot to me. I planned increasingly difficult hikes in the mountains. At that time, hardly anyone slept outside when they hiked in the wintry mountains, but Eric and I were inspired by Nansen and Mehren. We had no need to find shelter before nightfall. We had learned to dig suitable accommodations in a windblown snowdrift, and we became experts in finding good, hard-packed snow.

My hiking companions believed that I pictured myself as a future polar explorer. With the exception of Arnold and Eric, I never discussed my growing resolve to visit other parts of the world with anyone else. I financed my holidays by writing about them in Saturday papers and magazines, illustrating them with photographs and amusing drawings. Sleeping outdoors in the snow was so unusual in Norway in the 1930s that readers were interested in learning how to carve blocks of ice to build an igloo – and we built them in the most exquisite places.

There was nothing quite like waking up on a wintry morning on top of Stor-Ronden Mountain and creeping from our igloo feeling that all of Norway was within our view. Although a winter storm could be wailing outside, an igloo or a simple snowhole was warm and comfortable as long as it had proper air circulation, through a little hole in the roof, and the entrance level was lower than the floor. With a single burning candle, the temperature inside will remain above freezing while the temperature outdoors is below freezing. This is because the inner walls turn to ice which acts as insulation and provides a reasonable room temperature.

I have always liked to have an alternative course of action in case things go wrong, and I can only remember breaking that rule once. On the raft journeys there would always be a log or a bundle of reeds to float about on if the ropes came apart. But once, on the summit of Glittertind, Eric and I took a crazy chance. With its permanent snowcap, Glittertind was at that time higher than its neighbour, Galdhøpiggen, and thereby Norway's tallest mountain, which was why Eric and I struggled our way up its steep wall of snow on skis with Kazan fighting his way after us with the sled. We planned to build an igloo at the top, but before we could reach it we were caught by a snowstorm. Soon we could not even see the tips of our skis. It was also impossible to see the edges of the cliffs, and the only way to avoid them was to continue our ascent.

When we finally reached the stone marker at the top of Glittertind, the storm was so extreme that we couldn't even stand upright and had to take off our skis. The marker was all we could see, and the snow fell so densely that it was difficult both to breathe and open our eyes. The surface was impenetrable, making it impossible to dig a snowhole or to cut blocks for an igloo. We desperately clutched our skis so that they wouldn't be swept away into an unknown world, and there was no time to think of an alternative. We untied Kazan from the sled, took a compass bearing based on the direction we had come from, sat on top of the sled, and let it go. We kept our speed down as well as we could and several times even managed to stop and wait for Kazan until finally it got out of hand and we lost control. This was the ride of a lifetime. We went faster and faster, at a wild pace, and ended up rolling over in deep snow on flat ground without knowing where we were. We thought we'd never see Kazan again. After waiting for an eternity the dog appeared, limping and struggling to reach us through the deep snow. We knew we were in the midst of a wild landscape, but we could only see ourselves, the sled and the dog. The world disappeared in a white shadowless void, without contours or any way of detecting the difference between over, under and behind.

A map and a compass are relatively useless at an unknown location in invisible surroundings, but we knew roughly where we were and set off in an approximate direction toward the neighbouring valley. Not surprisingly, our track led us into higher terrain and as we progressed it became steeper and steeper. Soon we couldn't even turn our skis. We were forced to sidestep, keeping our minds on the task at hand and trusting that an avalanche would not sweep us away. Poor Kazan had no chance of keeping the sled upright, so his strength was drained by the time the three of us through our combined efforts made it over the ridge and down the other side. The storm had abated and been replaced by a thick fog. Once again, everything was white, until what we assumed was a hallucination presented a large house in the distance. As if by a stroke of magic it turned into a small cabin right before our eyes. As the fog lifted, we saw that we had reached the Spiterstulen tourist lodge. Many years later we were told that this ridge had never before been crossed on skis.

Did that turn you into a careful man?

More careful. Later on I set out on a ski trip alone with Kazan. To some this might seem even more foolish, but it had a specific purpose.

It was in the mid-1930s, and an early Easter snowstorm had been forecast in the mountains. I had accompanied a cousin to a railway station on the Dovre line. We had spent some time in a snowhole in Trollheimen, and brought Kazan on a hike up to Snøhetta. My cousin was returning to Trondheim, while Kazan and I were going to cross the plateau of the Dovre mountain range and continue down to Gudbrandsdalen. I had only reached Hjerkinn when the storm set in. I sought shelter in a mountain lodge in front of a warm fireplace, enjoying waffles, cloudberries and cream and cocoa. The snow beat against the walls of the lodge, and Kazan lay quietly under the table awaiting his turn. A dog should know that he will always be cared for and never beg. Kazan knew that I also looked forward to presenting his approaching meal. It would be quite a change from the dried fish packed on the sled. By the time we had finished, the storm had reached full gale force. It howled and screeched against the walls and roof of the lodge, and no one was allowed to venture outdoors without holding on to the rope that was tied to a door on the side building.

It was then that I recognized the storm as a personal challenge. The Dovre plateau had no cliffs or barriers. The mountain was above the tree line, and its bushes, rocks, lakes and fences all lay under a mantle of deep snow. The men at the lodge tried to keep me from leaving, but nothing could stop me. Neither the locals nor the gusts of the storm could prevent me from strapping Kazan to the front of the sled and my skis to my leather-lined ski boots. After a few strokes with my ski poles in the heavy snow, I was out of sight.

I was forced to lean forward against the storm; the pace was slow. Even Kazan had to struggle and pull with all his wolf-like might to make any headway. In ideal conditions on level terrain he could pull a loaded sled and my own weight effortlessly. Today he had to break through deep powder snow, and the snow falling from the sky was trivial in comparison to the stinging gusts of ground snow that whipped around us. Sometimes Kazan fell out of sight and my only recourse was to wait for him to appear, often with an overturned sled. Each reunion was an occasion of joy because we were equally afraid of losing one another.

What was the point of this wrestling match against the elements?

I kept repeating the words: 'This will make the boy a man! This will make the boy a man!'

I knew I had found my true self in the nature of the mountains, but not yet in the city. When I first returned to the city and my studies from my mountain hikes, I walked with self-confidence among the rows of buildings and felt that this was nothing compared to what I had experienced in the mountains, but by the next day the buildings had already become too much for me. They seemed to lean over me, making me feel small and insignificant. All I could do was yield to them and enter their world. Kazan probably felt the same way when he looked at me and peed on the corners of houses.

It was time to defeat this insecurity – almost cowardice – that overcame me whenever I was on asphalt or living-room floors. I had to train up my self-confidence and realize that I was the same person, whether I was walking on heather, grass, pavements or living-room carpets.

It must be that I still had some growing up to do. I was surely suffering from the after effects of a spoiled childhood.

'This will make the boy a man!' No reason to go any further. We were still undefeated, and being in the midst of the primitive forces of the mountain, simply able to lie down and sleep, was a triumph in itself. It was impossible to dig a shelter or build an igloo in this light snow. I managed to find the small tent on the sled, but it was impossible to set it up in the storm. No problem, I thought. I just crawled into where it lay on the ground and pulled Kazan in after me. And there we lay while the storm swept drifts of snow over us like soft quilts, me in my reindeer sleeping bag and Kazan in his coat of Greenland fur.

Then my heart began to throb. I had heard a train whistle. The Dovre line between Oslo and Trondheim was somewhere around here. The whistling came closer. Where were the tracks? The sound grew stronger; I could even hear the locomotive's engine. The train was bearing down on us at full speed!

Kazan was just as frightened as I was. We had to find our way out of both the sleeping bag and the tent. Since the tracks were buried deep in the snow, I panicked with the realization that we could just as well stay where we were. We certainly didn't know which side the train was on. It is on occasions like this that even an atheist finds himself hoping for the existence of a god, and promising to be good if he survives. I was more dead than alive when the hammering of the pistons reached a crescendo as the plough thrust masses of snow toward us and the train's car and wheels created an inferno of sound as they passed. No one on the train knew that outside, in the stormy night, just beside the tracks, a boy lay buried beneath the snow with a dog in his arms, simply because he wanted to be a man.

5

In the Footsteps of Darwin

From the vantage point of our orchard on Tenerife, we could see the pine forest reaching right up to the bare mountain. From there, Teide, a snow-clad peak, soared to 3,700 metres above sea level. In my earliest childhood years it took us three days to travel from our home by the Larvik Fjord to our Hornsjø mountain cabin. The trip demanded two overnighters, several changes of train and a seven-hour journey by horse and carriage from the Hunder railway station. Today we can get to Hornsjø from Tenerife in a day. But the idea does not tempt us. Bulldozers, new buildings and dilapidated old ones had not left much of the Hornsjø that I reminisced about while relaxing under the blue skies in my hammock and speaking to my aku-aku.

You have not said much about girls.

There was pitifully little to say about girls in my boyhood. When we were still in our prams, I had a pretty little brown-eyed girlfriend with black hair cut like a pageboy. Once I saw her naked and although this was very interesting, I couldn't tell which side was her front and which was her back. When I turned six and went to school,

I started to understand more and realized that it was a disgrace for a boy to play with girls. They had dolls and we had cap guns. Boys and girls were not allowed to attend the same class; we even had different playgrounds, separated by a high brick wall.

The difference between the male and the female became so overwhelming that I was torn with shyness when I had to ask a girl to dance at Miss Dødelein's dancing classes. My parents sent me there in patent leather shoes and a sailor suit for three consecutive years. I was awkward, sneaking out into the hallway to draw the steps of the waltz and the tango on a piece of paper. In spite of my efforts, I tripped over my own and other's feet, and never learned to execute the steps the way I had drawn them on paper.

This awkwardness would give me my first big opportunity with the opposite sex.

Girls and boys were allowed to be in the same class from middle school onwards, and during my high school years I had more contact with girls. There were dances and other fun get-togethers, but I missed almost all of them because I declined any invitation that could possibly involve dancing.

So my school years came to a close without any experience with the opposite sex. My anticipation of forming a relationship with the right woman grew steadily stronger. When I graduated from high school, wearing the traditional red-tasselled cap and partaking in the joy of having no more exams, I performed in the school play. I helped to write it, and had the lead part as the pioneer balloonist, Professor Piccard, a real person who had recently become the first man to guide his balloon into the stratosphere. In my version, however, he was so absent-minded that he forgot to return and ended up at the heavenly gates of St Peter and the angels. This was my first and only theatrical endeavour, and it was a success.

All the graduates from the small towns in the area were invited to the final party for my class in Larvik. We had dinner, wine, a youth orchestra and dancing at a beach restaurant in Stavern, the outermost point on the Larvik Fjord. Everyone danced after dinner. Even Arnold. I was left alone with a glass of beer, trying to seem above it all and staring coolly at the boats that passed the glass balcony in the light summer night.

Then Arnold came over and introduced me to a graduate from another town and his dancing partner. I saw only the latter. Liv had curly blonde hair, bright blue laughing eyes, lips that were naturally red and a countenance that reflected both wisdom and determination. She wore a flattering white summer dress; had it been possible I would have equipped her with enormous white wings and she could have stepped right into the role of an angel in my school play.

She wanted to dance.

I desperately tried all sorts of excuses.

'Shall we dance?' she repeated.

I was determined to keep her by my side.

'Couldn't we take a walk on the beach?' I asked in panic. To my relief she agreed.

Reflections from the stars and the restaurant lights danced on the water. It was a beautiful evening and she appreciated its beauty too. We went back inside and found a place to sit.

'Would you like to join me in an experimental return to nature?' The words just fell out of my mouth.

'If so, we would have to go all the way back,' Liv answered, adding that this was not to be a Hollywood farce.

I was overwhelmed. She was willing to return to a primitive life in a primal forest – and with me. We could find a South Sea island, or some other place where such an experiment would be possible after my planned studies of geography.

I sat in silence. One look at Liv's friendly but determined face convinced me that her answer was genuine. It was a sacred moment. But then the night with Liv came to an end. She would be graduating the next year, and had been invited from the neighbouring town of Brevik by an amiable young man who took his defeat like a gentleman and later became a friend. The bus was waiting; some had a long way to go, but Liv and I were going to keep in touch.

It was difficult for young people from different towns to keep in touch at that time. How would Liv's parents react to a long-distance call from a boy they had never met and who lived in another town? Being a girl, she could not call me.

Almost two years would pass before I saw Liv again.

Meanwhile the boy had become a young university student. After exchanging the red-tasselled cap for the heavier black cap worn by university students, I walked up the grand stairway in the university building in downtown Oslo near the royal palace. Most of my friends were going to study law, medicine or the humanities, and they were at the new university complex that was being built at Blindern, on the outskirts of the city. I was the only zoology student among them, and I felt the gravity of what was waiting for me behind the impressive oak door on the right at the top of the stairway. I had no idea that Fridtjof Nansen had also used this door until his death just a few years earlier. I did know that he had studied zoology and that, unlike Amundsen, he had been a professional scientist in his field and the author of important scientific dissertations. He had even held the title of professor in zoology, and I was about to meet his successor, who would become my advisor.

Why were you going to study, you who were supposed to go back to nature?

My plan was more involved than going to Africa, taking off my clothes and looking for food. I had to know more about the blank spots on the map of the world, and have an emergency plan in case my attempt as an explorer failed.

I was filled with anticipation when I pushed the door into the department of zoology, and thought back to the time when the door to my room in the stables had a *Museum of Zoology* sign. Here I had expected to be confronted by rooms filled with stuffed animals, but the first thing I saw was a human skeleton. It was placed inside the door like a silent butler, with all of its bones, including those on the skull, labelled in Latin. It was popularly known as 'Olsen'. I understood that human beings represented the latest stage of animal evolution and that this stage could not be displayed as a nude body. All the other animals on the floors and shelves were also shown in skeleton form, except for some stomachs and creepy embryos suspended in jars of alcohol. The first intact creation that I saw was my future professor, in her office. A woman greatly admired by my mother, Kristine Bonnevie was one of the three women in Norway who had attained the title of professor. I bowed with respect at the door and shook hands with a firm but friendly woman holding an old-fashioned lorgnette. Silently I hoped to myself that she would have more to offer the ear than she did the eye.

She asked why I wanted to become a zoologist and warned me that there were few available positions unless I planned to teach in high school.

I told her of my childhood dream of becoming an explorer, and about my interest in animal life, from insects to the larger mammals I had been studying in the wilderness over the last few years. She then let me understand that her own interests leaned more toward microscopic anatomy and research into the laws of heredity. However she welcomed me to her lectures and recommended that I consult with her colleague in the office next door, Professor Hjalmar Broch, a specialist in coral polyps.

As I was leaving her office, she called me back to look at a small amateur photograph. I clearly saw a moose in the background.

'What is this? A moose or a reindeer?' she asked.

My first test, I thought, before answering, 'A moose, of course.'

'How can you tell?'

'By its stance, its general impression.'

Embarrassed, she explained that someone had sent her the picture for expert identification but that the table in her reference book for the definition of mammals only said that moose and reindeer could be distinguished by the fact that a reindeer's nostrils were close together while a moose's were on either side of the snout. 'And in the picture one can't see the nostrils,' she added with a smile.

On my first day at the university I had already learned something important: being a specialist is not the same as being omniscient. To the contrary. The terms are contradictory.

I had looked forward to learning more about animal life from a zoology professor than I had from a man of the mountains such as Ola Bjørneby. It turned out that the country's leading authority on animals couldn't see the difference between moose and reindeer without studying their nostrils.

Nevertheless, after my mother, and until Liv came back into the picture, Professor Bonnevie may have been the most important woman in my young life. I was unaware of her importance then, but in retrospect she staked out my future path within a few days. To begin with, she thought of a subject for my thesis that gave me both a reason and an excuse for going to Polynesia. Secondly, since she saw human beings as part of the animal world, she trained zoology students in physical anthropology by teaching us about the indexes of the cranium and the heritability of blood types. Genealogy was her main interest, and chromosome composition was more important to her than animals in their natural habitat. After a while, branching out from pure zoology to the study of human origins and cultural development became a logical transition.

Liv came to Oslo to start her studies the following year, and when we finally renewed our acquaintance, I introduced her to my mother and Kazan, but not to my professors, because her father had decided that she was to study social economics. We immediately picked up where we had left off that summer night at the graduation party, and I could tell her that the plan was well on its way.

I had not mentioned my idea of leaving civilization in order to study it from a different perspective to anyone other than Liv and my two friends from Larvik, but my academic programme was set up to provide the knowledge needed to find a suitable location. By then my opinion of my university professor had changed radically. She was extremely knowledgeable, even though her area of expertise was not what interested me most. Zoology had become so specialized that senior scientists in the same laboratory had lost contact with what their colleagues were doing. Research solely for the sake of research. One was only to present what one had found; maybe someone could make use of it in the future.

Liv was shocked when she heard that I sat staring into a microscope, counting the number of hairs on the backs of a few thousand small banana flies – flies that our class had hatched in jars to control the validity of Mendel's law of heredity. Per Høst, the oldest in our group of seven, earned everyone's admiration when he opened his jar and let all the small yellow flies out the window, because – as he said – we all knew that Mendel's law was correct, so this was a waste of time. Per had grafted a fifth leg on the back of a salamander, and it moved on its own, independently of the four others. He once placed it on the shoulder of an unsuspecting fellow who had tasted a bit too much of a laboratory cocktail at a hotdog and beer party at Per's house. The cheerful student did not bat an eye when he saw the monster move the leg on its back. He calmly set his glass down and carefully studied his shoulder, but by then Per had removed the creature. It was Per who had to suffer the consequences, because the man became so ill that he rushed across the room and leaned out the window. Per lived on the seventh floor, and in the morning the family on the ground floor complained to the man on the floor above, and complaints were passed up from floor to floor until there was no one left for Per to blame. He worked his way down to street level with a bucket and a mop.

Only Per, Yngvar Hagen and Edvard Barth shared my interest in animal life in the forest. Per's brother-in-law was a manager in the city's main camera shop, and we were able to borrow 16mm movie cameras by trading film clips of moose, viper, owls and whatever we might find in the great outdoors on Sundays and during holidays.

Our other classmates chose to write about more curious subjects. For example, a totally normal and pleasant fellow by the name of Støp-Bowitz decided to study the colour structure of tube worms in the surf. He probably had little use for this later in life, but he did well anyway; one has to study something.

We all realized that specialization was necessary for the progress of science. There was no point in taking a superficial view; one had to limit the field and delve into the material. Even then, however, I was beginning to see that something was wrong. Specialists were in the process of learning more and more about less and less, and the price they had to pay was that ignorance gradually ate its way into their own fields of learning. This was bound to happen because the specialists discovered that there was still so very much that remained unknown to mankind.

Of course specialists must continue to delve into their material, but they must not lose sight of the forest for the trees. Universities also needed institutions that did not examine small pockets of information but kept sight of the overall picture and systematized the findings of other specialists. Someone had to put the pieces together.

By the time Liv came to Oslo I had already added geography to my studies on the advice of both of my zoology professors. I had studied enough mathematical geography to understand the consequences of the fact that the earth was round. Ancient geographers had discovered this long before Columbus, but when it came to the Pacific Ocean no one had taken on board the consequences of that fact, not even the anthropologists when they presented their theories about migration across the enormous ocean. They drew arrows on the map and talked about the straight line along the equator and the circuitous route along the continental coast running northward from tropical Asia and then back down again to tropical South America. In reality, a straight line from the coast of Southeast Asia to South

America would cut through the centre of the earth because the world is round and the Pacific Ocean is so large that it covers an entire hemisphere. Southeast Asia and South America were antipodal at the equatorial line since they were 180 degrees apart, therefore a route over the North Pole was no longer than one along the equator. If one followed what the geographers called the 'great circle', all the curves along the surface of the Pacific from the Philippines to Peru were equally long. But everything that could float, from coconuts to primitive vessels, would get a free ride with the wind and current, from America to Asia in the equatorial belt and from Asia to America with the warm Japan Current from the Philippine Ocean and up to the northernmost section of the Pacific.

I would soon learn that this mathematical knowledge of geography was necessary, even though I detested the textbook. When I became better acquainted with my elderly geography professor, Werner Werenskiold, he confessed that he had purposefully written it in such a complicated manner in order to show his colleagues in other fields that geography was also a science.

The geography classes were even more informative and the knowledge I gained there had an immediate effect on my plan. It forced Liv and I to eliminate all areas for our project except the thousands of islands spread out in the enormous Pacific Ocean. Werenskiold taught us about the trees in the primal forest and how their closed canopies of foliage high above ground prohibit the passage of sunshine, preventing the gathering of flowers and berries from the ground in the jungle. You have to climb the trees to find sustenance and, once there, you realize that the monkeys have taken anything edible and left nothing for their tail-less relatives on the ground. Liv understood why I had rejected the blank spots that still existed in Africa and the unexplored jungles of South America. In the jungle, food grew at a lever higher than we could reach.

After learning that I was interested in going somewhere in the Pacific Ocean, Professor Bonnevie gave me the idea of following in the footsteps of Darwin. Charles Darwin, my mother's great hero, had been on the Galapagos Islands off the coast of South America when he developed his theory on the origin of the species. The scattered islands of Polynesia were even further out in the ocean. Some had risen from the bottom of the sea through volcanic activity, and others had been built up by coral polyps, but they all had risen from the ocean without any form of native land animals. How had plants and animals come there? Bonnevie had just read a work published by the Bishop Museum on Hawaii by an American zoologist who had studied land snails on the isolated Marquesas Islands and observed how they had developed into new species and strains from island to island in relationship to their elevation over the ocean.

The Marquesas Islands. We were all equally excited – my mother who thought about Darwin's theory on the origin of the species, my professor who had the idea, and Liv and I who had been pinpointing Pacific islands that turned out to have been influenced or touched by civilization, lacking in drinking water or uninhabitable for some other reason. It soon became clear that Professor Werenskiold's mathematical calculations of great circles and the effect of the earth's rotation on the ocean's currents and winds were important.

Nevertheless it may have been the university preparatory courses in logic and philosophy that were most useful in my later life. The philosophy of ancient Greece was best suited to my way of thinking. I liked Diogenes, who was content to sit in his barrel and enjoy the sun, and Socrates, who peered into a shop window and was pleased to see how much he could do without.

Simple logic allowed me to conclude that a balsa-wood raft could manage to float from Peru to Polynesia. In the first place, the botanist F. B. H. Brown, the world's leading expert on the flora of the Marquesas Islands, had discovered that several useful South American plants, which could not have reached the Marquesas Islands without the aid of humans, were already growing there when the Europeans arrived. And secondly, the world's leading expert on pre-European navigation had proved that there were no other boats at that time other than balsa rafts. Ergo: the balsa raft had to have managed the crossing even though everyone else – without having tried it – believed the opposite.

You weren't actually thinking of attempting the crossing yourself?

Absolutely not. I still had not learned to swim. I planned a future with my feet planted firmly on the ground. But barefoot.

One summer, when Liv had grown close enough to my mother for me to risk inviting her to Hornsjø, I asked her to take off her shoes and walk barefoot through the heather and undergrowth just like me. I believed that we should harden ourselves and build up thicker skin on the soles of our feet. We also tried to make fire by rubbing dry sticks of spruce, birch and juniper together, without success. Otherwise I was so well prepared that I was even giving lectures about the Marquesas Islands at the university before we left home.

It was probably one of the first and most fortunate coincidences in my life that Bjarne Kroepelin's Polynesia library happened to be in Oslo and was available to me when I was studying. This was the world's largest collection of literature on Polynesia, and my parents happened to know the owner, a prosperous wine importer. Bjarne had been to Tahiti when he was a young man, and Kroepelin had fallen in love with Tuimata, the beautiful daughter of the chieftain Teriieroo. This would come to have a double influence on my life, because over the years this love affair would lead to the development of Kroepelin's collection of books about Polynesia, and Teriieroo would come to be my adopted Polynesian father. Tragically Spanish influenza came to Tahiti while young Kroepelin was there, and the Polynesians died like flies. He and Tuimata helped load the dead on to wagons until Tuimata herself fell ill and died. Bjarne Kroepelin never forgot her. He wrote a beautiful little book about Tuimata, which ended with the words: 'And where Tuimata lies, there my heart lies buried.' He dedicated the rest of his life to collecting his

Polynesia library. He was in contact with dealers in rare books and buyers the world over, and bought everything that was printed about Polynesia, no matter what the price.

During the seven semesters that I spent with my fellow students in lecture theatres following lectures in biology and geography, I spent just as much time alone sitting with a notepad in a leather chair at an old-fashioned desk, surrounded by Kroepelin's bookshelves.

These studies were useful references during the later years of controversy. My opponents in the rest of the world saw me as a sailor with Viking blood, and the anthropologists in Norway discredited the competence of zoologists when it came to issues about prehistoric vessels. I was well prepared to defend my theories after having read everything that explorers, missionaries, circumnavigators and scientists had published up until the 1930s, and I had kept up with additions to the Kroepelin library in the years that followed. When Kroepelin died, his entire Polynesia library was moved to the research section at the Kon-Tiki Museum.

Geographically, Polynesia had to be as close as one could get to paradise on earth, even though its population had been partially eradicated and ravaged by diseases that Europeans had brought with them. I knew that 80 per cent of the population of the Marquesas Islands had perished because of disease, and for this reason we concluded that there would be enough wild fruit trees in the depopulated areas for our survival.

I was fully aware that the question of who the Polynesians were and where they had come from was still unsolved. And I wondered why the anthropologists paid no heed to the observations of the botanists. I myself planned to collect everything of zoological interest that could be stored in crocks or glass containers. The question of how the Polynesians had come to Polynesia did not interest me very much. We had more than enough work figuring out how we could get there. In the 1930s no travel agency in Norway had heard of the

Marquesas Islands. Their expertise was based on Norwegian coastal steamships, a few isolated trips to islands in the Mediterranean and emigration to America. Scheduled air travel did not exist, and certainly not across the oceans. When I said farewell to neighbourhood children who were leaving for America, we knew that it was a farewell for life.

This was the situation we were dealing with when Bennet's Travel Bureau in Oslo learned from Paris that the closest one could get to the Marquesas Islands was Tahiti, and that a ship from Marseilles sailed there once a month to unload cargo and passengers going to French New Caledonia. The only other alternative was to take a Norwegian freighter that had a scheduled route to San Francisco, Samoa and Tahiti every month or so. We chose to disembark on Tahiti after a six-week voyage on the *Messangerie Maritime* across the Atlantic and through the Panama Canal.

That sounds easy.

Not that easy. Liv was only twenty years old and still a minor, and I only had fifty crowns a month in pocket money from my father.

I remember Liv and I sitting by a window at the Theatercafé in Oslo, watching drab people rushing past with umbrellas and overcoats without greeting one another. I ordered soda pop and creamy layer cake and tried to convince Liv, who looked a little uncertain, that we would be able to persuade our parents that we should get married and travel to the Marquesas. Liv envisioned her father's harsh reaction, and she smiled and shuddered simultaneously. But we concocted a plan and I pulled Kazan out from under the table, followed Liv to the trolley and walked home through the palace park to begin working on my mother.

She was easy to persuade. Professors Bonnevie and Broch had confirmed that after seven semesters the zoology lectures would simply begin again from the beginning, and their word was enough for her. Also, Broch supported Bonnevie's plan that I could get a doctorate by studying the origin of the species on the Marquesas

Islands – if I went there and collected material. Liv had already captured my mother's heart and, in consideration of the seductive South Sea girls, she thought it was very wise to marry Liv and bring her with me.

Persuading my father was more difficult. Considering exactly the same South Sea girls, he meant that marrying before I left was like crossing a stream to find water. He agreed to finance the journey as a part of my studies, even though it was unusually long, but my marriage would have to wait until I returned and found a job. For once I made no progress with my father. My arguments simply made no impression on him.

However I knew that my father's greatest wish was to become friends with my mother again. The fact that she still refused to see him provided a good opportunity.

'Mamma agrees,' I said carefully.

He answered immediately: 'Then I have to speak to her.'

I was already prepared. She had agreed to invite him for coffee by the fireplace, and that was all it took for total agreement between my parents and myself. I've never had a better time sitting in front of the fire.

It was harder for Liv. She wrote a beautiful letter to her lonely parents in Brevik and told them that she had met a boy from Larvik called Thor, and that we were thinking of getting married and going to the Marquesas Islands. Liv's mother, who was a very intellectual and gentle woman, later described her husband's reaction when she read the letter to him. With a red-flushed face, he left his large and roomy armchair and walked slowly to the bookshelf and searched the volume *M* in an old encyclopaedia from the end of the last century. Finding it, he read out loud that the Marquesas Islands were remote islands in the Pacific where there were still 'cannibals and immorality'.

My future father-in-law simply refused to lose his only daughter to cannibals, and my future bride almost lost her father to a heart attack. We dropped the discussion for a while, until my father, now satisfied with our scheme, allowed my mother to persuade him to pay a visit to Brevik. Here he would use all of his charm so that everyone could agree that the plan was good, and that my father would pay for the honeymoon. We ended up getting married on Christmas Eve, in a simple ceremony in the family's living room. It was snowing the next morning as they all waved goodbye to two youthful newlyweds who took the train south into Europe to board a huge ocean steamer in Marseilles with tickets to Tahiti.

A ticket to paradise, we thought. But by the end of the expedition we concluded that admission into paradise cannot be bought. Those who have found paradise have found it within themselves for free. Everything I had seen and read had taught me that paradise and hell do not have separate locations on this planet. They are always in the same place, and one cannot simply avoid one by moving away. The two of them turn up like inseparable companions, no matter how far you have travelled. But they cannot always be seen at the same time, so you have to settle down for a while to be sure you experience both aspects.

The tickets that my father purchased in Norway brought us to Tahiti in French Oceania. In the 1930s, Tahiti was still the way it was when Kroepelin had buried his heart with Tuimata. There were no cars in the narrow streets between the small wooden houses in the capital, Papeete, which was dominated by Chinese vendors selling their wares from small hand carts. There was one hotel, where you could sit up in the bed and look over the wall into the adjoining room. There was no regular contact with the distant Marquesas Islands, and many weeks could pass before a captain on a schooner was ready to sail there and load his ship with copra. There was still no suitable road for driving cars around the whole island, but one could make it all the way to the Papeno valley on a picturesque bus filled with colourful *vahines* à la Gauguin, with live chickens and pigs on laps and the rooftop.

We squeezed into the bus and got off in Papeno, still the home of Chief Teriieroo, the father of beautiful Tuimata and the most powerful of Tahiti's seventeen chieftains. Large and generous both in spirit and flesh, he was a full-blooded descendant of the ancient Polynesian chieftain families. We arrived with gifts from Bjarne Kroepelin and were received with open arms and automatically declared part of the family. Four weeks were to pass before a bus brought the message that a schooner would be sailing for the Marquesas. In the meantime we had learned a great deal. We were both barefoot and wearing colourful *pareu* and Liv spent her time with Faufau and the women of the house around the glowing hearth on the kitchen floor, while I went with the chief and his sons into the forests and the fields.

The most important thing I learned on Tahiti was how to swim. And I did not learn this skill voluntarily.

I fell into the Papeno River because I stepped on a spiny snail shell and got caught by the current. I ended up underwater in a large basin just before the water ran into thundering breakers at the outlet. I swam automatically to save my own life and managed to pull myself up into the heather before it was too late. Swimming was so easy and so much fun that as soon as I saved myself I dove into the basin again and swam around.

It was harder to learn how to climb a coconut palm. The first time I managed to climb one, I encountered a hornet's nest between the coconuts. Since I couldn't climb down again quickly, I slid down the notched trunk and landed on the ground skinless and bruised and was forced to let Teriieroo pull out the nail on my big toe with pliers.

We finally departed on a schooner for the Marquesas Islands. We were set ashore in a lifeboat on an island devoid of white people, radios, or any other form of contact with the rest of the world.

Can you remember what you thought?

That the world was incredibly large. The ship journey alone had taken more than two months. And on Tahiti I had heard that the Marquesas Islands were so isolated from the rest of the world that no one there had known about the outbreak of the First World War in 1914 before it had ended in 1918, even though Papeete had been shelled by German warships.

Farewells are always a little sad. Had I not been forced to stay in control for Liv's sake, I would have probably given in to the lump in my throat when we were left alone on the beach looking out over the ocean and watching the lifeboat return to the schooner. The ship hoisted its sails and disappeared beyond the horizon. Maybe he would return in a year, Captain Barnder had said. We turned away from the ocean and discovered brown faces along the edge of the forest under the coconut palms. They were staring at us. We had so many questions, but no common language. What I remember best is noticing that the crowns of the palms were filled with coconuts and thinking that, for now, we would not starve.

It was strange to recall all of these small details so many years later. It seemed that I had lived many lives since then, though in another sense it seemed like many of them happened only a few weeks ago.

'What are you lying there thinking about, with a notepad and a pencil on your stomach?' a happy voice asked. When I looked up, my aku-aku disappeared into the green foliage of the avocado tree and I was left alone in the hammock with Jacqueline's happy face peering through the branches.

'I was thinking about Fatu-Hiva,' I admitted, 'my first attempt to find paradise.'

'But you didn't find it with Liv on the South Sea islands. You say that one has to look for it in one's innermost self, and that the closest one can come to an outer paradise is by cultivating one's own piece of land.'

Certainly. Therefore it was not the island Fatu-Hiva and my experiences there that I wanted to recall. I simply wanted to clarify what

I had learned after a year of full board and lodging in the unlocked and abandoned guest house in the jungle.

Jacqueline didn't want to interrupt; she just wondered whether cheese and salad would be enough for supper. She had barely left before my aku-aku reappeared.

So you didn't find the paradise you sought on Fatu-Hiva, even though you say that it's the most beautiful and fertile island you have seen in the Pacific Ocean?

Yes, we found paradise when Fatu-Hiva rose into sight on the ocean like a floating basket of flowers, and its wonderful tropical aromas were carried by the breeze to meet us. It was on the beach of paradise that we waded ashore in tropical sunshine toward rows of palms welcoming us to the jungle garden that was uninhabited further into the valley.

Small fluffy clouds sprang like peaceful white lambs over the high wall of brick red mountains that divided the island in two behind the green canopy of the jungle. Even when the magnificent sounds of birdsong paused in the afternoon, when the midday heat and magically formed heavy dark clouds that concealed the mountains and chased the lambs away, even when the brook continued gurgling down the valley, just as happily as before, we were still in paradise. Weeks passed and we were filled with the same love of nature and the feelings we had in the wilderness at home. We never felt lonely or homesick, even though our surroundings were totally different from the pine forests we had loved. Bread fruit, bananas, oranges, and papaya hung over our heads, and there were no monkeys to get to them before we did. We literally enjoyed the fruits of what had been brought to the island from the east and the west, by people who had contracted contagious diseases and been sent to the eternal hunting grounds in the last century. With the exception of fern nuts, nothing that was edible to humans had grown on these isolated islands in Polynesia until people came here.

If there was a paradise on earth then we had discovered it up in the Omoa valley, and no one kept us from settling there. We found a tall platform of huge stone blocks – a pae-pae. The valley had many of these structures, which once held palm-covered huts above the mud in the rainy season. This one was right next to a spring with cold, crystal-clear water that ran into a brook filled with crayfish. The last queen of the island had lived here, according to those who had outlived her and moved to a small village down by the ocean. This is where we built our first home of bamboo, covered with braided palm leaves, and with an opening that gave us a view over paradise. It was our own Garden of Eden.

But the real Garden of Eden probably had no mosquitoes, unless it was mosquitoes that finally drove Adam and Eve away. For weeks we had roamed around naked and barefoot in the middle of the valley, which was ours alone. The only four-legged creatures were lizards and small fruit rats, except for the descendants of lost household animals brought by the Europeans that had survived in the wilderness. No snakes. In my entire collection, the only poisonous insects were some huge poisonous millipedes that usually stayed under rocks and never attacked, except for one time when a drunken and evil-minded native called Napoleon placed a few of them among the banana leaves in our bed in the hope of pleasing the God of the Catholic priests by driving Protestants away.

The mosquitoes came in thick swarms when the rainy season started, and that was the end of paradise. We were well on our way to perishing in an inferno of itching and stinging. I experienced hell in the Garden of Eden when my fears culminated in the sight of Liv rolling on the floor in the bamboo hut, moaning with pain and covered with mosquitoes. I had never seen her frightened or heard her complain, but we had to give up. Today survival in the garden of paradise on a South Sea island requires insect netting. Down in the village we were given some netting by an extremely helpful copra vendor, the island's only half-blooded inhabitant. He was a son of

Paul Gauguin's friend Grelet, who had lived with the natives in the village at the turn of the century.

But not only were mosquitoes chasing us from paradise. We knew it was only a matter of time before we would become infested with filaria, the worm that causes the dreaded elephantiasis, a disease that had devastated the village. Every tenth person either carried arms that were as thick as thighs or humped around on enormously enlarged limbs that were just as fat around the ankles as the waist. Leprosy had also taken its toll down by the coast, and of course there was no doctor or hospital. Life became intolerable when Liv developed huge boils on her legs which the natives called *fe-fe*, and they burst and turned into open sores that refused to heal. We left the jungle and relocated to the coast in the Ouia valley, on the windward side of the island where small white clouds came sailing with the trade winds from South America. The constant easterly wind blew all the gnats far into the woods and for a few wonderful weeks we experienced paradise again.

Ironically, it was the villagers who had warned us against moving over to the windward side because the ocean was rough all year round and nobody could risk getting into a canoe to fish. The only one person still living there was Tei Tetua, the last survivor of the era of cannibalism.

'Your father should have seen this,' I said to Liv as we crossed the mountain ridge and down the cliffs to the Ouia valley. The old man was running toward us, stark naked except for a strip of dark cloth protecting his most precious parts. His face shone with joy at seeing people in the valley and he welcomed us with the usual phrase: *Hamai te kaikai*, 'Come and eat'. But this was no empty phrase to Tei Tetua. He was a Polynesian of the old school, the only person I would meet who had entered the twentieth century as if the Europeans still had not arrived in the Pacific. He lived with his adopted twelve-year-old daughter Tahia-Momo in total isolation from the rest of the world.

Liv's father had not read a total falsehood about cannibals on the Marquesas. Officially the last instance of cannibalism occurred at a large party in the Puamao valley on the neighbouring island of Hivaoa in 1887. The last person identified as having been eaten was a Swedish carpenter who had been consumed in 1879. Tei Tetua told us modestly that he had only ever tasted a person who had been beaten to death in the neighbouring valley when he was a child. His father, Uta, however, had been a veritable cannibal who not only consumed his fallen enemies as a ritual, but because he preferred the taste to pork.

The bristly hogs of his forefathers grunted and dug freely in the Ouia valley, where Tei Tetua, with his dogs and lasso of bast, was the only hunter. It is unthinkable to imagine better pork than that the old man served, with fresh breadfruit rolled in banana leaves and baked in his earth oven. He helped us build our own hut in the shape of an open bird's nest with three walls. It was raised on high poles to keep the wild hogs from coming in when we were sleeping.

We never made our own food again. The little Polynesian charmer Tahia-Momo brought us all our meals on large taro leaves from Tei's hut, which was also just inside the beach of rolling stones and only a stone's throw away from our pole hut. Food was plentiful, and there was more variation than in the jungle on the other side of the island, where no one had lived since the move to the leeward side of the island in the last century. Tei Tetua kept chickens, and up in the naked ferny hills on either side of the Ouia valley, there were masses of wonderful cherry tomatoes and *enata* pineapples. The botanist F. B. H. Brown had concluded that this fruit must have been brought by people from South America before the Europeans discovered that there were islands in the Pacific.

And then there was the ocean finally cresting and breaking on the beach for the first time after having rolled in great swells from the coast of South America 8,000 kilometres away. The breakers made the round stones constantly roll and rattle on the beach in a rhythmical concert complete with its own waterfall. The ocean spray provided fresh circulation in all the salt-water puddles in the lava formations that flanked the valley, and they were filled with life. Crabs and fish crawled and swam among sea snails, sea anemone and sea weed. Compared to the continent's jungles, the ocean was a more suitable foster mother for us two-legged creatures without climbing skills.

Luckily there are many friendly people on our planet, and I have met many of them, but none are as incredibly kind and generous as this former cannibal. We could shudder a bit while sitting on our haunches, chewing on a meaty bone and listening to his stories from another time and another world. He described how Papa Uta, with a beautifully carved wooden club that is now a valuable museum piece, went off to war to get revenge on enemies in Hanativa, or walked all the way to the Omoa valley, where Tei now had his only remaining relatives.

Tei Tetua was no heathen. Everyone in the island group was now Christian. A priest from the Catholic mission in Hivaoa had come over the mountain and converted him. He had learned that in French Tiki was called 'Dieu' and, just to be on the safe side, he had dug out his own grave next to the wall of his hut and placed a cross right over it, which he proudly showed us. Tahia-Momo would come here and help him if he had too little strength to crawl into it when he felt that death was approaching.

He firmly claimed that according to his own forefathers the first people had come across the ocean with Tiki from the east, from Te-Fiti, where the sun rises. I knew from Kroepelin's library that the German ethnographer von den Steinen had heard a generation ago from old people on the Marquesas Islands that there was a large country behind the sunrise that was called Fiti-Nui, 'The Great East'. The American ethnologist E. S. C. Handy, who visited Hivaoa later, heard that the inhabitants' forefathers had come from this large country in the east called Te-Fiti. Handy was so surprised by the assertion that their fatherland was in the east, in the direction of South America, that according to his own words he had to ask twice. Again it was firmly maintained that one had to steer in *te tihena oumati*, 'with a course toward the sunrise', to find the ancestral homeland.

Tei Tetua was just as certain about this. We were mosquito-free, sitting at the edge of the woods and looking over the endless ocean in the direction of where the sun appeared at dawn. The small clouds faithfully followed the wake of the trade winds across the night sky. And when Tei Tetua told us about what he had learned in his youth, it was obvious that he had learned his lessons well, without the letters of the alphabet. Without having read botanical works, he could tell me things I myself had learned from reference books. He was fully aware of the fact that the wild pineapple and the tiny tomatoes up on the hillside had been brought by his own forefathers, whom he called *enata*, 'people', as opposed to foreigners. Even the younger generation in the Omoa valley was aware of the source of the useful species. They had two types of pineapple, *faa hoka*, but only one was called *enata*, because it was their original fruit; the other was called *oahu*, because a missionary from Oahu in the Hawaiian Islands had brought it to them. They also had two types of American papaya, the larger one called *vi oahu* and the smaller with the taller trunk called *vi enata*. The nickname *enata* was consistently given to species that botanists had identified as having been brought by boat from the species' place of origin in South America before the islands were visited by Europeans.

It was Tei Tetua who taught me that what we call oral tradition contains reliable information that is too easily disregarded and thrown into the same category as legends, folk tales and myths. Legends in Polynesia are just as dependable as many of the accounts we accept simply because they were written in pen and ink by medieval historians.

What did you learn about your own world by seeing it with Tei Tetua's eyes?

That we clothed ourselves to be able to fool ourselves into believing we were no longer as primitive as the people of nature. We refused to understand that we had changed no more than our surroundings; we were neither better nor worse than we had been. Generation after generation of human beings have been born with the same spiritual and physical characteristics that are described in the legend of Adam and Eve, which was passed down by Abraham's forefathers. The chromosomes carried by the twins Cain and Abel still exist in us.

We tell ourselves and others that we have made progress in the art of killing our enemies. During the last century we sent missionaries to all of the island groups in Polynesia to preach that it is wrong to club others in the head even if we don't like them. But then, a few decades later, we returned in uniforms, explaining that wearing this clothing they could kill as many as they wanted to – as long as the enemy was wearing different uniforms and saluted a different flag.

We found it difficult to explain that we had long-range cannons so we could avoid knowing who we killed, and that it was better not to know. Tei Tetua was the son of a warrior chieftain who always knew the names of the persons he beat to death.

Anthropologists' dissertations maintained that the tribal wars on the Marquesas Islands were a result of overpopulation, and Tei Tetua's stories seemed to confirm this. He showed no surprise when I had to admit to the fear of a new world war, since a generation had passed since the last one. Our friend in the Ouia valley also thought this credible. He had drawn his own conclusions from my attempts to describe life in London and New York.

We had multiplied so rapidly that our forests were rapidly disappearing, and we had so little space that we built our homes in rows without any room between them, and eventually we built them on top of one another and they became skyscrapers.

I assured him that although we didn't eat humans, we did eat cows and hens and any animals we thought were tasty. We were fond of animals and didn't like to slaughter them, and we liked fishing. Hearing that, Tei Tetua thought it stupid that we didn't do our own fishing, instead giving others the pleasure of pulling in the fish and then bartering with the fisherman. The idea of money and prices was unknown to our friend, so I didn't complicate the conversation by talking about middle men and stores.

Tei Tetua agreed with my criticism of cannibalism. Then, when he asked what we did with all the people we killed during war, I shocked him.

'We bury them,' I had to admit.

'Just dig them all into the ground?' I could read in the old man's face that I had disappointed him.

6

At the Bottom of Jacob's Ladder

From tribal wars to world war – that was quite some progress?

This time my aku-aku had ventured in to my study, where I was looking through my notes and papers to freshen up old memories. It had been a long time since I had seen these papers or thought about these things.

It was quite a twist of fate. After pursuing a course of studies that would allow us to avoid civilization in the certainty that a new war would break out, we let mosquitoes and the danger of infection among peaceful, primitive natives chase us away, only to end up risking our lives among mines and bombs in the same civilization we had left.

Just a year after our return from Fatu-Hiva, Norwegian newspapers were reporting that German tanks had rolled into Poland. These were the tanks that we thought would make a new war impossible. Better weapons did not guarantee peace.

We bought a nice little log cabin with a peat roof high up on the mountains above Lillehammer and turned it into a year-round residence. We had a splendid view of Lake Mjøsa and the town, and an almost impenetrable pine forest behind our cabin that gradually thinned out into juniper bushes, heather and flower meadows as it approached the high mountain near Hornsjø.

I worked in a small outbuilding in my own study, which was separated from the woodshed and the outside toilet by a panel wall. I had total peace. I thanked destiny that I had an education to fall back on. I made a living by writing a book and giving slide lectures about our attempt to return to paradise.

But I was also hard at work on a scientific manuscript. I had ledgers filled with notes from Kroepelin's library, and had left the field of biology in order to study Polynesian anthropology. The manuscript, which was in English, was already becoming extremely thick with all its quotations and references. It had the working title *Polynesia and America*.

I had done something that was totally different from the conventional research at that time. I had tried to solve the Polynesian riddle as a detective would. The groundwork had been done by researchers from totally different branches of science, and I was trying to correlate the results. The method did not follow the rules, but it gave good, well-founded results.

Everyone at that time agreed that at least two immigrant groups had reached Polynesia, that the later group had come such a short time before the Europeans discovered the islands, and that everyone still spoke the same language, even though they lived thousands of kilometres apart and were spread over the eastern half of the world's largest ocean. Since each individual researcher had attacked the problem within his special field, none of them, so far, had arrived at the same conclusion. The only findings that were not contradicted were those of the philologists, since they could prove that although the types of people and cultures were totally different, the Polynesians had diffuse language roots in common with the Malaysians in Asia.

The route of their migration was still a mystery. The Polynesians and the Malaysians lived at opposite ends of the enormous Pacific Ocean, with the native Negroid population in the Melanesia islands as a large 4,000-kilometre barrier between them. In all of this enormous area in between, there were no traces of any Polynesian passage. This in itself was very mysterious, because the Polynesians arrived at their islands furthest to the east in the Pacific Ocean as a pure Stone Age culture as late as the European Middle Ages. Therefore they must have left the coastal areas in Asia *before* the Asian Stone Age ended, between 3000–2000 BC. Where had these seafarers been in the meantime?

This was the crux of the Polynesian problem. Some of their forefathers must have journeyed out into the Philippine Ocean around 3000 BC and continued on to some unknown area, where they remained for almost 4,000 years. Where?

Researchers were divided between two theories. Some thought the Polynesian forefathers had sailed so rapidly through the Austro-Melanian and Micronesian island area that they left no traces. But this made no chronological sense. The second and opposite theory proposed that they had spent thousands of years on the journey by moving from one island to the other against the wind, and in this way changed themselves and their culture from Malaysians to Polynesians by a 'micro evolution'. But in that case, nothing made sense.

The controversy was at its most intense at the time when I was gathering information from the Polynesia library and went off to the Marquesas Islands myself to get an inside view of Polynesia as a biologist and geographer. At that time, the most renowned Polynesia researcher was the New Zealander, Sir Peter Buck. He supported those who thought that the Polynesian forefathers must have passed through Melanesia, but he admitted that his only reason for doing so was that they certainly could not have come through Micronesia. Buck's prominent colleague, the French ethnologist Dr Métraux, based his views on studies of blood types and wrote that any attempt to place the origins of the Polynesians in Melanesia 'was a crime against known facts'.

This complicated controversy was totally meaningless to me. There is no reason to believe that Melanesia and Micronesia created any obstacles. The world was round, and the current from the Philippine Ocean ran north of all of these islands and reached Hawaii via British Columbia.

British Columbia. No one had thought of a Polynesian stop-over all the way up there in the north. The warm ocean current beyond the Philippines flowed so quickly and majestically past Japan to the archipelago along the coast of British Columbia that the canoe people up there went barefoot year round, even though they lived as far north as the Hudson bay and Labrador on the opposite side of Canada. After my year in Polynesia, I had to find a way to visit and learn about these American Pacific islands. No Polynesian researcher had considered them, even though they lay in the middle of the route and had a maritime population that had come from Asia in the Stone Age, and continued living in the Stone Age until the arrival of the Europeans.

The Fred Olsen Oslo shipping company had cargo ships that served British Columbia. My parents knew old Fred, and his son Thomas was the first to hear about my theory. I myself thought it was so obvious that I was afraid that others would steal it before I published it. Thomas Olsen agreed with my idea, and I was given tickets to Vancouver for Liv, myself and Little Thor, who was now one year old, for a token fee.

We had not yet left Norway when England declared war on Germany, so the ship was directed north to Scotland to avoid submarines in the English Channel. Tei Tetua's tribal war would pale in comparison to what was to come.

My family and my theories received an exceptionally warm welcome in scientific circles in British Columbia, first at the university in the growing city of Vancouver, and then at the Provincial Museum in idyllic Victoria on Vancouver Island. The university still lacked its own anthropological faculty, but I met the foremost expert on local Northwest Indian languages, Professor Hill-Tout. The friendly old language researcher immediately identified two publications that had been written by himself and a colleague in Ottawa and pointed out the marked difference in language between the various tribes along the coast of British Columbia, despite their mutual relationship in both race and culture. The strangest thing, which they each had discovered independently, was that the language of several of the tribes showed a distant but definite relationship to the languages in both Polynesia and Malaysia.

The elderly professor maintained that there was no doubt about it. He had concluded that Polynesian canoes must have come up to British Columbia, but realized now that canoes from this area could just as easily have made it to Hawaii. Captain Voss from Vancouver had recently sailed a similar canoe from Vancouver and past Hawaii and, with the northeast trade winds behind him, his journey ended all the way down with the Maoris in New Zealand.

This was a good start, and, if possible, things became even more promising at the museum in the capital city. The ethnographical and archaeological collections from all of the coastal Indians were locked in cardboard boxes in the cellar, but the museum's director had the key, and he was a zoologist.

As a colleague and because I had brought a jar of fruit rats in formaldehyde from the Marquesas Islands, I was given a place to study at Dr Cowan's large desk and access to the excellent library.

As a researcher it was like arriving in heaven when I sat in the director's office devouring source material that I could never have found in Kroepelin's Polynesia library. The islands along the coast of British Columbia lay outside the Polynesian researcher's area of interest, which was the South Sea islands. They had simply forgotten that the earth is round, that the Pacific Ocean curves, and that a flat map tells lies about distances. When considering this, it becomes clear that the islands off British Columbia are not at the end of a

1. As a child I was brought up on goats' milk. I am pictured here with my father, a brewery manager also called Thor Heyerdahl.

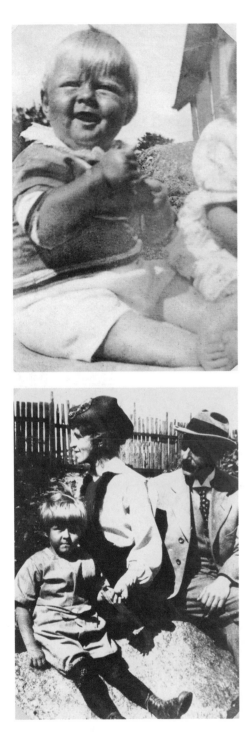

2. Me during the summer of 1915.

3. With my parents in 1918.

4. With my mother Alison in front of my childhood home in Larvik, 1920.

5. My wildlife mentor, Ola Bjørneby, in 1932.

6. With the catch of the day.

7. Me in 1935, aged nineteen.

8. My faithful Greenland dog Kazan, 1936.

9. With Liv at a carnival onboard the *Messangerie Maritime* on our way to Tahiti, 1937.

10. Chief Teriieroo and his wife in Papeno, Tahiti, 1937.

11. Liv at Fatu-Hiva, 1938.

12. Liv chewing on sugarcane, Fatu-Hiva, 1938.

13. With Liv in paradise surroundings at Fatu-Hiva.

14. The Ouia valley, Fatu-Hiva. Our cabin is on the right.

15. The former cannibal Tei Tetua.

16. Liv has a bath in a stream in the Omoa valley.

17. At my desk in the cabin close to Lillehammer, 1939.

18. With Liv, Thor Jr and our dog Kazan II.

curved and indirect route from the Philippine Ocean but on a line that is just as straight as the equator.

It was at this museum that I seriously understood the fact that ever since Captains Cook and Vancouver came here and were surprised to see how much the Northwest Indians reminded them of Polynesians in both race and culture, researchers in the twentieth century have confirmed the same, often convincingly, in their dissertations about the Northwest Indians and their culture.

What others had pointed out, without crossing the geographical border for Polynesian research, I came to see with my own eyes when I left the museum and went to live among the Bella Coola Indians further up the coast with my little family. The winter passed, and then things changed.

The news about my scientific theory had been well received in the local press, and one journalist located me in the Bella Coola valley. By tearing up layers of turf down by the riverbank, I uncovered rock carvings and found masks of gods with concentric rings for eyes, just like the ones I found on Fatu-Hiva. We found the same unusual axe blades of stone and bark beaters that were used on the Marquesas Islands, and we seemed to recognize both our own adoptive father Teriieroo and our old friend Tei Tetua among the Indians in the valley.

The news reached the *New York Times*, but it was accompanied by a commentary from the Polynesia anthropologist Margaret Mead, who had just become world famous for her book about love life in Samoa. She refuted my theory, claiming that I had probably found artefacts left behind by Captain Cook after his visit to Polynesia. I never managed to answer that it was doubtful that Captain Cook had sat down by the river and copied Polynesian rock carvings. More important things were happening, both for me and in the world at large.

I met Margaret Mead, my first academic opponent, in Oslo many years after the war. At that point we could enjoy the fact that we had done research in totally different areas. She had to admit that she knew as little about rock carvings in British Columbia as I knew about love life in Samoa.

Liv and I were about to experience a sudden and totally unexpected change in our lives. I had been bear-hunting with the half-blood Indian Clayton Mack, who later became quite a legendary figure through his book *Grizzlies and White Guys*, which included the story of our adventure. Our hunting trip ended with Clayton shooting and injuring a bear that then chased me in circles around a tree stump. Clayton felled the bear, and it screamed so dreadfully that the sound echoed from the mountains, and I was vaccinated against any form of hunting for the rest of my life. Clayton and I paddled back from the uninhabited Kwatna valley with the bear in the bow of the canoe. As we swung in between the cliff walls along of the long and narrow Bella Coola fjord, someone called to me from the dock.

'Norway has surrendered!'

I cupped my hands like a megaphone for my mouth, and called back: 'To whom?'

That anyone could attack such a neutral country as Norway, which had not been at war as an independent country since the Viking era, was totally unthinkable to me. Hitler had been regarded as an almost comical figure, and the United States had still not entered the war. The following week, Liv and I and our little boy boarded the coastal ship when it passed Bella Coola on its way south. I wanted to get back to Vancouver and report for military duty at the Norwegian consulate.

In fact I received a rather cool reception at the consulate after mounting the stairs and reading the name on the door: von Stahlschmidt.

The consul assured me in English with a German accent that Germany and Norway were friends. I should calmly return to my Indians and remain there until the war was over.

I had come into Canada with a student visa and a return ticket to Norway, but now I could just as well throw them away. In addition we only had enough money for a few days in Vancouver, and since Liv was pregnant, the situation became critical.

Worst of all, an American journalist who had been in Oslo on the day of the invasion had written sensational and totally false reports that Norway had welcomed the Germans. His story hit the headlines in both the American and Canadian press. And of course the Germans reported nothing about how the Norwegians sank Germany's largest warship, *Blucher*, in the Oslo Fjord with over 1,000 men on board or about the battles that continued for many weeks further north in Norway.

Now we were just as unpopular as we had been popular when we first arrived from Norway. We did not even dare speak Norwegian to one another on the trolley. More than a year would pass before this hatred of Norway died away and slowly turned to admiration after the United States was swept into the war and President Roosevelt proclaimed, 'Look to Norway!' in a speech to his countrymen. He pointed out that the Germans would have won the battle of Europe if the Norwegian merchant navy, which then was the third largest in the world, had not escaped from Norway and joined the Allies.

In the meantime, on a personal level, we came to see some of the shadier sides of life. We immediately moved out of our hotel and found an inexpensive room facing a back lot down in the harbour area. A gas light, a horrendous bed, a table, a stool and an old bassinet for Little Thor made up the furnishings. From the curtain-less window we looked down on to a large coal shed, illuminated by a single light bulb. Our landlady was suspicious, ill tempered and whiny, and when she heard that we were Norwegian, she became even more distrustful.

No one knew how long the war would last. I had to find a temporary job. There was work to be found for those who queued outside the unemployment office. After studying the people in this line, I stopped shaving, put on an old cap and placed myself at the end. As the queue advanced, everyone was asked about their occupation, and they all called themselves carpenters and plumbers, whether or not they had ever held a saw or a wrench. When my turn came and I said I was a zoologist, they had no idea of what that was. Ethnologist made no impression either. When asked if I knew how to use a wheelbarrow, I was proud to answer affirmatively. However I never got a job because I had entered the country on a student visa and had no work permit.

The days passed and turned into weeks. Our last traveller's cheque had been cashed, our funds had dwindled dangerously, and Liv was expecting our second child. We had to ration the food. This really helped me understand how fortunate I had been to grow up in a social class that could take a daily breakfast, lunch and dinner for granted.

We had felt hunger pangs on Fatu-Hiva in the rain season, but there were still crayfish in the brook and a few coconuts falling from the palm trees. Here there was only asphalt and closed doors and windows. Without having experienced it, it is hard to imagine the emotions of a man with a hungry family at home and an empty stomach himself, staring through a restaurant window at a plump, golden chicken slowly rotating on a grill while an indescribably wonderful aroma seeps out through the door every time it is entered by partially hungry people and exited by contented diners who have eaten their fill.

When people who have endured this experience join forces with revolutionaries, whether their names are Joan of Arc or Fidel Castro, they are not making a political decision. People who are not hungry never revolt.

Standing there with my last shillings, not even enough to pay the rent, looking at displays of wonderful food in store windows and not being able to run home with something for Liv and Little Thor, brought the unfairness of modern society into a frightening light. I wasn't alone in this situation. Thousands and millions, statistically over half of the earth's population, were in a situation like this, or even worse off. We who have enough write and speak like prophets about a time when a lack of resources and overpopulation will create a world catastrophe. But catastrophe is already here for that part of the world's population that never writes in newspapers and whose words are never heard, even from the top of a soapbox.

One day while I was standing in front of a bakery shop window, I understood that we, my little family, were actually in great danger.

Liv was incredibly brave, as she was on Fatu-Hiva. Never a complaint, never a sour word. I paced the floor for hours at a time, sometimes in anger and near desperation. And then came the darkest day of them all, a Sunday. The rent was due the next day. Our funds had been reduced to a few coins. Thirty cents. I just walked back and forth. Liv went out and used all of our money to buy three loaves of sweet bread. With Little Thor between us we walked out into the sunshine and sat down on a bench in Stanley Park facing the canoe that had sailed from here and all the way down to New Zealand. To hell with the whole theory. The totem pole that was next to the canoe seemed more fitting for the mood of the day. Grotesque characters climbed over one another, and the victor, with clenched claws and the greedy teeth of a beast of prey, crowned the pole. I was ready to repent, to beseech and beg the creative powers of heaven and earth for help, wherever they were to be found, out in the universe or within myself.

The next event might have been a coincidence. But coincidences like this have often turned up in acute situations later in life as well, so it pays to pray for them to happen.

When the landlady knocked on the door the next morning to collect the rent, we were flat broke. There was no way out, our time was used up, and we were ready to give in.

The landlady had a letter for us as well as the rent demand. It came from the Fred Olsen shipping company, and its agent in Vancouver had traced us with a telegram from the London office.

Shipowner Thomas Olsen and family had escaped from occupied Norway to England. All his ships were assigned to the Allied convoys through Nortraship, which was in charge of the entire Norwegian merchant navy. The telegram stated that the agent was to trace the whereabouts of everyone who was stranded in Vancouver as the passengers of Fred Olsen and had no possibility of travelling home. In addition, I was to receive a monthly loan of whatever amount I needed to survive until the war was over.

It was like a wonderful dream. Life could go on. In a rush of joy and with a mixture of gratitude and modesty, I asked to borrow fifty dollars a month. Even then it was a very moderate sum, but we had learned that one dollar consisted of 100 cents. We had purchased three loaves of sweet bread for our last thirty.

With renewed courage I finished my first two articles in English, a scientific article for *International Science* and a popular article for *National Geographic* magazine. Both were accepted, and from *National Geographic* I received a 200-dollar cheque. Just after this Liv was admitted to the maternity clinic, and the money came in handy for the hospital and for equipment for the new baby, Bjørn, nicknamed Bamse in honour of a bear cub we had seen climbing up a tree with a daisy in its mouth one day on a trip into the forest in the Bella Coola valley.

The sunny days in the Bella Coola valley were now a distant memory. They were replaced by a new life that was, in a way, totally different. A work permit arrived from Ottawa, and thanks to the father of a Norwegian student I had met at the university when we arrived, I found a job and a sponsor. The father, Robert Lepsøe, was employed as an engineer at a factory far up in the Rocky Mountains that had 7,000 employees. It was a frightening complex of factory buildings. Before Lepsøe's arrival, it spewed out so much sulphurous smoke that the forest and green fields had died out far over the border and into the United States.

Lepsøe had managed to install a filtering system so that most of the sulphur was collected and driven away in railroad cars. This was an important source of profit. Solely on that man's reputation, I was entrusted with a job in the factory's gang of handymen, and I really learned how to use a wheelbarrow. We were seventeen men with just as many mother tongues. We worked every day in the factory's so called 'ball gang' and we never had time to get bored because we had different types of work every day while the others had assembly-line jobs. My first job was to help load sacks of cement on to a railroad car. I looked around for a wheelbarrow, but the sacks were to be carried on the shoulder. My knees almost collapsed when a huge giant of a Pole threw the first sack on me. It was even worse to stumble beneath the heavy load and make it up the narrow plank to the railroad car while the others stared and teased the newcomer. I could barely stand when the day was over, and my body had swollen so badly that it was difficult to take off my clothes.

I didn't have to carry the sacks the next day. The cement was to be transported in larger containers.

'Come here, Mac, and you'll get a better job,' the foreman said. I followed him and explained politely that my name wasn't Mac, but Thor.

'I don't give a damn what you're called,' the foreman shouted. 'To me you're Mac!'

A better job was joining a long line of men who strove to feed cement into an enormous, rotating cement mixer. Each man had the contents of a sack dumped into his wheelbarrow as he passed, and the aim was to stay in line while walking up some narrow planks to a scaffold, where the cement was dumped into a mixer, before continuing down the other side with an empty wheelbarrow. The whole operation had to follow a rhythm and ran at such a fast pace that sweat ran and tempers erupted. Time and time again I had to back up my wheelbarrow to get more speed to make it up the plank, while the man behind me swore and cursed because I had broken the flow.

After a half a dozen rounds I was so tired that my wheelbarrow ran off the plank and tipped over the load of cement. The foreman screamed at me, but it was time for a cigarette break, which was allowed every fifteen minutes on this hard job. While the others enjoyed their foul-smelling cigarettes, I cleaned up the mess and threw myself down on my back and enjoyed every single deep breath until it was back to work again!

But I have never had such good food as what I ate then.

Everyone knows that hunger is the best cook. But it is a cook whose services cannot be bought.

Like most people who can afford to do so, I can enjoy sitting back and savouring something delicious like oysters or real caviar, or drinking a glass of champagne or a dry Martini. But I will never forget the superlative delight of the meal breaks at the Consolidated Mining and Smelting Company, when we threw ourselves down on the heap of bricks and opened our lunch boxes: bread with butter and cheese, and a bottle of cold chocolate milk.

Hard work takes the greatest toll on those who have never really used their muscles. By the third day I started to feel like a new man. I had built up stamina and I would not tire so easily. But the pleasure of using my muscles was short-lived. The foreman picked two of us for a less strenuous job. An experienced fellow whispered that he thought we were being sent down into some huge tanks that were on the factory grounds, and that rumour had it that they were only cleaned every fifth year and it was a devilish job.

We were equipped with long-handled scrapers and tall rubber boots that went up to our groins. Our first order when we were on our way down the ladder inside the tank, was at all cost to stay on our feet because the stuff at the bottom was sulphuric acid. If we slipped and fell, the acid would burn away clothing, skin and flesh instantaneously.

Before letting go of the ladder at the bottom of the dark tank, I touched the bottom with one foot. It was covered with a thick layer of slime, slippery as soap. We stepped with great care on to the tank floor, while the foreman hung over the edge far above us and shouted his orders, which we didn't quite understand because there was an echo like thunder within the metal tank. We understood that the acid had to be scraped out through an outlet on the far wall of the tank. It was a horrendous job. With our legs apart we slid as if in slow motion, supported by the scrapers that we pushed in front of us, toward the opening, pressing the muck carefully forward so it wouldn't splash. If we pressed too hard, we slid backward, and the slightest loss of balance would cause us to tumble down into the evil brew. I felt that, as if by a misunderstanding, I had landed in a great kettle owned by civilized cannibals.

There were worse assignments to come. I was also sent into a furnace. The factory, which first and foremost was a smelting plant, was also running some experiments, which resulted in the formation of cinder deposits in some of the smaller furnaces. I was sent inside one of them to remove the metal refuse from the walls, equipped with an air hammer, a chisel and a light bulb as well as a gas mask for my nose and mouth, because inside it was dark and dusty. As soon as I started hammering the walls, I found myself exposed to a more intense form of one of my early sketches of our progress from paradise: dust, noise and numerous harmful sensory attacks on humans. The air hammer provided an incessant explosion of cannons in my ears and, combined with the dust, lack of ventilation and my dripping sweat, it almost drove me crazy. I could not even hear my own voice, and all I remember is shouting the same two words at each explosive bang: 'I hate! I hate! I hate!'

When I finally finished and could crawl out, I thought of the fact that tens of thousands of farmers had voluntarily left their fields to crawl into mines or furnaces. They came to the cities to join in the dance around machines like the tribe of Moses around the golden calf. But later, in the shower, having removed the worst of the filth, both inside and out, I realized that the solution was not to be found in returning to nature either.

Not all the jobs at the factory were as tough as the ones in the tank and the furnace. The best one was to be in the gang that was left over after the most important assignments were filled. We were sent to clean used bricks. We sat with a brick on our lap and chipped off remnants of old cement. Whole bricks were then placed in beautiful piles, while broken ones and chunks of cement were thrown on a heap. We worked our way gradually into the huge pile, and the guys became experts in piling the bricks around us so we were less visible when someone wanted a cigarette.

I was working with a strain of humanity that was new to me, one not all that different from businessmen and academics as one might think. For most of them work had been hard to find until the war created employment. The men whose company I enjoyed the most, maybe because they were used to travelling and had a sense of humour, were classified by the others as hobos, the skilled workers' occupational title for professional vagabonds. They had criss-crossed Canada and far down into the United States by train, often by hanging under the railroad cars or hiding in the cargo.

As time went on I also came to like the rough foreman and we developed a better understanding of one another. He had reason not to give a damn what I was called. No one knew his name either; he just went by the name of Mystery. 'Because no one knows who the father was,' it was said. When he was angry, he spoke Italian. I did not realize how clever he was until I discovered that he could not read. I caught on one day when I happened to see someone give him a note that he just stuck into his shirt pocket. When he thought no one was looking he stuck both arms down to the elbows into a barrel with something gooey in it that dripped from his fingers, and then he came over to me and asked me to take the note from his pocket and read what was on it. He was in his glory when driving the factory's small locomotive. He had learned what words such as 'Stop' looked like.

Mystery probably meant well when he sent me up into the fresher air on the roof of one of the factory's new buildings after having seen how I hated the stench of all the spooky gases that gathered in and around the factory. A visible layer of clouds, consisting of dust, smoke and poisonous steam, descended into the valley to the small town of Trail, where all the workers lived. Only the white-collar workers could live on the plateau with its beautiful houses and green lawns at the same altitude as the factory. I chose to take a longer commute to the factory, and placed Liv and the two little ones up in Rossland, high above the factory smoke stacks. The sulphurous smoke from the factory was still a health hazard, even though conditions had improved after the United States had won a court case when the damages literally crossed the border. Older factory workers often had silicosis because of the dust in their lungs. One day, after work, a tall thin rod of a man with all signs of the disease looked at me with his pale face and said: 'One day more with another dollar earned, and one day closer to death.'

Fresh air was fine, but I was far from happy when Mystery gave me a job as a bucket hoister and sent me climbing on ladders and loose rickety planks up to the roof of the factory building. I cannot remember whether it was six or eight storeys, but the air was more than fresh enough because it was in the middle of the Canadian winter and we were 1,400 metres above sea level in the Rocky Mountains. I was already somewhat afraid of heights. As a student, I had almost fallen 1,000 metres from the mountain shelf over the Romsdal valley. Here my new job was to lie on my stomach at the end of the eaves with my head hanging over and my legs pointing uphill to nail tar paper under the eaves. A big roof and a lot of nails. My new boss was an expert roofer, and he walked upright with a long spreader and smeared glowing hot asphalt along the paper's upper edge so that the next layer would bond to the edge of the first one. We gradually worked our way further up from the horrible eaves, and I had time to notice the temperature. It was extremely cold and there were strong winds, but my namesake, Mac, who cooked the asphalt for us over a fire down on the ground, was experienced in the business. He heated bricks over the fire, and bundled them into a sack that I hoisted up with the asphalt buckets, so I kept a warm brick in my overalls and, when it cooled, exchanged it for a new one.

Then Mystery remembered that I could write. When the roofing job was finished, I was given a ledger and a pencil and was placed outside a furnace like the one I knew so well, both inside and out. One of the engineers wanted Mystery to keep a written report that recorded temperatures shown on a gauge when the ore started melting and observed the way the magma moved and the colour structure of the melting mass. Mystery simply came to me every day, collected the information and handed it on. And each time, he looked at the page and nodded satisfactorily, 'Looks good. Looks good.'

One day I wanted to check if Mystery really could not read. I handed the ledger to him upside-down. He didn't turn it around.

'Looks good,' he said.

However, on another occasion the engineer himself arrived and wanted to meet the person who was writing the reports. Mystery introduced his assistant. 'You write well,' the engineer said, and I was promoted. Mystery had to find a new assistant, but there were others in the ball gang who could write.

I ended up as a supervisor in a newly built magnesium factory. I had no clue as to what was going on, except that we were making magnesium powder, which was useful in the war against the Nazis.

The job did not last long. One fine day my bus pulled up at the factory stop but the factory was gone. Only some torn-up iron remained. The whole magnesium factory had exploded during the night shift. I'll never forget the descriptions of the day-shift workers who had been the first to arrive on the scene. A severed hand had been hanging over one of the iron roof beams.

That was the end of the magnesium powder, but I got a different job.

By then we had moved to Lepsøe's summer cabin beside Arrow Lake, so far from the factory that we had skunks under the floor and I had to get up under a night-time sky, while the coyotes howled, and take a bicycle, a boat and then a bus to get to work. I never became a white-collar man, but I made so much money that I paid off the entire loan to the agent in Vancouver. Then I bought a bus ticket over the border and travelled straight across North America to New York to volunteer my services to my country at the Norwegian consulate.

The Norwegian royal family and the whole Norwegian government had escaped to England, and the military high command was also in London gathering sailors and refugees from Norway to fight with the Allies. As I waited for an answer, I took a temporary job as timekeeper at the Bethlehem Fairfield Shipyard in Baltimore. It was a sedentary job which consisted of checking squares on the workers' time cards that showed whether they had worked on the propeller, the hull, or the superstructure of the ship. I could almost spend the whole day reading American anthropology with a clear conscience while the others were building ships. I had visited two professors at Johns Hopkins University who guided me toward the most relevant reading material. Both took the time to listen patiently to this time-keeper from the shipyard who had obviously read a great many books in their field. Professor Ruth Benedict was the first one to give me an important lead. The Polynesians must have come from an area that had a hierarchical society, ruled by a superhuman priest-king. This was a remarkable characteristic that the tribes on all the islands in Polynesia had in common with their neighbours in Mexico and Peru.

I arranged for Liv and the little ones to come to the States. Bjørn should have been baptized long ago. On the day we carried him to the font in the Norwegian Seaman's Church in Baltimore, the Japanese dropped their first bombs on American warships in Pearl Harbor in Hawaii. America joined the war. I thought about Teriieroo and Tei Tetua; bombs were probably raining down on Polynesia as well.

It was bad enough when the island warriors were sneaking up on their enemies in silent canoes and clubbing people they disliked on the head and then eating them.

But what would they have said if they had experienced Pearl Harbor?

7

Dance With the Devil

Each and every opponent of aggression and revenge is also a freedom fighter. A man of peace cannot allow strangers to break into his home and make everything darker. When the psychosis of war spreads over the world like an eclipse of the sun, casting shadows over the human soul in country after country, then even your own allies will help you envision the enemy as evil itself. It was bad enough to know that our country was occupied, but we were also told that people in Norway were surviving on leaves and bread made from tree bark.

War is a dance with the devil. The hatred of a common enemy becomes more important than feelings of friendship for a friend.

When I was a little boy, it was the Russians and the Red Army who had frightened the grown-ups. My father never even allowed me to stand at the bottom of the hill with the other boys on 1 May and watch the parade with red banners. The grown-ups' anxiety that they might even start a revolution was infectious. The whole free world sided with the Finns during the winter war when they camouflaged themselves in white and beat the red devils back.

But the situation changed rapidly. Only one week after Hitler had made the mistake of attacking the Soviet Union instead of Britain, the words 'Red Army' acquired an entirely different sound. Now it was almost like talking about red *angels* who were helping us fight the Nazis. Few among my small group of acquaintances could explain the difference between the Nazis and the communists, but Stalin and the Russians were now our allies in the battle against Hitler and the Germans.

Many years later, when Stalin and Hitler were gone and I had settled in northern Italy, I finally realized that most Russians and Germans were against both communism and Nazism. I thought about the fact that I was living among wonderful people who had once been our enemies, and thanked my fortune that I had never been forced to kill any of them. And I never met an Italian who had fought for fascism. Those who had a choice went into hiding and worked against what they considered to be a German occupation. Essentially, most people had been in agreement, and I wondered why millions of people ended up fighting one another and, for the second time, started a world war.

Did you yourself have an answer?

Of course I sided with those who wanted to chase all of the aggressors back to where they belonged, but I clearly recall that I never associated the word 'enemy' with any national boundaries. In fact, when the war was over, I decided to watch how long it would take before we cut off the wings of the Reds and re-equipped them with horns and devil robes. I had danced with them under the northern lights without seeing either horns or wings. They were frostbitten soldiers just like us, who had learned which uniforms to shoot at and who looked forward to getting home in one piece.

The warrior spirit was more genuine among the Polynesians and the Northwest Indians. They would not even use a bow and arrow because they wanted to look their enemy in the eye when they hit him on the head with a club. On our part, we dropped bombs from airplanes on families who were enjoying themselves at the dinner table, or we launched rockets from our own country that killed thousands of women and children. But at the same time we made amends for regressing into such barbaric behaviour by becoming humane, initiating regulations for social welfare and even for appropriate conduct at work. The smelting plant at Trail is my best example. From being an inferno of smoke, health hazards, and class differences, it has in the course of the past fifty years become a model of green lawns and happy workers. The forest has even returned to its surrounding hillsides.

After the war I was just as reluctant to become a career soldier as I had been to become a politician after having seen the conditions at the smelting plant. Nevertheless, even though I had seen the working conditions in the armies, navies and air forces of several countries, I became a career soldier. As with my civilian career, I just managed to rise enough in rank to experience service as both an enlisted man and an officer. Were I to choose again, under similar conditions, I would rather have been working independently for the good of my country than joining the ranks of those who received or gave orders in uniform. Experience has taught me that it is not wise to speak your mind to your superiors when enrolled in boot camp to learn discipline.

I requested an assignment that would allow me to work with a team of dogs in the forests and mountains behind enemy lines. I explained that I was all thumbs when it came to technology, and that I could not even drive a car or change a radio battery.

With this information, they sent me to radio school for further education in electronics.

Special telecommunications equipment had been made in London and it was on its way to Canada, where it would be used when the battle for liberating Norway began. It was strictly secret, and only ten men would be selected to use this equipment. I was one of them, and for unknown reasons, our cover name was I Group. We were drilled in the mysteries of 'Right, left, about turn' at a Norwegian boot camp in Lunenburg in Nova Scotia. After learning how to march, we were given air force uniforms and trained as air telegraphists at Camp Little Norway in Toronto. With certificates attesting that we were also trained navy telegraph operators, we were sent far into the forest to a secluded rest camp for Norwegian air soldiers, next to a small, idyllic lake. With four technical experts in army uniform, the eight of us who had passed all the tests and were wearing air force uniforms learned every development of modern radio technology, from constructing and using secret transmitters with hidden antennas to television technology, which was then in its infancy. We ran around in the Muskoka forests with specially constructed megaphones, shouting, 'One-two-three, can you hear me?' so loudly that people in Huntsville wrote us letters saying, 'Sure we hear you, and they also do all the way down in Gravenhurst.'

I came closer to drowning than ever before on a canoe trip with some fellow soldiers in the Algonquin National Park. We followed a map that showed the trails where we could carry our canoe between lakes and rivers in the great forest. The main attraction of the trip, in addition to sighting bear and moose, was High Falls, a thundering waterfall that fell vertically into a deep gorge where we saw huge logs splintered into sticks. According to the map, we were to follow a trail for about fifty metres along the riverbank above the waterfall and launch the canoe there. The trail ended at a steep mountain wall. There was nowhere else to go, so the map had to be correct. We all thought it was crazy, because the current was unusually strong after the spring floods. I suggested that we cut the trip short and turn back. Per and Rulle insisted that we had to be in the right place, so rather than ruin the trip I gave in.

We were smart enough not to paddle in the middle of the stream, so we used our hands to haul our way along the bank. A few hundred metres further up, the canoe was caught by a side current and even with all our strength we could not make it back to land. Rulle saw the danger immediately, and dove into the water while he still could reach shore with a few strokes. His dive tilted the canoe and I found myself struggling in the cold water, dressed in my air force winter uniform and wearing heavy boots. I was a terrible swimmer and, weighed down by my clothing, I experienced a totally new kind of hydrophobia. The waterfall! High Falls roared ever closer. There was no possibility of being saved. Rulle ran along the riverbank like a mad man, but the current only drew me further away, straight toward the cliff where I would be crushed like the logs we just had seen.

I swam like crazy, but I knew that all hope of reaching land was gone. I understood that in a few seconds I would experience death and find out what happens when life comes to an end.

That thought was enough to start a search within myself for that creative, all powerful force called God. I searched within myself, not up in the air or on the land. All Rulle could do was run after me, reaching his arms helplessly over the river without coming any closer.

A new source of resolve flowed into me. I felt unlimited powers surging into my arms and legs, and I began to swim calmly and invincibly, crossing the current at an angle.

The water became even more agitated, the roar overwhelming, but the riverbank stopped moving away – stood still – Rulle's hands almost reached me – a little more – a little . . . There! Our hands locked together. In a united effort I was pulled ashore, deathly tired.

But Per!

The red canoe had tipped over and was bobbing at the edge of the cliff. A huge boulder kept it from being swept away. We grabbed hold of the bow and pulled. It was surprisingly heavy. When we righted the canoe we found Per wedged under a seat with the only remaining backpack.

When we had finally roused him, we caught sight of three

magnificent deer. They were perfectly still, like a monument on a mountain ledge, on the other side of the waterfall.

'I'll take this as a sign that all three of us will survive the war,' said Per.

A few months later he was shot down with his plane over Norway.

The most vivid memory I have from my time as an enlisted man was the artist 1132 Stenersen. He was a willing soldier, but he wanted to contribute to the war effort in his own way and not by standing at attention. The most important thing for a soldier to learn is blind obedience. Your first lesson is standing at attention – heels together and toes at a sixty-degree angle, body as erect as the barrel of a rifle, eyes fixed straight ahead at a randomly chosen point, your mind empty in preparation for an order. We stood this way, like a row of tin soldiers, and stared straight ahead. Only Stenersen was a constant source of restlessness. Wearing a uniform jacket that was far too long and a cap that was too small, he stood there staring toward something or other in the distance with a smirk on his face that clearly told the sergeant what soldier 1132 thought of all of this. The sergeant approached him angrily and pointed to the toes of his huge boots, which were not at a sixty-degree angle. Stenersen was put in the guard house because he insisted that his feet were at sixty degrees, it was just that his boots were too large. Furthermore, he had no doubt that the Norwegians would manage to drive out the Nazis, even with their feet at forty-degree angles.

Stenersen stayed in I Group until flight school, but when he showed up for morning inspection wearing the red-bowed cravat of an artist, his uniform was taken away and he was ordered to paint a magnificent Norwegian landscape on the pilots' link trainer.

The class difference I had experienced in the factory also reigned in the military. There were three different kitchens and dining halls, for enlisted men, sergeants and officers respectively. As soon as the air force telegraph operators had completed their training and been made sergeants, they were no longer allowed to eat with I Group, because we were still privates. It was also strictly forbidden for an officer and an enlisted man to have any social contact.

Few men with stripes and stars on their uniforms were admired by us enlisted men. I only remember two. The camp commander, Colonel Ole Reistad, was one. From him I learned that respect of a subordinate can be maintained and even increased by giving orders in such a way that the one who receives them still feels that he is an equal as a human being. The other was Major Viggo Ullmann, the only person in the camp except for myself who had brought his wife and child to Toronto. We lived in apartments in the city. He broke all rules and we visited one another when I had evening leave. While the adults ate dinner, my little ones played on the floor with his two girls, Liv and Bitten. Who could have known then that Liv Ullmann would grow up to become a famous figure in the movie world and the two of us would one day sit together on a mound of snow in a free Norway to open the Winter Olympics?

My clearest memory from Vesle Skaugum training camp in the Muskoka forest was a visit by a six-year-old Norwegian who caused just as much of a sensation when he arrived unannounced with his mother as he did many years later when he took his seat on the royal stand with his two children during the same Winter Olympics. Liv and I, our little boys and Peik, a bear cub they had as a playmate, lived in a small log cabin some distance from the camp. Prince Harald did his morning runs with the camp commander along a trail past the cabin every morning. They glimpsed Peik sitting politely at the table and being groomed by the boys. Its black fur was as clean as a fox pelt, so Liv allowed me to let it sleep at the foot of the bed so it could get used to people. Peik had not been friendly when I acquired it from a lumberjack for a bottle of whisky. Liv had more trouble with our sleeping arrangements when the bear became too heavy to lie on my feet and I removed my pillow and let it sleep there.

I was given a day off to show the prince and princesses how Peik could do tricks. The princesses begged for a canoe trip. They had seen me paddle out with the bear and how it jumped into the water and pulled me back to shore with a rope. With the Princesses Ragnhild and Astrid on board, and Peik in the bow, I paddled slowly and carefully past the dock where Crown Princess Martha sat on a stool crocheting while little Prince Harald was preparing to film the event with his new camera. Honey was Peik's favourite food; honey on my finger had secured a lasting friendship with him the first time we met. As we approached the dock the film camera started buzzing like a bee, and the bear rose up on two feet in the canoe, and we all tipped over. I had no way of knowing whether the princesses had learned to swim yet, but it turned out to be great fun for everyone, because the water was so shallow that the three of us could wade ashore.

The worst was yet to come. Peik was dripping wet when he wandered over to the Crown Princess, who had nearly finished her crocheting. The bear shook itself, spraying water everywhere, and with its long crooked claws he got a good hold on the crocheting. A veritable battle ensued. Helping the Crown Princess rescue her handwork was to little avail. Luckily Liv saved the situation with a piece of honey cake.

Then the day arrived when air soldier 2209 Heyerdahl, formerly army soldier 1136, along with his seven colleagues in I Group, knew more about electro-technology than anyone else in the Norwegian forces. The only thing we did not know was how to put our newly acquired knowledge to use. Sadly it seemed that no one else did either.

Now that the war has long been over and I Group's invaluable equipment is lying on the bottom of the ocean, north of the North Cape, I think that I can reveal something of our curious contribution to the war.

When the ocean liner *Queen Mary* set a record by carrying 18,000 passengers, I was one of them. After receiving an urgent telegram from London requesting I Group's immediate presence, we became eight of the 18,000 allied troops from camps in Canada, Australia and New Zealand who were one night secretly transported to a collection point in Halifax. From here we were squeezed aboard the huge steamship and sent into the line of fire overseas. The eight of us shared a single cabin but we could only use it on alternate nights because we had to take turns with those who had to sleep on deck, leaning against their gear without any room to stretch out. I will never forget the seasickness and the long lines to the toilets. We could brag about being a high-priority target for German submarines, so the luxury liner raced full speed ahead with all lights out on a zigzag course to avoid submarine torpedoes.

We arrived after five days and were met by a swarm of Allied fighter planes. The first thing most passengers did when we were safely ashore was to have a cigarette. Any light from a cigarette had been forbidden during the crossing.

So now we were overseas. But no one knew who had sent for us. Two of our own officers were dressed in army uniforms, so we decided to get out of our air force uniforms and into army ones. This time I became army soldier 5268. This probably made the confusion even worse, because now no one could locate us in any military records. Upon our arrival in London we were greeted by the Commander-in-Chief of the army with the words: 'You have long been awaited and long missed.' Four days later we were told that no one could find out who missed us. Therefore we were sent to the Army School and Training Company in Scotland and told to wait patiently until the case was solved. A short time thereafter we were given new weapons and army gear and sent to a Norwegian communications company in an isolated castle in Scotland.

We were welcomed with open arms by the communications commander, who assured us that he had plenty of officers but far too few enlisted men. Every morning Captain Pettersen placed all his officers and soldiers in elegant rows, and sergeants and lieutenants turned snappily on their heels and reported that everyone was present and accounted for.

I Group had regular army gear and none of its fine technological equipment, so we were either put on kitchen duty or sent to work for Scottish farmers. We only saw the officers at morning inspection, because we ate in different rooms of the castle. After a month we were given travel orders and left Captain Pettersen's castle, but only to be quartered in the beautiful Scottish village of Callander. A few days later we were moved to the university town of St Andrews, where we met up with Captain Pettersen and his communications company. We were all quartered at Westerlea House, a huge old castle with many wide stone stairways and long corridors with unpainted wooden floors. Here we were ordered to wash floors and stairs every day – not sweep but wash, because without wet floors no one could verify that they had been washed. After a while, the whole castle smelled of rot and mould.

Complaining and begging to be put into the line of fire was no help. As the I Group representative, I kept meeting the company commander, explaining that we were forgetting everything we had learned. So we were given the key to a Morse code transmitter. As air force and navy telegraph operators, we had learned to send and receive Morse code at such a tempo that it made a steady drone, so we had to learn to type with all ten fingers in order to get it down on paper fast enough.

Here my problem was not only being cut off from all contacts in Norway, but also that none of Liv's letters from Canada had reached me. I knew that as a soldier I was being paid the same as a recruit was paid at home in peacetime, and it simply was not enough to cover everything, even though Liv and the children lived inexpensively in the cabin in the Muskoka forest. Therefore I had sold my whole collection of valuable ethnographica from the Marquesas Islands to the Brooklyn Museum before I enlisted. I had lugged the collection with me after leaving Norway. Among other things it included extremely valuable pictures of gods, a king's robe made of wavy black human hair bound with cocoa fibers and a magnificent crown of carved tortoise shell and mother of pearl. Little did I know that Thomas Olsen had invited Liv and the boys to live with his family at their lovely country home outside of New York for the duration of the war.

My days as a scientist seemed distant and unreal while I was living with my shoes pointing out at a sixty-degree angle and staring out into emptiness because I was ordered to do so. St Andrews University kept my soul alive by allowing me to borrow stacks of books. In my diary from that time I wrote: 'I'm starting to study anthropology again since it seems our mission here has been sabotaged. After dinner the others carry on as before, washing stairs basically.'

Unrest started to brew among our special secret group from Canada. Morning inspection continued as before. The communications captain did not want to exercise his soldiers under the command of the major of the corps of engineers quartered at the same castle, so he exercised I Group and his other enlisted men behind the castle. The shouting of orders from both sides of the building resounded in the twilight as if it were battalions rather than six or eight men being ordered from the lieutenant to the company commander and then back again to the lieutenant. The captain used a flashlight to inspect every soldier in I Group and make certain that we had the communications emblem sewn into our sleeves. Afterwards two enlisted men were picked for the daily washing of the stairs while the rest were allowed to return to their quarters and relax.

This could not continue. Stair-washing and kitchen duty were bad enough, but there were rumours that the waiter in the officers' mess had been transferred so now we could also expect to do that job.

That would be degrading. We agreed that if just one of us was given the job, he would refuse and the rest of the group would support him. It would be the only way to bring the problem to the attention of the army high command. Earlier, while cleaning Captain Pettersen's office, we had found a letter of complaint that we had sent to London in his wastepaper basket.

It all came out at inspection the next morning. As the order of the day it was read out that 5269 Beyer-Arnesen would have duty in the officers' mess.

The answer came loud and clear, as from a man on death row: 'I refuse.'

The words hung in the air. Beyer-Arnesen was ordered to leave the ranks and report to the captain's office. At first the captain tried to be reasonable. It was an honour to serve in the officers' mess. Beyer-Arnesen stuck to his point. Refusal to carry out an order in a time of war is punishable by death. Beyer-Arnesen stuck to his point. The captain grabbed the telephone and called the military police. The soldier watched calmly. Beyer picked up his gas mask, helmet and toilet kit and was led to the guard house in St Andrews.

As the group representative I was called into the captain's office to bring the soldier to his senses. I told the captain that Beyer was old enough to know what he was doing, and that if he was arrested then our whole group had to be arrested because we had all agreed not to carry out that order. I was informed that the matter would be brought to a military tribunal and that the rest of us had not yet refused to obey the order and would not be given a chance to refuse. Furthermore, if we had been serving in the German army, Beyer-Arnesen would have been shot. When I asked whether he thought the Nazis were good examples for us, I was simply told that 'war is war'.

I Group met to consult. Since I was in communications, with the proper stripes on my arm, I borrowed a tool box and went straight downtown to the military gaol, where I explained that something was wrong with the wiring in one of the cells. I was let in and went from cell to cell. All the wiring was in order until I reached Beyer's cell, where I stopped and slipped in a bar of chocolate and a pack of cigarettes. Beyer told me he was a childhood friend of a lieutenant in the supreme command in London who was the son of the Minister of Defence, Oscar Torp. I now had a letter to bring to him.

Captain Pettersen was pleased to grant me leave to visit London. Lieutenant Torp was shocked when he heard that his friend was in prison in Scotland, and immediately arranged for a meeting with his father. The Minister of Defence was, if possible, even more upset when I read out loud from my diary. He assured me that I Group had a truly important role to play and that there must be some misunderstanding. He would personally take the matter up with the commanding general of the army and the war attorney. My mission was to return quietly and see that I Group behaved in an exemplary fashion until the matter was resolved. Even before I left London I learned that orders had already been passed down and Beyer had been released.

Back in St Andrews our enforced idleness continued. Five months had passed since we had done anything more important than washing floors and raking leaves. As we lay like mutineers in our bunks, we discussed the humiliation of doing nothing and not making use of our expensive education while our peers from the flight school had long been in the front line. We had heard about the great contributions that our own air force and the Norwegian navy were making, not to mention all the men in the underground resistance movement behind German lines.

We read in the newspapers how the British Foreign Minister Anthony Eden had pointed out the invaluable efforts of the Norwegian merchant navy, which alone transported 40 per cent of all the oil to the Allies. Why were we not called upon, with our telegraph operator licences? British Admiral Dickens said in a speech, 'Our loss of men and ships has been heavy. It is therefore no exaggeration to say that Norway's effort has been indispensable.'

Even when one of us was sent to wash the corps of engineers' latrine, which we never used, we did not protest. Shortly before Christmas in 1943, I was called in for questioning by the military police, and asked whether I Group was still unwilling to serve in the officers' mess. In that case we would be accused of mutiny. We remained loyal to Beyer.

I Group received its travel orders just after the new year, and we were each sent in a different direction. I was delighted to be transferred to a Norwegian mountain company in the Scottish Highlands. They were well-trained soldiers, and the company chief, who was nicknamed Tarzan, enjoyed everyone's respect and admiration. We had many sports activities and trained and ran like wild men in the mountains. I became a person again.

One day during the morning inspection we were ordered to stand at attention. When Tarzan took out a document to read aloud, we all understood that something serious was at hand. Sentencing orders from the army high command in London. Soldier 5268 Heyerdahl was sentenced to sixty days of detention, with one year's probation, for – Tarzan paused deliberately – for having refused to serve in the officers' mess.

In spite of standing at attention there was unrest in the ranks. Some grinned so openly that Tarzan quickly put the men at ease while a smile played in the corners of his own mouth.

The eight of us had each received a year of probation, and the supreme command now made certain that we would have no more opportunities to create problems before the end of the year. We were brought together again, not under Captain Pettersen but under the command of a small, wiry and stocky lieutenant who wore a British DSO among all the Norwegian decorations on his chest and the communications emblem on his sleeve. Lieutenant Bjørn Rørholt had just returned from a trip behind the German lines and was one of the heroes of the resistance movement. We soon discovered that he was a dedicated soul, bursting with energy, and one who resolutely looked for a new task as soon as an old one was solved. He greeted us with a twinkle in his eye, because he had heard about us when he arrived in London and had assumed the responsibility of getting us into the war.

After a refresher course in electronics with our secret suitcase transmitters and antennas, we were sent off for a few days as vacation guests in private homes. We had to sneak out at night and climb up into the shelter of trees to transmit messages. We made contact by Morse code with uniformed British servicewomen who received our coded messages from their stations at various castles around England. The women that we enlisted men had the opportunity to meet at the pub later were not much to brag about. For my part, all I could brag about after the war was that I had neither killed any enemy soldiers nor seduced any of the beautiful women Rørholt had bravely introduced me to. Even though I wore the uniform of an enlisted man, with him being a lieutenant and a member of the SOE I was accepted by these young upper-class women probably because they thought it was some kind of camouflage.

And then all of us who were sergeants were sent to parachute school.

We were all scared to death as we lined up in front of the plane and Lieutenant Rørholt reminded us that from now on everything we did was voluntary. The one fellow who was brave enough to admit that he didn't dare and then stepped out of rank may be the one I admired most.

Sitting on the floor beside the open door of the plane and waiting for orders was a dreadful experience. The parachutes were small and had openings in them so we would fall quickly when the enemy shot at us. A thundering noise beating us senseless was all we heard until finally the parachute opened. When it did, it seemed as if Our Lord himself had grabbed a firm hold of my neck. I descended with the wonderful feeling of having been a bird in a former life – until the ground came rushing up toward me and I hit it with a jolt as power-ful as if I had jumped from the third floor.

There were many jumps. One night we jumped and there were only three candles to mark our landing target. Many of the men hurt themselves because they hit the ground before they could get into a proper landing position and roll around in time. I did well because during the flight I kept my eyes shut until the moment I jumped out into the dark. The most difficult part was the initial ground training. Imagine following an order to jump out of a window from a high tower with a loose coil of rope in your hand and trusting that it would work out fine because one end of the rope was tied to your back and the other was attached to the shaft of a pro-peller that would spin around and start breaking the fall when the coil straightened out. Fortunately it succeeded.

The most frightening jump of all was the one we were chosen to do as an experiment. We were to jump with our weapons and all of our gear in a sack that was secured with a noose around our legs. Just before we hit the ground we were to loosen the noose and let the sack hang by an eight-metre rope so that it would hit the ground at the same speed but just ahead of us. Two members of I Group ended up in the hospital with broken legs. It could have been much worse for me. My parachute didn't open. It simply hung over me like an empty sausage skin. While the earth came rushing toward me, I could hear the instructor on the ground screaming into a megaphone and telling me to pull the ropes apart and I also needed to consider the rope that was holding the heavy sack to my legs. The parachute opened at the last moment and I got my legs free, but everything went black when I rolled around on the ground the way I was supposed to.

One day, when I was stretching out and relaxing on a stack of hay between jumps at the parachute school, a short and skinny officer wearing a lieutenant's uniform covered with war decorations walked over to me. His face was pale but with sharp features, and the pow-erful setting of his jaw revealed a clean-cut character with a strong will. The man was Knut Haugland, the famous radio operator from the heavy-water sabotage mission at Rjukan that had prevented the Germans from making the first atom bomb. Here was a Norwegian, a member of the underground resistance, who had done a great service for his fatherland. The British Prime Minister Winston Churchill had given the Norwegian heavy-water factory top priority during the war, and Lieutenant Haugland had already met Churchill and our own King Haakon in London. He had also been congratulated and decorated by the British King. When I met him, he had just returned from yet another assignment in Norway. Three years later, when he was the radio operator on the *Kon-Tiki* expedition, he told us how the Gestapo had surrounded him in his hide-out with the secret radio transmitter in a ventilation shaft at the women's clinic in central Oslo. He shot his way out and disappeared over the hospital wall while bullets scattered around him.

We became good friends. Later he insisted that I had been day-dreaming about Polynesia in that stack of hay, and that I had said that if the old bearded men of academia were unwilling to believe me then I would build a raft to prove my theory. I made no note of this in my diary, but what is certain is that Knut was going to parachute into Nordmarka on the outskirts of Oslo and lead the coordination of about one hundred secret radio stations in Norway. He asked me to be his second in command, and I accepted.

These were the days when Soviet troops were marching through Finland into the northernmost part of Norway. Two hundred thousand men of the 20th German Gebirgsarmee were in full retreat from easternmost Finnmark, but they had found new strongholds after having scorched and burned all houses they passed on their way, including all of the town of Kirkenes. For the time being, there was no contact between the Soviet and German forces. The situation on the polar front was extremely unclear, and in all haste a small Norwegian force had to be sent over from Britain to look after Norwegian interests.

The 1st Norwegian Mountain Company was sent to Murmansk on an Allied convoy, and Lieutenant Rørholt received orders to follow them with two men to establish communication between the burned-out and gutted part of Finnmark, which the Soviets had liberated, and the Norwegian government in London. All of I Group were immediately promoted to the rank of ensign, and Ensign Heyerdahl and Ensign Stabell were ordered by Lieutenant Rørholt to accompany him.

So the parachute mission with Lieutenant Haugland never took place, but war is war, as Captain Pettersen would have said. Furthermore, I still had the sixty-day sentence hanging over my head.

After the war, when I invited both Haugland and Rørholt to join the *Kon-Tiki* expedition, they both agreed. Later Rørholt withdrew but it was Rørholt who organized our communications on board by supplying a suitcase radio transmitter left over from the war and setting up an amateur radio network. Haugland joined the expedition and manned our communications systems.

The mission with Rørholt became more dangerous than the journey on the raft with Haugland would ever turn out to be. In November 1944 Rørholt, Stabell and I travelled to Scapa Flow on the Orkney Islands, and then further north to Murmansk on an enormous American aircraft carrier in a convoy consisting of about eighty Allied ships. Half of them were warships, the others were cargo-bearing Liberty ships, which I recognized from my time at the Bethlehem Fairfield Shipyard.

We had barely stepped aboard before a telegram arrived stating that Ensigns Heyerdahl and Stabell had been promoted once again, this time to lieutenants. Lieutenant Rørholt was promoted to captain. This would come to cause unexpected complications when we were set ashore on Soviet territory.

We sailed northward into the Norwegian Sea and the polar night, which was dark and sinister as the convoy passed the polar circle. All of the ships' lights were extinguished and the sky and the ocean were indistinguishable in the night-time darkness. In the afternoon, a patch of red sky appeared to the south, and we could make out the shadowy black silhouettes of large and small ships on the endless ocean. Two heavy locomotives were on the deck of the nearest cargo vessel, on their way from the United States to the communists in the Soviet Union. The world had become transformed into steel and ice, cannons and black seas.

As an outdoor person, I was shocked at the winter equipment we had been given in haste as we left England. I barely had enough time to buy a few rolls of chewing tobacco, which I could use to barter for a reindeer-skin sleeping bag from the Laplanders. The one I had been given consisted of loose filling that fell into the bottom if I held it upright. We heard that arctic gear was being sold in a small depot down by the keel on our aircraft carrier. We were led down ladders through two open watertight bulkheads, and as Rørholt and I were trying on long fur mittens we heard a heavy crash on the iron hull. Instinct told us to climb up the ladder, but the bulkheads were immediately closed and sealed over us. Another loud thud resounded against the outside hull, and explosion after explosion echoed through the iron ship. We heard depth charges from our own escort ships. Enemy submarines were in the waters.

I had always thought that being enclosed in a submarine during warfare would be the worst thing imaginable, and my suspicions were confirmed while we sat down by the keel, closed in like rats, and the battle raged on above and below us. Suddenly, silence reigned. After a while the bulkheads were opened and we were let up into the cold polar night. The convoy was on its way into the Murmansk Fjord with its priceless cargo. We learned that Soviet warships had come out and joined the battle on our side.

We left the Americans in Murmansk, and I went over to a bearded hulk of a guy in a fur coat to practise the list of fifty Russian words I had compiled during the voyage. The man understood none of them. He was English, and had escaped from German captivity and managed to get through the Soviet Union to reach the convoy in Murmansk without knowing one word of Russian. 'Just smile to them,' he said, 'then they'll help you.'

I met my first Russian when we boarded a Soviet torpedo boat that had been badly damaged by German cannon shells. It was on its way to Petsamo in Finland, the port that the Soviets had captured from the Germans. On a long six-hour journey on rough seas, I sat next to a Soviet officer who looked as though he were tough and suspicious. I was cold and hungry. I followed the Englishman's advice and smiled in a friendly but perhaps uncertain manner, as I had never seen a communist before. The Russian beamed a large smile, grabbed my arm, and dragged me down into a cabin. He lifted the blanket off the bunk and pulled out a huge loaf of black bread, broke it in two, and gave half to me. We perched on the edge of the bed, chewing dry bread and smiling at each other while the ship pitched heavily through the waves of the icy sea.

At midnight we arrived at Petsamo, the Soviet's only ice-free harbour. The small Norwegian corvette *Tunsberg Castle* was moored there, waiting to transport thirteen large boxes of valuable technical equipment for I Group to the front in Finnmark. There was only room for one of us aboard, so I gladly let Stabell board the ship with the equipment while Rørholt and I took to the road. I climbed up next to the driver on a Soviet military vehicle, which was full of bullet holes and had no windshield. It was freezing cold and we were accompanied by flickering northern lights.

We sat in silence after greeting each other with smiles. Neither of us could carry a tune, but still we sang 'Volga Volga' and Norwegian and Russian folk songs. I tried to make use of my fifty Russian words along the way, but they never fitted into the conversation. The vehicle bumped and jolted through the polar night, and we kept on like this without seeing anything to reveal that we had crossed into Finland and were no longer in the Soviet Union. We stopped for a rest in Russian mud huts, where we were served hot millet and huge clumps of coal-black bread. Everyone in the convoy was clothed in fur and we crept close to one another to keep warm. I will never forget the atmosphere of eeriness and intense joy on the afternoon we rattled over a long Soviet pontoon bridge and the Russian pointed to an isolated little house that could barely be seen in the dark.

'Norvjeskij dom,' he said triumphantly. I understood those words. Norwegian house!

Home again. My mother and my father lived in this country. But southern Norway was far away, a few thousand kilometres still held by the Germans. I had never been in northern Norway, the land of the midnight sun, and now I was to experience it as a smoking pile of ruins. Coals were still glowing in the scattered ashes. The Germans had pulled back and burnt everything in their path, the scorched earth tactic. Only one house remained in Kirkenes, and everything else had been destroyed. The fleeing Nazis had also brought all the civilians they could find southward with them. This called for a good three days of marching through the no-man's-land of mine-fields between the Soviet and German fronts.

I found Rørholt quartered in an abandoned German bunker with Colonel Arne Dahl, the chief of the Norwegian Mountain Company, who had arrived with another Murmansk convoy just before ours. They had had no direct communications with London, but had to communicate through the Soviets, who had their own headquarters in the vicinity. We all waited for the arrival of *Tunsberg Castle*.

A few days later the sad message arrived that the *Tunsberg Castle* had been sunk. Five Norwegian navy men had been killed, and the thirteen boxes belonging to I Group were lying at the bottom of the ocean.

Surprisingly, Stabell showed up just before Christmas, in Russian clothing, but without as much as a wire-cutter from the equipment. He had been on the aft deck when the alarm sounded on the *Tunsberg*

Castle and had stormed up to the captain on the bridge and stood firmly at attention to take military orders. At that moment, thirty metres of the aft deck was blown away. Further explosions followed, and before he knew it he was struggling for survival in the ice-cold water. A Soviet vessel rescued him before he froze to death. He could also report that when our huge Allied convoy had steamed back out the Murmansk Fjord, the Germans were waiting for it outside and attacked with a swarm of submarines and fifty Junker 88s. The English reported that twelve German submarines had been sunk or damaged, but also that several of the convoy's cargo ships had been lost, including two Soviet ships. The destroyer *Cassandra*, which suffered the loss of sixty-one men, was towed back to harbour with the whole foreship blown away and corpses still stuck between the twisted iron on the wreck.

Our joy at seeing Stabell again was great, and we duly celebrated on Christmas Eve. A Lapp came down from the mountains with a reindeer roast, and the Soviet commandant who had heard about a Norwegian Christmas feast brought a keg of vodka and a sack of Russian rice to celebrate with us. We were told that the Russians would pull out of the country as soon as the German troops had been evicted, then we sang Norwegian Christmas carols and Russian folk songs and wished one another peace on earth.

On the second day of Christmas, a messenger from the Soviet high command appeared with orders for Lieutenant Heyerdahl to return to England immediately. He was not listed on the personnel record that the Norwegian high command had cleared through the Soviet embassy in London. Colonel Dahl, as the Norwegian superior officer, immediately sent a message back that Heyerdahl's name was on a supplementary list, and that in any case the lieutenant could not be spared because of a lack of officers. The Soviets found a *Sergeant* Heyerdahl on the supplementary list, but no officer. Something was obviously wrong, and the lieutenant had to return immediately to England. Orders from Moscow.

This was pure lunacy. I worked out a plan with Colonel Dahl. Hoping that the Soviets would accept his explanations, I was ordered to participate as second-in-command for an élite Norwegian commando group of tough characters. The order was, 'Attack on your own initiative.'

On the last day of 1944, our small seven-man commando group crossed the mountain by the Smal Fjord and, with a requisitioned truck, reached the furthest outpost of seventy men from the Norwegian mountain company. No-man's-land lay behind us, and the Germans were in front of us on the other side of the fjord. We were well hidden in abandoned German dug-outs, and we rested before carrying out our commando raid. Three German destroyers were anchored by a lighthouse on the other side of the fjord, and our assignment was to row undetected across the fjord in a small dinghy, surprise the guards while they were asleep, and blow up the lighthouse.

I suffered intense mental agony in anticipation of the raid. The German soldiers who were sleeping in the guard house were strangers to me. Of course they were enemies, but probably not volunteers, and they would be court-marshalled and shot if they refused to obey an order. It was bad enough to refuse to serve food to one's own officers. I tossed and turned that night, arguing with myself about what was the worst evil: throwing hand grenades through the window on to a defenceless, sleeping enemy, or waking them first with a scream and exposing my own friends to mortal danger. Then a message came on our field telephone. Colonel Dahl had been given an ultimatum by the Soviet high command: the Norwegian troops were to split up into patrols and search for Lieutenant Heyerdahl.

The message was clear and left no alternative. I bid a quiet farewell to the leader of the commando group, Lieutenant Alfred Henningsen, who was left to do the job alone with five men. I jumped on to the truck with the driver, who had to go back through the minefields in no-man's-land in the winter darkness. Pure insanity! But I had to push on and reach Kirkenes before being held responsible for splitting the Norwegian front line into patrols to find me and send me back to London for a Soviet visa!

We heard nothing more from Henningsen and his five men for the duration of the war. Later we learned that the Germans had discovered the boat and opened fire. The boat sank and half of the crew drowned; the rest were captured by the Germans. Henningsen was one of the survivors. He later became a member of the Norwegian parliament, representing Troms.

It had started to snow and the heavy truck got stuck in a snowdrift. The driver and I discovered an abandoned snowplough stuck in the frozen ground, and we pulled and tugged on it until we suddenly noticed that a mine was attached to it. We spared ourselves any further efforts.

We managed to keep on going, constantly having to dig ourselves free from drifting snow; we never saw a single snow marker. The bridges over the Guljok and Tana Rivers had been blown up, but we made it through birch thickets and open fields down to the frozen rivers and up again on the other side. Except for once, after we had crossed the Tana a second time and the truck got stuck and would not budge. In the end we found a Lapp's turf hut and borrowed a horse to pull the truck loose. On the following day we broke through the ice in the fjord outside Nesseby. I nearly experienced my childhood fear of water and ice again, but we were still close enough to the riverbank to make it to shore, soaking wet. We heard horse bells, and three small Lapps came to help us, but even before we had started to rescue the truck, the Lapp's horse and sled also went through the ice and its runners broke. We fashioned new runners from birch logs and, after striving for six hours, we managed to save the horse and sled. The truck was abandoned for good.

I reached Vardø on foot one morning, and fell asleep on the kitchen floor of the first house I entered.

Before I managed to cross the fjord on the final stretch to

Kirkenes, I met a mysterious unshaven ensign who had hidden in a cave of snow during the German retreat. When he left his place of hiding he found himself, like me, in no-man's-land. After we gained each other's trust, he introduced himself with the cover name Torstein Pettersen. Immediately we were on good terms and we developed a lasting friendship. Later he would come along on the *Kon-Tiki* journey under his real name, Torstein Raaby.

In Finnmark, Torstein kept his stories to himself while we were together during the winter war. Later I came to learn that, after his training in England, he had been secretly parachuted into the Tromsø area in Norway. He had stayed under cover close to the place where the German cruiser *Tirpitz* was based, and for several months he sent daily reports to England with a small hand-carried transmitter and by using a receiver antenna at night that belonged to a German officer. He was also, like Rørholt and Haugland, highly decorated by the Allies. His messages finally helped the British air force bombers sink the *Tirpitz*, the second of Germany's proudest warships to rest at the bottom of a Norwegian fjord.

When the Norwegian headquarters learned that Lieutenant Heyerdahl was back in Kirkenes and preparing to join a Soviet transport back to Murmansk to catch the next convoy to England, there was both relief and commotion in the camp. Since the loss of I Group's equipment, there had been no communication with any country other than the Soviet Union. I was stopped by military personnel and civilians who wanted to send messages or give me assignments in London. Someone claimed that on the most recent shipment over to Murmansk, boots for left feet had arrived at the military depot without any matching ones for right feet. Whether or not that was a dig at the communists will remain a moot point, but a lieutenant could confirm that on that same day he had gone out on patrol with eight men and one sleeping bag; the eight had been picked because they fitted into the eight pairs of boots that he had been supplied with. Furthermore the patrol had only three rounds of

ammunition and cups and cutlery for only four men. The military
police wanted to report the number of Norwegian Nazis who had
been taken prisoner in the Kirkenes area. The division doctor sent
information about health conditions and a plea for sanitary equipment, while the depot manager lacked the most incredible basic
things, from weapons and ammunition to boot polish, mittens and
snow glasses.

On 11 January 1945, a Soviet military vehicle arrived at the
Norwegian headquarters to pick me up, and to my amazement I was
not alone. There were also two lieutenants from the Norwegian navy
who were not desired by Moscow either. The three of us were to be
returned to London on the same convoy. Moreover, three Norwegian
'blue majors' crept into the transport vehicle. They did not look like
military personnel, but wore their officers' distinctions on a blue
uniform because they were important civil servants. They were
accompanying a military division to London and the Norwegian
government with important observations about the civilian population. We rattled along together in the freezing cold and dark, six
Norwegian officers and one Soviet driver, driving eastward, over the
pontoon bridge and out of Norway. Days and nights were indistinguishable and we saw only snow and endless rows of military trucks
and fur-clad soldiers. We rode and rode, and every once in a while we
stopped to eat, drinking tea in snow-covered bunkers in the company
of half-naked Soviet soldiers sitting on benches along the walls. We
finally saw lights and realized that we had crossed the border
between Finland and the Soviet Union and must have reached
Murmansk.

A Soviet naval officer tore open the car door and hurried us out,
because we were late and the convoy was already on its way out of
the fjord. He pulled out the three lieutenants first and let the three
blue majors remain in the car, because he had good news: they had
been given permission to return to Kirkenes! One of them, in fact a
bank director representing the Bank of Norway, gave an overbearing

smile and tried to explain to the friendly Russian that this was a misunderstanding: it must be the three majors who were returning to England, and the three lieutenants who had been given permission to remain.

'No misunderstanding, is order from Moscow,' the Russian answered firmly. And the incredible thing happened. The car door was shut, and the three 'blue majors', thoroughly frozen through and in despair, were sent on their way back to Kirkenes.

We, the lieutenants who had taken it for granted that the permission to remain was for us, were equally confused and disappointed. Nevertheless, with all our gear, we were firmly helped on board a Soviet submarine chaser that sped at full throttle northward in the Murmansk Fjord to catch up with the convoy that had already left Polyarno. The first thing I saw when I picked up my gear was that one of the majors had placed his own bag next to mine. It contained secret reports, a pistol and personal effects, and I quickly picked it up as if it were my own.

The submarine chaser was going at full speed, and in less than an hour we caught up with the two English destroyers at the rear of the convoy. Without slowing down and in high seas, one of the navy lieutenants was hoisted aboard the *Zebra*, while myself and the other lieutenant were hoisted aboard the *Zambezi*. We both fell asleep immediately in the officers' lounge.

The ship tossed heavily when we left the fjord entrance, but German submarines were waiting beneath us and I woke up to the booming thuds of depth charges. The first ones came from the *Zebra*, but then a submarine turned up aft of the *Zambezi* and sent coded messages out over the Arctic Ocean. Soon there were even more of the escort ships in the convoy who would have contact with the German submarines.

My countryman from the navy was incapacitated by seasickness. The transition from the Finnmark plateau was sudden, but I managed to get my sea legs and followed an English officer into the chart house where I could study the structure of the convoy. The escort, protecting a large number of cargo ships that were returning home empty, consisted of one aircraft carrier, one cruiser, eight destroyers, nine submarine chasers and a number of smaller escort vessels. We hung our hammocks in an open corridor on deck with orders to sleep with our life jackets on close to our designated 'dive-in' spot should it become necessary to jump into the sea.

There were many reasons that none of us slept well; one was that the corridor was so narrow that when the ship rolled the hammocks thudded from one bulkhead to the other at such a rapid tempo that as soon as we fell asleep after hitting one bulkhead we were woken up by the other.

We soon heard close and distant explosions in the sea around us, coming from all angles. The Englishmen took it all with a wry sense of humour: 'We have landed among a school of mackerel,' the captain said.

But Our Lord would never have let this kind of fish into the ocean. These devilish, mechanical monsters had been devised by human brains with no other thought than to send human souls into oblivion. I wondered what Tei Tetua would have thought about the bearers of culture from the outside world if he had been lying in the hammocks with us.

A loud explosion interrupted my thoughts. The ship shook and a spout of water stood in the air on the side of the boat.

'That was us,' a proud sailor explained, and I had to get up to the bridge to see what was happening. There was intense activity on board. Orders were shouted and repeated. From catapults on deck, heavy barrel-like depth charges were slung in a tall arc out into the racing blue waves of the Arctic Ocean. A few moments later the water rolled over and around us as if it were boiling, and some spouts of water shot up higher than the bridge. To lessen the risk of being hit by torpedoes, the *Zambezi* constantly changed course without leaving the convoy.

To mislead the main force of the German submarines, which was lying in wait beneath the sea further from land, the aircraft carrier ordered the convoy to change course and steer eastward along the Kola peninsula in the direction of Siberia, rather than taking our route westward. Then our course was changed again, and we hit pitching seas for almost 200 kilometres straight north. Once here, we encountered heavy seas, and the following night the ship rocked back and forth at thirty-five-degree angles.

It was almost impossible to keep a tight convoy. We changed course and sailed two days to the southwest, but rather than calming, the storm increased. On the third day I heard the cry 'Man overboard!' Three crew members had been taken by the heavy sea, but they were tossed on board again by the next wave and managed to stay on the ship. The rolling was intolerable. On the bridge they measured forty degrees in each direction, and it was almost impossible to hang on to anything. In a heavy snowstorm we were visited by a German scouting plane that was only five kilometres away before it disappeared.

An attempt to set the mess table for the three of us who had come to eat was a complete failure ending in pure comedy. We tried to hold on to dishes and cutlery until a giant wave sent all tableware, chairs and rugs flying through the mess. At the last moment I managed to twist my legs around the legs of a mess table that was screwed to the floor, but the ship doctor was swept over the deck and ended up stuck between the rug and the bulkhead. He was followed by a sea cadet who came rushing forward on foot with marmalade on a knife. As if this were not enough, the galley boy sailed through clad only in his shirt, dancing around broken dishes and sandwich spreads in his bare feet. Before we really understood what was going on, I heard the dry comment from the ship doctor about the galley boy's dance: 'Is this supposed to be a striptease, or what?'

The next great wave sent the galley boy back where he came from, and the door ended the performance with a dramatic clap.

The next day the ocean was calmer. A submarine rose immediately to the surface and sent new messages while following just under thirty kilometres behind us and at a speed of eighteen knots. It dove back down when an aeroplane was sent up from the aircraft carrier. Submerged it couldn't reach a speed of more than about six to eight knots, so when the convoy increased its speed to twenty knots we escaped. But our position had been discovered, and before long we were detecting submarines on all sides. The *Zambezi* was first.

I was on my way up to the bridge after having inspected the watertight bulkheads with the next in command when I heard a strangely metallic sound and the hull shuddered and heaved greatly. My first thought was that we had been hit by a torpedo, but it turned out we were the ones who were firing. The crew on deck worked the mine launchers and sent out one depth charge after the other, while the sonar screen on the bridge showed that another submarine on the starboard side was slowly being drawn by the asdic. Nevertheless the commander ordered us to cut out of the convoy and chase the other submarines. *Zambezi* rolled and tossed in the deep valleys between the waves, while the look-out and the instrument crew were vigilantly checking for acoustic torpedoes. Soon we got an echo bearing and changed our course toward a submarine that appeared on the screen while we were beginning to launch our bombs. We followed our course until we had the submarine right underneath us, then the bearing instrument failed and before we could repair it we had lost contact with the convoy. We increased our speed to twenty knots and caught up with the rest of the convoy as we passed the Polar Circle going south. At the same time the wind increased to a blistering storm. The waves became mountainous masses of water that heaved and thundered against the destroyer so that it reared like a stallion in battle with a sea monster.

Toward evening it was reported that the aircraft carrier had been forced to turn and ride out the storm. Shortly thereafter orders came that any ships that could manage it were to continue southward in convoy formation. By ten o'clock we also had to give up, and *Zambezi* left the convoy with most of the escort ships and headed north to ride out the storm. For a while this led to pure chaos. *Zambezi*'s bearing instrument failed again, and in the darkness we cut straight through the convoy, barely avoiding a collision with a transport ship that suddenly appeared out of the towering waves. The heavy seas were now more dangerous than the submarines, so lanterns were lit on all the surrounding ships.

It was impossible to get any rest in the hammock because I had to protect myself against knocking against the bulkhead with both hands, so I was awake when a colossal wave washed on board and shattered our ship's only motor boat. When one of the bomb throwers that had been riveted fast broke loose from the deck, it made a large gash and the water rushed over the crew below deck with every new wave that swept over us. We had become our own worst enemy. Depth charges that had been cleared for detonation had broken loose from their moorings and rolled freely around on deck. They were no longer weapons of defence, but became uncontrollable enemies tumbling wildly from one railing to the other while the ship rolled and masses of water cascaded over the deck. It felt like we had been taken by surprise and thrown into a meaningless game of life and death. I think everyone aboard felt as helpless as I did. For a moment I evaluated my chance of surviving if I jumped overboard and tried to swim away from the doomed ship.

Just then a few metres of deck railing tore away and the first of many heavy barrels rolled overboard. Normally, when a depth charge is launched into the ocean the destroyer sails full speed ahead in order to be as far away as possible when the explosion occurs. The *Zambezi* was only making three knots against the storm, and the bomb rolled into the sea right alongside the ship. The result was what might be expected. One by one the bombs rolled off the deck, splashed into the sea and exploded as they sank because of the water pressure. The sea, which was already wild, became an indescribable inferno, and with each explosion I became more and more anxious about the hull. The crew made heroic attempts to catch the bombs that were still loose on deck, but when someone was washed overboard they had to give up. This time the fellow was not thrown back on board, and all attempts to save him failed. It was a horrible experience to catch a few glimpses of him for a moment, struggling and bobbing in a crazy dance in the icy water just a few armlengths from the side of the ship. I heard the cry 'Man overboard' and then he was gone. Impossible to find him in such conditions. In a matter of minutes he would be coated with ice.

'Too bad,' one of the officers said quietly when he heard who the man was. 'He . . . he was such a good accordion player.' The officer could find no better way to express the hopelessness we all felt.

The seas now beat over the destroyer with such force that it was impossible to send anyone out on deck, even with a line. In total twelve bombs rolled slowly overboard. The cruiser ordered any ships that were still together to change course and continue to the Faeroe Islands on their own. Two cargo ships collided in the snowstorm. The side of one was ripped open and it reported that it was sinking. Before we reached the Faeroe Islands it was reported from the bridge that we were registering echoes on three sides. The captain wanted to save our remaining valuable bombs, so *Zebra* took over and launched depth charges with another destroyer all the way until it reached the entrance at Torshavn.

I flew from the Faeroe Islands over Scotland and on to London in order to get a visa from the Soviet embassy and return to the front. Of course, I also used the opportunity to deliver the documents and other items the blue majors had involuntarily sent with me to the Norwegian government.

I did not learn why my original papers were not approved by the Russians until long after the war when I was invited to the Soviet Academy of Science to defend my theories against the opposition from Soviet scientists. I discovered that my mismanaged promotion from 'ensign' to 'lieutenant' had confused the Russians. The word 'ensign' is just as unknown in Russian as it is in English, where the equivalent would be 'second lieutenant'. In Russian letters, Ensign Heyerdahl became Henrik Heyerdahl. And how could that possibly be the same man?

In London, as the first to return with an account from the northern front, I broadcast a report over the BBC in English, French and Norwegian. It became a dramatic experience for my old mother. She spent all of the war years living with one of my nieces in her house, just beside ours on the hillside above Lillehammer, and had set up a secret hideaway in her attic for paratroopers in the underground resistance movement. One of them had just completed his mission with a portable radio and was planning to escape over the border to Sweden and back to England the next day. When the Norwegian announcer on the BBC reported that Lieutenant Thor Heyerdahl would send a broadcast about Finnmark the next day, the paratrooper postponed his journey, and on 6 February 1945, my mother heard my voice for the first time in six years and knew that I was alive. As a reward for her contribution during the war, this seventy-two-year-old woman received a signed picture from Winston Churchill with a personal note of gratitude for what she had done for the Allies.

The next mission was to get back to the front with a valid visa, but this time I was not forced to wait for the next convoy to Murmansk. In London, to my surprise, I was met by Captain Rørholt. He had managed to get back to London via neutral Sweden in the hope of finding new communications equipment for the Norwegian forces in the polar north. We made plans and, with Rørholt's blessing, I wrote a report from Finnmark containing an order to myself to find my way to Sweden to train Norwegian refugees in the use of parachutes and radio transmitters. Rørholt read the report at a meeting of leaders of the Norwegian army and navy, American air force officers

and the British SOE. The orders I had written myself were signed by
the general and the day after I spoke on the BBC I flew over
German-occupied Norway to Stockholm as a lone passenger in a
small British plane with no lights. In a borrowed civilian suit, and
with a pistol and a Norwegian lieutenant's uniform in my suitcase, I
was driven to a camp for Norwegian military police just outside
Stockholm. Officially Sweden was neutral, and although the country
thereby avoided German occupation, which much of the continent
had had to experience, it also provided a haven of safety for
Norwegians and refugees and contributed all sorts of hidden help.

Rørholt had discovered that there were about 10,000 Norwegian
soldiers disguised as 'policemen' in Sweden, and they were prepared
to step into action as soon as they could come out into the open. My
task was to select a suitable group for assignments with parachutes
and radio equipment on both sides of the northern front. Rørholt
was to provide radio equipment later and we would get it up to the
isolated forces furthest north in Finnmark.

I was received with enthusiasm everywhere in Stockholm. Just
outside the city, at the Norwegian police post in Axvall, I put on my
Norwegian army uniform and this created quite a stir. I was able to
choose sixteen of the best police soldiers, all students who had also
recently finished a five-month radio course and eleven trained cryp-
tographers. I began training them in receiving and transmitting the
Norwegian and English procedures, and they were also put through
hard physical training.

Rørholt called three weeks later. He had the equipment, and had
established contact with two independent officers who had been
told of our secret plans. One was Ensign 'Pettersen', the man I had
met alone in Finnmark with his portable transmitter after he had
sent his final report on the *Tirpitz* before it was bombed. He became
our contact on the Norwegian side of the Swedish border. The other
officer was the long renowned Norwegian-born pilot Bernt Balchen,
who was now an American colonel. He had Allied planes at his

disposition, but he operated out of a secret air base on Swedish territory. I was to bring my soldiers there, and the group was to be ready to travel at 0600 the following morning.

Meanwhile, the group had expanded, and I bore the responsibility for the command and training of thirty-five men. It would be impossible to lead thirty-five police soldiers through Sweden in civilian clothes. I took the chance that most people in a neutral country would not notice the difference between a bluish Norwegian police uniform and a khaki-coloured Allied uniform with Norwegian flags on the sleeve. And I was quite right. No one raised an eyebrow when our little troop marched through the streets of Stockholm to the central station, where a railway car had been reserved to carry the company farthest to the north in Sweden.

My little Norwegian force was quartered in secrecy at a hidden Swedish air camp at Kallax, all the way up near Luleå, close to the border to Finland. The Swedish air force soldiers were not just a little surprised when they came out one morning to find a long row of Eskimo igloos along the edge of the runway. I had started to teach the soldiers wilderness survival, and had every reason to be sceptical about our equipment.

Rørholt's arrival took a while, so the time was used for ground training, parachute jumps and hard physical endurance training. Cut off from any communication with high command in England, I promoted the brightest of the fellows to sergeant and some of the others to corporals in order to establish order in my company.

Then Rørholt arrived with the equipment. Balchen let us train some of the men in trial jumps from one of his Dakotas before we dropped them with transmitters behind the German lines or up by our own isolated liberation forces. Then Balchen personally flew me to Kirkenes, where I was immediately embraced by the same smiling Soviet officer who had sent me back to London four months earlier.

'Welcome back, Lieutenant Heyerdahl,' he said. 'Now your papers are in order.' He had received a message from Moscow.

It was a small but well-trained communications troop that now camped outside the ruins of Kirkenes. The gear was first-rate, a mixture of American polar equipment, good British and Soviet weapons and wonderful Swedish provisions. I was in the peculiar situation of not being under the command of any particular military unit. Colonel Dahl and the Norwegian high command in Finnmark still had their headquarters near the Soviets in the Kirkenes area, but the Norwegian Mountain Company had advanced alone down into no-man's-land after the Soviets had stopped their advancements on the other side of the wide Varanger Fjord that divided Norway from the Soviet Union. After Rørholt and I agreed that I maintain my command over the crew, and he continue with the responsibility for equipment and the co-ordination of all the outposts, with permission from the Swedish high command he remained in the barracks we had been allowed to borrow in the Swedish flight camp, and this is where he established the main base for our operations.

After landing on the Norwegian side of the border, I started a crash course boot camp for a score of volunteers from Finnmark, and continued on behalf of Rørholt to establish small radio stations. Rørholt received a message from one of our stations behind the German lines that armed Norwegian Nazis were on their way north from Narvik to sneak up on the advancing Norwegian forces. If they found out how few troops there were, the large German forces would move northward again and wipe them out before the Soviets could make it through the mine-obstructed no-man's-land.

With the blessings of both the Soviets and Colonel Dahl, I ventured down to the front line again. Just then Ensign 'Pettersen' reappeared as a lone wolf, and with Lieutenant Stabell, who now was back in Norwegian uniform, he joined my little troop. The spring thaw had not yet come to the mountain plateau, and to avoid a third journey through the minefields of the German no-man's-land, we requisitioned two fishing boats to transport us down the coast.

We put a radio patrol ashore in Båtsfjord to keep a lookout for the

Norwegian Nazi spies. No Allied warship had made it further than this point. We were in waters filled with mines that were still patrolled by German submarines and kept hourly radio contact with Stabell, who was out of sight, following on in another fishing boat. We had agreed to meet in Hopseidet, but on the outskirts of Hopseidet I had a premonition that we might end up in a trap and sent a coded message to Stabell to continue beyond Nordkyn and into the long Porsanger Fjord. This would seem like pure lunacy to everyone, including the Germans who were positioned on the west side of the fjord and would not suspect that military troops would enter the fjord right in front of their noses.

German observation posts or spies must have discovered our destination before we changed course. That night, three German submarines slipped into Hopseidet and set navy troops ashore. They disarmed the few Norwegian guards, and eyewitnesses reported that some drunken sailors took six civilians into custody and eventually shot them because they gave them no information. By then we were already far beyond Hopseidet and on our way along the eastern bank of the Porsanger Fjord.

Just as it had been pitch black day and night when I came to the front in January, it was now light at all hours of the day and night. Turning out the lights on the two fishing boats was of little help when we sneaked into the seemingly endless fjord right ahead of the German front lines. Now, in May, it was so light at night-time that one could see for miles both at sea and on land.

We went ashore from both boats at nine o'clock in the morning. We were met by an incredible array of barbed wire obstructions and landmines. Just the day before two men had stepped on to a landmine. We found two parachutes that had fallen straight to the ground without opening, and a smashed generator revealed that this was part of Rørholt's airdrop from Balchen's plane. We all returned to the boats, and continued all the way in to Hamnbukt, at the base of the fjord. Here we carefully went ashore and set up camp near some Lapps. When I contacted Rørholt in Sweden later in the evening, we were told that the German forces in Denmark had capitulated.

We celebrated the news with the Lapps, who treated us to nips of their special drink, klonk. It was a silent celebration since the cannon on the other side of the fjord were still loaded and our closest neighbours were probably not in as good a mood as we were.

During the days and nights that followed I witnessed modern warfare at first hand. We think with disgust of the time when barbaric heathens chopped off heads with swords, and like to believe that warfare in our days has become cleaner. In fact those who launch the rockets and lay mines can conduct war wearing white gloves.

I had the rain of rockets in London fresh in my memory when I came to the minefields in Finnmark. I had seen the V-2 bombs fall at random while London's innocent civilian population sought cover in underground stations or shelters, like the Christians in the catacombs in the Roman Empire. I also saw the Allied airplane squadrons fill the sky like prehistoric dragons on their way for revenge, using the same tactics and with the blessings of the military priest.

One night I was able to view almost 5,000 years of technological progress in a single image that I would never forget. I had always dreamed of seeing the famous ancient ruins at Stonehenge, and while in London on leave from stair-washing, I took a train to Salisbury and hitch-hiked in my Norwegian army uniform to a barbed wire fence that surrounded the whole area because of a neighbouring military base.

Firmly intent on not returning without having experienced the prehistoric megalith temple, I decided to make use of my commando training in a peaceful manner among my own allies. I noticed a large cardboard box thrown in a ditch and, when night came, I pressed myself through the barbed wire fence between two layers of cardboard. After admiring the thousand-year-old stone giants reaching skyward in a protective ring around me, I crawled on to the altar stone itself. After eating the supper I had brought along, I rolled out my sleeping bag and lay down to meditate on the passage of time. In the night sky above me I saw the same unchangeable constellations that Our Lord had placed there before life was created on the planet. They were all there with the sun and the moon, and may have been a greater source of fascination to the ancient engineers of Stonehenge than they were to us. Then a single star moved slowly among the others, from horizon to horizon. This one had been created in my own generation; it was a V-2 on its way to London.

I had seen modern war from a new perspective on the altar stone at Stonehenge. When I went ashore deep in the beautiful Porsanger Fjord with Lieutenant Stabell, Ensign 'Pettersen' and our soldiers, we walked right on to a stage set for modern man-to-man combat, but we also let our cunning technological equipment fight it for us.

We landed in a partially snow-covered valley, similar to the Bella Coola valley in British Columbia. This time, however, we were not hunting bears. The valley's entire beautiful birch forest had been vandalized and razed down. Only a few scattered giant spruce remained. The Germans had set out incredible amounts of mines and booby traps. They must have had many men up here. As we advanced, we encountered many abandoned camps surrounded by minefields, and littered with twisted tin and iron, cars, tanks, posters, paper, broken glass and huge piles of bottles.

Norwegian reinforcements had arrived with new convoys via Murmansk, and they had advanced southward over the mountain plateau to the Lapp city of Karasjok, which was closer to Sweden than we were. Rørholt had airdropped a communications patrol to them from Balchen's planes, and these men were in the process of clearing the airport, which was totally covered with mines. There were daily reports of civilians and soldiers being killed, and both the snow and the white birch trunks could bear witness to a bloodbath.

Up here in the north the war was not fought against living enemies but against the atrocious mechanical equipment they had left behind. A tempting bottle, a useful item, anything at all could have invisible threads connected to a diabolical booby trap that had been placed to tear off an arm, ruin a face or shatter a body.

The true heroes on the modern front line were the men who detonated these cunning toys of the devil and the medics who ran through invisible and terrible labyrinths to save lives. The enemy can become a friend the instant he receives the ceasefire order, but for the mechanical wizardry that remains buried underground without any other purpose than to maim or kill, peace is an unknown concept. It continues in the service of evil until it has been detonated or disengaged. A long week had passed since soldiers of flesh and blood had ended their armed engagements. I made a note in my diary to remind myself always to support those who work for peace. In this way I would be able to enjoy a future life with fellow human beings from all countries and all sectors of society. Never again would I join a dance with the devil.

On the northern front, the difference between war and peace went unnoticed. My entry for 6 May was the following: 'Stabell was shaving . . . when we heard an explosion from the field. Everything became eerily still until the mountains threw the boom back. When I came out of the tent, Lieutenant Asbjørnsen and two medics were on their way right out into the minefield where hidden devilry could explode anywhere under the sand or in the junk piles above the ground. We ran toward the explosion. When we had run a few hundred metres, a cry came to us from some twisted skeletons of red iron, remnants of what had been a hangar. "Rolf has hurt himself," he moaned. He had fragments from the explosion in his eyes, and his nose was gruesomely cut open . . . We climbed over a hill of sand and found a man on his back about eight metres from a hole in the ground. The white birch trunks were stained with mud and splashed with blood. The poor man's face was no more than soot, mud and blood, and his hair was a wet mass . . . He was fully conscious and complained of pain in his legs. Blood gushed through his torn pants. We took a knife and cut off his pants, underwear and socks. Large open sores were filled with mud. No use cleaning anything here. We bandaged him as well as we could to stop the worst bleeding, and then the medics carried him back, carefully following in our own footprints.'

As early as 7 May we had heard a vague rumour on the radio that the Germans in Norway had capitulated. The bugle player ran out to the campground and blew 'cease fire' but we managed to calm him down immediately, because the German vanguard was just the other side of the closest hills to the west.

On 9 May both us and the German vanguard still had weapons ready on either side of the hill, but we were the only ones with constantly newly wounded and medics in action. Then we heard thousands of jubilant voices on the radio from Oslo: Norwegian troops from England had just landed and were on their way into the capital; liberation was being celebrated ecstatically by the Norwegian people. We rejoiced with our countrymen but exchanged crooked smiles to one another when we heard the announcer's triumphant comment from the south: 'At this very moment, the first Norwegian troops are returning to Norwegian soil!'

We had crawled out of the tent and were dancing with joy when I caught sight of a solitary Lapp running down the hillside with a reindeer carcass on his back.

'Peace has come! The war is over!' I shouted in joy to him.

He took his pipe out of his mouth and asked: 'Who won?'

Yes, who won?

Many of us soldiers have asked each other that question since. The Red Army had quickly changed from being devils to angels when the Germans marched into the Soviet, but as soon as the Germans left they became devils again. We needed the Germans in

NATO to defend us against our former liberators on the northern front. No one reacted when a few years later I settled for a longer period of time among our former enemies in Italy, and it was considered just as natural that a German, a Soviet Russian and an American were with me on the expedition with the reed boat, *Tigris*.

What became of the enemy?

We carry an enemy within us until the next time the devil, with his magical powers, releases it to participate in his diabolical dance. Precisely who we choose as an enemy is unimportant as long as we have someone to vent Cain's legacy of hate upon. If we were able to believe the word of the Bible, Cain beat Abel to death, so there are no other sons of Adam for us to be related to.

War and peace blended into one for us. A 'cease fire' order came over the radio on 13 May, but it had the surprising addition that the order only applied to companies that had at least one division. Since there were not that many soldiers in Finnmark, the instruction did not apply to us. That day I noted that seventy mines had been found around a single bomb crater that was to be repaired in the road.

Stabell, who had been thrown into the Arctic Ocean by a mine when we first came to Murmansk, could have been blown to the sky with 'Pettersen', alias Raaby, and myself during the two weeks we shared a tent on the banks of the Porsanger Fjord. On 22 May I wrote in my diary: 'Moved to new campsite. The corps of engineers has set up camp by our old site. They had a mine-seeker exercise today, and great was the surprise when they found a large teller-mine under the sand in the middle of our old tent.'

In theory a teller-mine should not explode for something as light and 'expendable' as a human body, but theories do not always hold true. An experiment by one of the newly arrived officers in Karasjok proved this point. He placed a German teller-mine on the ground and explained to his soldiers that it adjusted to the weight of a valuable tank or a heavy car. To prove it, he stepped with both of his feet onto the mind and it exploded. Twenty-two were killed and nine were wounded. One of our paratrooper telegraph operators was there and he contacted Rørholt at the main base in Sweden. In record time, he and Balchen managed to get two doctors and a nurse down to us. They landed, uninjured, in deep snow. Before a mass funeral could take place in Karasjok, the church graveyard itself had to be cleared of land mines.

On 13 July, about two months after the liberation was announced on the radio, I applied to the Army high command in Oslo for an honourable discharge. My request was turned down. They needed me in Finnmark. I then requested two weeks' leave to visit my wife and children who had come home from America and my old parents whom I had not seen in six years. Leave was granted.

I went south via Sweden to Oslo. With two lieutenant stars on my collar I went straight to the office of the high command. I was met by two ensigns with one star each, and I ordered them to get the discharge forms, told them what to write, had it stamped and sealed and delivered into the neighbouring office.

A few days later, in the bosom of my family, I received my discharge forms in the mail, signed by two high-ranking officers at the high command.

I was a civilian again, a free person, with my own name and no number or title.

8

No Time to Think

Once again I was lying in my hammock in my garden in the Canary Islands. My eyes were open, and my memories of the meaningless days of the war disappeared into the surrounding foliage – or maybe they simply withdrew into the endless labyrinths of the mind, where they remain hidden, like invisible pieces of film footage.

When I slapped shut my diary containing the notes I had made of the manhunt in the Arctic Ocean, my aku-aku disappeared. I thought he had been shaken and scared by my recollections of friends and enemies who were possessed by orders to kill, but when I glanced at my watch I knew that it was the haste within me that had chased my invisible companion away. A clock has a scarecrow effect on an aku-aku, to whom time does not exist and who lives in a world where one day is a thousand years and vice versa – just like the story of creation and Einstein's calculations.

Life had never before been so busy, and time had never flown so quickly as it did now, fifty years since we drifted from Peru to Polynesia on the *Kon-Tiki* raft. Being ruled by the clock, I climbed out of my hammock and frightened my two faithful four-legged friends Kan and Oro, who had been sleeping peacefully at my feet.

We ran to the house. They had more than enough time to spare, but I had things to do. My travelling schedule had been unusually hectic, and I hard barely managed to unpack after a visit to Japan and the United States before having to pack for Peru and Easter Island. There was no chance for a peaceful moment with my aku-aku. With time passing more quickly than jet planes and faxes, I was barely managing to keep up.

The fiftieth anniversary of the *Kon-Tiki* journey was observed and celebrated on a far greater scale than the journey itself had been. Back then we were satisfied just to have survived the expedition, but that was nothing compared to the fact that fifty years had passed. I often felt guilty about leaving our two dogs and the wonderful pyramid valley on Tenerife to drag Jacqueline through this commotion of festivities and journeys. We were crossing our shrunken planet at all angles, flying far above all the oceans I knew so well from first-hand experience. All of this was to mark the fact that a long time had passed since the raft voyage to Polynesia.

It is always relaxing to sit back in a comfortable aeroplane seat and realize that no duties and no appointments can be taken care of before the plane touches the ground. I felt that I was approaching home when we sailed over the Andes toward Lima and the endless Pacific Ocean appeared ahead of us. It was impossible to count all the times I had visited the Pacific Ocean, especially along South America's coast from Chile, Peru and Ecuador and further north along Central and North America all the way up to the Canadian archipelago off the coast of British Columbia. It was here that I thought the Stone Age people from Asia had stopped on their way to the New World, before currents and winds brought them straight down toward Polynesia. I had travelled there both by boat and balsa wood raft and, in later years, often on aeroplanes. I was now familiar with the opposite shore as well, the other side of the ocean and of the planet itself. I had studied the remains left by the earliest navigators on Okinawa, on Che-jo outside South Korea, and especially in Japan.

Just a few weeks ago I had lectured at the University of Tokyo on the significance of the ocean currents on migration in the Pacific. After that I squeezed in three jubilee lectures at the National Geographic Society in Washington on the way to our new home on the Canary Islands. Once home we had to pack our best clothes for the Kon-Tiki Museum's royal dinner in Oslo and all of this was on our way to Lima, where the airplane now touched ground and thundered down the runway. Here we were to celebrate *Kon-Tiki*'s launch from the naval harbour on 28 April 1947.

More than any other time when I had been back in Peru, memories flashed before me in rapid succession. Back then, I had just got out of uniform, a wolf's clothing from another life. I had conquered my childhood fear of water just a few years earlier. Joining me on *Kon-Tiki*'s maiden voyage were the war veterans Knut and Torstein; Erik, whom I'd played pirates with in childhood; Herman, whom I bumped into at the Norwegian seaman's restaurant in New York; and Bengt the Swede, who stumbled upon me as he came paddling in his canoe up the Amazon River while the rest of us were about to leave the raft in Lima. Today they were no longer with me. Torstein had ended his days in the barren ice of Greenland, Herman in the empire of the sun god Kon-Tiki by Lake Titicaca, and Erik in our birthplace, Larvik, where we had both dreamed of distant voyages to foreign lands. Only Knut and Bengt were still alive. Knut had retired in Oslo after being instrumental in creating both the Kon-Tiki Museum and the Norwegian Resistance Museum.

It was hard to believe that so many years had passed, and that I had survived uninjured both the ocean crossing and the following storm of attacks from all of the people who were irritated that the raft had remained so buoyant. The Pacific Ocean remained unchanged, and it curved westward beyond a blue horizon the way I had first seen it when I flew from Ecuador to Peru to find a suitable location for the jungle logs that were to carry us across the ocean. But Lima and the port city of Callao had grown into a huge metropolis, with a population twice as large as Norway's. Crowded rows of sky-scrapers and tenement buildings had swallowed the barren area one used to pass through to get from the hotel to the harbour. Missing in this ocean of skyscrapers was our old, traditional Hotel Bolivar, which in my memory still soared majestically above low houses clustered around a colonial plaza against a blue sky.

Even the impressive presidential palace was now disrespectfully overshadowed by towering concrete walls, the captive of a network of congested traffic that coiled snake-like around the residential areas. From here they greedily and insatiably made their way over the plains, pushing growing smog and slum areas toward the desert mountains. Wealth and poverty grew side by side at the same rate, as in developing countries elsewhere in the world. Party politics and changing governments tried to solve the problems of big cities with more industry and more machines. In addition, the rich built more skyscrapers and the poor built more slums, unfazed by all the experts' calculations.

As manager of the Kon-Tiki Museum's archaeological excavations in Túcume on the northern coast, I had been back to Peru numerous times in recent years. After many years in Italy, Peru became a new home and I had a long list of good friends among both the very rich and the impoverished, so these changes were not shocking when I returned to this fantastic former Inca empire for the *Kon-Tiki* celebration. Still, this was hardly the same country or the same people Herman and I met when we arrived to build an Inca raft with our nine huge balsa logs and were denied permission by the minister of the navy. In accordance with the view of the National Geographic Society's scientific council and all other nautical experts, he thought it was suicidal to venture on an ocean journey on such a vessel. Now, fifty years later, it was this navy's turn to celebrate the anniversary of the launch of the raft. The National Geographic Society had been a few days ahead of them in Washington. The first event would be a reception in the presidential palace, since the country's president at the time, Bustamante y Rivero, had been the one to finally order the minister of the navy to let us build the Inca raft in the naval harbour.

A chief of state with Japanese blood now ruled from the magnificent old palace. President Fujimori was an unknown quantity, but as in so many other countries he had been elected because the people had lost confidence in their well-known politicians. He won the election as a completely unknown political figure with billboards showing a new face that had no resemblance to the Spanish or the Incas.

Governing a country with such a diversified population and history as the former Inca Empire was not an easy task. Up until this point in time, I had met five of the presidents who had tried. Only the first one, who let me build the *Kon-Tiki*, had survived his elected years with dignity. After the meeting with Bustamante y Rivero, my next encounter with Peruvian politics occurred in my own home in Oslo. One afternoon, a few years after coming home in one piece from the *Kon-Tiki* expedition, someone rang my doorbell. I was delighted to see my jolly artist friend, 1132 Stenersen from the boot camp days in Canada. I recognized him by his wide smile and his wide tie, but I did not recognize the short foreigner he had brought with him.

A nice guy, I soon learned. They had met at a bar and he wanted to meet me because I had launched *Kon-Tiki* from his homeland.

Over a cup of coffee by the fireplace in the living room, our new acquaintance wanted to know who I knew in his native country. Not wanting to seem like a braggart, I had to admit that I could only name the minister of the navy who at first had refused me permission to travel, and the fit young air force minister who had arranged for my audience at the palace.

'Two of my best friends,' the little man answered humbly. I was sceptical and pretended to believe him. After this I couldn't resist mentioning the president's name.

'I am the one who got him elected,' my guest answered just as calmly. I had to ask him to repeat his name; it was a difficult one.

'Victor Raul Haya de la Torre,' was the answer. This was the man who had founded APRA in the 1930s; for several years it had been the largest political party in Peru. He was a refugee in Norway and had been here long enough to speak broken Norwegian.

APRA, with the charismatic young hero Alan Garcia in the presidency, had been in power when I returned to Peru in the late 1980s and applied for permission to start archaeological excavations in Túcume. Neither the president nor the other government members had heard of the name Túcume, and when the minister of culture rolled down his wall map neither the village nor its huge neighbouring pyramid complex were marked on it. However, when we started digging and found the mummy of the last loyal viceroy of the Inca period buried on the top of the largest pyramid, the president became curious. The former vassal king sat in his colourful robe of feathers in the grave, high above the plain, with his *tumu* sceptre and crocks of food, wearing a silver crown and displaying huge silver plugs in his prolonged earlobes. According to the legend recorded by the first Spanish conquistadors to march by, these pyramids were built by the grandson of King Naymlap, who had sailed down the coast from the north with his whole entourage on balsa rafts. On a temple wall we found magnificent illustrations of large reed ships navigated by mythical men with bird-like heads – just like illustrations on the temple walls in Egypt and on the cliffs of Easter Island.

This became too exciting for the inquisitive young president. Alan Garcia and his immediate staff came to stay the weekend in the simple but roomy adobe dwelling by the pyramids. I had built this house for myself and my foreign workers with sun-dried clay bricks.

None of the inhabitants of Túcume or the whole desert valley of Lambayeque had ever seen so many police and military men in different uniforms. They all spent the night around and inside our fence, up on the roof, behind the bushes, and in the stable, barn and chicken coop. Six kilometres of telephone wire wound its way to Túcume and up to the president's bedroom. At mealtimes there was barely room between the walls and our long dining table for all of his servants and special musicians. In the kitchen our own little Túcume cook disappeared among all the professional master chefs who created dishes she had never seen before.

Early the next morning, our loyal local driver Pizarro was sent off to the closest town to get the president's favourite bread for breakfast. When the whole escort was ready for the morning trip to the pyramids, Pizarro sat behind the wheel of the big expedition truck that would lead the procession. We were barely out of the house before the president wanted to know which vehicle I would be in, and when I pointed to my four-door pick-up he hurried over and pulled the alarmed Pizarro out of the driver's seat. With me at his side, he started the motor and the ever responsible Pizarro became so confused that he jumped into the back seat in order to keep some control over the situation. The car-happy president sped off to the gate in a spray of desert sand, and the motorcycle escort took a roaring short cut through the algarobe trees in a desperate attempt to take the lead. The guard at the gate had already managed to swing it open, and the whole population of Túcume had gathered outside the gate to catch a glimpse of their president and to welcome him. The cheering crowd will never forget their surprise when the whole escort came racing past the gate, with the president himself behind the wheel of the first car and their friend Pizarro sitting humbly in the back seat waving shyly to his friends.

Just a few weeks after the popular president had visited us, there were re-elections in Peru. The APRA party lost, and because of various accusations that rained down on him Alan Garcia had to flee the country to escape imprisonment. Among all the election posters showing pictures of Garcia and other well-known politicians, a completely unknown Japanese face appeared and he won the majority of the votes. In Peru, as elsewhere in the world, most people had

19. Liv and Thor Jr on a fishing trip in British Columbia, 1940.

20. With Thor Jr, 1940.

21. With Clayton Mack on our way home from a bear hunt in the Bella Coola valley, 1940.

22. In January 1941 I published my first article in *National Geographic*.

23. The soldier and artist Bjørn Stenersen and Thor Jr on a boat trip by the camp in the Muskoka forest, Canada, 1942.

24. The baby bear, Peik, plays with Bjørn ('Bamse') outside the Vesle Skaugum camp in the Muskoka forest, 1942.

25. Father, sons and bear.

26. A winter exercise in Little Norway, 1943.

27. With Peik, 1943.

28. Lieutenant Heyerdahl in uniform.

29. Clipping from an article on the *Kon-Tiki* expedition in *Life* magazine, 1947.

30. After the *Kon-Tiki* expedition, at Raroia, 1947. The oar was carved by me and shows bearded natives from Mexico and Peru.

31. During the twentieth anniversary of *Kon-Tiki* in 1967.

32. The crew on board the *Kon-Tiki*: Herman Watzinger, Knut M. Haugland, Torstein Raaby, Bengt Danielsson and myself. The photo was taken by Erik Hesselberg.

33. 'To my friend Thor Heyerdahl. Greetings from Cheif Teriieroo.'

34. Receiving the Vega Medal from the King of Sweden, Gustav VI Adolf, in 1962.

35. With Lex
'Tarzan' Barker in
Hollywood.

36. Showing my daughter
Anette a model of the
Kon-Tiki.

37. On a turtle's back during the Galapagos expedition, 1952–53.

38. Marriage to
Yvonne Dedekam-
Simonsen, 1949.

stopped believing in the promises made by the politicians they knew.

Therefore, on 28 April 1997, fifty years to the day since the *Kon-Tiki* was towed to sea from the naval harbour in Peru, I was to meet President Alberto Fujimori in the palace. It was an exciting time. Only six days had passed since he had ended the terrorist coup at the Japanese embassy with gunpowder and bullets. Hostages had been held for 126 days. No one had seen him in public since the dramatic end of the tragedy. As could be expected, it was not a happy man making jovial comments who met the Norwegian ambassador and myself in the inner chambers of the palace. President Fujimori, erect as a soldier and with an inscrutable facial expression, asked us to sit down for refreshments. A little time usually passes before conversation warms up at such a purely official courtesy visit, but a smile broke through when I reminded the president that we had met before, when we sat together eating raw fish from the same dish because of a misunderstanding.

That had happened some years before; I still had not met Jacqueline. It was while the cholera epidemic raged in Peru, and rumour said it was spread by eating fish from along the coast. This was not a happy time in Túcume. The kitchen assistant was down with typhus fever, and Pizarro had just recovered from an attack of cholera when he drove me to a farewell dinner for the village priest, who had been forced to leave because of bomb threats. The Shining Path terrorist group had marked its presence in Túcume by placing a flag on the nearest pyramid, and after Padre Pedro had received written warnings about bombs at his home the bishop ordered him to leave the village.

I was just leaving my place at the farewell dinner for the priest, feeling pleasantly full after eating kid and drinking corn beer, when flutes and drums started and I was to start the dancing with a *marinera*, a mixture of Spanish bull-fighting and Norwegian folk dance. I just managed to avoid this, because a message came from the fishing village Santa Rosa, down by the coast. It was an invitation to 'a surprise' at 1500 hours, signed by 'Nicolas, President of the reed-boat fishermen's union'.

Pizarro was already waiting with the car, and I invited the woman who had been seated next to me along for the surprise. She was a local architect who sketched plans of the ruins we excavated, and who believed like me that we were on our way to see a regatta of fishermen sitting astride their reed *caballitos* and paddling out to sea. I had gained a special relationship with these men, since they were now getting public aid to cultivate the nearly extinct *totora* reeds that they used to build their traditional inexpensive fishing vessels.

The police had blocked the road down by the coast on the way in to Santa Rosa, and no matter how much Pizarro argued that I was the guest of honour we were not allowed to pass. Pizarro found a detour and he made it to the main street from a side road. The street was jammed. A brass band with a tuba and bass drums came marching along, but we were too late to join with them. I couldn't see a thing, but pressed my way through the crowd, dragging my friend behind. We managed to squeeze in immediately in front of the band, and we joined the procession with relief, keeping step with a small group in front of us. We then saw that one of them was President Fujimori, marching next to the mayor of the village.

It was too late to get out of the crowds as we were surrounded by cheering onlookers. We were forced forward with the parade, flanked by waving people and with the band at our heels. Only the president and the mayor were allowed to enter the town hall, and there we were, locked in by the masses of people. I looked up, and the two of them stood on a little balcony right above our heads. The mayor looked down into my face as I dutifully waved like everyone else. In a second he was gone, and he showed up at my side whispering that I should wait in the village restaurant. And then he returned to the president. We managed to push through the crowds and into the restaurant, where there were two long tables and many people.

Everyone sat at the same table, but there were no chairs for us there, so we placed ourselves at a table where no one else was sitting.

We remained at our places, declining any offer of food or beverage. We were still full from the dinner for the priest. The door opened and in came President Fujimori and his young son, escorted by the mayor, who seated them across from us before stepping back respectfully and leaving the room.

Quite a surprise, I thought, before I realized that this had to be a misunderstanding. Fujimori obviously did not realize this, and looked far from happy when I introduced myself. He thought this was part of his programme and broke into Japanese with his son while they both hungrily threw themselves over their portions of the president's favourite dish, *seviche*, raw fish marinated in the Peruvian manner.

An embarrassing silence followed, but suddenly the president seemed to catch on and he asked whether I had been on the *Kon-Tiki*. When that fact was confirmed, the son was given a quick and lively briefing in Japanese, and then Fujimori pushed his own dish toward me so that we could eat together. I tried in vain, both in Spanish and with simple gestures, to assure him that I was not hungry, that I already had eaten, but to no avail. There we were, eating raw fish from a shared dish in the middle of the cholera epidemic, and it became more and more obvious to me that this was a misunderstanding. Nevertheless the conversation flowed easily on, about sea food and the exploitation of ocean resources, and I made a number of points to support his theory that cholera was not carried by the fish from the ocean but by unsanitary overland truck transportation. Túcume and all the roadside villages had been infested, but the fishermen along the coast below us had escaped the epidemic.

Then I happened to look out the window and see the knit caps belonging to Nicolas and the fishermen. They were outside, peering in; obviously only the village élite were at the other long table. Slowly it dawned on me that the 'surprise' that was waiting for me was not the president. He had only come to eat fresh fish with his son. They had arrived by helicopter, wanting to be alone, and then the mayor had mistakenly placed me right next to his tray of delicacies because during the march I had been in the midst of the president's entourage.

The comedy started to get out of hand when I saw the door open slowly, and a tiny older woman tiptoeing toward me, virtually crawling behind the table. It was Doña Perla, an activist from a totally different social class than the one she worked for when she fought to improve the rights of the reed-boat fishermen. Almost unnoticeably she placed a note in my hand and I only managed to nod in agreement before she sneaked out.

'Can you introduce Nicolas to the president?' the note said. I could not refuse, even if my life depended on it.

Then Nicolas appeared at the door, standing respectfully with his cap in his hand. He walked over to the president who got to his feet when he saw that I did. What was I to say now?

'This is the president of the reed-boat fishermen's union,' I said, 'and this is the president of Peru.'

Not much else was said. But Nicolas was walking on cloud nine when he went back out to the others. Since the president had almost had as much to eat as I had, he headed for the helicopter while I was carried in the arms of the fishermen down to the beach. Indeed, the surprise was that magnificent reed boats were ready for the regatta. But first, we went into the fishermen's bar, because Nicolas was now an acquaintance of the president.

Fujimori did not forget Nicolas. He presented him with a brand new truck to transport clean fish from those who fished with the *caballitos*. And Doña Perla had government help with the recultivation of the *totora* reeds, and a promise to abstain from giving rich people permits to build on the land where Nicolas and his colleagues had always harvested reeds.

*

Fujimori had loosened up and regained his human characteristics when the ambassador and I expressed our gratitude after the meeting. We had to hurry over to the National Museum, where a special exhibition with models and pictures from the *Kon-Tiki* and *Ra* journeys was to be opened that morning, the occasion of the anniversary. Half jokingly, I asked whether the president could come, and as expected, I received a crooked smile for an answer.

The exhibition was displayed right inside the museum's large entrance hall, and it was crowded with people who had to make way for us when we came. Jacqueline waited on the podium with the museum director and our good friend, Consul General Stimman, afraid that we would be late. The public had just managed to close their ranks when the shouts of police and a roar of motorcycles caused everyone to turn around once more and make a new passageway. President Fujimori arrived unannounced, and went straight to the museum director, who brought him up to the podium. He was just as surprised as the rest of us.

This is how President Fujimori, who had not shown himself alone in public for a long time, came to open the exhibition, first with a speech about the *Kon-Tiki* expedition and its goals and results, and then with the scissors that cut the silk ribbon.

The anniversary celebration was still not complete when we gratefully put down our champagne glasses and the president returned to his palace. The original departure of *Kon-Tiki* had taken place at the naval harbour in Callao, and we were now on our way there. To celebrate the fiftieth anniversary of the expedition, the navy's historical institute had published a short book I had written about pre-Columbian navigation in Peru. The admiralty had arranged for a ceremony at the exact place where the raft had been launched.

In the consul-general's car, we took the bends in the road so rapidly that we held on for dear life, and when we entered the large gate to the naval harbour, exactly by the slip between the brick walls where *Kon-Tiki* slid into the ocean, the navy orchestra was already waiting, ready to play.

This was a commemoration. For the occasion a small stand of seats had been mounted on the upper end of the slip and it was already occupied by navy officers in starched white uniforms with gold on their shoulders and medals on their chests. Jacqueline and I found our waiting seats between the admirals in the first row.

In an opening speech by Admiral Arrospide, president of the navy's historical institute, our attention was drawn to the historical fact that it was from this harbour that the Pacific islands were discovered, or as he expressed it himself, 'were first visited by Europeans'. After the conquest of their country, the Spaniards heard from the historians in the Inca Empire that uninhabited islands that no Europeans had visited were a few months' journey out into the ocean. The historian Sarmiento de Gamboa collected such precise directions for the journey to these islands that he persuaded the Spanish viceroy in Peru to outfit two expeditions under the command of Alvora de Mendañas with himself as the guide. The first Mendañas expedition reached Melanesia in 1567; the second reached Polynesia in 1595.

The admiral pointed to a bronze plaque with an inscription to the memory of the Mendañas expeditions on the brick wall to the left of the slip. On the opposite side was a curtain that he asked me to open. I did, and the inscription was in memory of the *Kon-Tiki* journey from Callao to Raroia in Polynesia in 1947. The military orchestra started playing the Norwegian and Peruvian national anthems.

This became too much for my aku-aku, who had kept calmly to himself both at the palace and in the museum.

What more can you ask for now?

I too noticed a lump in my throat.

There is, however, never any reason to feel perfectly safe. The celebrations nearly came to a premature conclusion. A television crew of eleven Russians had come from Moscow for the occasion. My good friend Yuri from the three reed-boat journeys was the interviewer. I had promised to accompany them up to the pyramids in Túcume and out to the statues on Easter Island. For the trip to the pyramids, the Russians had rented their own little plane. A Norwegian journalist would not give up until he got the one remaining seat for a price.

Night fell and I sat enjoying the view over the dark Pacific Ocean while we flew northward with the lights from the mainland on our right. After a while I discovered that the lights had disappeared from the right side and were now showing up on the left. I realized that we were flying full speed back where we had come from. I only hoped we would reach the airport before we ended up in the ocean without any balsa-wood logs to rescue us.

When we were safely on the ground we were informed that another plane was ready to take us up again, but we had to wait for a new pilot. While Jacqueline and I sat patiently with the Russians and waited, the journalist went over to our plane to take a look. Through his newspaper we later learned that fuel had been pouring out from under the engines. Without being prepared for it, we had been closer to death than when we sailed on the raft from Callao fifty years earlier.

9

David and Goliath

The celebrations were still going on when we made an emergency landing at the airport in Callao. When we were on the next plane, we made a quick visit northwards to the pyramids in Túcume, and then south to Santiago de Chile and all the way out to Easter Island, all in two days.

According to legends in this loneliest place in the world, the forefathers of the inhabitants of Easter Island had taken two months on their westward sail toward the sunset. They were escaping with their king, Hotu Matua, and his queen, Ava-rei-pua, after being defeated at war in their homeland. Times change, but not people. It is no more difficult for the people of today to believe that people back then could manage a journey lasting two months than it would have been for them to accept that we could fly up and down the entire coast of the Inca empire and out to Easter Island within two days.

The giant statues stood patiently and waited for us, as they had before, and they kept the Russian film crew busily occupied with their cameras on all corners of the island. I managed to find time to relax in familiar surroundings, and once again to climb the abandoned stone quarry by the volcano of Rano Raraku.

When I first came here with my own expedition ship and four professional archaeologists, it had taken us many months to become acquainted with these petrified stone giants in the mountain wall and down by the foot of the volcano. Up on the side of the mountain and in the dead volcano's crater wall, they lay twisted in all directions with their hands on their stomachs, staring blindly up at the sky like the unborn children of a sculptor. But down at the foot of the mountain, they stood upright with clenched lips, ready to move onward as soon as their midwives had finished polishing their backs.

I found a rock shelf with a view of the plain where I had slept one night, stretched out beside a stone statue. What a masterpiece of art and technology! Ever since their first period on the island King Hotu Matua and his men had mastered the art of sculpturing and transporting these massive stone statues, mounting them upright and spreading them around the terrain. Our excavations had shown this. Memories of how the descendants of the 'long ears' had shown us how their forefathers had created these giants with sharp axes made of hard basalt and jacked them up to standing position with the aid of boards and rocks flooded back. Many years later our own experiments had confirmed their legends that the statues had 'walked' where the sculptors had wanted them to go. All they needed was a little support from a very modest number of transport workers, who slowly nudged the upright statues forward with rope.

Jacqueline climbed up to my hiding place, asking about the location of the statue that had a reed ship with three masts carved on to its body. She knew that it was the discovery of this stone sailor bearing a tattoo of his own ship on his chest that had inspired me to sail with a reed ship over the Atlantic and Indian Oceans. This came after my first Easter Island expedition. In addition, she had been present when the reed ship cycle had been completed in Peru. This was the time when Alfredo called to us while he was digging his way down a temple wall in Túcume to tell us he had found a carving. First he found bird-like heads, which were soon seen to be attached to human bodies, and then, while he carefully removed sand with a digging spoon and brush, we saw that these birdmen were on the deck of a reed ship with rows of oars in the water.

I understood that coming to Easter Island was important to Jacqueline. It had been such an essential part of my earlier life. I saw how thrilled she was to experience all the places I had told her about and described in my books. More than anything else, she appreciated meeting those of my original Easter Island friends who were still alive. She became best friends with old Lazarus, who in a much younger version had led the 'long ears' when they re-erected the huge statue that had been lying face-down at the foot of his own temple platform in Anakena Bay until 1956. This was the first of the island's roughly 600 *ahu* statues that were raised back to standing position after they had been toppled over by the 'short ears' in their uprising against the 'long ears' only a few generations before the arrival of the Europeans.

A shout of joy told me that Jacqueline had found the statue with the ship carving. Luck was with her, and with me too. By pure coincidence we had come to Easter Island with the Russians the day before a huge three-masted reed ship was to be launched in Anakena Bay, where King Hotu Matua had landed in his time. It had been built by my Spanish friend Kitin Muñoz and modelled after the reed ship on the statue. It was exactly the same size as the caravel that belonged to Columbus, the *Santa Maria*. Now the golden reed ship *Mata Rangi* bobbed gently in the waves in the bay like a reincarnation of the three-masted ship on the chest of the stone giant.

A few weeks later it came to light that my worries had been justified when I pointed out that Kitin's giant ship had no thick rope along the railings on either side. This rope would prevent the short reeds from being pulled apart in high seas. After studying illustrations from the temple carvings in Egypt and on stone statues in Easter Island caves, I had placed copies of the rope on my three reed ships. Three days after Kitin and his crew from Lake Titicaca and Polynesia had sailed on to the great ocean, they were caught by a heavy storm with wild seas and the waves split the vessel in two. The crew on an ordinary boat would have gone down with their ship, but the skipper on the *Mata Rangi* left the afterdeck to sail unmanned and gathered his crew on the foredeck. They stayed afloat on half a boat for three weeks until they were rescued and brought back to Easter Island with plans to harvest reeds for a new voyage.

In the early days of seafaring, back when kings in Peru and the Middle East had workers and time enough to build pyramids as large as mountains, it was also inexpensive to build large ships. In fact, they also had reeds and time enough to build sturdy vessels as large as the *Santa Maria*. Today, time has become money, both on land and at sea, and haste has lowered standards of maritime safety. More people lost their lives on sinking ship hulls in the Middle Ages than in ancient times, when they could stay afloat on bundles of reeds.

A lack of time is one of the essential drawbacks of civilization, and it might be the most difficult product for us to export to people who live beneath the open sky. We, who are on the cutting edge of progress, accept noise, polluted air, canned food and heart attacks as long as everything moves fast enough for us to accomplish even more. Things move too quickly. Future generations will find it impossible to digest all the entertainment and all the pastimes. They will lose their minds in their search for a peaceful, normal life. Our nervous system is not constructed to tolerate so much noise and so many fleeting impressions, so much murder, sex and constant excitement.

You can eat yourself to death, but you can also entertain yourself to death.

It was quiet up in the abandoned quarry, among all the lifeless statues. I could barely hear the wind whispering behind the rock wall, or the weak sound of the distant surf. Then time disappeared too. I remained there, stretched out and staring into the clear blue sky of eternity.

Here we were, celebrating the fiftieth anniversary of the *Kon-Tiki* expedition. So much had happened since then. My memories from after the journey were not only good ones. I encountered unexpected attacks from scientists all over the world, and at the same time my marriage to Liv started to fall apart. When we finally met after the long years of separation during the war, nothing had been the same. We no longer had the same view on life, and our experiences had been totally different. I had seen the dirty reality of war face to face. She had, without me knowing it, had a carefree life with the children as a guest in Thomas Olsen's wonderful country home outside New York. She saw heroism and patriotism, where I saw meaningless death and suffering among both friend and foe. Liv had lost faith in the existence of any god since he had allowed such a horrible world war to happen, while I was reinforced in my faith in a god who forbade mankind to kill, whether voluntarily or following orders. In the end we agreed that, instead of arguing, we should part as friends. And if we should find new companions, we would use one another as advisors in our choice.

I met Yvonne a short while after the *Kon-Tiki* journey at a dinner party with friends in the Norwegian mountains. When I presented her to Liv, the judgement was immediate: 'You have found yourself a real angel!'

I could attest to that. Yvonne was both beautiful and a pure incarnation of peace and amicability. She finished her studies of penicillin in Glasgow and moved with me to New Mexico, where we married in all haste at the sheriff's office in Santa Fe. We found a stone cabin up in the mountains, where I worked on an enlarged version of my comprehensive *Polynesia and America: A Study of Prehistoric Relations*. From my study I could look out over the valley to Los Alamos, where Oppenheimer and his colleagues had produced the first atomic bomb. Nobel had had little success in creating lasting peace with his invention of dynamite, and now one hoped for better results with the atomic bomb.

I started my first and eventually ongoing co-operation with professional archaeologists at the Museum of New Mexico in Santa Fe. Yvonne developed an absorbing interest in my theories of the Polynesian migration, and from the very beginning was my heartiest supporter in my battle against academic opponents.

When we moved home to Norway, I bought a group of old historic houses in the Majorstuen district in Oslo. The red wooden buildings, dwarfed by huge chestnut trees, were placed in a horseshoe around a large courtyard. Yvonne and I lived here while I planned and later revised the results from the Easter Island expedition.

In the meanwhile, Liv had met James Stillman Rockefeller, popularly called Pebble, who had just visited the Marquesas Islands on a trip around the world with a small sailing boat. He was so impressed that Liv had lived there for a whole year that he fell for the brave woman. Liv had my due blessings and ended up in the United States as his wife.

The attacks from my academic *Kon-Tiki* opponents found new sustenance in the publicity around the Easter Island expedition. They became so intense that two young Norwegian archaeology students who suggested that I had willingly sailed the *Kon-Tiki* onto a reef to create a sensation had entire pages placed at their disposal in the Oslo newspapers. At this point I decided to find a peaceful place to work abroad.

In 1958 Yvonne and I discovered the small village of Colla Micheri on the Ligurian coast in northern Italy. High on the ridge of a peninsula, we found the ramshackle remnants of old medieval houses, with a view over wooded hills all the way up to the ragged peaks of the maritime Alps and over the blue Mediterranean to the wild mountains of Corsica. The old Roman road that once had been the only connection between the two papal cities, Rome and

Avignon, passed straight through one of the houses. A memorial plaque over the door on the tiny local church stated that Pope Pius VII had rested here and blessed the inhabitants when he passed through in his papal chair on his way home from Avignon in 1814. Another chair that he had used lay abandoned inside the house, beside old figures of saints.

After Napoleon had constructed a new road down by the coast and an earthquake had ravaged the countryside, the village remained virtually deserted. We bought and restored all the uninhabited houses. At one end of the property there was a huge Roman watch-tower, and on the other was a medieval bird-hunters' tower, which became my workplace for many years.

When I first arrived on Easter Island with Yvonne, we had our two-year-old daughter Anette with us. She trudged along and called the statues that now surrounded me in the quarry, her 'big dolls'. It would become my life's greatest sorrow when we lost her while she was in the prime of life. It was painful to think about, lying here and looking up into the sparkling swarm of stars.

There had also been a clear starry night the last time I was here. I could see all the stars of the southern sky at the same time. There is something strange about time. We can see all the stars at once, but still there are thousands of light years between them. We see the past of everything out there among foreign heavenly bodies, but not at close range, on this planet, where we ourselves live. We see farthest into the past when we look at the stars that are most distant from us. Maybe the starting point is even closer, but still beyond the scope of vision. Perhaps the future is stored in a place we cannot see, in the chromosomes, and time is unleashed by genes that are programmed for all development, whether from a seed to a tree or from plankton to a human being. Science has discovered that rays from the sun impregnated lifeless particles in the ocean that eventually triggered the development of simple cells into complicated genes and chromosomes and finally led to the creation of all the species of the world. Could the sun have created time that comes and goes as well?

Are you asking me?

I should have expected the aku-aku to show up at such a peaceful moment. This was where it belonged. It was here, when we excavated a kneeling statue that no one had seen before, that the former mayor Pedro Attain and Lazarus introduced me to my aku-aku.

But of course I knew the answer. I was well aware that it was no modern scientist who had made the discovery that the sun was the father of all life. All cultures that built pyramids in honour of the sun knew that, back when the Christians' forefathers were worshipping Baal and my own ancestors were praying to my namesake with the hammer.

Sumerians and Hittites and the creators of the ancient cultures from the Indus valley in Egypt had been sun-worshippers and honoured the visible sun as the symbol of the invisible god of creation. It was unfair when the Christian European conquerors murdered the Incas because they claimed that the sun was their father, while they themselves introduced the cross, the forerunner of the electric chair, as the symbol of the god of love. I think that Christ himself would have preferred the sun rather than the cross they nailed him to as a symbol of his morality and the tolerance between all of us who are born under the same sun.

On our first expedition to Easter Island, Ed Ferdon had excavated the ancient place of worship, Orongo, on top of the Rano Kao volcano. He uncovered a sun observatory and relief carvings of three-masted sickle-shaped reed ships from the oldest period. These revealed that the people who had painted reed ships depicted their most important god Make-Make with the huge, round eyes of the sun. On Fatu-Hiva I had learned from old Tei Tetua that Tiki was a human god, while Atea, 'The Light', was his creator. Just like the relationship between the three identical human gods Tiki, Kon and Viracocha in ancient Peru.

My philosophizing about a connection between the time that passes and the sun that has put everything on our planet into motion was just as old as sun-worshipping. Legends about the attempts of their forefathers to capture the sun in order to stop time can be found in the mythologies of both Polynesia and Peru. This task was too much even for the pyramid builders, who had to be satisfied with devising the calendar we have inherited from them, based on years, months and days.

You should be happy as long as time passes. If it stopped one day when you were in pain, you would regret it. And if it stopped while everything was going well, you would be bored to death.

The aku-aku was absolutely right. Memory is finely attuned when it comes to preserving the past in our brains. The ability to remember and the ability to forget. The art of using both for the benefit of oneself and others. The ability to forget evil and remember goodness contributes to a better life, both with others and for oneself. I had to smile when I thought about how carefree my fifty years in the limelight seemed to myself and my friends today. Fifty years filled with excitement, adventure, meetings with wonderful people, good friends, good food, sunshine and joy, both at home and abroad. It was all true. But it was not the whole truth. Were I to dig deeply in my memory, I would after all be glad that time had passed.

I remembered the storm that raged from all directions after we had crawled ashore in Polynesia, alive. And it only increased in strength in the years that followed, when I brought archaeologists into the Pacific Ocean, and after each expedition became more and more certain that the Polynesians were right in claiming that all of the islands in Polynesia were discovered from the east, while the Europeans, who themselves had arrived at all of the Pacific islands from the east, claimed that the Polynesians must have discovered them from the west.

I have always considered the legends of the natives as possible guidelines and scientific dogmas as possible false leads, but I have never relied entirely on the truth of either. When I have doubted the accuracy of the dogmas, I have tried out various seagoing vessels and excavated and searched wherever oral tradition has suggested there might be something to find.

The first lead I followed, when I was preparing for my voyage to the Marquesas Islands at Kroepelin's Polynesia library, was that all of the Polynesians agreed that their forefathers had come from the east, while all of academia disagreed upon where in the west the Polynesians had come from. Missionaries who recorded the Polynesians' beliefs and legends in the last century, found complete agreement among the Polynesians, from Hawaii in the north to New Zealand in the south, from Samoa in the west to Easter Island in the east. One missionary, Ellis, wrote in 1827: 'It is a remarkable fact that all of the journeys that are spoken about in their stories of sea voyages, whether they are part of the native's oral traditions or from more recent times, have without exception gone from east to west.'

The foremost scholar on Polynesia at the time when I decided to build the *Kon-Tiki* raft was Sir Peter Buck. In his popular bestseller *Vikings of the Sunrise*, which I read with fascination when it was published after I returned from the Marquesas in 1938, he quotes the text of a Maori song about the direction to the Polynesian's homeland:

> *Now I direct the bow of my canoe*
> *Against the opening where the Sun-god rises,*
> *Tama-nui-te-ra, Great-son-of-sun,*
> *Do not let me sway from that direction*
> *But sail directly to the land, to the homeland.*

This was why Peter Buck called the Polynesians 'the Vikings of the Sunrise'. But at the same time he believed that the Polynesian homeland lay in the west, because in New Zealand, as in the rest of Polynesia, as well as Peru and Egypt and wherever traces of sun worship had been found, it was believed that the souls of the dead followed the sun to the west. What he forgot was that in all of Polynesia they believed that the sun set in a tunnel that led it through the underworld and back to its own home in the east, where it rose. This journey with the sun was only for the dead. The living staked their direction directly eastward, as the song told them to do.

Buck had published his textbook *An Introduction to Polynesian Anthropology* only two years before the *Kon-Tiki* expedition. Here, like all other researchers, he accepted the dogma that a balsa raft could not reach Polynesia. Therefore he opened by reinforcing the idea of a boundary between Peru and Polynesia that could not be crossed: 'Since the South American Indians had neither the vessels nor the abilities to navigate right across the ocean between their coast and the closest islands in Polynesia, we can rule them out as the possible first settlers.'

When the *Kon-Tiki* voyage tore down this academic boundary against the east, showing that the whole ocean around Polynesia lay open without protection of any kind against the wind and currents from South America, we who had experienced the incredible sea-worthiness of the balsa raft believed that all interested parties would be happy. After a week of commotion and publicity, I was very pleased to receive a telephone call saying that the first reaction from the academic world had come in a newspaper interview with Sir Peter Buck.

I was a little less pleased when I finally saw the clipping from the *Auckland Star*, which made it extremely clear that Sir Peter Buck thought the raft voyage was no more than a joke. He threw his head back and laughed aloud, the journalist wrote.

And then Buck's counter-argument followed: 'No fishermen I have ever known have had women on board. And according to their own theory, the landing should have taken place on uninhabited islands – so exactly who became the mothers of the Polynesian people?'

This was when I first realized that, in our age of specialization, the man who knew the most about Polynesia was so ignorant about America that he knew nothing about Pizarro, who had captured a balsa raft on the way from Peru to Panama with both women and men on board – before the Spaniards themselves had reached the Inca Empire. The raft carried thirty tons of cargo, which Pizarro's men robbed, and they also captured five women whom they trained to be interpreters before their final offensive against Peru. And additionally: would it have been easier for the fishermen to procreate if they came to uninhabited islands against the wind?

The joke from New Zealand quickly caught on in the otherwise sombre world of science. Nevertheless the balsa raft continued to float in the imagination of the general public. Many must have thought of this raft as a warship manned by Vikings from the east who were trying to ram their logs of soft balsa into the wooden canoes of Sir Peter's Vikings from the west, which were so heavy that they would sink if they took in water.

I never heard more from Peter Buck, though I was told that he attended the première of the *Kon-Tiki* movie in Honolulu.

Opposition to the so-called *Kon-Tiki* theory spread with the speed of modern communications throughout the whole academic world, eastward to America and westward to Australia, and from Western Europe it swept through the Iron Curtain to the Soviet Union. The daily press became my staunchest ally. They gladly printed all the attacks, but were even happier when I came back with my replies. Many malicious attacks followed, and the debate became little more than a personal attack that rarely rose to an academic level. The replies became so time-consuming that I had to seek refuge in a cabin in the Norwegian mountains to make the time to write a travel narrative about the *Kon-Tiki* expedition. This would provide income and an opportunity to inspire interest in my weighty scientific manuscript, which no one at the universities would read and no one at the publishing houses would print.

Among all the commotion, it was my Norwegian publisher Harald Grieg, at Gyldendal Norwegian Publishers, who first ventured to publish the travel narrative. He had published my book about the adventure on Fatu-Hiva before the war and had bet 5,000 kroner that there would be a new book about the raft journey even before it had started. In the United States the manuscript was rejected, among others, by the New York publisher Doubleday, because there was no sex on the raft journey and there were no drowning casualties.

But then Adam Helms in the small Swedish publisher Forum got hold of the text and sold a record number of copies in Sweden. And when the Chicago atlas publisher Rand McNally decided to print it, the book jumped to the top of the bestseller list, where it remained for weeks. My British publisher, Sir Stanley Unwin, calculated that if he made a pile of all of the books that had been sold about the raft journey, it would have been taller than Mt Everest. As time went on the *Kon-Tiki* book was published in sixty-seven languages, including Esperanto, Eskimo, Telugu, Singalese, Gujarati, Marathi, Mongolian and Urdu, as well as several editions in Braille.

It must have been a fantastically good time!

I'd be happy to forget most of it. The more popular the six of us raft voyagers became to the general public, the less popular we became among the scholars, and I still had my serious manuscript about the theory behind the *Kon-Tiki* expedition. No one wanted to read this; its size was discouraging enough, and it had references to more than a thousand sources from different branches of scientific literature.

On the other hand, the travel narrative was written for a wide audience and had none of the academic jargon that would reflect my associations with professionals in the field. At that time it was still against all the rules for a professional to write for a larger circle of readers. Science was to be cultivated for the sake of science, and one was never to venture outside of one's own speciality. I was aware of this but disregarded it in order to remove the boundaries between

Polynesia and America as well as between the academic branches that would have to work together before there would be any chance of solving the puzzle of migration in the huge area of the Pacific Ocean. I also wanted to keep ordinary people informed, since they often had more insight than the specialists.

As time went on, the opposition from academia made the raft experiment look like no more than a sports adventure. I was described as an unknown adventurer, an unschooled daredevil who was stepping into an area where I did not belong. It was paradoxical that I, with my former fear of the water, should be celebrated as a seafaring hero while the fantastic vessel that had carried us to Polynesia like a magic carpet was still seen as no more than a bunch of wooden logs. It was tragicomical that I, who had never hoisted a sail before we crept aboard the balsa-wood raft, was being invited to yacht clubs and celebrated at cocktail parties with admirals, while doors to the academic clubs were locked and university professors shrugged their shoulders.

While I was virtually alone in defending myself and my theories, the Twenty-Ninth International Congress of Americanists convened in New York. For the occasion, an exhibition had been set up at the American Museum of Natural History called 'Across the Pacific'. The title could imply that the *Kon-Tiki* expedition was discussed, and the well-known Danish anthropologist, Professor Birket-Smith, was interviewed when he came back to Copenhagen. The answer to the question of how the experts had appraised the results of my expedition became a headline: 'THE KON-TIKI EXPEDITION IS TO BE SILENCED TO DEATH'.

After this, a bomb went off in another corner of the Nordic countries. Finnish anthropologist Professor Rafael Karsten could not contain himself, and broke his Danish colleague's appeal for silence with a long interview in Helsinki's leading daily newspaper. 'THE HUMBUG AROUND KON-TIKI' read the headline.

The press described Professor Karsten as a world-renowned

authority. I had heard his name in connection with a planned expedition down the Amazon River. Before we had hoisted the sail on *Kon-Tiki*, the professor had said that it would be a miracle if we survived on the open seas on a balsa raft. Now he stuck to his words, adding that since miracles rarely occur now, the entire journey must have been pure humbug! The raft must have been specially constructed so that it could tip over but still carry us along while overturned. He added that if only half of what I wrote in the book was true, it would have been a miracle.

A few of us *Kon-Tiki* voyagers got together to compose a powerful reply to the accusations, but before we had completed it the news stories had grown out of control. 'KON-TIKI EXPOSED,' the headline read in another Finnish paper. 'CAUSE CELEBRE IN THE SCIENTIFIC WORLD: THE KON-TIKI VOYAGE IS HUMBUG, SAYS A FAMOUS FINNISH RESEARCHER,' was written in Sweden. 'IS THE KON-TIKI THEORY A PUBLICITY STUNT?' a Danish paper asked. And the echo came from my own country: 'HUMBUG, HUMBUG!'

On the day of the attack from Professor Karsten, I was in Stockholm on a lecture tour with our amateur movie of the *Kon-Tiki* voyage. Never have I felt the earth disappear so completely beneath my feet as when I saw the newspaper. What would my mother think? She who was an atheist, but who put truth at such a premium level? The only time I ever saw her cry was when I lied to her as a boy and told her that I had been playing in the neighbour's garden, when in fact I had been riding my bike out on the road to Stavern.

When I went to bed alone in my hotel room that evening, I felt as if an army of unknown enemies had hit me with a lethal blow. I was on the verge of wishing that I had drowned, as my opponents had expected, instead of having to experience this degradation and shame. At that point I had little faith in any god of justice, and I was unsure that there was any god at all. Though when we hit the reef in Polynesia and the surf pulled and tore at me and the whole ocean tried to drag me loose from where I was clinging, I had taken a brief glimpse behind the veil of life and experienced a sensation that something was going on there. I had promised myself that if we all survived the towering walls of waves I would never forget that moment. I thought back to the endless gratitude I felt when I waded ashore on the Raroia atoll with all my men alive. I went down on my knees on a golden beach, which was not rolling with waves, and dug my fingers down into the warm, dry sand. Where had the extra power that I had begged for in the face of death come from? The white birds that flew across the blue sky as we lay and regained our breath on the beach reminded me of the doves of Christianity bringing messages from Heaven. But the help that I felt as a physical force out there in the ocean had not come from above; it came from within. Perhaps the Heaven with a capital H of the Bible and the Koran should not be mistaken for the heaven with a small h that we can all find within us?

I twisted and turned in my hotel bed. Couldn't sleep. Thought. How was I to deal with the following morning? How was I to counter those kind of accusations in the press? I had nothing to read, looked at my watch on top of the bedside table, and opened its drawer. A Bible was there, as is often found in hotel rooms. Black and gloomy, as if it were meant for funerals and sorrow.

That night, when I opened the Bible at random, when everything in my life seemed as black as the cover of the Bible itself, I thumbed through the pages to distract myself and see if I would bump into something that with a little imagination could be interpreted as a form of guidance.

I opened it up and placed my finger on the facing page. It was about David and Goliath.

I laughed to myself a little and stopped thinking. Then I pulled the quilt up over my ears and fell asleep.

10

The Scholars

I was still resting in my world of memory, stretched out on the rock ledge on Easter Island in the silent company of the stone Goliath, when voices down the hill revealed that the Russian television crew was approaching with Jacqueline. I climbed down among all the other unfinished stone giants that were lying scattered about, eyeless with noses pointing skyward. A fossilized battlefield of fallen giants.

Symbolic, I thought. I took the Russians to film the island's only kneeling statue. After the battle against the 'short ears', he had literally got back on his feet, even though it was to a kneeling position, and seemed to be begging for mercy. It came from the oldest period on the island, and we were the ones who had raised it up to its current position when we excavated it on my first expedition to Easter Island. All the other statues on the island were busts without legs, cut off horizontally beneath the groin. They had hands with long fingernails resting beneath roomy stomachs. Carved by the first settlers on the island, the kneeling giant was totally unlike all the others, but it was remarkably similar to the kneeling sculptures the pre-Incas had raised in Tiahuanaco by Lake Titicaca in the Andes. All the other statues were exactly the same type and resembled nothing else in the outside world. This entire army of Goliaths appeared to be copies of the same model, either lying there legless and blind on the mountain shelves, or buried in landslides with only their heads above ground.

To show the size of the statues for the Russians' film, I stood next to the one lonely giant who knelt with his hands on his thighs and his head lifted as in a humble prayer to the sky. I felt very small. Sun-worshippers had made this giant, and they were the ones who brought the art of sculpture to this lonely island. All of the other fallen giants who had been re-erected on their *ahus* later stood there with straight backs and defiant closed lips, as if they had no respect for any others than themselves. Just as Captain Cook had thought, they represented the god-like kings of 'long ears' and the more powerful they had been, the higher their monuments towered over the rest of us mortals.

The Russians wanted to continue filming by Anakena Bay in order to secure a few frames of the broad-shouldered giant who was the first *moai* we had re-erected on his *ahu*. He was the first to stare at Europeans through his deep, empty eye sockets. When I first saw these meaningless empty eye sockets, I was struck by the fact that I had seen similar deep holes in the heads of stone giants from the Hittite Empire in the inner Mediterranean. I had also seen them in several stone statues and figures of both stone and wood from the oldest cultures in Mexico and Peru, though in those cases the eye sockets had been inlaid with white eyeballs of bone or shell with life-like pupils of black obsidian. Only when one or both of the eyes had fallen out, did the empty sockets look exactly like the ones on Easter Island.

I told the Russians that a book I wrote in 1975 had presented my conviction that the Easter Island statues once had inlaid eyes and that this idea had been rejected by opponents who argued that inlaid eyes on stone statues was not a Polynesian custom. Pointing out that it was an American custom and that Easter Island was one of the thousands of Pacific islands that were closest to America made little difference. Two years later, the young Easter Island archaeologist Sonia Haoa was to find the first huge eye from a classic middle period statue when she was assisting in Sergio Rapu's excavations at King Hotu Matua's *ahu* in Anakena. Later, when she was excavating for us, she also found the first eye to have fallen out of a statue head from the earliest period.

But a great deal had happened since then. The discovery in Peru of the mummy mask from Sipan with inlaid eyes inspired me to start the excavations at the pyramids in Túcume. To get blue eyes on their royal mummy mask in remembrance of the blond god-like people who had visited their forefathers, the seafarers furthest north in Peru had sailed all the way down to Chile to find South America's only source of blue lapis lazuli. Otherwise in Peru one had to make do with black obsidian for use as inlays for pupils.

Lazarus and his people had managed to re-erect the broad-shouldered giant without technical aid, and the lone statue was now on its former platform in the easternmost part of Anakena Bay. Later archaeologists with modern cranes had continued to lift other *moai* back on to their *ahus* around the island. For those of us who were used to the gaping empty eye sockets, it was now an almost frightening sight to see the whole row of raised Goliaths standing in rank like soldiers on parade, with straight backs turned to the bay, stiffly staring toward us with eyes as large as tin plates.

This was the second time in a thousand years that small two-legged creatures made of perishable flesh and blood had given eyes to the statues. If they had been able to see us and open their clenched lips, they would have been able to tell us how little mankind had changed in the course of a millennium.

While the Russians filmed the statue and there was so much commotion around Kitin Muñoz's reed ship, no one noticed that I had sneaked up the hillside and lay down with a view over the blue bay, a heavenly mirror partially framed by Anakena's golden yellow sandy beach. It was far from easy to collect my thoughts about the most difficult period of my past when it was so exciting to live in the present, to see the stone giants in place where Hotu Matua had landed and watch a real three-masted reed ship dipping in the breeze.

How did it go? Did David beat Goliath with his slingshot?

I have never tried to kill anyone. All my battles have been in self-defence. If I have been aggressive, it is because there have been many attacks.

The attacks from Professor Karsten ended abruptly when the Nordenskiöld Society, the Scientific Academy of Finland, invited me to Helsinki to refute his accusations. I turned up for the meeting, but Karsten was not there. He preferred to meet behind closed doors at his home. The secretary-general of the Academy took me to the entrance of an apartment building. We were both let in, but a voice from upstairs insisted that I come up alone. A smiling old lady greeted me and I loaded my slingshot with academic arguments in my defence. The miracle occurred. Goliath dwindled into a peaceful old man who sat with a cup of tea and rocked in a rocking chair. I was also given a cup, but not a chance to discuss my Pacific Ocean theory. He had not called the *Kon-Tiki* expedition humbug. Newspaper editors wrote the headlines. He confirmed this fact later in a newspaper article. I just sat there devouring pieces of cake while the man who had been my greatest opponent told me stories about his travels.

On the surface, it looked like peace had arrived when Karsten gave up the fight in Northern Europe, but I knew little of the battle for honour that was taking place behind the scenes of Pacific Ocean research. There the war was being waged among the big names. I thought of them as a united front, standing shoulder to shoulder, collectively dragging me into the limelight in order to behead me in public.

In the beginning it was obvious that their team effort had been unsuccessful. Denmark's leading anthropologist, Professor Birket-Smith, had suggested to the press that the *Kon-Tiki* expedition should be silenced to death, but his colleague, Professor Karsten in Finland, had started a serious newspaper debate throughout Scandinavia. The vice-president of the Swedish Academy of Science, Professor Carl Skottsberg, also stepped into the debate on a strictly scientific basis.

Skottsberg deserved his position as one of the foremost experts in Pacific research. I had quoted him frequently in my thick, unpublished manuscript, but there was no way he could know this. When Skottsberg came forward as my next opponent in the newspaper controversy, he had one advantage. He had been to Easter Island, and I had not been there yet. For the time being I was most familiar with the islands further out in the ocean where, according to Skottsberg, I had first spent a year as a wild man, and then returned later on a lumber raft.

Skottsberg had written botanical works as well as a travel narrative from Easter Island, and since he was reviewing my travel narrative from the *Kon-Tiki* journey, it was expected that he would choose Easter Island as my Achilles heel. I was praised for being a capable sailor, but I was not a real scientist. My evaluation of the problem of manoeuvring the statues on Easter Island was faulty, as were their measurements. Before expressing my opinion, I should have read the book about Easter Island by the famous French ethnologist Alfred Métraux.

I answered in the same Gothenburg paper that it was precisely from Métraux's book that I had found the information about the transport problems with the statues, and the measurements I had given had been taken from Skottsberg's own travel narrative.

I never received a proper reply from the professor, just a short note that brushed away any further discussion by stating the Latin names of three plants that proved that Easter Island was populated by people from Asia and not from America. The debate was thereby over from his point of view.

Skottsberg could not know that he had now entered an area I had studied intently before any journey on the balsa raft. I could quote his colleague, botanist F. B. H. Brown on Hawaii. Two of the plants that Skottsberg mentioned were species with seeds that could be spread over the ocean without the aim of humans, and the third, *Hibiscus tiliaceus*, was just as common in prehistoric South America as it was in Asia.

Skottsberg did not return to the debate until eight years later. By then, my manuscript *Polynesia and America* had been published under the title *American Indians in the Pacific: The Theory Behind the Kon-Tiki Expedition*. Skottsberg wrote a positive review and now supported the *Kon-Tiki* theory with an important botanical argument: the Easter Island inhabitants built their reed ships with the freshwater *totora* reeds. The reeds were only indigenous to South America and therefore had to have been brought to the crater lakes on Easter Island by their own forefathers.

Meanwhile, the net was still closing around us; the newspaper duel in Sweden continued for weeks. Sweden had a history of botanical experts ever since Carl von Linné assigned Latin names to all plants and animals, and Erland Nordenskiøld created a school of South American anthropology through his archaeological studies in the border areas of Peru and Bolivia, which brought rich collections to Gothenburg. His student was the archaeologist Stig Ryden.

When botanist Skottsberg left the debate on the first settlers of Easter Island, archaeologist Ryden approached the matter from another angle. His speciality was Tiahuanaco by Lake Titicaca, precisely where legends said that the white and bearded Kon-Tiki had ruled before he wandered down to the coast and disappeared with his followers out across the Pacific Ocean. Ryden was the only archaeologist in the Nordic countries who had personally excavated in

Tiahuanaco, and now he came forward and claimed that those legends did not exist. The Indians in Tiahuanaco were just as beard-less and red-skinned as other Indians. The head on the Kon-Tiki statue from Tiahuanaco, the one we had used as a symbol on the sail, had no beard; it was simply some sort of a nose ring.

A capable archaeologist unravels unwritten ancient history with an excavating spoon. Reading history is something different. It was easy to provide Ryden with quotes from the numerous Spanish chroniclers who had recorded the Inca's legends of the white and bearded *viracocha*, whom the Incas believed had returned when the Spanish conquered the land. It was just as easy to refer to Ryden's predecessor in Tiahuanaco, American archaeologist W. C. Bennett, the man who had excavated the Kon-Tiki statue and described it as a sculpture of a man with a beard. The head on our sail was an exact copy of Bennett's drawing in his scientific report.

I had the last word in the duel in the Gothenburg paper concern-ing whether or not the pre-Inca artists of Peru depicted their god with a nose ring or a beard. I asked Ryden to go down into the store rooms in his own ethnographic museum to look for a catalogue number that I had found in my own notes. I wish I could have seen his face when he found what I had sent him to find: a pre-Incan Mochica jar from the coast of Peru that represented a man with a full beard that could even make Santa Claus jealous.

It was no laughing matter to be a Norwegian scientist in Sweden, even though week after week full lecture halls gave warm applause to those of us who had been on the raft journey. It was even less enjoyable to be a Norwegian at home when I was accused of every-thing from dishonesty to ignorance in the daily press of all the neighbouring countries. In Norway there was little help in my former zoology professors giving me honourable praise as an aca-demic and inviting me to lecture about my theories at the university. Although my former geography professor, Werner Werenskiold, came to a powerful defence in the press, I was still on my own.

None of those professionals were specialists on the migrations in the Pacific Ocean.

I was ready with my slingshot and waiting for the next Goliath to appear when a wondrous event occurred in Stockholm. One evening in the lecture hall of the Swedish Academy of Science, one of its real giants, Sven Hedin, sat and joined in the applause after I had shown an amateur movie of the raft journey to Polynesia. As unpopular as Hedin was for his political views during the war, he was both popular and with good reason world famous for his adventurous explorations through the unexplored areas of Central Asia. A few days after the lecture I received a card in the mail from Hedin, reminding me that where great deeds are done one will always hear the wolves howl and feel the claws of the ravens, but that this was a part of the game.

In the late autumn of 1949 I received an unexpected call from the secretary-general of the Royal Swedish Society for Anthropology and Geography, Associate Professor Calle Mannerfelt. He was an elegant and sporty-looking young contemporary geographer, who brought the message that Sven Hedin had suggested that I be invited to the Society to defend my theory before the leading experts of Sweden. At the same time, Mannerfelt invited me to dinner at his home the next day in order to meet Sweden's youngest professor, Dr Olof Selling, who had returned from Polynesia the previous day. It was obvious that I was going to be tried out against this young scientist first before the major confrontation that Hedin had organized. Selling already had a brilliant career behind him, despite the fact that he was three years younger than me. He had received a doctorate in botany as the first person to introduce the technique of pollen analysis in Polynesia. And he was the only twentieth-century botanist to have discovered a completely new order in the plant kingdom; fifteen new plant species were named after him. In competition with far older colleagues, he had just been hired as director for the paleo-botanical division of the National Museum in Stockholm.

My private life had taken a totally new path when I met Yvonne. Now my life as a scientist took a path that was just as unexpected when Yvonne and I dined with Calle and Ebba Mannerfelt and their guest Olof Selling in their beautiful home outside Stockholm. The somewhat retiring and stuffy professor of botany had a contagious smile that bore witness to his special sense of humour. His replies and penetrating eyes also revealed an unusually acute mind. It was easy to understand that with his memory and insight, he was ahead of his age and our time.

Our introductions were formal and full of anticipation, but Ebba and Yvonne became friends immediately. And when we men sank into our deep chairs with a cocktail, not much time passed before the three of us, who had been meeting for a preparatory joust, quickly understood that we had a common background in geography and biology and that we spoke the same language.

Any final uncertainties melted around the dinner table as quickly as the ice disappeared in the white wine cooler. Following Swedish custom, the host suggested we refrain from using titles, and I who had no title was more than willing to comply. The basis for a lasting friendship was established that evening.

I opened the conversation by asking Olof if he knew the botanist F. B. H. Brown.

Forest Brown? Olof called him Forest. My F. B. H. Brown, the author of three volumes on the flora of the Marquesas Islands, the man whose solid genetic evidence had given me the faith and courage to experiment by bringing sweet potatoes, bottle pumpkins and coconuts from Peru to Polynesia by raft, turned out to be Olof's personal friend. My personal friend, Tei Tetua, son of the cannibal Uta on Fatu-Hiva, had affirmed that Olof's friend Forest was right. This was getting to be fun.

The geographer Calle was no less interested. To him the earth was round, and therefore the distance along the equator from Asia to South America just as long as the one from the equator all the way north to the Bering Strait and south again to the equator on the opposite side, even though it seemed like a detour. Calle understood that the ocean was crossed by invisible currents that would drag everything afloat westward from South America to Polynesia in the southern hemisphere and eastward from Asia via the northwestern American archipelago to Polynesia in the northern hemisphere.

Then the great day arrived, 23 September 1949. Not a single seat was spare as the secretary-general opened the meeting in the Royal Swedish Society of Anthropology and Geography. When I stepped up to the podium I caught an encouraging look from the famous Sven Hedin, who sat directly in front of me in the first row. That helped. The other faces melted into a many-headed creature with eyes reflecting everything from curiosity to friendly expectation and demonstrative contempt.

It went well, almost too well. Where were my opponents? It was so surprising that no one protested that I was almost more confused than comforted.

The unexpected outcome was my first scientific award: the silver Retzius Medal, for organizing and carrying out the *Kon-Tiki* expedition with scientific objectives. No scientific award that I received later in life has pleased me more and meant more to my ongoing uphill battle than this first official recognition from academia.

But the battle against an increasing stream of specialists was far from over, and I was a hair's breadth away from losing Olof as a colleague. A senior botanist who had been passed over when the Academy of Science hired Selling as director for the National Museum's paleo-botanical Division announced that Selling was being insane. Olof had changed the locks to his division after his old rival had locked himself in at night with his own key, and borrowed herbariums and documents without informing the new director.

According to Swedish law the Academy of Science could fire an employee if one of its own members produced a document claiming the person to be insane.

Known as one of Professor Selling's closest friends, I was visited by the psychiatrist who only laughed when I asked if he really believed that Selling was insane. Of course not, but it was his job to write a report and he wanted my opinion. He got it. It was ignored, and Professor Selling was publicly declared insane with large front-page headlines in all Swedish papers. The papers were full of protests. Could the Royal Swedish Academy of Science, a venerable academic institution since 1739, do something as barbaric as to declare a colleague insane when he was sane? I was given access to some of the documents in the case and saw that my own statements had been manipulated. One of the accusations against him was that he had written two favourable articles in *Svenska Dagbladet* about the *Kon-Tiki* theory.

The storm against the Royal Swedish Academy of Science became so violent that the Academy did not dare fire him, even though the judgement of insanity remained unchanged. The popular Swedish author Vilhelm Moberg, who in 1996 was named the all-time greatest author by the Swedish public, wrote a play about Olof Selling's battle that was translated into English and German and even performed on stage in Moscow. The newspaper started an appeal that raised 150,000 Swedish crowns to engage independent doctors for a second psychological examination. Professor Olof Selling was declared completely normal, and the insanity charges were annulled. A few years later he received the Academy's highest award, the Order of Knight of the Swedish North Star.

Attacks against me in the Swedish press waned, and this had some influence in my own country, where the Norwegian Geographic Society invited me to lecture on the *Kon-Tiki* expedition. After this I was declared an honorary member, and consequently invited to the Royal Norwegian Academy of Science, where my excited aging mother sat in the first row with King Haakon and waited for a storm of attacks from Norwegian research scientists. Our two leading language researchers had promised to refute my migration theory. After the lecture, they both remained seated in silence. The king looked at them until one of the experts got to his feet and said in a friendly tone that since the lecturer agreed that the Polynesian language had distant roots in Southeast Asia, he had no objections to my suggestions of migration routes over the ocean.

'Do you agree, professor?' he asked, facing his long-term colleague who was a specialist in Asian languages.

He rose rapidly, said 'I agree,' and sat down.

My mother could leave with pride, after having made a solid contribution to the applause. The Norwegian publisher, Harald Grieg, who had been the first man to publish an edition of *Kon-Tiki* had to reset the type and run a second printing. My initial relief of being accepted on the academic front would have been considerably less if I had been aware of a new storm that was brewing behind the scenes and across international borders.

The movie about the *Kon-Tiki* journey had brought me to Paris, where French ethnologist Dr Alfred Métraux was the director of UNESCO. The book's tremendous sales had awakened the interest of the movie industry for the amateur film from the journey. With this, public interest increased, as did the academic opposition's indignation about a researcher who appealed to the masses without having published any scientific work. However my scientific work was by this time at the point of being published, lying as an enormous pile of loose manuscript pages with my Swedish publisher Adam Helms.

However the amateur film from the *Kon-Tiki* journey was a fiasco when it was shown in its unedited form in New York. President Truman's enthusiasm for the *Kon-Tiki* journey had been reflected in the American press, where the *New York Times*, *Life Magazine*, and other leading newspapers and illustrated publications had given the expedition tremendous exposure. The film producers were insistent and the Norwegian Embassy organized a screening of 800 feet of unedited 16mm film for the country's most interested buyers.

Watching the film became a veritable nightmare. I had been given twenty minutes of instruction when I bought my small wind-up camera with a loading magazine and three changeable lenses in a photography store in Oslo before I left. We were now gathered for the showing and saw that over half of the film was completely damaged by water, and what remained was shown in slow motion. It looked like it had been filmed by someone swinging in a hammock on a train at slow speed, moving in and out of tunnels, and the film was broken by blinding periods of light where one could barely discern the mouth of a shark, a bearded head, a naked foot or a squirming fish.

One after one, the onlookers silently tiptoed from the room, and the hours passed. In the end I sat alone with a single buyer from the RKO company, who offered 200 dollars for everything in the hope of being able to splice the usable parts into a ten-minute news report. No deal was made.

I had no choice but to swallow the first bitter disappointment. With a friend who had a small splicing machine, I went to work in my small hotel room in New York, splicing whatever film frames could be used for a silent movie. Without being able to watch the result, we barely managed to glue the last parts together before I hailed a cab and drove to the renowned Explorer's Club, where ever since my time on Fatu-Hiva I had been the youngest member. I had never been more surprised. After sitting in a packed but totally silent hall, suffering from the realization that the most dramatic parts of the film had ended up in the bin, I heard the applause break loose. I was still burdened with all of the expedition debt, and I accepted a contract with an experienced lecture tour agent who gave me a high percentage of the lecture fees since I paid all of the hotel and travelling expenses. Therefore he accepted all requests, and in a matter of three months I criss-crossed the United States giving over 100 'movie lectures'. I slept on aeroplanes and trains as often as in a bed, from New York to San Francisco, back to Washington DC, and then over to Los Angeles again. Once, when Toronto, Canada was followed by a lecture in Chattanooga in Tennessee, I made a profit of seven dollars, even though the minimum lecture fee was 200 dollars.

Europe was next in line, and the auditoriums were sold out in Stockholm until former prince Lennart Bernadotte had the idea of offering a movie version to Hollywood. He was not discouraged by my pitiful story about the highest bid being 200 dollars. While my friends from the raft took turns lecturing to packed audiences in Sweden, the former prince followed me to Copenhagen, where Queen Ingrid, the princesses and a few others were placed so close to the screen in the first row that some of us became seasick from the motion of the waves in the amateur film. At one embarrassing moment we heard a splash, and when the usher came running in with a bucket of sawdust the queen asked if this was part of the show.

Lennart Bernadotte wanted to correct the raft's violent dance across the screen and increase the speed of the film since I had filmed in slow motion. He bought Europe's very first optical printing machine, which could make a 35mm copy of a 16mm film by rephotographing every third frame and replacing the duplicates in order to achieve the film speed of a standard movie projector. The next morning, I went on to Vienna and he returned to Stockholm after drawing up a handwritten contract, half in Norwegian, half in Swedish, about dividing equal shares of the movie profits. We lost the one-page contract, but in the meantime a small new company, Artfilm, which consisted of Lennart and his friend Olle Nordemar, had enlarged and stabilized the 16mm film to 35mm for the movies. They sold the result for a fifty-fifty share to the Tarzan movie producer Sol Lesser in Hollywood, who then sold it further for a fifty–fifty share to the distributing company RKO. RKO and I would have both enjoyed greater profits if we had made a direct fifty–fifty deal from the very beginning.

The contracts rolled in, in as many languages as the book, and we ended up with two Oscars for a documentary film, one for the producer and one for the cameraman. Since I was in the middle of the scientific controversy, I refused to show up in Hollywood and received my Oscar from the hand of Tarzan's producer aboard the raft at the Kon-Tiki Museum.

Later on I did visit Hollywood and Sol Lesser offered to hold a cocktail party in my honour. He asked who I wanted to meet in this movie metropolis but my ignorance in this area was tangible. After a little hesitation I blurted out Walt Disney. He came and proved to be an extremely humble and gentle person who kept the sense of humour he must have had to himself. He greeted me very seriously and thanked me for the publicity I had given him in the *Kon-Tiki* book. Publicity? I asked. I couldn't remember having mentioned him at all. Oh yes, he said, on three different occasions you mention me by name when you describe the most fantastic and imaginative creatures in the ocean as things that not even Walt Disney could have come up with.

There was a world première in Stockholm on 13 January 1950, with the Swedish royal family, Sven Hedin and Olof Selling among the invited guests. I only attended a few opening nights, but the French were so interested in the film that an innovative company had been allowed to truck the raft around country roads while we were constructing a home for it in Oslo. The raft arrived with apples between its logs after it had passed a fruit orchard and ended its final triumphant journey on the Champs Elysées.

Despite the reception at the airport, my own arrival in Paris the day before the movie première was not among the happiest of occasions. Alfred Métraux had started a powerful offensive in his home country. Once again, I was portrayed as an adventurer lacking scientific capabilities in a professional French journal. One of the journalists showed me a copy of the day's *Carrefour*, where Métraux, commenting on the movie première, labelled me a 'mauvais savant', an inept scientist. I was asked to comment, and I promised to do so in the company of Métraux if they could arrange a meeting.

The next morning I was brought to Métraux's office at UNESCO. He was there with Dr Walter Lehman, the leading specialist in South American archaeology at the Musée de l'Homme in Paris. The *Carrefour* journalist was there too, ready with his pad and pencil.

Immediately after the introductions, I opened my briefcase and pulled out an advance copy of my coming work, *American Indians in the Pacific* – 821 pages long and with a list of more than 1,000 quoted sources and a great many illustrations. My two opponents became silent and confused, and after they had asked their complicated questions and been given their answers, it was my turn to take the floor. I had brought a large stack of pictures of different stone statues from the Marquesas Islands and Easter Island, and from the entire Andes area from San Agustin in Columbia to Tiahuanaco in Bolivia. Métraux had claimed that there was no similarity between the stone statues in the two different areas. I placed the stack of pictures on the desk and asked them to separate the Polynesian ones from the South American ones.

Dr Lehman grabbed the stack immediately and wanted to begin sorting them, but then he hesitated and pushed the whole stack over to Métraux. This was, after all, his speciality. Métraux took the stack with a smile.

'This is from Polynesia,' he said, putting the first picture down on the table.

'No!' I said triumphantly. 'It is from San Agustin!'

'This is also from San Agustin,' Métraux said, unaffected, putting the next picture down on the table.

'No!' I countered again. 'I took this one myself on the Marquesas Islands!' I then added that if two of the world's foremost authorities in the field saw no difference, might they be willing to admit that there was a similarity?

They agreed. Métraux looked at his watch and suggested pleasantly that the four of us should go down to the UNESCO bar and have a drink. We did. What a delicious drink.

The same evening the cinema was filled to capacity and the atmosphere was one of expectancy. There was a large gathering of French explorers and mountaineers, including the polar explorer Paul Emil Victor and the Anapurna climber Maurice Herzog. Paul Emil introduced the movie, and I made two new lifetime friends.

The next morning *Carrefour* was slipped silently under my hotel room door. David and Goliath, I thought, when I saw the story of the confrontation at UNESCO. A large picture of Métraux on the upper left, lifting a large glass for a toast. A smaller picture of myself on the bottom right, returning his toast with a small glass. 'A Métraux half convinced by Thor Heyerdahl,' the headline read. And then the journalist admitted that when the two experts were asked to distinguish between the South American and Polynesian statues, they failed just as often as they answered correctly. Furthermore, Métraux had retracted on his earlier statement and admitted that his opponent was a true scientist.

When Adam Helms and his small Swedish publishing house, Forum, risked publishing my large scientific tome on the theory behind the *Kon-Tiki* journey, the book was very amicably reviewed by Métraux in the same Swedish paper where his attacks had first appeared. He pointed out that if he had not been prepared for it, it would have been unfathomable that such a young man could have managed to collect between two covers so much important scientific material from different branches of science.

His partner from the Easter Island expedition, the Belgian archaeologist Dr Henri Lavacheri, never joined the opponents and he visited me in Oslo after my own expedition to Easter Island to study the material I had brought back. He later wrote the introduction to my work on the art of Easter Island in 1975.

Achieving peace in France did not bring an end to the conflict. The more attention the book and the movie about the *Kon-Tiki* expedition received around the world, the more fiery the opposition became among a growing number of experts who felt they had become the objects of public ridicule. In their eyes the public was delighted that I had dared to step on the toes of the learned. Professor Birket-Smith's plan at the Twenty-Ninth International Congress of Americanists to silence the *Kon-Tiki* expedition to death had not succeeded, and when the Thirtieth Congress was planned in Cambridge in August 1952, the organizers decided to try a far more effective method. I was invited to participate as a lecturer at the Congress, where all the foremost experts in the world would be present. My *American Indians in the Pacific* had finally been published, though only the week before, so hardly any of the participants would have become aware of its existence.

The invitation provided an unexpected challenge. In the guidelines it said that every active participant had the opportunity to hold three lectures. I signed up for all three.

When the next circular came from the Congress, with its printed programme, I noticed that they had chosen, of all people, Professor Birket-Smith as moderator for the section where I would present my lectures.

If I ever felt humble in the past, then I felt even more so when I was on my way to Cambridge to speak in front of the collected world élite in anthropology. Two hundred participants from thirty countries would be participating, and when Yvonne and I arrived most of them were already standing in the university corridors speaking in groups like old friends. The manuscripts for three controversial lectures were in my bag. Curious glances revealed that a few people recognized me, some with a cold smile or an empathetic twist on the corner of their mouths.

No one knew Yvonne. She waited in the corridor while I found a place to leave my bag and my slides. As I returned, she suddenly heard a voice that said, 'Let's turn our backs. Here comes Heyerdahl.' Shortly after this, Yvonne was drawn into a conversation with the friendly Swedish anthropology professor Sigvald Linné. While they were talking, an elderly participant approached Linné and said, 'I'm sorry that I didn't say hello, I thought you were Thor Heyerdahl.'

I was not feeling very confident while I waited my turn on the podium. I had three lectures to deliver, while the others rarely had more than one. The atmosphere was clearly one of expectancy: someone was about to be held up to scorn. There was an unusually large group of journalists with cameras, a rare sight at these events. This increased both the hostility towards the adventurer and the hope that he would be slain on stage before their very eyes.

Two other lecturers were to speak before it was my turn, but their topics were so specialist that only a handful of listeners had gone in to listen to them. The rest of the participants remained in the corridors and obviously waited to experience something of a circus. When the first lecturer had finished after half an hour, Yvonne and I were among the few remaining listeners who faithfully waited for the second lecturer, who for some unknown reason never turned up. Normally this would have resulted in a half-hour break before I was to stand in the line of fire, but Birket-Smith went up to the podium and, as he looked out over an almost empty auditorium, asked me to come up and begin.

I made my way up to the lectern and started reading to Yvonne and half a dozen uninterested listeners. It was as if I was reading to myself. I had worked hard to prepare the lectures, and the people who were supposed to listen were still in the corridor.

I may have been reading for about five minutes with the same lack of interest as the listeners when I saw Yvonne sneak out. A moment later the huge entry door was opened widely, and people literally poured in behind Yvonne. There was such a clamour of feet and chairs that I had to wait until silence settled in the crowded room, with people lined up against the walls and crowded door openings. When I tried to continue, there were cries from the hall that I should start again from the beginning, and Birket-Smith asked me to start over again.

I saw many bewildered faces in the auditorium. Rather than the bearded savage they had expected, there was a freshly shaven young man in a blue suit on the podium. According to the papers, he looked more like a well-dressed bank clerk than a seafaring explorer. Whether the audience or the lecturer was the most surprised is difficult to say, but I was bewildered by the total silence in the auditorium after the first lecture. Not one malicious comment, and only a few careful, friendly questions that were easy to answer.

The next day, after the second and third lectures, the audience and I had both had time to warm up. These last ones were given without a break, and they were an in-depth consideration of the possibility for American financial aid to the native population of Polynesia. No one raised any counter-arguments. To the contrary, the first response came from the renowned Canadian researcher on race, Professor Ruggles Gates, who admitted that the latest blood analyses provided sound support for the speaker's conclusions. Greatly relieved and totally exhausted, I cleared the way out of the room for Yvonne and myself. The reporter from Oslo telegraphed the news of my survival back to Norway, noting the fact that my opponent, Professor Birket-Smith, had thanked me for unusually important scientific work. Without exception, the newspapers in Finland that had spread the accusations of humbug published positive reviews of the scientific work and underlined that the critics had been silenced.

Later I learned that the little old man who had not greeted Linné because he thought he was me was the famous French ethnologist

Paul Rivet. I never did meet him; he had overtly avoided all of my three lectures. I was informed that he had later proposed a resolution that the Congress declare Heyerdahl's theories unacceptable. The proposal was denied on the grounds that the Congress could not deal with resolutions coming from someone who had not attended the lectures in person.

Nevertheless, I still had not won my battle. Just a few days after the Congress in Cambridge, the Fourth International Congress for Anthropologists and Ethnologists opened in Vienna.

Like many others who had been at Cambridge, Yvonne and I bought rail tickets directly to Vienna. Before boarding the train, we heard from a friendly scientist from Vienna that one of my keenest opponents, Professor Robert von Heine-Geldern, had been appointed vice-president of the Congress in Vienna. He had printed a circular with intense criticism of my theories and they would be distributed at no charge to all the Congress participants.

I immediately changed our tickets, and Yvonne and I flew directly to Vienna instead.

After landing, I dropped Yvonne off at the hotel and continued in the taxi directly to Heine-Geldern's office. I was received by a stooped but active elderly professor with alert bespectacled eyes, who immediately gave me a copy of the circular which was ready for distribution. When I asked for time as a lecturer to refute the attack, he answered negatively, in triumph. If I had wanted to speak at the Congress, I should have requested this when I was invited. It was now too late.

Two students who had been waiting impatiently outside the door were shocked when they overheard that I was refused the opportunity to defend myself. A delegation of students went to the professor and suggested scheduling an open debate during the Congress. They were turned down.

That evening the students brought me to a secret meeting with their favourite professor, Dominik Wölfel, in an abandoned wine cellar. The students were loath to be seen in public with Professor Wölfel because he was far from being a good friend of their own professor, Heine-Geldern. Wölfel was known as one of the old-timers with the sharpest eye for realistic cultural contacts. I had quoted his studies on the culture of the original inhabitants of the Canary Islands, which he thought was a possible stopover point between the old and new world of antiquity. As we sat and made plans with muffled voices in the dim glow of a lantern, I was reminded of a group hiding in the catacombs during the Christian persecutions. I learned that the Museum of Ethnography in Vienna was ready to distribute its yearbook to all the participants in the Congress. Neither the museum director nor the yearbook's editor were particularly close to the vice-president of the Congress, Heine-Geldern.

I visited the museum director the next morning and received permission to submit an article for the yearbook. He was probably unaware that it had already been printed, and sent me to the co-editor, Dr Etta Becker-Donner, a friendly and well-known specialist on South American Indian cultures. She pointed to the stacks of yearbooks in her office, but agreed to insert a separate response to Heine-Geldern before the books were taken to the Congress halls.

This was Friday evening, and the Congress was due to open on Monday morning.

Luckily my German publishers, the Ullstein family, were in Vienna, and we were on very good terms with them after the tremendous success of their edition of *Kon-Tiki*. After meeting the publisher and the production manager I was promised that my offprint would be printed by Sunday evening if they could have it by Sunday morning.

I went to bed early on Friday evening to ensure a good night's sleep. Heine-Geldern had written his attack before he had read my newly published scientific work, which I had brought along to Vienna. On Saturday I effortlessly drew quotes from my own text as answers to all of Heine-Geldern's arguments; I had already dealt with them. The professor's only new contribution was an admirable list from sources all around the world, giving examples of days when the wind had turned and blown in the opposite direction of the trade winds that carried the *Kon-Tiki* raft to Polynesia. To this new and unexpected argument I simply commented that if one used this research method rather than visiting the Pacific Ocean oneself, then it would also be possible to compile a sufficient list of hurricanes to prove that the Pacific was uninhabitable.

Yvonne and I were among the first to arrive in the flag-decorated auditorium on Monday morning. We were cordially received by the Congress president and vice-president, and they expressed their slightly confused appreciation for the printed article.

Heine-Geldern was extremely pale when he walked up to the lectern and declared the Congress open. He did not respond to my offprint because he had used up all of his ammunition and realized that he had run out of credible arguments in his final attempt at turning the winds in the Pacific Ocean.

Heine-Geldern's great chance for revenge finally came eight years later. In 1960, the Thirty-Fourth International Congress of Americanists was held in Vienna, and this time Heine-Geldern had been appointed Congress president. When the invitation came in the mail, I considered the pros and cons and decided to attend, also as a lecturer. This time I chose a topic within the field of biology, where I knew I had the upper hand over Heine-Geldern and his disciples.

I have often wondered whether Heine-Geldern had purposefully gathered all his disciples in the first row. When I stepped up to the podium I felt more openly unpopular and hated than ever before. If looks could kill, they say – I was on the verge of thinking this was true as I leafed through my manuscript and looked out over the audience. I read as if I were in a fog, convinced that these people, who were staring at me intensely with cold eyes, would not be listening to a word I said. And then the incredible happened. I had just about read the final sentence when I looked up and saw Heine-Geldern rapidly approaching the lectern. He grabbed me by the hand as if I were a long-lost friend, and gave my lecture such overwhelming praise that I would never come to reach these heights again. His disciples on the first row must have been just as surprised and confused as I was. I had not realized that my lecture on the ethno-botanical proofs for contact between South America and Polynesia had killed the isolation theories of Heine-Geldern's worst enemy, the super-isolationist E. D. Merril. In his joy over me putting this American botanist to the wall, he completely forgot that I had travelled across the Pacific Ocean in the wrong direction. On this occasion the wind was blowing so favourably in my direction that I still recall being hugged up on the podium, even though I am assured that it was only a handshake.

Skottsberg, the botanist who had found his support in the ethnologist Métraux, also lay down his sword. He re-evaluated his own studies of the Easter Island flora, and became the first to point out that the island's only two freshwater plants, the *totora* reed and the medicinal plant *tavari*, were South American species that could only have been brought by pre-European seafarers. The *totora* reed was the most important cultivated plant on this unforested island, and it was used along the desert coast of Peru for houses and boat-building. Attempts to claim that freshwater plants could have arrived on the Easter Island crater lakes as pollen stuck to the legs of birds failed, because no seabird can reach this island from South America. Furthermore, without the aid of humans, the pollen from freshwater plants would have been taken over by South American food plants such as sweet potatoes, cassava, pumpkins and chilli peppers, all of which were already cultivated on the island when the Europeans arrived.

The battle with the great Goliaths finally ebbed out in Europe. But the web I had been caught in during the years of battle had also spread across the Atlantic Ocean and gone straight through the Berlin Wall and behind the Iron Curtain.

In the United States the book and the movie about the *Kon-Tiki* expedition were received with just as much enthusiasm as they were in Europe. The expedition participants were invited to the White House, where President Truman welcomed us to the Oval Office. He gave a speech where he praised our courage and our seamanship, and he showed us his book of news clippings from our whole journey.

However the enthusiasm among American scientists was slightly more subdued, even though their attacks were much more moderate than they had been in Europe. This country had originated the dogma that the South American balsa raft could not stay afloat all the way to Polynesia. The world's leading authority on navigation in prehistoric Peru, Dr S. K. Lothrop at Harvard University, had written a special dissertation on the balsa raft and concluded that it would sink after two weeks on the ocean, therefore it could not have brought Peru's original inhabitants all the way to Polynesia. Lothrop was quoted by all the scientists in Pacific Ocean research, and Sir Peter Buck and all the others built upon his theories. Among them was the friendly, aging Professor Herbert Spinden, whom I stayed with in New York when I tried unsuccessfully to get him and his colleagues to read my comprehensive, but unpublished manuscript. When I claimed that Polynesia's oldest inhabitants had come from South America, he only smiled and said, 'Well, you could try to sail with a balsa raft from Peru to Polynesia.'

I had accepted his challenge.

My greatest surprise in the whole academic battle that ensued after the journey was that Professor Lothrop and his wife invited my wife and I for cocktails in their apartment in New York. There he showed me an exact model of the *Kon-Tiki* raft on the piano. He had built it himself. This friendly and gentle scientist was the first to admit that I, with the raft journey, had convinced him that my theories were correct.

When we were building the balsa raft in Callao, the famous American archaeologist Dr Richard P. Schaedel was excavating ancient Inca ruins in Peru. When asked by the press if he thought we would survive the raft experiment, his answer was just as negative as that of everyone else. After the journey had been safely completed, Schaedel was asked what the *Kon-Tiki* expedition had proven. He answered, 'Nothing. Except that Norwegians are capable sailors.'

We met many years later in Peru, and by then he was so convinced that there had been early seafaring in this country that he suggested that we could work together on archaeological projects on the islands off the coast. In the 1990s, Schaedel's colleague and my good friend and coworker Dr Daniel Sandweiss from the United States uncovered archaeological proof of a Peruvian coastal maritime culture, dating as far back as 10000–9000 BC. These coastal people subsisted almost entirely on fish from the ocean.

Did you find a little time to satisfy your adventurous spirit in the midst of all the scientific controversy?

When involved in researching prehistoric civilizations, adventure adds spice to the sober world of science. After the breakthrough at the Thirtieth Congress of Americanists in Cambridge, I was invited to act as honorary vice-president at the Thirty-First congress in São Paulo in Brazil in 1954. There I presented among other things the material from my first archaeological expedition to the Galápagos Islands in 1952. A journey to the interior of Brazil had been planned for all the congress participants, and Yvonne and I were among those who had signed up for the trip. To our great disappointment, the journey was cancelled because of the suicide of President Getulio Vargas.

To make up for missing the journey we had looked forward to, I managed to charter a small single-engine aeroplane to fly us and our

guide to Santa Isabel, a small Indian village by the Araguaia River in
the southwestern Amazon basin. The trip did not quite work out as
planned.

Provisions and equipment that had been bought for the occasion
had to be left behind at the airport. Not wanting to overload the
plane, the pilot refused to allow us to bring anything but a fishing
rod and a rifle. After a while, when the jungle canopy of green roof
lay far beneath us, the plane made a complete about-face and the
motor became silent.

'Don't be afraid,' said the pilot. 'I've made twelve emergency land-
ings before.'

Back at the airport he changed all the sparkplugs, and we headed
off again. The pilot navigated by looking at an old school map with
villages marked as red rings on a green background. After some
hours the plane touched ground in the middle of the rain forest, in a
clearing that resembled a potato field. In the immediate vicinity
there was a bar with a local beauty behind the counter, and for some
unknown reason the pilot told us that it was impossible to get the
plane back in the air.

A long, carved log canoe was by the riverbank, and I saw this as
our only chance to get out of the jungle. Two Caraja Indians were
willing to paddle us in the direction of the Amazon. We crawled
aboard with rifle and fishing rod, and moved rapidly down the river.
For several days we saw nothing but green jungle, brown water,
colourful parrots and screaming monkeys. At night-time we slept on
the bank, either on the sand or on mattresses of branches. Staying
close to the edge of the river in case of unwanted visitors, we found
it hard to fall asleep with the unusual sight of shining eyes that lay in
pairs and stared at us like bright marbles on the water's surface.
They were caimans, the alligators of the Amazon, who slipped
silently through the water without taking their eyes off us. The day-
time heat was suffocating and we had no other water than whatever
we could scoop up from the chocolate-brown river. The first day we

used handkerchiefs to filter out the mud, but after a while we became so thirsty and tired that we drank directly from the river.

During the next few weeks of being locked in the Amazon's incomparable virgin forest, we were to experience an incredible world. The first person we saw was a stark naked man who stood staring at us from a sandbank in the river. When he saw us he ran into a hut and came out again just as naked as before, but with a belt around his stomach. There were more huts further into the forest and we were welcomed with a large meal of fried fish, turtle eggs and cassava roots. We fell asleep in hammocks in the great outdoors, but were woken up in the moonlight and became witnesses to a strange drama. At regular intervals, two naked young girls ran like frightened gazelles past our hammocks and the forest filled with an eerie, mumbling song. Out on the sandbank, four swaying figures danced with towering decorations on their heads and straw capes covering them completely from top to toe. We were never given any explanation for this peculiar night-time pageant.

However we did learn a lot about the art of survival in close contact with overwhelming natural surroundings – searching for roots and turtle eggs, hunting crocodile with an axe at night and experiencing almost supernatural meetings with dolphins and flying fish in a lake that had been cut off from the river during the drought.

Our days as guests of the jungle Indians were an extreme contrast to the glittering business areas of the skyscraper city São Paulo that we had just left.

Not to mention the sober world of science that we soon revisited.

11

Behind the Iron Curtain

You're finally going to do something sensible again.

The old familiar voice had returned after several weeks of silence. Sensible?

I was on all fours, making my way upward among the lava boulders on the Teide volcano on Tenerife. Jacqueline was at my heels. It was a meaningless undertaking really; it was Sunday and we could have slept in and relaxed in our garden hammocks down in the pyramid valley.

I keep Sundays sacred. It is a principle. I put away whatever I am working on. This may be a combination of respect for the symbolic seventh day with cold calculation. It allows me to feel the call of the wild, to recharge my body and soul, so that I can attend to the work of the coming week with renewed energy.

I had no desire for any more talk for the moment. I had enough to do breathing in the thin air and placing my feet so that loose rocks would not fall down on Jacqueline's head right beneath me. Odd that my aku-aku sprang back to life right here. My schedule had been so busy that I had forgotten the aku-aku since I climbed down the slopes of the crater between the statues on Easter Island.

Maybe it was this crater wall that had us thinking about one another again.

But now it was Christmas and the end of a memorable anniversary year. A new year was on its way and I might have enough time to get back to work again.

What a wonderfully beautiful view. Even the colourless black lava boulders around us had stiffened into so many shapes in their wild dance down the mountain wall that they gave life and richness to the emptiness high up here beneath the blue vault of the sky. We had left a world of almost tropical lushness down in the Güimar valley. Further up the hill on the outer side of this enormous witch's pot, a dense pine forest grew up to about 2,000 metres above sea level, loosening its grip just under the rim of the crater. The crater's interior was a gigantic bowl, twelve kilometres in diameter, half-filled with dried lava. Teide's highest peak soared to 3,700 metres and was the highest point on Spanish territory. We were climbing upwards from the witch's pot of cracked porridge that was both black and burnt brown and had a sprinkling of ashes coloured like sugar and cinnamon. The only sign of any organic growth in the bowl were some dense, perfectly round bushes that occasionally stuck out of the porridge like unkempt trolls' heads on their way up from the centre of the earth, captured in dried lava before they had time to get their noses up into the fresh air.

Ocean, mountain, forest or desert – I like it best when I can still see something of humanity's birthday gift from the creative powers. A lover of nature is someone who shares Our Lord's taste. Enter a synagogue, a church, or a mosque, and you will hear that Our Lord created everything that is outdoors and then declared a day of rest, proud of his own work.

My invisible twin was in quite a gabby mood while we were climbing the rock-strewn slope. The aku-aku was as light as my own thoughts, while I myself was wheezing in the thin mountain air and feeling pleased whenever I could sit down without shame because Jacqueline was falling behind. She certainly was tough, and had more willpower than muscle.

Why constantly ever higher?

I had to admit I thought that climbing high on a mountain and getting such a panoramic view was a special treat. As in science, although it is also beautiful far down in the narrow valley, in the long run there was a danger of becoming narrow-minded.

We reached the ledge of a high lava peak and the view opened incredibly at all angles. I pulled Jacqueline up beside me and we sat down to catch our breath and enjoy the sight of the world beneath us.

'It makes you feel safe to sit on top of an island and see the ocean all around you,' she said.

As usual, I agreed with most of what she said. Maybe I had an atavistic feeling that no one could come out of the dark forest and take us by surprise. Perhaps we have hidden memories in our inherited genes, from the time when our biological ancestors crept up from the depths of the ocean and drew their first breaths on the beaches. One thing was certain: the great ocean was the source of life, and as long as there was life in the ocean, there would also be conditions for life on land. But if the ocean died, the plankton would wither in the sunlight near the surface of the ocean and stop helping the forest to pump oxygen into the air. Then it would be of little help to the future generations that Our Lord had equipped with lungs in exchange for gills.

We were both stretched out on our backs on the lava boulders, staring at the blue sky and the blue ocean. The curtains on our eyes gradually closed, and Jacqueline fell asleep.

You were in the Soviet Union in the middle of the Cold War. How do you really feel about communism?

I have seen communism from within and also in countries that have razor-sharp demarcations between communism or capitalism. Having seen frightening poverty and inhuman conditions in places where a tiny upper class refuses to acknowledge that people are starving on the streets and simply steps over them, I have realized that a society where people die on a street or a country road from hunger or a society that cannot provide food and shelter for everyone is a sick society. When a person is ill, he needs medicine. To me, communism is a strong medicine. When this medicine has been taken long enough for everyone to have food and a roof over his head, then it is time to stop taking it. A healthy society does not need that kind of medicine.

Other than that, I really have no political platform. I have yet to find a political party that stands for everything I want and is against everything I am against. They are all a mixture of good and bad. I remember sitting with my Russian interpreter, Lev Zjdanov, and his aging mother, a small, wilted and thin woman. She told us that she had participated in the Revolution and that she had grabbed a red flag with enthusiasm, because now they were finally going to be able to live in humane conditions. Her enthusiasm made me think of Joan of Arc, and I suspect that I would have grabbed a flag myself under similar circumstances.

The *Kon-Tiki* book was forbidden in the Soviet Union, and I was an unknown figure during Stalin's lifetime. When Nikita Khrushchev came to power and allowed the book to be translated, it went to the top of the bestseller lists in all the Eastern European languages. The edition was the first to sell more than a million copies. With this, my peaceful days ended and controversy started among the literati of the Soviet Academy of Science.

It was launched by the literati in the deepest sense of the word, because they were specialists in letters that they were unable to read themselves. In the whole of the Pacific, which fills exactly half of the world's surface, any form of writing was totally unknown until the arrival of the Europeans. The only exception was Easter Island, where around twenty wooden boards with hieroglyphics have been found; not even Easter Island inhabitants could decipher these. A team of language researchers and cryptologists in Moscow had attempted to understand this *rongo-rongo* writing, but no one paid any attention to them until their criticism of a book that had passed through the Iron Curtain from the West hit the newspapers. My brave translator Lev Zjdanov sent, by censored mail from Moscow, copies of the attacks translated into Norwegian, and the controversy started over again.

At that time, no Russian researcher had been free to travel outside the Soviet Union, least of all to Easter Island. The mail was slow and the attacks from the Soviet researchers increased and became more aggressive as I started answering them. There were always a few weeks of delay, since the censors thought that everything I wrote was a special code.

Then something totally unexpected happened. The supreme director of the Soviet Academy of Science, Mstislav Vsevoldovich Keldysh, the man who had launched the first Sputnik into space, entered the arena. He invited me to Moscow to meet Soviet academics face to face.

I accepted. The year was 1962, in the middle of the Cold War. I had not met any Russians or communists since the battles in Finnmark, so it was a new experience to arrive alone with my Russian translator as interpreter in a hall filled with Soviet scientists presided over by President Keldysh himself.

When Keldysh opened the meeting by giving the floor to a comrade who was the head of the anthropological division, a powerful hulk of a man rose to his feet. With a muscular physique and an impressive Stalin moustache, he was a stereotype of the Western image of a communist. With a voice as deep as a sailor's in a storm and his clenched fist held up to me, I knew that these introductory words to his comrades were far from flattering. There was a deathly

silence when he was finished and went back to his seat. As my interpreter gently translated to Norwegian, I heard a totally new
argument against an early migration from America.

My theories of migration routes in the Pacific Ocean did not
comply with the teachings of Lenin. According to Lenin all emigration began with pressures caused by overpopulation or enemy
invasion.

An expectant silence filled the room. What could I answer? The
interpreter looked unhappy. The discussion was dead before it had
begun.

I frightened myself and everyone else by saying out loud: 'I had
no idea that Lenin was an anthropologist.'

Still there was total silence until the interpreter, with a low voice,
repeated my words in Russian. Then I saw some of the audience
hold their mouths to hide smiles. A feeling of unease began to grow,
and Keldysh immediately invited me to take the stand. I had understood the situation. Academics were present. The Stalin lookalike
who had opened the debate was not a scientist but a faithful communist who had been rewarded by the party and made manager for
this section of the Academy. Each and every professional field within
the arts, culture and science had a leader who resembled Stalin, if not
physically then mentally. The man with the giant moustache had
done his duty – he had referred to the teachings of Lenin – and now
he had no more to say.

Nor did anyone else object when, without wavering from Lenin's
line, I used Peru as an example of how since time immemorial, overpopulation and pressures from the country's interior had been a
typical problem for the fisher population in the narrow river valleys
along the desert-like coast of the Andes. Cultures replaced one
another in succession until the Spaniards came to power in the Inca
Empire in the 1530s. The Spaniards learned that the Incas' history
was preserved in the sun temple in Cuzco, on wooden boards that the
Spanish subsequently burnt. But the *amauta*, the Inca Empire's

scholars, could refer to frequent migrations in the country. The last had taken place only three generations before the arrival of the Spaniards. Inca Tupac Yupanqi, the grandfather of the two Inca brothers who welcomed the Spanish, had then left his own empire in the mountains and found his way through all the narrow valleys along the desert coast. He then conquered the Chimu Empire and all of the settlements along the coast from the equator and southwards for 4,000 miles. When the coastal population told him there were populated islands far out in the Pacific Ocean, he forced them to build hundreds of balsa rafts and then sailed on the ocean for nine months with a flotilla that included half of his army and returned with dark-skinned prisoners.

I had no idea whether my Russian listeners knew any of this. It was a docile assembly which sat in silence and let me continue. I added that every so often Peru still suffered dreadful natural catastrophes along its coastline, when floods from the mountains and El Niño currents from the ocean flooded the valleys and drove the whole population away from their homes and on to their rafts. In the so-called El Niño years, the mighty ocean current ran directly from Peru to Easter Island. Then I added that we must not believe that people in the old days and in foreign countries had less courage, curiosity, greed and need for adventure than we had today. And back then there was nothing to stop them if they had wanderlust.

No one protested. Keldysh demanded to hear the arguments from those who had been the keenest opponents of my theory of the origin of the Polynesians. Several got to their feet, but there were no new attacks; those who had something to add were satisfied with their answers.

Soberly and calmly, the man who had sent the first manned capsule into space directed the debate about who had sent the first vessels out into the Pacific Ocean in the Stone Age. He refrained from making any personal comments during the discussion, and waited until everyone had spoken before giving his. At that point there was no doubt about his personal opinion. He reprimanded the anthropologists in his own Academy unconditionally, pointing out that they were poorly prepared for the debate and lacked any basis for their earlier criticism. Speaking directly to me, he said smilingly that the next time I set off on an expedition he hoped I would bring a Russian along.

That ended my little private cold war with opponents in the Soviet Union. It was definitively over, and the proof of the fortunate outcome was the Lomonosov Medal from the State University in Moscow. Even though I had become a Fellow of the New York Academy of Sciences, it must have been President Keldysh who saw to it that I also received an honorary doctorate at the Soviet Academy of Science while the Iron Curtain was still in place.

A few years later, when I planned to sail with a multi-national crew over the Atlantic Ocean on the papyrus reed ship *Ra*, I recalled President Keldysh's words. I wrote and reminded him of his suggestion to bring along a Russian, and I asked him to choose a Russian medical doctor who spoke English and had a sense of humour. And thus Dr Yuri Aleksandrovich Senkevich, smelling faintly of vodka and slightly intoxicated, stepped down from the aeroplane ladder in Cairo to meet me for the first time. Keldysh had won in the political tug-of-war with the highest political leadership, and Yuri became the first Russian to be let out of the Soviet Union on his own to participate in a private capitalist raft journey. I had asked for a Russian with a sense of humour to avoid getting a fanatical party politician, and because a good laugh does not weigh much and counts for much on any expedition. Yuri later told me that he had served himself generously aboard Aeroflot because he was afraid of not being amusing enough.

Yuri later became chief doctor for the Russian civilian astronauts, and after our three reed-boat journeys with multi-national crews he was invited to the United States by American space researchers to discuss future long-term co-operation for peaceful co-existence among individuals of different nationalities living under stress and in overpopulated areas.

The learnèd *rongo-rongo* experts who had been my most bitter opponents in the Soviet Union would become important supporters when it came to deciphering the Easter Island wooden board hieroglyphics.

At the Thirty-Second International Congress of Americanists in Copenhagen in 1956, a completely unknown name in science showed up with a sensation. A German wartime deciphering expert, Thomas Barthel, claimed to have deciphered the mystical *rongo-rongo* alphabet. The sensation grew and reached the world press, when he could reveal that one of the boards related that the forefathers of the Easter Island population had come from Raiatea in Polynesia, in 1400 AD. In other words, the totally opposite direction and far later than I myself claimed.

Even the celebrated Musée de l'Homme in Paris mounted Barthel's deciphering of the writing on a board in its Easter Island exhibit. The fuss died down when Russian language researchers went to work on the *rongo-rongo* writing with computers. They discovered that the texts were written in an unknown language, unlike that which now was spoken in Polynesia, and without knowing which language they were written in it would be impossible to decipher the hieroglyphics.

Barthel's fantasy had intrigued a whole world; even his own students have disclaimed his translations and are fighting among themselves with suggestions that are equally fanciful. The *rongo-rongo* writing of Easter Island remains a mystery.

When I was invited to travel around the Soviet Union after the *Kon-Tiki* movie, I did so on the condition that I could travel freely and that the programme would be of my own choosing. I learned a lot by experiencing the world on both sides of the Iron Curtain, during both the Second World War and the Cold War. There are no sensible national borders between friends and enemies.

My first loyal friend at the Academy of Science was the ethnologist Genrikh Anochin, a war veteran and a specialist in Nordic languages and culture. He was responsible for the fact that when I was in Moscow I met not only scientists but, to an even greater degree, members of the authors' guild and the artists' unions. Vodka and caviar were plentiful, and there was a general atmosphere of tolerance, but the rooms were small in the crowded workers' dwellings and hidden dachas in the forests around the capital. They accepted that I was both a Fellow of the New York Academy of Science and an honorary doctor at their own Academy of Science, but no one cared to talk about science or politics.

Out on the endless Russian plains, and on distant journeys by plane or train to other republics in the Soviet Union, the Russian translator of my books came along as interpreter. We were the peasants' guests on the *kolkhose*, and we visited small orthodox village churches, which to my amazement, were filled with people and the pleasant aroma of incense. The lighted candles were so plentiful that the walls glittered like gold, and the colourful icons in these simple peasant churches would be the envy of museums all over. Inside the heavy church doors there was a tangible atmosphere of memories of the past and hopes for better times to come.

We travelled westward by the night train to Leningrad to study art from the islands in the Pacific Ocean that had been brought to the Tsar's museums in the previous century. And we rode eastwards on the Trans-Siberian railway through all of Siberia, passing endless forests and fences and seeing the steam from the locomotive every time fur-clad passengers either got off or on at the ice-cold new settlements. We rode all the way to Vladivostok, to the point where the Soviet Union and China met in the northeastern corner of the Pacific Ocean. In the ocean, Japan, the Kuril Islands and the Aleutians formed a bridge over to the American coastal archipelago in British

Columbia, the pre-war home where I had become acquainted with the natural sea route from Asia to America and Polynesia. I was amazed when I saw that here the Soviet régime, which was notorious in the West for its total contempt of environmental considerations, was building a lumber-processing plant in its easternmost territories, where environmental concerns had been given top priority.

It was too cold up there on the coast of Siberia to suit me. I would have much preferred to drift by on the warm Japan current, right off the coast, and then to wade to North America in snow and ice over land.

I treasure my fondest memories of the Soviet republic Georgia, when Lev and I went on a fishing trip along a crystal-clear brook in the Caucasus Mountains with actors and musicians from Tblisi. We lay in the grass and ate fresh trout that we caught so quickly that we had trouble frying it. Like Vikings we drank Georgian wine out of cowhorns that had a tendency to tip over, so we had to empty them before breaking off chunks of bread or eating the fish. According to the local custom, we had to bring a toast to each of the guests, to the women, to peace, to friendship between our people, to King Olav and President Khrushchev, to our forefathers and our descendants, to love of all kinds, to the growth of the soil, and to a long and happy life. It turned into a long and enjoyable outdoor lunch. Even my dutiful companion Lev forgot the time. Speeding across fields and around corners back to the railway station in Tblisi, we arrived just as the night train to Moscow was departing. I quickly thanked everyone for their hospitality, and while Lev jumped on to the closest moving railway carriage, I ran after the next one with my suitcase while the train increased its speed. I was due to give a lecture in Moscow the next day and managed to throw the suitcase on board, but by the time I finally managed to grab the railing by the wagon door the train was going so fast that I ended up hanging on with my feet in the air. It was impossible to put them down onto the step. I hung horizontally by my hands, as if I were on *Kon-Tiki* in strong winds, my uncontrollable body waving on the outside of the wagon. I thought my final hour had come, but the conductor, with the help of other passengers, managed to haul me in.

I escaped with a few bad bruises, although a nurse came to attend to my one leg, which was bleeding right through my trousers. She put a large bandage around my leg and I was still wearing it under a clean pair of trousers the next day, when I appeared in a blue suit to present the lecture in Moscow. A dark suit and tie was still the proper attire at such occasions east of the Iron Curtain. Cap and overalls were not called for.

As the evening's guest of honour and his interpreter, Lev and I were placed in comfortable, adjacent chairs in front of the first row. Just before I was asked to speak, I noticed that Lev was carefully leaning over with his eyes pointing toward the cuff of the left leg of my trousers. It looked as if he were about to remove a piece of lint from my black sock. In fact it was only a white piece of thread, but it was not a short one and when he started pulling it grew longer and longer. Then I understood that he had not realized that he had found a loose thread of the bandage. He sat there calmly and silently pulling and rolling the thread into a ball. We were both calm, but I tried to yank my leg away so he would figure out that he was about to unravel the whole bandage. Finally understanding, he bent over quietly and shoved the bundle back into the trousers. I sat up and worried about the walk up to the lectern, in case the ball of bandage thread would fall down and drag along the floor.

I could still almost feel that bundle in the leg of my trousers, but now I was the one to fall asleep. Jacqueline woke me up for the climb back down. Still stiff from the ascent and having napped in sitting positions with our legs raised on the lava boulders, we stumbled down just in time to meet the shadow of the crater edge rising upward as we reached the marked trail. And then we experienced the completely fantastic fanfare of colours after the sun had set beyond the crater edge in the west. We said good night to the silhouettes of a whole rank of coal-black trolls which we had not seen in the day-light. We knew that when the sun's rays started to play on the cone-shaped walls of Teide the next morning, we could recognize the silhouettes as some of nature's most bizarre sculptures in the form of statues and monoliths of dark and light brown lava.

The next day, without any particular goal or route in mind, we set off across the bottom of the crater itself to enjoy a close-up of nature. The world around us soon disappeared behind lava protru-sions and piles of yellow sand and black boulders.

We had brought our lunch, and became incredibly hungry. It was the last but one day of the year, but the sun up here in the clear air was still so strong that we sought the shade of a large bush. Jacqueline fell asleep on a soft mattress of dry branches, without realizing that two small, happy birds were also resting in the bush. One of them almost sat on the tip of her nose without understand-ing that it was her beak.

I met President Nikita Khrushchev at the Kon-Tiki Museum. He was visiting Norway with his loyal Foreign Minister Gromyko. Khrushchev had allowed the *Kon-Tiki* book to be translated into Russian and now he wanted to see the raft as he had a certain feeling of kinship with it. Gromyko always walked behind him, without saying a word, but when we went down into the basement to see the Easter Island sculptures he leaned forward and whispered that the interpreter they brought with them was the one who had translated my book *Aku-Aku* from the Norwegian. The interpreter was kept busy because the jovial Soviet communist boss asked and queried and broke all rules of etiquette and his own timetable. He obviously would have enjoyed himself more if he had been barefoot on the raft with us than in a political meeting where, in order to ventilate his feet, he had to get angry and smack his shoe on the table.

39. In front of the Colla Micheri estate in Italy, with daughters Anette (born 1953), Marian (born 1957) and Helene Elisabeth, called Bettina (born 1959).

40. In the watchtower at Colla Micheri.

41. At work on the unknown *rongo-rongo* text in about 1955.

42. At the Kon-Tiki
Museum in Oslo: King
Haakon, Prince Philip,
Queen Elizabeth and me.

43. Shaking hands with the Soviet leader,
Nikita Khrushchev, in Oslo, 1964.

44. At a science
conference in Moscow,
1964.

45. Receiving the Lomonosov Medal in Moscow.

46. Decorated as Commander of the American Maltese Order after the arrival in Barbados after the *Ra II* journey, 1970.

47. The Madan people in the swamps of Iraq.
48. With, among others, the Prime Minister of India, Indira Gandhi, in New Delhi.
49. Raisa and Mikhail Gorbachev with me and Jacqueline in The Hague, 1994.
50. Testing samples of goats' milk with Fidel Castro in Cuba, 1985.

51. A window display of the book on the Túcume pyramids, 1995. Oxford University Library is seen reflected in the window.

52. My childhood fear of water was conquered a long time ago.

53. Marriage to Jacqueline at El Aaiún, Western Sahara, 1996.

54. With the President of Peru, Alberto Fujimori, and Cabinet Minister Grete Knudsen during the fiftieth anniversary of *Kon-Tiki* in Lima, 1997.

55. On Easter Island with Jacqueline and Yuri Senkevich, 1997.

56. On a horse in Túcume, Peru.

57. With Jacqueline in front of our home in Tenerife, 1994.

When we were about thirty minutes behind schedule, Khrushchev stopped at the exit and asked if he could come on the next raft journey. Interpreters and journalists pressed forward and long poles brought microphones down right to the tip of my nose. What could I answer to a question like that from the world's leading symbol of Soviet communism?

'What could you do aboard a raft?' I asked.

'I could be the cook,' the answer came. Well then, Khrushchev could cook.

'What could you do as a cook aboard?'

'I can cook on a Primus.'

'Don't worry about the cooking as long as you bring along enough Russian caviar,' I jested.

We shook hands on that and, as the first proof that he hadn't forgotten the agreement, later that day I received a whole bucket of caviar and a case of anniversary vodka from the Soviet embassy in Oslo. As if that wasn't enough he also proved that he could satisfy my condition for a Russian to have a sense of humour before being invited on a raft journey.

A totally unexpected invitation arrived from the Department of Foreign Affairs later in the day. It was for an informal and very exclusive reception for the Soviet head of state in a hidden mansion in the Folk Museum park, just a few hours after our visit to the Kon-Tiki Museum. The whole park had been closed to tourists for the occasion. Khrushchev was in high spirits and enjoyed himself fully when we all gathered on the lawn after the meal to watch a 'Halling', a folk dance performance by a couple of Norwegians in traditional costume, accompanied by a fiddle player.

There was no doubt about who had invited me. There were no other outsiders and no press, just a small group of politicians from both countries and myself, who stood in the background and peered between the heads of the other guests.

When the couple were finished leaping around and doing the gymnast-like kicks that the folk dance consists of, the Soviet head of state went out on the lawn, signalled for the fiddler to play, and then went over and engaged Foreign Minister Gromyko for a 'Halling' dance. Gromyko despaired; he hardly looked like the athletic type. After Gromyko declined, Khrushchev calmly went over to the Norwegian Foreign Minister Hallvard Lange and bowed deeply. I knew Lange as an experienced citizen of the world who was accustomed to most difficult situations, but this was too much for him. He blushed and stood stiffly while the fiddler played cheery folk songs on the lawn.

There followed one of the funniest things I had ever seen since my boyhood days in Larvik, when we sat in the front row at the movies and ate peanuts and laughed until we cried at Charlie Chaplin in one of his silent films as music came from a piano in the corner.

Little round Khrushchev would not give up. This time he went over and bowed deeply to our tall, slender Prime Minister Gerhardsen. Khrushchev barely reached up to Gerhardsen's stomach. When Gerhardsen accepted, I couldn't help myself. I bent over in laughter and stomped my feet on the ground like a boy, while the Norwegian hosts politely struggled to smile and the Russian guests stood in full seriousness and watched their own head of state jump around like a ball in the arms of the tall Norwegian.

Later, I met Khrushchev's daughter and son-in-law in Moscow. She was in charge of an ecological journal and he was the head of the communist paper *Izvestia* and the only person ever to give me a political classification. I was invited up to the editorial offices and he brought me out on a balcony overlooking Moscow's rows of houses and the main street, almost traffic-free.

'All of this we have managed since the Revolution,' he said.

'You saw Karl Johan's Gate in Oslo with your father-in-law,' I said, and he had to admit that he had been impressed.

'We managed that without a revolution,' I said.

Then he laughed and turned to his co-workers. 'Heyerdahl is an incorrigible social democrat,' he explained.

The relationship between East and West was still frosty when I visited the Soviet republic of Azerbaijan by the Caspian Sea for the first time, meeting the republic's president, Heydar Aliyev, one of the non-Russian members of the Supreme Soviet. Without being aware of their family relationship, I had driven around this fascinating republic for a week with his brother, Hassan Aliyev. He was the president of the country's Academy of Science, which had invited me to come and see the world's oldest datable rock carvings of ships. In Gobustan, just a few kilometres south of the capital Baku, the enormous Caspian Sea had over the millennia pulled away from cliffs to reveal layers of ancient settlements. Since these settlements were above the ship carvings, the ships could be carbon-dated. Some were more than 5,000 years old, and were reminiscent of the oldest Egyptian rock carvings of reed ships by the Red Sea, with a sun symbol in the bow. Others could be mistaken for our Nordic Viking ships. Seafarers had been in this area for a good many generations.

Travelling with Hassan Aliyev, I became acquainted with the people and landscape of a fascinating country. He was an agriculturist and even then, in the 1960s, he was one of the leading environmentalists of the Eastern Bloc. The only thing that made me suspect that his personal connections went higher than the Academy of Science was that every time he saw a column of smoke on the horizon he immediately whipped out his notepad and made a sketch of the location. If the factory pollution could not be corrected it would be shut down. I was faced with the fact that us Westerners had not always been a good example. This was where Alfred Nobel had started the earliest oil explorations, and great stretches of land were pitch black and barren.

The day that I was leaving, Hassan asked carefully whether I had anything against meeting his brother. I then realized something was awry, and my suspicion was confirmed when we ended up at the presidential palace. It was a very formal meeting, which featured strict rules of etiquette. The president and I each entered an enormous formal hall through our own facing doors and then met in the centre, after having measured one another carefully, for a powerful handshake. Then we sat down simultaneously at opposite sides of a long table, with politicians on his side and scientists on mine.

After speeches and toasts and an ever increasing number of empty bottles appearing between the sandwich platters, people started to move around and it became impossible to tell who was a scientist and who was a communist politician. Raised in a conservative home in the West, as I was, where communists were regarded as a different form of humanity, it was in itself a frightening experience to shake the hand of a real bona fide communist leader and to sit at his table and talk to him in the same way that I would to anyone else. In fact I was very impressed with him. He was very much a leader, both physically and spiritually.

Later, after the fall of the Soviet Union, Heydar Aliyev became the elected president of the free Azerbaijan. He became so popular abroad that England and Norway competed to gain his favour. The West wanted to continue oil explorations where the founder of the Nobel Prize had started them. An English delegation sent to Aliyev was headed by Margaret Thatcher, and the Norwegian delegation was informed that they were also welcome if I came along. Aliyev remembered the meeting at the presidential palace as his only visit from the West during the Cold War.

Therefore I returned to Azerbaijan and found myself sitting next to President Aliyev again, at the same long table but this time as the spokesman for an official Norwegian delegation and with Jacqueline at my side. It was in late November 1994 and Aliyev's favourite older brother was no longer alive, but our previous conversations about the environment were still alive in the president's memories.

Our Norwegian delegation hoped for a licence to exploit oil from the rich wells at the bottom of the Caspian Sea, and we earned many points because of our long experience and conscious and honest desire for environmentally clean drilling.

Aliyev and all of the ministers demanded that I spoke first at all meetings with the opening words 'Dear Azers'. Azerbaijan was the home of the Azers.

I repeated the word 'Azers' so often that it sounded like 'Asers', the people who lived in the original homeland of the Vikings, the land of the Asers. And I remembered the rock carvings that resembled our Nordic Viking ships. And then at the museum in Baku Jacqueline discovered that the models of Azers hunting during the Stone Age were mostly blondes, and the museum director explained that the Azers were of Nordic descent, until the invasion of the Arabs. At the same time I heard from our own delegation that the easiest way for Statoil to transport drilling equipment from Norway was via the old Viking route from the Baltic Sea, down the Volga through Russia and on to the Caspian Sea.

I sent a fax from Baku home to Norway, and asked that the first six pages of Snorri's *Sagas of the Kings* be faxed back to me. Before he died in 1241, the Icelander Snorri had written in his history of Norway that far down, to the east of the Black Sea and all the way down by the border to the Turkish Empire, chieftain Odin ruled. The forefather of Harald Hairfair and the whole Norwegian royal line, he had been threatened by the Romans and wandered northward with his people, through Russia, Saxenland and Denmark, up to the Scandinavian peninsula.

Everyone talks about where the Vikings went, but no one asks where they came from. They did not simply rise out of the ice at the end of the Ice Age. Could they have come from the area around the Caspian Sea? Could this have been an early starting point for the long-distance travellers with light skin and blond hair that the Chinese now were starting to excavate from the frozen tundra in inner China and that in prehistoric times appeared as Berbers along the whole coast of Africa and all the way out to the Canary Islands?

I have often felt that leaders in the communist world have worn an official iron mask when they have received the press and politicians from the West. I've had the opportunity to meet several of them in less formal circumstances, and got to know them as individuals. A few of them became extremely popular in the capitalist world since the fall of communism. Heydar Aliyev was one of them; Mikhail Gorbachev was another.

During the Conference on the Environment in Rio de Janeiro in 1992, Gorbachev was appointed to lead the foundation of a world-wide organization for the environment. A short while later I received a letter from him, inviting me to become his personal advisor at the inaugural meeting of the Green Cross International in Kyoto. To me this was a strange meeting. I had seen his face so many times on television and in so many newspapers that it was like a reunion with an old friend. I could hardly resist throwing my arms around him, but it was not necessary. He had read all of my books and seen all the movies from my expeditions, so he also felt that we were old acquaintances, and we met in a heartfelt embrace.

Gorbachev's warm personality and his honest smiling eyes did not seem to belong in the world of politics. He proved this by setting a greater price on human beings than on artificial boundaries and the arms race. When those of us who had been invited to participate at the meeting were in his company, it became obvious that he was a leader who fought on the side of all of humanity against an enemy that threatened all of us, regardless of nationality or politics. He was aware of the fact that, with the rapid development of modern technology and the population explosion, our generation was in the process of putting the essential conditions of human life at risk.

I had been an active member of other environmental groups, ever since Prince Bernhard of Holland appointed me as international advisor to the World Wildlife Fund about twenty-five years before. At that time Neil Armstrong and I took part in a meeting in London where all of the European royal families were invited to raise public awareness of the WWF. There was so much blue blood present that when Bob Hope entered the stage and looked out over the audience he quipped that it was like seeing a living deck of cards.

This meeting had been organized by Prince Philip. In all my years as an active member of the WWF, he was the driving force behind the organization. He also had foresight when it came to moving the definition of ecology away from the narrow desire to protect large game from the hunters toward a full understanding of protecting humans by taking care of the ecological systems of the planet.

Prince Philip also played a key role when the *Kon-Tiki* raft lay half hidden in a shed outside the Seafaring Museum in Oslo. After having visited it alone, he later returned with Queen Elizabeth and King Haakon and caused such a stir of publicity that the income from ticket sales made it possible for Knut Haugland to build the Kon-Tiki Museum.

Now, in Kyoto, we saw that even a former arch-communist understood that the world had to join forces and take care of nature. During the meeting, Gorbachev obviously agreed with my own main point, namely that other environmental organizations were already working on saving threatened animals and plants, or certain rivers and forests. The greatest threat to humanity lay in the fact that the winds and the currents in the oceans paid no attention to national boundaries. The wind that blew in Asia one day swept across Europe the next, and from experience I knew that the current along the coast of Africa ran into American waters as rapidly as a raft can move. On the *Tigris* journey we had noticed a change in direction of the monsoon. This meant that our planet could experience rapid climate changes with unknown dangers to islands and continental coastal areas. In practical terms, however, it turned out to be necessary to start the work of Green Cross International at national levels, until the nations united as a single world.

Mikhail Gorbachev had a deep spiritual belief in the necessity of protecting nature. He told me that this began when he experienced the wonders of nature in the small garden around his childhood home. Once, we were in a synagogue in The Hague during a Green Cross International conference and saw the Jewish worshippers performing their religious rituals. When we came outside, we stood beneath a large tree. I have a weakness for big trees, and the bigger they are, the more I feel for them. I couldn't help myself, and with a crooked glance at the tree I turned to Gorbachev, 'This is my temple.'

He quickly gave me his hand and answered, 'Mine too.'

At the same moment I discovered that the rabbi was standing close by, and I hurried to add, 'But we still have to admit that there must be something behind this, something that has built this temple.'

Then all three of us shook hands, in full agreement.

As an advisor for the Green Cross, I was asked by Gorbachev to help him to attract the world leaders that I knew to join the organization. I mentioned his earlier comrade Fidel Castro, whom I knew to be just as intensely interested in protecting nature as Gorbachev himself. Gorbachev liked the idea, also because he regretted the break between Cuba and Russia after the fall of communism. He very much wanted to meet Castro, anywhere and at any time. I promised to try to arrange a meeting. The last time I saw Gorbachev during the conference, he was on an open-air platform, giving a final speech to a large gathering. When he stepped down and marched out with his official delegation he happened to pass by me in the crowd of people. He lifted his one thumb to the sky and mumbled, 'Remember your promise!'

This would be the first and last time I attempted to get involved in international politics, and it was not a success.

Fidel Castro was strongly interested in the goals of the Green Cross, but he immediately said that Gorbachev was not very popular in Cuba since the recent period of political turmoil. Instead he suggested that I give an interview about the Green Cross in his country's political newspaper *Granma*. When I came right out and asked whether he was willing to meet Gorbachev, he answered, 'Well, one has to like a man with eyes like his, but he has caused Cuba so much hardship.'

I've rarely met two people who had so much in common, not least a strong appreciation of nature and a conviction that it must be preserved. But I never did manage to bring them together.

12

A Red Island on a
Blue Planet

When we stopped to take a breather, far above the tree line on
Tenerife, we relaxed and began to take life one step at a time, and I
had plenty of opportunity to talk to both Jacqueline and my aku-aku.
The trade-wind clouds passed peacefully and silently like small
patches of cotton across the sky, and they evoked many associations.
I recognized them from the year on Fatu-Hiva and from the voyages
in prehistoric vessels that followed the sun and the endless tropical
clouds. From Africa over the Canary Islands and west to America,
and further on out over the Pacific Ocean, to Easter Island, Tahiti,
Fatu-Hiva. Far down there where the waves broke against the coast,
I knew that the surface of the ocean itself beckoned in the same
direction. With the Canary current to Barbados, where we landed
with *Ra*. And to Cuba, where Columbus landed.

Cuba. Could you have landed there with Ra?
    Actually, I could have. But the funny thing is that it was the *Kon-
Tiki* journey across the Pacific Ocean that brought me to Cuba.
When Fidel had carried out the Revolution in 1959, the book about
the *Kon-Tiki* expedition was the first book he had published – in a

pirate edition, of course, which he himself admitted with a smile when we met.

While I still lived in Colla Micheri, I continuously received dinner invitations from the Cuban embassy in Rome, but it was a long trip from my little village in northern Italy to the capital, so it was easy to send my regrets. I didn't really understand the embassy's interest in my person, and suspected that it was based on political motives. Little did I know that Fidel was behind it. One of his main interests in life was the ocean, and he had built a well-equipped ocean research ship.

One day the Cuban ambassador travelled up to a little town at the foot of the peninsula where I lived. Could I meet him for dinner down there? As it was only four minutes away, it was difficult to find an excuse. He was waiting at the restaurant table with the chief of Cuban foreign contacts, who was visiting Europe. During the aperitifs they placed a tape recorder on the table between us, and on behalf of Fidel Castro they invited me to visit Cuba. The microphone was on, and I answered that I had been to Cuba during the Batista era, the year before the *Kon-Tiki* expedition. On the way to New York, I had been a passenger on a cargo vessel that was rerouted to Cuba, and I was put ashore in Santiago de Cuba. The owner of the shipping line, my good friend Thomas Olsen, made sure that his agents provided me with train tickets right across the country to Havana and put me up at a first-class hotel while I waited for the first available seat on a plane to New York.

I had never seen worse poverty or misery or greater contrasts than when I entered the luxury hotel. Even in the lobby I was run down by a countless number of uniformed piccolos, all wanting to carry my solitary suitcase and openly competing in showing me photo albums of beautiful ladies. When I tried to slip away, they came whispering and asking if I preferred young seven- or eight-year-old girls.

Still speaking into the microphone I accepted the invitation with the hope of seeing a changed Cuba.

*

Yvonne was a typical girl from Oslo and she had friends and relations back there. She considered our property in Italy as a holiday home, but I insisted that it was our permanent base. In the years after the *Kon-Tiki* expedition, I had travelled alone, and Yvonne could not join me on my numerous sea voyages. This left her in Colla Micheri with our daughters, Anette, Marian and Bettina, wonderful children who kept us together, even when we started to slip apart. My long and frequent absences were probably the main reason that the marriage to Yvonne came to an end. She was a model of patience, but in the long run it was difficult to live with a man who was rarely at home and who was often risking his own life. Differences about rearing children also made their mark, as in so many other marriages. I tried to be a strong guardian of morality, but played the role poorly with my many absences. I must take the whole blame for our separation.

For Yvonne, Colla Micheri ended up as a wonderful place for a holiday, while I once again travelled out into the world.

At this time, without any commitments to Yvonne, I met Liliana, who would be a part of my life for several years until I finally left Europe and settled permanently in Peru. With her raven-black hair and her warm, southern eyes, there could not have been a greater contrast to Liv and Yvonne. She had an exotic background. Her great-grandfather was an Indian trader who ran a caravan route between Calicut in India and Carthage in Tunisia. His son married the daughter of a Berber chieftain, and Liliana's mother was their child. She ran away from her father who, as a rabbi, refused her permission to marry an Italian Catholic. Liliana was born on Italian soil, and when I met her looked like a fantasy figure from *A Thousand and One Nights*. I was not alone in my opinion. Princess Caroline of Monaco, who later became her friend, said it directly: 'You're like the real princess in a fairy tale. I only have the title.'

Liliana was with me when I went to Cuba for my first visit to Fidel Castro.

After arriving, we were driven to a house in the outskirts of old Havana, near a lake and with beautiful surrounding gardens. It was a residential area with houses that had belonged to old families that chose to leave when Castro came to power. We lived in one of the residences that had been fitted out for guests to the country. I was to meet Fidel Castro at his office the next morning.

As we were entering the house, the wind picked up outside, and it became stronger and stronger, sweeping twigs and branches into the air. Then the rain poured down. It was a terrible storm. People came in and taped the windows – a hurricane was expected. Liliana went into the bedroom, climbed into bed, and drew the quilt over her head. Suddenly the door flew open, and a huge man wearing a sou'wester and full rain gear appeared. He greeted us, saying his name was Chomi, and that the El Commandante wondered if we would like to see the hurricane from a car. I asked myself who this Commandante might be, thinking of course that it might be Castro. So I replied that if El Commandante thought it was safe – surely he would not have invited me if it wasn't – then I would be pleased to come. We drove off.

Cuba had been hit by the extreme hurricane Kate. Entire trees lay across the streets and we constantly had to turn around to find new routes. Finally it looked as if we were down by the breakwater in the old city, where the waves usually broke right against the wall damming up the Malecón, the promenade. But now it was impossible to see where the ocean ended and land began; everything was flooded. The car became stuck in mud over and over again, and we had to get out in the spraying surf and pouring rain to push. Chomi said we had to give up. He wondered if I wanted to come home with him for a cup of hot coffee. I thought that it would be interesting to see how a Cuban driver lived, and accepted the offer.

All the high-tension wires and masts were down, and there were no lights in any windows. We parked in front of a brick wall by a low house, where we rang and knocked on the door. An old lady appeared with a candle and in English asked us to come in. First a small hallway, then through a small room with all sorts of strange things on the walls. Thereafter through a large room, and here there was no end to all the strange objects. Huge pictures, photographs of Fidel, curiosities from around the world dedicated to Fidel, and pottery from different pre-European periods from Peru and Mexico. As I was shown into another room, I suggested that this was the home of a well-travelled intellectual.

'No, I'm not an intellectual. I'm a doctor. I'm El Commandante's private doctor and accompany him on all his travels. He keeps his souvenirs here.'

We finally came into a living room with big, comfortable chairs, not a large living room, but a cosy one with a pleasant atmosphere. The sweet woman, who turned out to be Chomi's wife, asked me to sit down.

'I'm sorry,' I answered, 'but I can't sit, I'm soaked through.'

'Maybe you want to borrow a pair of dry trousers from my husband?'

And then I was guided back into the hallway and shown into a little toilet with a flashlight. I was given the dry clothing, and I closed the door. Off with my own soaked trousers and on with the dry ones. However Chomi was somewhat of a giant, so it was impossible to keep them above my hips and I had no belt. I clutched them with one hand to keep them up, and went back out with a smile. As I entered the hallway, the front door was opened by the lady of the house and in came Fidel Castro, wearing a uniform and cap and with a full beard, just as he looked like in his pictures. We were standing, face to face, and then Fidel opened both his arms to give me an embrace. I couldn't let go with my one hand, but I tried to embrace him with the other.

That was my first meeting with Fidel.

Castro asked immediately if Chomi knew how the botanical garden had fared. Chomi had nothing to report because all of Cuba's telephones were dead. He was ordered to go out and take a look; I could come along if I wanted to. Then Castro disappeared.

The storm had died down and we drove and drove until we were far outside of Havana. We came to an enormous complex, a mixture of a nature park and the most marvellous botanical garden I had ever seen. The amazing complex was totally undamaged, as it had not been in the direct path of the hurricane.

'This will please him,' Chomi said. 'Next to the ocean research vessel, this botanical garden is his great hobby.'

When we had seen that everything out there was in good shape, I was driven back to the guest house. The next morning Chomi reappeared in our doorway. The whole country was in chaos. The meeting at the office was cancelled. El Commandante was to inspect the damage after the hurricane, and wondered if I wanted to come along. 'Find your toothbrush and clean underwear and come immediately.'

I ran in to Liliana and said that I would be back soon.

With Chomi at the wheel we raced on. We saw terrible destruction. We drove in a four-car escort, police or military in the first car, Fidel in the second, ourselves in the third and another escort car in the rear. For three continuous days, I was as close to El Commandante Fidel Castro as one could be. The hurricane had raged along the whole southern coast of Cuba and hardly a dwelling or an industrial complex had escaped damage or destruction.

The first night we slept in some tin shacks belonging to the military. Early the next day, Fidel was waiting outside the shack that had the long table where we all were to eat. He would not go in before the guest. When we sat down I saw five glasses in front of Fidel's place. The rest of us only had one glass each. I asked if he was planning on using all five. We were going to drink goats' milk from a farm school, Fidel explained, and he wanted to judge which type of goat gave the best milk. I told him that as a child I was raised on nothing but goats' milk.

'Then you shall also judge,' he said, and I was also given five glasses. The two of us sat like wine connoisseurs tasting the goats' milk. The difference was slight, but I made my choice, which happened to be the same as his. All that was left to do was to finish breakfast and race on.

I will always remember the small fishing village where all the small wooden houses had been blown down and crushed. People ran back and forth from all directions, calling out 'El Commandante, El Commandante'. There was no end to the enthusiasm. We jumped out of our cars and went to see where the destruction was worst. An old woman was clutching her small radio. It was broken, and Fidel gave her a strong comforting hug. She lit up and said: 'Now it doesn't matter that I've lost everything, because I've met El Commandante.'

Further on we came to a brick house and Fidel gathered the local leaders in its attic, around a table with a short candle in its centre. The ground floor was just one big chaotic mess. It was like being back at the front in Finnmark, the same spirit of co-operation in a time of catastrophe. Fidel sat through the night and organized his countrymen.

'How many trucks can you get over there, and there? Where is the closest cement supply? How many bags?'

And so it went on. He had an ability to organize and give orders that made people flock around him in their eagerness to fight for a common cause.

In the evening on the third day we came to a place where his little private plane could land, and he, Chomi and I flew back to Havana.

During my first visit I discovered that the world knew little about Cuba's archaeology because of the country's scientific isolation. This fact led me to work with local archaeologists, and it resulted in many visits and meetings with Castro.

I came to look upon Fidel as a rather uncommon dictator. He

lived in extreme simplicity; no one knew exactly where, but I assumed it was in the area where we ourselves were staying. I have dined with him and his closest friends countless times, but never with one single politician or military person as a fellow guest. His circle of friends consisted of artists, authors and scientists. His private parties were always held at Chomi's, where I'd first met El Commandante as I firmly gripped the waist of my trousers.

We often had to wait for dinner until ten or eleven, because he worked virtually around the clock. Every once in a rare while a message would come at around midnight, telling us to start eating without him, while cold food was sent to him at his office.

Even Castro's keenest opponents recognized his great contribution to the country's schools and its health-care system. One time when I was in Cuba, long before the Pope's visit, I was amazed to learn that this communist had made it possible for Catholic nuns to work in hospitals. When I asked him about this, he answered quietly: 'Many old people in the hospitals feel a sense of comfort when they are visited by the nuns.'

Even though I had no success in getting Castro to receive his former colleague, ex-communist Mikhail Gorbachev, Castro did agree to meet Norway's master capitalist, Knut Kloster. Kloster had purchased the giant ship *France* shortly before this meeting, and now he planned to build the largest passenger ship in the world, *The World*. He dreamed of routing it between Miami and Havana to build a bridge between the United States and Cuba.

Fidel's favourite meal was spaghetti with tomato sauce and parmesan, and Liliana always brought a rich supply when we flew directly from Italy. That is how Castro came to meet the Norwegian shipping magnate for a spaghetti dinner in his own guest house. After the meal, when Kloster unfolded the drawings for this incredible ship, Castro was clearly just as impressed as I was. When the two of them started discussing whether profits from arrivals and dockings should be distributed to all of Cuba's hotels or remain in the local port, I had trouble figuring out which one of these men was a capitalist and which one was a communist. The two of them ended up lost in a conversation about religious mysteries, and when they started on the questions of the origins of life, star swarms and the Big Bang I suggested with a smile that they return to earth.

Kloster continued with his giant ship-building plans, but the bridge across the Florida Strait remained a dream.

My small attempt to build a bridge between scientists on either side of the same strait was more concrete. In spite of the blockade, I brought two American archaeologists to Cuba for a meeting with El Commandante, and this led to a five-year contract for archaeological co-operation between the Carnegie Institute and the University of Havana. The first result of this co-operation was the book *Art and Archaeology of Pre-Columbian Cuba*, written in partnership between two American and two Cuban archaeologists, with an introduction by myself.

In the 1980s I kept travelling back and forth between my research studies in Cuba and excavations on Easter Island. One day, while waiting for a ride to the airport with my packed suitcase in the guest residence in Havana, the door suddenly opened and revealed the towering, well-known character with a beard and a green uniform. He sat down and asked for a cup of coffee.

'Where are you going now?' he asked when he saw the suitcase.

'To Easter Island,' I answered.

'Hmm,' he said and stroked his beard. 'Then you must not say you have come from Cuba. Easter Island belongs to Chile and the governor is married to Pinochet's daughter.'

'No,' I answered. 'The governor is a friend of Pinochet's daughter, but he is in fact married to an American woman. He is, by the way, an archaeologist himself and my closest associate on the island. He knows very well that I'm coming from Cuba.'

Fidel was pleasantly surprised and asked if I thought the governor would appreciate a case of Havana cigars, but I wasn't certain that Sergio smoked. Then he asked, 'Does he drink?'

'Yes, certainly.'

At that, Fidel sent for a bottle of Havana Club from the kitchen. The driver who was responsible for getting me to the airport on time started to become visibly nervous. When the bottle arrived, Castro grabbed his fountain pen in a hurry and wrote on the label:

'Best regards to the governor of Easter Island from Fidel Castro.'

I barely managed to get the bottle into my hand luggage before we swept off to the airport, for a stopover in Panama and then on to Santiago de Chile.

I came all the way to Easter Island without anyone examining my hand luggage. The governor had arranged a reception with hula dancers and a party at the hotel, and I only had time enough to set my luggage down before he came toward me with a whisky glass in his hand. I remembered the gift and asked him to come into the room with me, where I gave him the bottle and told him to read the label. Before I realized what was happening, I heard a crash and saw pieces of glass and liquid flying in all directions. That was it for the gift from Fidel, I thought. But it was the whisky glass that the governor had dropped. He held the bottle of rum from Castro with both hands.

'When you go the next time,' he said in jest, 'you'll have to take a case of Chilean red wine from Pinochet to Castro.'

I reminded him of that when I was leaving, but then he smiled and said that he doubted Pinochet's sense of humour was as sophisticated as Fidel's.

13

In the Garden of Eden

We were up on the mountains in Tenerife and could see the blue ocean curve like a giant circle in all directions, and we realized that neither the planet nor we who live on it had changed dimensions over the ages. We think that we have made our world smaller because we can travel fast to compensate for a lack of time. But previously people could afford to travel slowly. They were rich in time.

Around about the year 1200, when Iceland's Snorri Sturlason wrote the *Sagas of the Kings* with a quill pen on parchment, three centuries were still to pass before the enormous royal empires of the Aztecs and the Incas became known to Europeans. But the horizons of Snorri's geography were not limited to the coasts of Iceland. He recorded geography of his time in detail, from the Nordic colony on Greenland and its discovery of Vinland in the far northwest of the Atlantic Ocean, to the coasts of Africa in the south, and the Black Sea and the Caucasus mountains bordering Asia. While he was in Iceland and immortalizing his own historical and geographical knowledge, his forefathers' relatives in Norway were still on trading expeditions, Viking raids and pilgrimages throughout this whole enormous area. The ocean lay there, open and without borders or limitations. And thousands of years before them, the same ocean had enticed others to journey out in the world. From the day when human beings learned to build means of transportation that could float, the continental coastlines became points of departure, and navigable rivers led inland through virgin forest and wilderness. Humans learned to paddle and sail before they learned to saddle a horse or discovered the wheel.

In 1977 I tempted fate on the ocean once again, on a fourth raft, and this became the longest journey of them all. Five months with eleven men aboard a boat of reed bundles, from Iraq to the Indus Valley and across the Indian Ocean from Asia to Africa.

Seven years earlier, with a crew from all corners of the world who were not seamen, we had sailed from Africa to America with the papyrus reed boat *Ra II* without losing as much as one reed. We arrived however, with a vessel so soaked that barnacles grew on the deck and the sharks could almost swim aboard. During the last week we spent most of our time up on the roof of the bamboo hut, consoling ourselves with the observation that the papyrus bundles that were carrying us were still afloat, even though they were totally saturated with water. We could have kept floating like this for weeks, with the deck at the same level as the surface of the water, but we pulled the saturated raft ashore when we arrived in Barbados and freighted it as cargo to Oslo, where it joined the balsa raft *Kon-Tiki*.

Something still must have been wrong with *Ra II*. The ingenious builders of pyramids from antiquity would not have kept on building reed vessels for hundreds of years if they hadn't succeeded in keeping the cargo dry on deck. Mythological motifs of god-like forefathers who navigate reed ships on the ocean are depicted on the oldest temple walls in Mesopotamia, Egypt and Peru, on metal signets from the oldest seafaring cultures in the Indus valley, and on the ceremonial bronze drums from the oldest known dynasty in

China. In the Middle East they often show reed ships that are so large that there are one or two cabins on the deck in addition to horned cattle and a large crew. In China they are also depicted with royal families and full crews on board, and all the details are just as realistic as in Egypt. The Inca culture in Peru often shows them with the king and his court on the upper deck, and below them a line of prisoners and water mugs fastened with rope.

But what did they do to keep the reed bundles from becoming waterlogged?

That is what I wanted to find out when I built my third reed ship, *Tigris*.

I had found all the papyrus I needed to build my first two reed ships from the sources of the Nile in Ethiopia, and I found experienced reed-boat builders from Lake Chad in Central Africa and Lake Titicaca in South America. But in both places the reed boats were pulled up into the shallows or on to dry land after the fishing trip. No one had any idea of how long a reed boat would float. In the academic world, the floating ability of the reed ships was estimated to be about two weeks, like that of a balsa raft. From our own experience we knew that in both cases the theoreticians had been mistaken. Both balsa rafts and reed ships could transport people across the ocean, but still no one could tell us what the old reed-boat builders had done to improve the floating ability of the reed.

Is it possible for people to forget something they have known for thousands of years?

I had to go to the marsh Arabs in Iraq to get an answer to that. I went to the Madan people who still lived undisturbed on the land of their forefathers, which the ancient Greeks called Mesopotamia, the Land Between the Rivers. While the rest of Iraq had become desert, these people lived on floating reed islands where the Euphrates and the Tigris combine to form one river that flows out into the Persian Gulf. The generals ruled the country with a firm hand from Baghdad, but in the endless marshes where the rivers met and both the Bible and the Koran placed the Garden of Eden life was just as peaceful as it had been at the time of the Sumerians. There were no roads into the reed marshes and no television antennas reached up to announce the presence of people, except for along the bank of the river itself. Totally hidden from the world at large, and concealed in a swamp of about 15,000 square kilometres, the Marsh Arabs had managed to maintain the culture of their forefathers for 5,000 years, undisturbed by the upheavals of history on the rest of the planet.

Two British explorers, Thesiger and Young, had recently come out of the marsh area with reports of almost Biblical conditions. Neither rock nor clay were available in the swamps, so the Madan people built their beautiful dwellings with artistically twined bundles of reed, following the exact same model depicted in art from the age of the Sumerians. In ancient times, the whole of Iraq was covered with large and small channels for navigation and irrigation. The Sumerians' first king arrived in this flat country with all of his followers on board large reed ships, and according to their own written history, built their first capital, Ur. According to archaeological datings this was around the year 3,100 BC. There are many indications that this was also when civilization began in Egypt.

In spite of the fact that there had been human life on earth for 2 million or maybe 3 million years, civilization started simultaneously and apparently suddenly and in a fully developed form, along the riverbanks in Egypt and in Mesopotamia, on either side of the Arabian peninsula. And in the closest neighbouring valley in the east, along the banks of the Indus River, the Indus civilization developed at the same time. The three oldest known civilizations started at the same time and had striking resemblances: worship of the sun, pyramid-building, city-planning of adobe dwellings, complex forms of metallurgy, writing and everything that characterizes civilization on an impressive technical and cultural level. And they all depicted their first kings as seafarers who arrived from their mythical home-land on large reed ships.

At first, the three fertile river valleys enjoyed a period of early power, but later the large navigable channels disappeared in Mesopotamia and the landscape became parched and buried in sand dunes and the influence of the Sumerians, the Babylonians and the Assyrians waned. As memorials to the transience of culture, ruins of the palaces and temples from their golden era rise from an endless desert surrounding the green marshes and the clusters of date palms and gardens around the cities and along the riverbanks.

When I first arrived in this area in the early 1970s to seek per-mission to travel into the marshes, a new revolution had just taken place in Iraq after the fall of royalty and the cessation of British influence. Two generals had established a dictatorship as leaders of the pan-Arabian Bath party, and the borders were closed to tourists. I received a visa at the Iraqi embassy in Rome because of my status as a researcher and because on my first visit I had brought along an entrepreneur from Mexico who imported machines from communist China. In the eyes of the Iraqi ambassador, China was then the real paradise.

We were warmly received by the archaeologists at the large museum in Baghdad, where we had a great deal to learn both from them and from the rich collections of Sumerian reed-boat models, as well as the descriptions and pictures on clay tablets and Sumerian cylinder seals. We were invited to lunch with the two generals who were enthusiastic about the idea that I might build a new reed boat and set sail from their country. They made strict conditions about the nationalities I could bring into the country to join the voyage, but withdrew these when I implied that I actually had a choice of start-ing either in Iraq or Iran, on the opposite side and further down the same Tigris River. It ended with them lifting both passport and cus-toms regulations and granting permission to travel into the marshes to meet the inhabitants and find help for building my reed ship.

I have never met people like the marsh Arabs. I also liked the other Arabs in the country, but my friendship with a general, Saddam Hussein, who later took sole power in the country, would come to an abrupt end. I was grateful that he had allowed me to meet a people who had lived untroubled lives in harmony with nature and their neighbours for thousands of years. Little did I know that the same general who had helped me meet these people would later give a brutal order to dry out the marshes and thereby destroy the fundamental necessities for life for the Madan people. In addition he became furious the following year because I burned the *Tigris*, and not least because all eleven of us from different nations who had been guests in his country sent a plea for peace to the United Nations. We, who had lived together peacefully for five months, claimed that if the arms shipments to the Middle East were stopped, people around the Gulf and the Red Sea would be forced to fight with clubs and swords as in the old days. This did not please the general.

When I first met Saddam Hussein, I was totally without prejudices. I only knew that he had tremendous power. I have to admit that when we first had lunch together, he made such a small impression – as a person – that I only recall that the food was good and he supported my project.

As a gathering place for the construction crew and the large amount of reed we needed, we were allowed to stay in an abandoned inn called the Garden of Eden, which lay on dry ground on the banks of the Tigris just before it runs into the Euphrates and the marsh area begins. Just a stone's throw away from the lonely wall of the house there was a cluster of date palms and a few leafy green trees bending over the river. Between them a huge moss-covered tree stump was fenced in as if it were a holy site. It was covered with candle drippings. According to ancient records, this was the spot marked by Jews, Christians and Muslims as the birthplace of Adam and Eve. A sign with text in Arabic and English left no doubt that the stump was the remnant of the Tree of Knowledge, and one could read that even Abraham himself had come here to pray. We were on historic Biblical and historic Koranic soil.

The trip down the quiet river from the wooden stump by the Garden of Eden to the meeting place of the rivers by Qurna and the marsh area was not a long one. We immediately understood why the people who lived in the compact brush of tall berdi-reeds had been allowed to live in peace in their own world, without border signs and defensive weapons. No one could enter the area without knowledge of the labyrinth of canals that were often completely invisible. The water level was so shallow that not even a raft could float; if one tried to wade, one sank through the peat-filled bed of the marsh. That was also the case for the hooves of horses and camels as well as tanks, so neither the Assyrians' war fleet, Alexander the Great's army nor the mechanized troops of the world wars had managed to disturb the peace of the Madan people. It would be the general in Baghdad who outmanoeuvred the marsh people by pulling the reed carpet out from under their feet.

In the marshes I travelled back to the time before the invention of the wheel, before street noise and antennas numbed the minds and streetlights blocked out the stars.

With an interpreter from the museum in Baghdad, I was picked up from the riverbank just south of Qurna, where the deep water ended. Two Marsh Arabs in long white robes stood upright in a slim canoe and punted their way forward with long poles in slow, calm strokes. After the simple greeting of placing a hand on the heart, the interpreter and I were seated in the bottom of the narrow *mashuf* to keep it stable, while the two barefoot men in their wingless angel outfits punted us away from our own world and into theirs. The reeds closed behind us in the wake of the canoe, higher than a standing man could see. Further in, the canals were sometimes both wider and deeper, and we were surprised to see that the water in here was crystal clear, not muddy or brown as it was in the rivers. Green plants grew on the bottom, and in the clear, shallow water, fish swam about while long garlands of crow's-foot snaked along the surface. We slid soundlessly forward between dense walls of reeds and cat's-tail, and for every slow push of the punt we felt that we were further on our way into the past. Not towards barbarism and insecurity, but toward a culture just as removed from the age of the apes as our own, but safer and less complicated. When we reached the first settlement, my Arabian interpreter was just as moved as I was.

First there were only a few thin scattered columns of smoke, showing that people lived in the marshes. We saw no trace of human litter, and not a single roof to reveal where the settled area began. There were no mounds or stones to stand on to get a view over the reeds, and the turbid bottom gave way like a mattress. We saw geese and ducks with wild swimming birds in all colours and sizes paddling fearlessly around us as if guns had not yet been invented. A solitary eagle sailed over us from the lifeless desert, and an ice bird on its migration perched and swayed in the reeds with an array of smaller birds, many with wonderful colours. Tall snow-white cranes and red-beaked storks stood like guard posts, motionless among the stalks, and fat pelicans scooped up fish with their large beaks. Once we saw a bushy coal-black wild boar push its way through in heavy leaps between the swaying stalks. And when we closed in on the settlement, we met mighty water buffaloes wading lazily in front of us with their broad, black backs glistening like wet seal fur in the sun. They stopped to stare with lazy glances, waved their wide ears and thin tails patiently to chase away the flies, and continued uninterrupted to chew the green watergrass that hung from their mouths.

Then suddenly the first houses appeared, a revelation in total harmony with nature. They blended into their surroundings just as naturally as a bird's nest in the reeds. Since there was no other building material, everything was built from reeds. The only solid ground that gave anchorage to a few date palms was on the outskirts of the marshes. Building houses in the marshes called for large piles of reeds for the foundation. The canals often ran out into small open lakes where reed houses were built on floating islands that were artificially constructed in thick layers of reeds that had to be replenished from above as the lower layers rotted and sank. Walls and roofs of large and small houses curved in harmonious arches from side to side. Compact bundles of reed were bent elegantly into rows of rib-like curves and covered with thick mats of reeds. Not one piece of wood, not one nail; everything was connected by reed fibres. All the houses had the same shape, whether small overnight shelters, spacious homes, or huge gathering halls resembling hangars, with ceilings so high that one could barely reach them with a punting pole.

This enchantingly beautiful architecture had survived in the marshes from the time of the Sumerians, each abode built as a small temple to honour the past, afloat with its own golden-grey reflection on blue water and a perpetually blue sky. The surprisingly transparent water flowed slowly to the Gulf and, to keep their building foundation from moving, they were fenced in with palisades of bamboo-like reeds stuck into the silt. The islands and their reed houses rose and sank within the palisades as the water level changed with the seasons. The slender *mashuf* punting along the canals between the buildings created a landscape that looked Venetian.

Some of the floating islands we first passed were so small that with the main house and the water buffalo stall on top they looked like a houseboat or Noah's Ark, with just enough room to be able to walk around the perimeter. A Marsh Arab can rarely take many steps before he has to get into a canoe. Deep in the marshes, in the open lakes, floating Madan families gently swayed on reed mattresses with their buffalo, ducks and hens, and when the owners opened the night gates on the hangar-shaped reed barns, the buffalo rolled into the water with the ducks to swim to their fodder while the shepherds paddled in their canoes.

I had spent the night with a sheik at the end of the gravel road leading to the ferry landing, Madina. He had arranged for the journey into the marshes, but first he served me a breakfast I will never forget. Coffee, tea, fresh buffalo milk, yogurt, egg, lamb, chicken, dates, Arabian bread, cakes and jam. I barely managed to stumble down to the riverbank and squeeze myself into the narrow *mashuf* that would bring me to Om-el-Shuekh, deep in the marshes. This was the home of Hagi, the oldest man the sheik knew. According to the sheik, if anyone would be able to remember the vessels of the past it would be Hagi, because he was more than one hundred years old.

As we slid out of the reed and crossed open water toward this old chieftain's abode, I was not really expecting much from the memory of such an old man. And my optimism did not increase when I saw that the old man looked like a Methuselah in a white robe and with a long white beard, sitting in front of the opening to his huge floating residence. When I jumped ashore with the interpreter from Baghdad, his island rocked beneath our feet. It was like standing on a hammock, and we swayed and grabbed for support while the man rose and walked briskly toward us.

As he greeted me with both hands, touched his heart and wished me peace, I looked into eyes that were so wise and friendly that time and place disappeared. He obviously deserved the great respect he was shown by all the other men who eventually arrived and sat down on the floor with us in two rows along the long wall of the huge hall. With our legs crossed, we sat and listened to the wisdom and wit of old Hagi, while the pile of cinders was brought to life and tea was served. There was no electric wiring here, but the stars in the sky winked in through the archway opening and the flickering fire caused shadows to dance on the walls.

Large fish were sliced open, folded out like huge butterflies, and placed end-up along the flames. The fish was brown and crispy on the outside but white and juicy inside, and it was rolled into oven-heated Arabian breads as thin as pancakes. It was so delicious that I ate as if the sheik in Madina had starved me. The wise old man paid attention to everything and made certain that the man at my side served me the best pieces of fish and fed me like a five-year-old prince. True to custom, a man came around with soap and a towel after the meal and poured a stream of warm water over a basin so each and every one of us could wash our hands.

Hagi made excuses for the simple meal, as if he had not noticed my appetite, and spoke of an even better meal in the future if I promised to return. I promised, and I did return, knowing that I had to. Good meals are one of the highlights of life, and not least of expeditions.

This was not the only reason I enjoyed being with the people in the reed marshes. I had lived with so-called primitive people in Polynesia, America and Africa, but these Marsh Arabs were not primitive in any sense of the word. They were civilized, though in a different way to us. As people, we were totally alike, both physically and spiritually. The road back to our mutual ancestors in the wilderness was just as long. It was our way of living that had changed, the daily existence of traffic jams and computers that earned us our daily bread. In our form of civilization there was no one who, like Hagi and his people, lived in the midst of their food supply. The more we remove ourselves from nature, the more complicated our existence becomes. It also becomes more difficult to bring fish and potatoes from rivers and fields to our dining tables. We have managed to complicate everything that once was simple in our existence, and we try to mend our mistakes with traffic regulations and computer programs, with doctors who get paid for repairing the damage caused by a poor diet and a lack of exercise, with lawyers to lead us through the jungle of laws and regulations. We race on with beating hearts and screeching wheels, finding vicarious thrills through sex and excitement on television, experiencing life solely through watching the lives of others. We believe we are rich when we have money in the bank.

'We're not poor,' old Hagi said, who owned no more than the mat he sat on. 'Our pride is our wealth. And no one in the marshes is starving.'

These people had an inner wealth. They envied no one. This is why their culture had survived, while the Assyrian, Persian, Greek and Roman civilizations that had flourished around them had disappeared. These centuries of stability bear witness to qualities that we lack: a respect for our forefathers and confidence in the future. We think that we have created the first civilization that will last forever, but we cannot stop ourselves from building on. We are building without a plan, and by doing this, new problems arise. Stress, youth crime, unemployment, the arms race, terrorist activity, overpopulation, climatic changes, decreasing resources and increasing pollution of air, water and earth.

In fact, we might be happiest when on holiday, when we can escape stress and the trivialities of daily life. This is when we turn to God's great outdoors, and go fishing and hunting in the forests or on the plains. Then we pity people we call primitive because they have to live like that all year round.

Hagi sat there with his hundred years, dignified, safe and satisfied, poking the cinders from the reed fire that had flamed up again on the clay hearth in the middle of the floor. No one here was missing anything they didn't know existed. The old man entertained us with tales of his experiences and his sense of humour. The fire shone on the faces of rows of silent Arabs, clad in kaftans and capes, sitting attentively between the columns of reeds along the wall. An elegant Arabian teapot was passed in front of me, and when the tea was poured into small glasses edged in silver, its aromatic fragrance thrilled my nostrils.

I looked around the large and airy building that was the old man's guest house. The ceiling was high, and seven strong reed bundles, thicker than a human body, arched elegantly from floor to ceiling and then back down again the other side. Like parallel ribs they bore a tight covering of braided reed mats. I felt as if I were sharing Jonah's experiences when he ended up in the belly of the whale, but this whale opened at both ends and had a gilt-edged view to a twinkling night sky. I wondered what the Marsh Arabs thought about the world out there.

As if Hagi had been reading my thoughts, he said that he once had been in Baghdad, and that when he was there he deeply missed the peace and safety of Allah's marshes. In his opinion the city bred greed, envy and dishonesty. In the marshes no one steals, he said. Everyone has what they need, and no one has more than enough. Praise Allah. The buffalo had enough fodder, there were masses of fish to spear, and chickens, ducks and wild fowl; boats filled with watermelons, braided reed mats and baskets from the marshes were exchanged for supplies of flour and tea.

In addition, and here the old wise man lifted his hand in blessing, there were beautiful women here. He himself had four wives. Along the walls there was merry whispering acknowledging his joy of life. The old man with the long white beard knew what he was talking about.

As we know, we should not succumb to temptations in the Garden of Eden, but on one occasion I was with the expedition's Mexican mechanic on a bridge by the outskirts of the marshes. He shared my sense of all that is beautiful and well formed, and when a beautiful woman came paddling past in a canoe he got out his camera. What he did not see, but I did, was a man with a raised spear running toward us as fast as he could with his long robe flowing behind him. I had to tear the camera away from the photographer, who only had eyes for the woman. We ran for our lives and left the beauty to her guardian.

The women were quite well guarded in the marshes. They were not allowed to eat with us, not even to serve the tea. As if to protect those of Adam's gender from falling for a severely punished temptation, they were robed in black. Only their faces and beautiful feet were visible when one caught glimpses of gliding shadows between the reed curtains or when they fed chickens, sat in a canoe or baked bread. In the marshes the flat bread was baked with a dough that the women smacked against the inner walls of the round clay ovens, which were open at the top like a jar. If one was attracted by the fine aromas from the ovens, one had to be quick to catch a glimpse of more than two sparkling eyes and teeth that shone like new snow in the sun before the woman managed to turn her head away or pull the black cloth over her nose. The women had the same fine, clean-cut profiles that characterized most of the Marsh Arabs. They were just as skilled as the men in paddling and punting large boats loaded with reed or reed mats, but they were only allowed to get together with the men and laugh and wave as we paddled past their dwellings when they were either very young or very old.

The ideas of whiling away the time or light entertainment had not reached them from the outside world, but smiles and laughter revealed that they got along well without it. Hagi was aware that we city-dwellers could not get by without earning money for a car and electricity. But he was not at all certain that his people would be any happier now that the government in Baghdad planned to bring electrical wiring and bricks for the construction of houses into the marshes. When people are happy, they smile, he said. No one had smiled at him in the streets of Baghdad.

'There are too many people in the city streets,' I explained. 'One can't smile at everyone there.'

But Hagi had walked in streets where there were almost no people, and no one had smiled there either.

The arched reed bundles that held the roof and walls together in the chief's dwelling were exactly like those tied side by side to form the shape of *Ra II*. I had found people here who could make the necessary constructions to build a solid reed ship, but they had only used them to build houses on their floating islands. They themselves punted around in the shallows with the *mashuf* made of planks treated with asphalt. But if they could help us learn the art of maintaining the floating ability of the reed, then we could help the Marsh Arabs learn the lost art of their forefathers' forgotten boat construction from the Titicaca Indians.

When I came into the marshes, I had wondered if Hagi and his people would understand my plans. He was willing to listen. With his appearance and mien, he could have been a wealthy oil sheik, a former diplomat or a retired scientist. In his long white robe he looked more like a Biblical prophet than a patriarch, as timeless as the Sumerian reed house we were in. I actually felt as if I was with Moses or Abraham. Of course old Hagi must have experienced real reed boats.

And he had. Three types were in use when he was young. Two were hollow, like baskets, and stayed afloat because they were smeared with asphalt both on the inside and the outside. One was a *guffa*, as round as a leather boat from Ireland, and the other a *jillabie* with an extended structure, which was the forerunner of the plank-built *mashuf* they used today. Both had survived since ancient times, and I had seen models of these 5,000-year-old boats in the museum in Baghdad and been aboard the last ones that were still in use on the river above Babylon. The third type was an *elep-urbati* and this one was not smeared with asphalt because it was made of tight bundles of reeds without cavities in the middle, and stayed afloat by itself.

This was the reason I had come! But didn't the reed become saturated?

'Not if you cut it in the month of August,' Hagi assured us, and everyone around the walls nodded. It was a matter of general knowledge. Everyone in the marshes knew, but we who had cut papyrus reed by Tana Lake in Ethiopia in December for *Ra* and *Ra II* had not known. In August, during a full moon, a special sap in the reed hindered water saturation. There was nothing written about this in the textbooks, but then they are not always the best places to find answers.

14

In the Wake of Noah

We continued to relive Biblical history when with ten companions from different countries we travelled onto the ocean from the Garden of Eden. From the legendary birthplace of Adam and Eve at the confluence of the Euphrates and Tigris Rivers, we set straight out to sea where Noah had introduced a completely new chapter in the religious history of the Christians and the Muslims. The story of Noah and all the animals in the Ark who survived the Deluge had thrilled me as a child. The same fairy-tale atmosphere came over me when I saw the Marsh Arabs on the bank of the Tigris tying the enormous bundles of reed for our ark, which we had named after the river that would carry us to sea. Noah symbolized the world's oldest known boat-builder. In the earliest era of seafaring, no ships were built with boards; Sumerian art shows both people and cattle on large reed ships.

There are no limits to the size of a ship being built with bundles of reed, and there were unlimited amounts of reed in the marshes. We had crossed the Atlantic Ocean on *Ra II*, which was twelve metres long and had one cabin. The *Tigris* was eighteen metres long and had two cabins on deck. In comparison to the pyramids and reed ships that were built for the most powerful Sumerian kings, we were launching a modest vessel in Noah's wake.

I will always think of the aging Hagi as the rightful successor to the Sumerian throne and the direct heir of the Garden of Eden. His dignity reflected an inner wealth and a time-honoured culture. Saddam, with his imported tanks in Baghdad, was protected by an arsenal of weapons as if he were a foreign soldier in a conquered empire. His Arabian forefathers had arrived in Mesopotamia victoriously with the teachings of the Koran, and taken possession of the ancient cultural centres of the Sumerians, the Babylonians and the Assyrians in order to redeem a promise from Our Lord to Abraham. When Abraham and his people came to the Mediterranean coast and the land of the Pharaohs on their journey, he claimed that according to the Bible and the Koran God had promised his family all of the land between the Tigris and the Nile. It was this ostensible promise that the prophet Mohammed wanted to redeem many generations later, and he even managed to expand the limits of the area to include the areas both west of the Nile and east of the Tigris. However, back when Abraham declared his promise to his descendants, he could not have foreseen that both the Jews and Arabs would come to count him as their progenitor.

When Abraham visited the stump where the Arabs had built the inn called the Garden of Eden, it was easy to construct and equip a reed boat on the river bank. Reeds were as plentiful then as now, and they could refer to a few thousand years of experience in binding hundreds of reed bundles to achieve the same elegant forms and lines on boats made of wood. From grave excavations, we knew that they had been experts in twining and braiding rope from fibres taken from the tough outer covering of the reeds. Also, farming, fishing and a lively trade up and down the rivers and out into the Gulf had made it possible to load all the necessities on to a vessel at short notice, and then to hoist sail and cast off for a long voyage.

In modern times it was not that simple. The oil boom in Iraq resulted in the demand for consumer goods being far higher than the supply. The boundary of the enemy country Iran was right in the middle of the river, and despite changing water levels and unaccountable sand banks, the line could not be crossed. The ships with trading goods were moored like sardines outside the river delta, waiting for weeks to come up the river and deliver their cargo. Merchandise that was unloaded in the ports along the Euphrates and Tigris was grabbed by local buyers before it had time to reach the stores. No one could make rope anymore; rope-makers were just as out-of-date as reed-boat builders, and the only people who had heard of the large Sumerian merchant ships, the *magurs*, were the scientists at the museum. Our shopping trips to Baghdad ended with empty baskets.

The art of building a sickle-shaped ship robust enough to maintain its shape on the open ocean prepared the way for the development of seafaring in both the Middle East and South America. But this art lives on only at Lake Titicaca. When the *Ra II* dried out at the Kon-Tiki Museum in Oslo, it became as flat as a pancake, and we had to cross the Atlantic again to find the same South American mountain Indians who had built it for us. The Indians from Lake Titicaca were the only ones who could set it back to its original shape, because neither scientists nor boat-builders in our days had any idea of the technique they used.

So the ancient barbarians had knowledge we don't have today?

The Aymara Indians from Lake Titicaca were far from being primitive barbarians. Their ancestors in Bolivia had founded the outstanding Tiahuanaco civilization, and built the Akapana pyramid that loomed over the plain by Lake Titicaca, just as impressively and in the same style as the pyramids in Mesopotamia and the oldest one in Egypt.

The Aymara Indians had also made the statue of Kon-Tiki with a beard that we painted on the sail of Kon-Tiki. The Incas gave him the symbolic name Viracocha, which means 'Foam on the Ocean', because he was a seafarer. After conquering all of the ancient kingdoms in Peru and the neighbouring countries, they enlarged the name to Con-Tiki-Viracocha, because they found that the coastal Indians called the same legendary god-king Con while the Indians at Lake Titicaca called him Tici or Ticci. When the Spaniards arrived, the Aymara Indians in the Tiahuanaco area told them that this god had come to their ancestors with his following of white, bearded men and crossed the ocean with the same kind of reed boats that they themselves had learned to make. He claimed to be the son of the sun, and after landing at Tiahuanaco, he built the large pyramid. He left them in the same way that he came. And throughout the whole Inca empire, the Spaniards heard the same story that the Aymara Indians told me on the shore of Lake Titicaca 400 years later. In the end, the godly priest-king wandered with his following to the north, all the way to what is today the republic of Ecuador. He then disappeared across the ocean, sailing westward from the coast by Manta.

It was easier said than done to invite the descendants of the god-kings to Iraq. August is the hottest month in the marshes, and the Aymara Indians live in ice-cold mountain air on an island in Lake Titicaca, 4,000 metres above sea level in the Andes. First, four of them had to be picked up by reed boat from their island out in Lake Titicaca, then we had to find a place for them to live for two weeks down in Bolivia's jungle so they could get used to the difference in air pressure and temperature. The next concern was to bring them to Baghdad with a plane that landed at night so that the car ride through the desert to the Garden of Eden inn would be over before the heat of the scorching sun became too much for them. Only three of the four men could build reed boats and they only spoke their native language. The fourth man was a Bolivian interpreter who would translate the mountain Indians' Aymara language into Spanish for me, so that I could translate it further into English for my interpreter from Baghdad, who spoke Arabian to the leader of the Marsh Arabs, who then translated it into their own Madan language.

It was an irony of destiny, I thought, that I would come to experience these language problems right here, not far from the ruins of the legendary Tower of Babel. When I visited its ruins, I found no more than a pathetic pile of sand, some scattered clay bricks and a sign reading 'The Tower of Babel' that had been put there by Iraqi archaeologists. It had probably been some sort of a step pyramid. I had now assembled a crew representing eleven different tongues, and in addition I had twenty Marsh Arabs who only spoke Madan and who were to learn how to build a reed boat from three Indians who could only speak Aymara.

I let the Aymara Indians sleep late on the first morning after the journey. I grew afraid when I peeked into their room and found it empty.

They were already sitting outside with a group of marsh Arabs in the shade of some date palms by Adam and Eve's tree stump. They were still wearing their warm woollen hats and thick, colourful ponchos in contrast to the Arabs in their snow-white linen robes. They were nodding and pointing while they talked, and everyone sat with a handful of reeds. The interpreters simply stared at them. 'These señores are very wise,' the interpreter from Bolivia assured me when I walked over to him. 'They understand everything we explain to them without understanding a word of what we're saying!'

'*Totora*,' he said to the ones dressed in white, holding up a reed.

'*Berdi*,' they answered, raising another one.

We never had any use for the interpreters. The world's foremost experts on reeds had met one another. They were just as smart as the rest of us, but when it came to skills, life had made us experts in different areas.

The worst thing was that I needed experts in other areas than reed-boat building. Not one sail-maker could be found in modern Iraq!

Modern Iraq had no sailcloth either; it was being trucked from Europe. In the meantime I searched in vain for someone who could sew a normal dhow sail for us, the typical sail for local vessels. No one had heard of anyone who could sew a sail in modern times. Sailing ships were just as outdated on rivers as camels were on highways. We were about a generation too late in Iraq.

I searched along the riverbanks all the way down to the Gulf and even crossed the border to Kuwait in the hope of finding an old-fashioned dhow with sails. The dhow had been a typical sailing vessel in these waters since time immemorial. The sail was most likely the transition between the first square sails of antiquity and the modern Latin sail. It looked like an old Egyptian sail hung aslant. When I came to Iraq for the first time all the Arabs in the area had sawn off the masts on their dhows and put in motors. Fuel was as cheap as the wind in the Gulf countries. Back then, however, I had seen white sails on Indian dhows that came all the way up to Basra to bring dates to Bombay. This traffic had ceased because of smuggling, and I had to turn to the Indian consul in Basra and ask him to find three dhow sailors through the seamen's employment office in Bombay to help us sew a sail and then to escort us out of the Persian Gulf, which was currently a nightmare of oil platforms and traffic.

The three dhow sailors were not on the plane we met in Baghdad, and a telegram from India confirmed that they lost contact with them in New Delhi where they had gone to get Iraqi visas.

Two weeks later our local assistant Ali came to the breakfast table and reported that he had finally found the men. They were just outside the door with their sacks, and one of them was called Saleman.

We tried all the European languages, and Arabic, and Toru tried Japanese, and Yuri Russian, but it was only Saleman who understood enough English for all three to sit down happily and eat with a good appetite.

After their meal their eyes filled with wonder when they saw the reed boat glistening like gold in the morning sun with its impressive hull. The shock came when Saleman wanted to know where the motor casing was to be built. No one at the seamen's office had said anything other than that the three of them would be sailing on a newly constructed dhow. They had never worked on a dhow with sails, and they had never been in the Gulf.

After a good deal of linguistic confusion, it became clear that the co-operation with our new friends had to be limited to clearing the table after breakfast. In addition to being our navigator, we appointed Norman as our sail master and he had the bright idea of bringing the three new arrivals down to the harbour in Basra. There they could help him as interpreters and get information about dhow sails from some of the Indian sailors who were anchored in the river. Yuri had managed to borrow a wonderful new Russian car from the Soviet consulate-general in Baghdad, and Norman drove happily off with the Indians on a main road crowded with trucks.

The next time we saw Norman he was standing in the doorway with his head wrapped in bandages. All that was visible was one ear and his nose, which was red and bruised.

'Where are the Indians?'

'They're being examined at the hospital.'

'What happened?' I asked horrified.

'The car turned over three times.'

'And the Arabian interpreter?'

'At the police station. He was driving.'

'And the Soviets' new car?'

'With its wheels up in the air. A total wreck.'

When the three dhow men finally came limping in, one with an aching foot, the other with an aching head and the third with an aching back, they were not in the least bit hungry. They simply pleaded with me to be sent on the first plane back to India.

After this we were ready for our next surprise: a message that a man in European clothes was on the other side of the house throwing sausages into the river.

I found a sunburnt man with a beetroot-red face who looked totally disoriented. He was standing there in the heat throwing salami sausages into the river. I interrupted him carefully just as he heaved a huge ham into the water in a true hammer-thrower style. He wiped his face and I had to nod in agreement, yes, this was a tough job in the midday heat. And then I heard his terrible story, which would affect us greatly. He was the truck driver who had come all the way from Hamburg with the wood for the mast and everything else we had ordered.

'Eine Katastrofe,' the man assured me in German. And I was in total agreement when I realized that it was our food supply that he was offering to the fish in the Tigris. While he was speaking I heard sharp cracks from his truck. He comforted me by saying it was the bamboo splitting in the heat. And then I saw an open case filled with tins of food that had grown to the size of cannon balls.

'Customs!' the German explained. Ali had to run and find a cold beer in the refrigerator before we could get another word out of him.

He was a special envoy from an excellent shipping company in Hamburg, sent with two drivers to make certain the cargo arrived at its destination quickly and safely. The truck was not refrigerated, so they drove continuously, taking turns in order to arrive within a limit of fourteen days. Everything went smoothly until they were in southernmost Turkey. Kurdish snipers along the country road had started shooting at them. Then they stepped on the gas.

There were already some bullet holes in the truck when they caught up with a large transport convoy that, like them, drove as fast as it could to get over the border to Iraq. In the confusion they had forgotten to obtain clearance from the customs officers at the Iraqi border, who were expecting them to arrive with a special order from Baghdad for them simply to break the seals. Instead they had just sped southward, in constantly warmer temperatures. They passed Baghdad, passed the detour to the Garden of Eden, and arrived at the crowded seaport down in Basra. A friendly policeman gave them directions through the harbour area where all the ships were moored waiting to unload and get through customs, and suddenly they found themselves outside the customs and excise building without a shady place to park. The man claimed it was forty-five degrees Celsius outside the truck and probably seventy degrees inside, and he assured us that both he and his two drivers almost died inside the truck on the third day in the customs yard. A friendly soul who spoke English had finally helped them to call the ministry in Baghdad, who rescued them from their involuntary stay in Basra. The two drivers had taken the most direct route back to Europe, and left it up to him to deliver the cargo.

And so he did, in this peculiar manner.

'All the food has spoiled,' he assured us furiously. Before anyone could stop him, the last salami sailed far out over the river.

With a single leap our youngest crew member was over the terrace railing and in the river. He returned with a huge roll of salami, holding it like a baby in his arms. The only one. The rest had been swept away by the current.

The Garden of Eden was far from the ocean. We had been able to steer straight out to sea with the east wind behind us in both Peru and Morocco. This time our challenge was to manoeuvre the reed ship with the current down between Iraq and Iran and all the way to the Persian Gulf. Then we had to make it through the long, heavily trafficked Gulf and the Strait of Harmuz before reaching open sea.

Our first problem after the launch in the river was that the water we were on was heavily polluted, and it became even worse as we approached the delta. Large white patches of foam drifted like loose ice on the surface, effluents from paper factories. Chemicals had transformed enormous amounts of reeds into wood pulp. I had once been on board a giant reed raft on this same river, on my way down to a paper factory. A friendly Arab had invited me for tea in front of a reed hut he had on a deck where everything was made of reed except for a clay area beneath some burning dried stubs. The giant raft consisted of reeds placed loosely in layers criss-crossing one another, and I measured it: thirty-four metres long, five metres wide and three metres deep. It rode high on the water because the owner had cut the reeds in August and he lived two months on board, waiting to be able to deliver his reeds to the cellulose factory. On our current trip, our major fear was that our ark would dissolve and end up as pulp before we reached the Gulf.

The fact that the fertile gardens of Eden and Babylon now lay buried in desert sand is interpreted by some as the punishment of Our Lord and by others as a result of the Sumerians' excessive agriculture. But it is our own generation that has travelled further down the Biblical rivers and smeared black oil on golden sand and on every green straw down beside the river delta. It looked more like a sewer outlet or the inside of a factory smokestack. Here Iran and Iraq were eyeing one another like Cain and Abel from either side of the river, competing over the sacrifice of the most virgin terrain to the oil pumps. Ships from the east and the west were lined up at their moorings, either pumping oil or waiting to get up the river with their cargo. Our only aim was to move with the wind, through the chaos, and out into clean open sea.

In tropical waters there is an interplay between the currents of air in the atmosphere and the currents in the ocean. Equatorial currents and trade winds keep one another company from east to west all year round across the Atlantic and the Pacific Oceans. The Indian Ocean differs because the monsoons dominate, and the ocean current is influenced by the wind that blows from south to north in the six summer months and from north to south in the six winter months. This is the only ocean area in the world where currents change direction with the seasons. Arabian and Indian dhows had taken advantage of those different tail winds when they sailed back and forth with their merchandise in and out of the Persian Gulf. The changes in the monsoon were a part of the clockwork of nature, and just as reliable as the sun and the moon.

But it seemed that the gods had deserted the Gulf area, Allah as well as the weather gods. They cared little about maintaining old traditions and acted as if the time of sailing ships had passed. The rainy season had surprised us by appearing a month early, and the Arabs in the area told us that the wind had been totally unpredictable for the past two years. Out in the Persian Gulf it felt as if we had ended up in a belt of calm that was not supposed to appear in November, when the north wind should have blown us straight out.

We had to make do with a few small gusts of wind. While sand had conquered the Sumerians' fields and cities, sludge had transformed the whole coastline by forming endless banks of silt outside the harbours. They stretched invisibly out just beneath the water's surface for many hundreds of square kilometres, all the way out to Failaka Island off the coast of Kuwait. We ended up here against our will because we were trying to avoid the dangerous supertanker that dominated the rest of the Gulf and had no possibility to steer around us. Some sudden and extreme gusts of wind from the south threatened to send us back toward Iraq and the shipping traffic, and they forced us closer to the dangerous rocky coast of Failaka than we wanted to be.

One night the helmsman woke us up because he heard the sound of the surf. First we heard a deeper rhythmical undertone beneath the sizzling orchestra of regular ocean waves breaking around us. The sound increased and became a consistent roar that came out of the night somewhere ahead of us. Land. Cliffs or reefs. We dropped anchor in the hope that it would catch hold in the mire, but we lost the rope and simultaneously both anchors. We threw out another rope with a canvas sea anchor – an open bag that was meant to slow down our speed. Luck was with us; the water was so shallow that the anchor settled into the mire and stayed there until sunrise, when we were able to steer free of the lone reef that rose from the endless banks of mud. All this, just to gradually end up even closer to the shallows along the coast of Failaka. No ship could navigate here, but we could have waded up to our knees if the bottom hadn't been a quagmire of soft mud.

We had ended up in the innermost crook of the gulf, where charts warned against pirates and showed that the steep coasts of Failaka were completely inaccessible, blocked by reefs and shallows. The only harbour on the huge island was on the other side.

And then the pirates appeared, just like a fairy tale, surely just as they have always appeared ever since the time of Sinbad and the Sumerians. They did not climb on to the reed ship with swords. They did not do anything, but just waited.

First we saw the lights of their kerosene lanterns moving between the cliffs on land, and we rocked our own lanterns in the naive hope of being saved from the breakers that were thundering against the reef. When daylight came we saw one small boat, and then another, dancing across the breakers between the reefs. Soon they both closed in, but not so close that they were within bullet range. They hovered close to us, and as far as we could see they did nothing but stare at us, even though they must have noticed that we were drifting slowly toward the thundering breakers. It occurred to us that we had ended up in bad company.

On our amateur radio transmitter Norman contacted a Russian voice from a Soviet ship that was anchored further in the Gulf. Yuri explained our precarious situation to the captain in his own language, and not many hours later we could see the outline of *Slavsk* anchored on the horizon, as close to the renowned Failaka banks as they dared to be. The captain himself and a full rescue crew with lifejackets came in over the shallows in a huge lifeboat.

After hearty hugs, one of the Russians was able to haul our sea anchor out of the mud, and the increasing wind took such a good hold on our boat's light hull and bamboo hut that we pulled the Soviets with us toward the reefs, in spite of the fact that they were trying to pull us out toward *Slavsk* with their motorized lifeboat.

Rashad from Iraq, one of my crew who spoke Arabian, offered to row the rubber dinghy over to one of the hovering boats and explain that we were not propeller-driven and would soon smash against the reefs.

Rashad returned and explained that they wanted a handsome ransom in Kuwait currency. Otherwise they had time to wait for the inevitable.

I was ready to negotiate, but Captain Igor from *Slavsk* became furious and would not let me strike a deal. He offered six bottles of vodka and two cases of wine. Rashad went over again, and came back with the message that the men over there were Muslims, and that Allah forbade them to drink alcohol. With this, they moved a little further away, and stopped, ostensibly to fish. The other boat dared to come within hailing distance, and Rashad explained that they had doubled the price. After this they disappeared. The Russians refused to give up towing, and both boats drifted toward the reef. Then a third and larger boat appeared, seemingly from around the headland from the Kuwait side. It came pretty close, and turned out to be a dhow with a sawn-off mast. The other men had looked like fishermen, but these looked like pure bandits.

A fat gangster type with a big turban and fairer skin than the others sat with his legs crossed on pillows and studied us with calculating contempt. His fat hands had never touched a fishing line. He was the archetype of a crook. The others were a mixed gang under his command. These people told us outright that they wanted a ransom, and our alternative was to drive into the breakers in the dark of night. The best-case scenario would be to survive and end up naked on the reef. The Russians had set their own anchor and ours was down in the mud again, but nothing held. I took over and ordered Rashad to negotiate. The sun would set in one hour. No coast guard would ever show up in these endless, unnavigable shallows. We had heard that organized gangs had been smuggling human labour from Pakistan to work in rich Kuwait in this very area. Failaka was a part of the sheikdom of Kuwait, and we had landed at its back door, which was closed for legitimate travellers.

The bandits did not lower their price. It had obviously been agreed upon previously. We had no Kuwait currency, but the robbers accepted Iraqi bills, which was hard currency in these parts. They demanded that Rashad come over as a hostage on the dhow. The boat came alongside and I placed the money, bill by bill, into someone's hand, who then passed it on to the fat person on the pillows. After a wave from him, Rashad was set free and jumped over to us.

Then the Soviets threw a towing line over to the dhow, and we hung on while the dhow, helped by the Russian's propeller, slowly pulled us out into open water just next to *Slavsk*. There was no time for farewells, because when we reached deep water the dhow was already at full speed on its way back to the shallows.

Igor set a course for the sheikdom of Bahrain without orders from Moscow, and did not let us go before we had reached the island's territorial waters, where *Slavsk* was refused entry because of its Russian crew, even though they had saved our lives.

We had arrived where written history had begun. Never has any arrival given me such a sense of reliving something dramatic in the history of man as when we came to Bahrain with a reed boat. The inscription on the Sumerians' clay tablets reports that after the Deluge their first king brought his people and their livestock to Dilmun. The Assyrians confirm this in *Gilgamesh*, the world's oldest example of epic literature. Danish archaeologists, first P. V. Glob and now Geoffrey Bibby, had started extensive excavations on Bahrain and found that the legendary Dilmun was identical to this highly modern Arabic sultanate. We had barely moored before Bibby took the first plane from Aarhus to see a reed ship, as if it were thousands of years ago, back on the coast of Dilmun.

It was quite an anachronism that the reed ship *Tigris* came to inaugurate what was then the world's largest dry dock. It was built to handle oil tankers of up to 450,000 tons, and we arrived two days before its official opening. Bibby landed at the ultra-modern Concorde airport, and we drove over to the other side of the island where it seemed that the clock and the calendar had been turned back 5,000 years. Simple fishermen still paddled out into the Gulf with boats tied from bundles of palm leaf stems.

In the centre of the island we were struck by how frivolously today's people cut their roots to the past in the blind faith that what they have now will last forever. Everywhere we went large palms had been razed. Only the stumps remained, and the landscape looked like a man's unshaven face. One could buy dates in the store. One could buy everything in the store, flown in fresh from the whole world, and there was enough money because the oil flowed in through huge pipes from the mainland. Dilmun had become an important stopover for the shipment of oil from the pumps on the Arabian peninsula.

But in the centre of the island we were struck with reverence. Here there were springs of clean fresh water that literally sprang from the ground and ran like brooks through the remnants of ancient irrigation channels. 'This comes from the high mountains in the inner Arabian desert,' Bibby explained. When it rains there, the water seeps through the rocks and follows underground water arteries that run beneath the desert and the bottom of the Persian Gulf before resurfacing here on the island like freshwater springs run by hydraulic power.

I drank some and sat down on a stump to think. Was it faith or superstition when the old Sumerians thanked the god of heaven for gifts? I had made a note of the text on a Sumerian clay tablet, which relates that the seafaring god Enki had asked the highest god of heaven to bless Dilmun with fresh water:

> *Let the sun god Utu who lives in heaven*
> *bring you fresh water from the earth,*
> *from the earth's water springs.*

Let him bring water up in your large pools,
let him give your city an abundance of drinking water,
let him give Dilmun an abundance of drinking water

Before we humans built our own world, we were grateful for all the miraculous god-like gifts nature had given us, regardless of what name we give to the god of heaven. Out in the middle of the salty Gulf, where desert and wilderness dominate all of the coasts in the area, the unexplainable law of gravity had been given the opportunity to pump drinking water up to the original inhabitants of Dilmun. And from the springs in Dilmun the fresh water still pours out of the ground on its way to the sea.

In the impressive ruins on Dilmun's original port city I felt life pouring into all the ancient texts about seafaring that dominated the translations of the inscriptions on the Sumerians' clay tablets. Bibby showed us that at high tide large vessels could be moored right beside the warehouses near Dilmun's city gate, while at low tide a regular keeled boat had to hurry out again so as not to be grounded and tip over with all its cargo. Now it was our turn to show him that a reed boat consisting of two huge bundles of reeds side by side can float higher over the shallows than a boat with a hull and a keel, and when the tide goes out it can lie on the bottom with all its cargo without tipping over.

It was not necessary to close our eyes to picture the traffic in the harbour when Bibby brought us through the remains of the ancient warehouses and pointed to the places where he had found trademarks and other identification proving merchant contacts with both Sumerians and the distant Indus valley, our destination on *Tigris*. I felt that I was part of the scene when I stood on the edge of the dock by the city gate and looked out over the waves that united the people of the world's oldest cultures. Before leaving Iraq I had delved into translations of the ancient text sources in the library in Baghdad. If I had not been convinced before, then I certainly was now.

Modern people are so strongly influenced by Darwin's theory of evolution that we believe that 5,000 years ago people were 5,000 years closer to the apes. In the interest of truth we have to revise our understanding. If we are to use a timescale for the development of human beings, we have to go much further back than we can by reading ancient texts. And if we talk about culture, then we cannot use a general timescale at all. Civilization was far more developed in parts of Asia, Africa and America in ancient times than it was in Europe in the Middle Ages. And it was seafaring that made it possible.

What had struck me the most by reading the ancient Sumerians' own words was that, deep within themselves, they could not have been as different from us as we like to believe. In his essay, 'The Seafaring Merchants from Ur', the Sumerian expert Oppenheimer claims that the most interesting information on the clay tablets from Ur is about the role that seafaring played in the city's life as a trading port in the earliest prehistoric era. Both the harbours and the inland canals had been dredged and maintained, and they were inspected by high-ranking officials who reported to the king. The harbour authorities taxed the importing ships, and the skippers had sealed documents concerning their ships and cargo.

The largest reed ships at the time of the Sumerians had a cargo capability given in *gur*, which when converted was about thirty or forty tons or more, and by comparison, this made our *Tigris* seem like a tiny boat. The Finnish language researcher Salonen described the largest reed ships as *magur*, and they were also called 'god ships', 'the sea-going ship', or 'the ship with the tall stems'. We had named our vessel after the river that was our starting point. The Sumerians had romantic names on their ships such as *The Protectoress of Life*, *Morning* or *The Heart's Delight*. The texts refer to passenger ships, ferries, fishing boats, warships, troop transport ships and private and chartered merchant ships. The cargo could be anything from lumber, copper, ivory, bricks, hides or textiles, to corn, flour, bread, fish, dairy products, wine or livestock.

I had become totally entranced by harbour life when we left to visit something that made a permanent impression on my personal view of both the past and the future: the world's largest prehistoric graveyard, an endless field of sand covered with grave mounds as far as the eye could see. Archaeologists had estimated the number of graves at about 100,000. Most of them only rose like tightly placed mounds in the terrain, but many were of impressive dimensions. The largest were grouped together in a place of honour by the sea, and they were obviously the oldest graves, built while there was still plenty of room. The others were scattered in all directions and looked like giant turtle eggs. All of them had been plundered by grave robbers.

I was aware that Dilmun was as holy to the Sumerians in ancient times as Jerusalem became to the Christians, and Mecca to the Muslims. Even the Assyrians made pilgrimages here, and their famous tablet vouches for this fact. Perhaps they wanted to be buried here in the native country of the first god-kings. Because it was here that the progenitor of the family of kings had pulled himself ashore after the Deluge.

Today no one showed any respect for this plundered field of graves. Those who had earned enough money from the oil boom flew to Mecca. I was immediately captivated by the largest of all the grave mounds, which lay close to the modern Arab settlement. Bibby brought me around to the rear and showed me how the contemporary locals had started an industry by breaking limestone from the pyramid-like structure that lay within the huge mound that they used for burning lime. This kind of limestone did not exist on Bahrain. Just like the Sumerian empire on the mainland, the architects of this colossus used *magur* to transport the beautifully carved stone blocks to the island's coast. I recognized the masterfully joined limestone blocks that I had seen in Iraq's famous Nippur pyramid, where they were hidden beneath a later layer of sun-dried blocks of clay.

One day, when I came back to Dilmun's abandoned field of graves alone, I crawled up on the giant mound where I could look down over the roofs of two-and three-storey whitewashed houses and out over the whole dead, cupola-covered landscape. I lay down to think.

Do you remember what you thought?

I thought that 5,000 years ago the written history of mankind began on this island, and I wondered what would be written about this same island 5,000 years from now, when the pipelines from Arabian oil reserves lying on the bottom of the sea were empty.

I thought about how we Europeans smile at oral traditions, and claim that history began with the written word. But unless we have written it ourselves with letters we learned from the Phoenicians, we don't take it seriously. I had the oldest known written version of the Sumerians' own history fresh in my memory since the days at the library in Baghdad. And when I lay on the giant mound with a view to over 100,000 forgotten graves, I decided that the least I could do would be to make sure that this written work would never be forgotten, since it was the oldest known version of the beginning of world history.

I thought how Jews, Christians and Muslims in their common inheritance of faith have all incorporated into their traditions the story of Noah's Ark and the Deluge, which Abraham brought with him from Ur in Mesopotamia. As a child, there was nothing that had captivated me more than the story of Noah saving all the animals in the world, but I had never dreamed that I would come to wonder how a story like that became a part of religious teachings. The Bible gives the story a place of honour just after the story of creation, while the Koran regularly mentions Noah and Allah's punishment with the Deluge. If we go back to Ur, where the original version of the Deluge had been buried with the clay tablets of the Sumerians for more than 2,000 years – when Abraham left Mesopotamia – we find that something happened that relates to all of us.

No one knew that the Sumerians had existed until an expedition from the University of Pennsylvania began excavations of the Nippur pyramid and found a library of 35,000 clay tablets, among them the original edition of the Deluge.

To the Sumerians this was not legend but the history of their own times that they recorded themselves. We know all the essential parts from the Bible, but the original version is more realistic. In the Sumerian original the name of the god-fearing king who saved the human beings from the flood is given as Ziusudra; he had no elephants or giraffes aboard, just his own livestock. And the Ark did not land on any mountain top, but on the blessed island of gods, Dilmun, in the Persian Gulf. From there the king's descendants later moved to Ur, which then was a port city at the river delta in the Gulf.

The details are sparse in the original version, but it relates that the Sumerians believed it was the sun god Utu who had advised the king to build a reed ship large enough to rescue both people and animals. The Deluge raged for seven days and seven nights. 'And the giant ship was thrown around on the waters.' When the Deluge ended and the sun god came and let light shine on heaven and earth, the king threw himself face down and sacrificed an ox and a sheep.

After the Sumerians were obliterated, it was the Assyrians' turn to write world history. And they inherited the beginning from the Sumerians. The world's oldest known epic work, the Assyrian *Gilgamesh*, is about the same awful Deluge that eradicated all previous history. The Assyrians believed it was the ocean god Enki who wanted to punish human beings, and they called the king who was advised to build the big ship Utu-nipishtim.

The Assyrians, whose main centre was further inland, allowed themselves certain historical falsifications. They let the Deluge rage over the country for six days and seven nights, until the great ship on the seventh day landed on a mountain top in upper Kurdistan. It was the Assyrian version that Abraham inherited when he departed from Ur, and it is therefore understandable that the Bible lands the Ark on Mt Ararat, while the Koran lands it on the top of Al Judi, which are

both well-known mountains in upper Kurdistan. But the author of
the epic gives himself away by admitting that they had heard the
story of the Deluge from the mouth of Utu-nipishtim while he still
lived in Dilmun!

Abraham caught on to some interesting details. The Assyrian text
says that when the king tried to get to shore, he first released a dove
and a swallow, but both came back to the ship. Later he released a
raven, and when that did not return the king understood that the
water level had fallen and the ship was on solid ground. He left his
ship with his following and made offerings to the sun god, who
promised never again to punish all of humanity because a few had
sinned.

In the Jewish version, a raven was released first but it came back,
and so did a dove. But on the seventh day he released a dove again
and it came back with an olive branch in its beak. Another seven
days passed before another dove was let out and never came back. It
was then that Noah left his Ark with all the animals and made an
offering in gratitude to God in Heaven, who promised hereafter to
keep peace with all of mankind.

Could Noah's Ark have been a reed ship?

At the time of the Sumerians all the gods' ships were *magur*, or
reed ships. And in the Assyrian version Utu-nipishtim received
orders to tear down his reed house in order to build his large ship.
The text reads: 'Reed house, reed house. Wall, wall. Reed house
listen! Wall listen! Man from Shuruppak, son of Ubara-Tutu. Tear
down your house, build a ship!'

The reed ship *Tigris* had not been impregnated with anything,
but it still floated well during the five months the eleven of us lived
on it before we set fire to the vessel as a demonstration against the
war in the Red Sea. But we would have been strongly tempted to try
Utu-nipishtim's recipe if all the ingredients had been available in
modern Iraq: 'Six sar tar I poured into the melting pot, three sar
asphalt I added. Three sar oil the blending crew got, except for one

sar which the cargo hold held and two sar hidden by the captain.'

In the New Revised Standard Version of the English edition of the Bible, Noah was ordered to build a slightly more modern Ark: 'Make yourself an ark with rips of cypress, a deck of reed, and cover it on the inside and the outside with tar.'

But what does science say about the Deluge?

When the British started the archaeological excavations at Ur at the end of the 1920s, Leonard Wooley found that the holy city of the Sumerians lay on top of a three-metre layer of a particular type of river silt. Beneath this layer, the British found the ruins of an even older settlement that had been buried by an enormous tidal wave that had thrown the silt up and covered the entire lower half of Mesopotamia with an estimated eight metres of water before the flood retreated, leaving the silt behind. This was the same type of silt that we had been stuck in just beyond the same coastline when we were towed out by the Russians and the pirates from Failaka.

The Danish archaeologist Glob, who had led the first fifteen years of excavations at Dilmun, was also the first one to take the Sumerians' recording of the flood catastrophe seriously. He connected them directly to the three-metre layer of dried silt which the Sumerians had settled on top of about 5,000 years ago.

And then many other strange things happened on the planet.

About 5,000 years ago, or around 3100–3000 BC, the oldest civilizations in the world were developing rapidly. Not only did the Sumerians come sailing from Bahrain to establish their first kingdom in the area at the mouth of Mesopotamia's rivers, but also the ancestors of the Pharaohs came sailing up the Nile and settled in Egypt. For a short time these people continued to tax the mighty kingdoms that suddenly appeared on both Crete and Cyprus. Immediately thereafter, if not simultaneously, other seafarers came up the lower part of the Indus River and established the third of the world's great civilizations in Mohenjo Daro. They all arrived from unknown origins with fully developed civilizations, but each had individually developed writing and used the motif of god-kings aboard reed ships in their religious art.

I doubt that I have ever wondered so much about anything else as I have wondered about what happened on our planet at that time. Something happened, we know that.

Out in the Atlantic Ocean something happened to cause Iceland to split across a crevice that continued across the bottom of the sea far out past the underwater Atlantic Ocean mountain chain. When the Vikings went there a few thousand years later, they established Europe's first parliament down in that crevice. When I visited, I learned that the Icelandic had discovered the trunk of a tree stiffened in the lava that had poured out back then, and carbon dating showed that the crevice had opened at around 3000 BC.

Something happened with the climate at that time too. Through pollen analysis, botanists have found that this was when rivers and lakes in all of North Africa started to dry up and when both the Sahara and Mesopotamia changed into desert landscapes.

Something also happened in the Pacific Ocean. Today the whole world talks about the El Niño current, which appears at regular intervals off South America's coast and causes storms with both flooding and periods of drought over the whole world. It had raged terribly in the village of Túcume a few years before I came to start the excavations in the area of the pyramids. When we stopped our digging, Daniel Sandweiss continued excavating further back through time on the coast of Peru. He and his American colleagues found remnants of a hitherto unknown fishing population that had subsisted on shellfish and ocean fishing along the coast for more than 10,000 years. By studying the presence of tropical shells in deep refuse mounds, they could reconstruct the occurrence of definite El Niño years through the last 5,000 years, as far back as about 3000 BC. Before that there was no El Niño current. For totally unknown reasons it was at that time that tropical masses of water first started to cascade down the coast of Peru, and this influenced the climate of the whole planet.

Modern researchers talk about approximate datings when we talk about the millennia before Christ, because our own accounting of time does not go back any further. Christians count year 0 from the birth of Christ, while Muslims count year 0 from Mohammed's flight to Mecca, which converted into the Western calendar becomes year 622 AD. The Buddhists start their time with the death of Buddha, which the West knows as 544 BC. But on either side of the globe, the ancestors of the Indians and Mayans had a calendar system based on astronomical observations so accurate that it forces us to wonder and reconsider history. Both systems seem to have started independently of one another in the same century, 3,100 years before Christ in terms of the Western calendar.

Then what happened?

The main interest of the Mayans was astronomy and history. The Europeans managed to burn their books of hieroglyphics that were written on paper, but the Mayans had also carved countless astronomical observations and mathematical calculations in stone on their temple walls and monuments. And they had calculated that one year consisted of 365.2329 days. This figure only gives us one day too few every 5,000 years, and it is 8.64 seconds closer to the truth than our present calendar. It then becomes interesting to note that the Mayans started their account of time with 4 Ahau 2 Cumhu, which when converted is 12 August 3113 BC.

The Hindus, who are the rightful heirs to the civilization in the Indus valley, also kept meticulous records of time. The historian A. Z. Chandra writes: 'Arybhatta, the greatest astronomer of his time, was in activity around the year 499 according to our calendar, and his calculation of the beginning of the Kali era was midnight after Ujjain, which ends after 17 February, year 3102 before Christ.' That is only eleven years after the Mayans started to count days, months and years.

The Hindus also have another tradition about the oldest eras of time. Converted to our time, it lets Brhaspatrikaka start in the year 3116 BC. And that is only three years before the Mayan's calendar starts.

Not only do the Sumerians start their history by telling us about a catastrophe of nature. Recordings of a flood that destroyed most of humanity are found in the introductions of the histories of both the Aztecs and the Incas. It is also repeated in the same version on every island throughout Polynesia. The only written text about America's discovery that escaped the fires is the Quiche-Mayan's sacred history book *Popul Vuh*, which was copied in Guatemala before the original disappeared. To me it is like a small piece of a lost world history in fairy-tale form. The god of heaven, Huracán, was not satisfied with the first people he created, for they were like wooden dolls, without hearts. He repented and sent a horrible flood as punishment: 'a flood was called forth by the Heart of Heaven; a large flood he created, that fell down over the heads of the wooden figures . . . This was to punish them because they had not thought about their mother or their father who was the Heart of Heaven, Huracán. And for that reason the earth's face darkened, and a black rain started falling, day and night.'

The ascension of kings in the culture of Guatemala starts with the leader of the group who stepped ashore on the Atlantic coast after the flood and in the dusk moved inward through the country in search for a new residence.

Now we're back to the Atlantic Ocean; now you can't avoid the legend of Atlantis.

It has been misused so much that it frightens scientists. But it would be just as unwise to discard it without analysing how it originated as it would to take on board without question all the versions that have appeared in the wake of Plato. In typical Hellenic style, in 400 BC, Plato spoke for historical figures such as his countrymen, Solon and Socrates. And Solon described his visit to Egypt, where the priests at the temple library in Sais mocked the Greeks for their historical ignorance. They excused the Greeks, since they had lost their own scholars when a terrible tidal wave raced in over the Mediterranean, and the Greeks and their neighbours were damaged the most. The only people who escaped were the shepherds in the mountains, and the Greeks had to rebuild their culture from its infancy. And then Solon learned that there had been an island in the Atlantic Ocean, outside the entrance to the Mediterranean. The priests told him that they had learned from their papyrus scrolls that the city of Athens once fought off a great power from that island that had come into the Mediterranean to attack the cities in Europe. And then we get the Egyptian version of the flood, in Solon's words: 'In a later time there came earthquakes and tidal waves of unusual violence, and during one horrible day and night all their warriors were swallowed by the earth, and the island Atlantis was in the same way swallowed into the ocean and disappeared. That is the reason that the ocean in those parts even today is unavailable, with silt obstructions just beneath the surface, remnants of the sunken island.'

No one knows exactly what happened about 5,000 years ago to cause civilizations the world over to use it as a starting gun for both history and the accounting of time. As a contribution to this riddle, the first project to be financed with FERCO funds from the pyramids on Tenerife, will be an international conference with participants from all fields at the University of Maine. The subject will be 'Climatic and cultural changes around 3000 BC'.

Maybe in the future science will find out more about the past so that we stop running about like wooden dolls, and think more about staying friends with our mother and father, who is the Heart of Heaven.

15

The Ocean and the Sky

I was sitting all the way up in the Northwest of America looking out
across the Pacific Ocean. All the way up there where Asia and
America bend together so that Siberia and Alaska almost meet.
Waves from the Japanese current rolled amicably over the broad,
white, sandy beach and up to my shoes, to where I was sitting on a
huge piece of driftwood, thinking about life.

The circle has ended, I thought, almost sadly.

The second circle. The first had ended with the celebration of the
Kon-Tiki expedition's fiftieth anniversary down in Peru. But now a
year had passed and I was back with the Northwest Indians, the
island people off the coast of British Columbia where I had started
looking for the Polynesian's closest relatives when I had been interrupted by the war that swallowed all of Europe.

To me, it was up here that the last immigrants to Polynesia had
chopped timber for their enormous double canoes and started their
journey with the currents and the wind down in Hawaii, where they
started the conquering of all the Pacific islands that were already
populated by raft voyagers from Peru.

Fifty years ago I had been accused of creating waves in a teapot.

At my feet, waves were still rippling in, nature's own creation. The Pacific Ocean lay there like a hemisphere of its own, occupying as much space on the surface of the earth as all the other oceans and continents together. Unaffected by all theories, the ocean current on this hemisphere rotated according to the laws of nature in two enormous circles that almost met on either side of the equator. South of the equator, the ocean ran counter-clockwise, helping seafarers from Peru to Polynesia. Up here the ocean rotated with the clock, helping everything that floated with the Japanese current on a return trip out to the same islands. I thought of the two glass balls that I had just seen at the home of one of the Indians up here, floats from fishing nets close to Japan's coast that the son in the house had found on the beach.

With Jacqueline and my American colleague, the archaeologist Donald Ryan, I had come to British Columbia to gather up the loose ends from my first visit to British Columbia. The reception in the scientific circles in Victoria and the university city of Vancouver was as sincere as it had been the last time, not the least at the Royal British Colombian Museum, where the present director was an anthropologist, not a zoologist. He invited my small group out to dinner after having shown us around the impressive exhibition halls in the new building. It was odd to revisit many of the artefacts that had been stored in cartons in the basement the last time I was here. This museum had not forgotten that, in 1939, I sat in the director's office with books and stone axes and claimed that the Polynesians had stopped off here.

On our journey further up on Vancouver Island and into the heart of the Kwakiutl Indians' island kingdom, two of Canada's foremost experts on the original coastal population came with us, anthropologist Jerome Cybulski and archaeologist Bjørn Simonsen. In addition, we were accompanied by the Kwakiutl Indian, Stan Wallas. Jerome was employed at the National Museum in Quebec, and had such a good relationship to the original coastal population – who now called themselves 'First Nation' – that they let him examine the skeletons of their forefathers. Bjørn was the archaeological inspector for the authorities and the museum in Victoria, because, better than anyone else, he knew all the tribes and every island and cove along the coast. Stan was an enthusiastic amateur archaeologist and Jerome's invaluable assistant.

Jacqueline and I were so tired during the long car trip up Vancouver Island that we could barely open our eyes whenever there was a bear on the road or we stopped to look at rock carvings or a magnificent view. Following our arrival from Europe we had an incredibly hectic week because I had squeezed in visits to four universities in the United States. First, clad in an academic cap and gown as the main speaker and honorary doctor at the annual graduation for 6,000 students at the University of Maine. Then with a new cap and gown for yet another honorary title received in pouring rain in front of thousands of umbrellas at Hartford University. The day after that I gave a lecture at the Peabody Museum at Yale University about the role of the ocean in the development of civilization.

The following day Don Ryan waited for us at Seattle airport to drive us up to the Kwakiutl Indians. He came from the Pacific Lutheran University in Tacoma, where I was going to give the annual graduation speech on the way back home. All we wanted to do today was to cross the border and get to the Indians who were the goal of the journey.

The great forest covered us on all sides, enveloping us completely when we crept to bed in the tiny Pioneer Inn at the northern tip of Vancouver Island. This was old Kwakiutl territory, and Stan would assume the lead here. He was staying with his own family at the new Kwakiutl reservation, Quatsino, nearby, but the next morning he met us before sunrise to take us to old Quatsino, where he had been born. He brought us on board a large and fast motor boat, and then we took off at full speed.

It is hard to imagine that Norway has even more fjords and islands along its coast than British Columbia. On the chart Quatsino Sound, with all of its tributaries, looked like a rock carving of a man with long extended arms. The head was resting against an elevation just by the eastern coast, while the long narrow body with its legs covered to the groin ended in the open Pacific Ocean on the western coast. We went to the head section first and had an early breakfast in the former coal-mining port of Coal Harbor. After this, during our whole long trip out to the ocean we saw no traces of people other than piles of shells at earlier settlements and a few abandoned buildings.

One of these was the former schoolhouse, a single forlorn remainder of the original Indian village of Quatsino, where Stan had grown up as the son of the chief. Not a trace remained of the other dwellings. I felt a lump in my throat as we tramped our way through bushes and arrived at the burial ground at the edge of the woods. Most of the area was covered by rotten remnants of old lumber and fresh bear droppings. But it was thrilling to see a newer group of well-preserved grave monuments shaped like huge fish or swimming whales. They were carved in wood and painted like figures on totem poles, though placed individually on top of poles stuck in the ground. Only one of them was a wolf, with its head lifted and seemingly howling at the moon. On the mainland the motifs carved along the totem poles were mostly animals of the forest, bear and beaver and eagles. Here animals of the ocean dominated. All of them bore garlands of recently picked flowers.

I asked no questions. This was the resting place of relatives who had not yet been forgotten.

'These are not pictures of idols,' Stan said calmly. 'People who come from the outside think that totem poles were worshipped, or meant to scare enemies away, but we believe in the same invisible god as you do. These animals are the symbols of our families. The tall totem poles relate the history of a family.'

We ate a picnic lunch on the beach and went over to another spit of land. We found a rotten plank roof, and when we looked underneath it we saw a well-preserved skull gaping up at us. We touched nothing, since Jerome would have to request the permission of the Indian council before we could take samples for DNA analysis. Later we took the boat out to a wonderful little island, and in the distance Bjørn caught sight of something shining white in a pile of shells that had been left behind by a prehistoric settlement. Even Stan had never been here before. The tiny island was covered with forest and underbrush, and as we were making our way under branches and over huge rocks we heard a cry from Bjørn. He had found an open grave with three skeletons and the remnants of old lumber under a ledge on a small hill. One of the skulls was as white as chalk and well preserved, but of a shape that was not granted to ordinary people. These coastal Indians were masters of many arts, and the quality of their work would fit right in with our modern taste. As in many other ancient cultures, the skulls of their own newly born infants were sometimes artificially enlarged, but in no museum have I ever seen a skull this long and slim; the beauty could almost have been wearing a stocking over the head. It felt wrong to leave an artefact like this behind without the care of relatives or museum curators.

Later, Stan brought us to his home, a spacious wooden house in the new Quatsino reservation. A few of the family's beautiful women transported my thoughts away from the surrounding pine forest and over to the palm-studded islands further south in the same ocean. On the wall there were pictures of the older generation. The grandfather, Jimmy Jumbo, and his wife, were both Kwakiutl from Quatsino, and a great-uncle bearing a bark cape could easily have been a Maori chief.

We were flying further north in the Kwakiutl Indian's archipelago in a small chartered plane, and when we parted Stan inscribed a small book and presented it to me – *Kwakiutl Legends*, as told to

P. Whitaker by Stan's own father, Chief James Wallas. I thought I was finished with the legend of the Deluge, but here it showed up again in even more realistic terms.

Up here, farthest away from the Sumerian Empire, it was not a king but the whole population that had sensed an approaching flood from the ocean. They bound all their canoes together with cross-poles and filled them with dried meat, fish, shells, berries and plenty of water in wooden containers. When the warning cry came from the look-out and they saw the flood close in like a wall, they hurried into their canoes. The flood lifted them up to the level of the hillside, and in the ensuing chaos they had to fight their way clear of uprooted trees and sections of their own wooden houses that were crashing into the canoes. When the ocean retreated, they ran around on all the elevations calling out in the hope of finding survivors. Some canoes had torn loose and either disappeared in the storm or ended up other places where new tribes were founded.

I may have been more attentive than other researchers when listening to what the so-called primitive peoples are trying to tell us in their way, because I have never met any who are that much more primitive than we are. After the old man on Fatu-Hiva told me how the god-king Tiki had come there, and I learned that the Aymara people at Lake Titicaca had also told the first Spaniards that he had come from there, I have listened carefully to the stories that have been passed down by people without a written culture.

Ever since I suspected that the archipelago along the coast of British Columbia had been a stopover for Asians before they ended up as conquerors of Polynesia, I have had a suspicion that the coastal Indians up here might also have something important to relate. When my new friend Stan gave me the book about his forefathers' oral traditions, I already felt on the first page that he had given me the key to a gold mine.

I had always suspected that the Kwakiutl Indians had been visited by a representative of the same wandering god who played a leading role as a bearer of culture from Mexico to Peru and out into the Pacific Ocean. The Kwakiutl Indians remembered him as *Kane-akeluh* or *Kane-akwea*; Stan pronounced the name *Kane-kelak*. The book was filled with stories about this god and his creations, and how he impressed the Quatsino tribe when he and his brother landed on the beach in Sand Neck about 2,000 years ago. He performed his miracles with a two-headed snake that he wore as a belt around his waist and sometimes used as a sling.

Folk tales? Myths? Certainly. But the sling has only been found in certain areas, and it is this weapon that accompanied the bearer of culture from Mexico to Peru. In pre-Incan art along the coast of Peru he was depicted as a seafarer and always had a two-headed snake as a belt around his waist.

I also concluded that the Kwakiutl tribe's wandering *Kane-akwea*, who had the sun as a representative, had to be the Polynesian's *Kane-akea*, god of light. *Akea* or *Atea* was the highest deity and the word for 'light' in all of Polynesia. In addition, I knew that *kane* was remembered as an extremely important human god in all of Polynesia, but especially on Hawaii, where he was so significant that the sun was called 'the resting place of Kane'. And the sun, known as *ra* in most of Polynesia, was called *La* on Hawaii while it was called *na-la* by Dawson's Kwakiutl tribe.

I had all this stored in my mind, like folk tales in science when we said farewell to Stan, and Jacqueline and I crept into the small plane with Don and the two Canadian archaeologists.

We took an alternative route, flying just above the treetops. We were on our way further up the coast, over the uninhabited Hakai Strait that was the final destination of our journey, over the Bella Coola valley where I had lived when the war broke out in Europe, then skimmed the tops of the waves and landed in calm waters in the fjord outside Bella Bella, the main centre of the surviving Kwakiutl tribes.

We were expected, and a group of representatives for the Elders welcomed us by the dock and brought us to their traditional long-house in the middle of the village, where we were to attend a meeting with dialogue and refreshments. The outside of the huge wooden building was decorated with totem poles and gigantic wall paintings of the tribe's animal symbols in typical Kwakiutl style, but just inside the door there were rows of fax machines and computers. The rest of the wall space in the large hall was packed with appointed men and women from the Kwakiutl reservations.

It was an unforgettable meeting, with one leg in the past and the other firmly placed on contemporary soil. At least half of the faces that were studying me, while I studied them, took my mind right back to Polynesia. They too were all aware of what I had observed in 1940 and what Captains Cook and Vancouver had seen as soon as they arrived here from Polynesia: there was a striking physical resemblance between the 'First Nation' people up here and those who had greeted the Europeans on the other islands further south in the same ocean. Everyone mentioned this, and since my last visit tourism and communication systems had had a visible effect. By now the local population had visited Hawaii, and they themselves had received visitors from Hawaii, Samoa and New Zealand. Guests were welcomed as relatives, and they felt as if they were among their own.

The dialogue in the longhouse proved that the Kwakiutl people still had their gift of speech. Their ancestors did not have a written language, but they were renowned for their powerful oratory, which was far superior to most other nations, and their professional speakers were highly respected in their society. The participants sat along the walls and heard about the background to my visit with composure and dignity. Their well-placed comments were made in the same spirit of composure, and they came from both men and women, from both sides of the hall. Everyone had something to offer that they had learned by questioning the elders in the family. It struck me that the people in the coastal reservations had woken up to a new life after a long period of hibernation. When I was with the Bella Coola Indians the time before, only the bear hunter Clayton Mack had a canoe, a purchased canoe in red canvas. Now the young men on the reservations were learning how to carve canoes from cedar logs from older masters, decorating them with colourful carvings in the traditional style of their ancestors.

Frank, a young boy who had been kept isolated on a little island for a year because he had stolen and abused drugs, had turned into a wonderful man. It was he who led the youth of the 'First Nation' along the whole coast, organizing canoe races and reviving the best of their traditions. Later we also met the Polynesian movie producer, Karen Williams, who had come to film the first canoe race. Her father was Maori and her mother came from Tonga, and she had become so convinced that this was her ancestors' homeland that she had stayed behind to film cultural parallels.

Ever since I sat on a dock in the neighbouring valley of Bella Coola with my oldest son Thor, who was then two years old, I had dreamed of finding my way out of the long and narrow fjord, and further into the mouth of the ocean all the way out in the Hakai Strait. That was sixty years ago, but we were now about to try to land a seaplane there, straight out from the Bella Coola fjord. When the gathering in the longhouse heard where we were going, three of the oldest were so eager to join us that we had to leave Don and Jerome behind on the reservation while two old men and an even older woman clambered into the plane and fastened their seatbelts.

In the grey weather and wind we danced our way over the hillside toward the Bella Coola valley. The pilot took his bearings and flew right out until we saw the shimmering light of the Hakai Strait between the larger islands. We descended without changing course, and with forested wilderness on both sides we flew along the whole Hakai Strait toward the open ocean. If anyone had fled the Bella Coola valley, which was closed in by mountains, this would have been the best route to the sea.

And that was precisely the reason for this trip. The Bella Coola valley carried on along the fjord between steep mountains far inland, and it was the largest and most verdant valley along the entire coast. Once, Salish Indians, strangers from the south, had managed to force themselves right into the heart of Kwakiutl territory and conquer this valley, thereby splitting Kwakiutl territory in two. One of the essential problems in the ethnology of the Northwest coast was how this could have happened. Most likely they had avoided detection from the coast by forcing themselves into the valley from the inland side. But what had happened to those who had to flee the valley?

I hoped to find traces of earlier settlements along the uninhabited Hakai Strait. With the three elders well secured, we flew just above the tops of the waves, with Calvert Island on one side and the two islands Nalau and Hecate on the other.

The pilot landed in a calm cove protected by a small protruding headland where the Hakai Strait opened to the Pacific Ocean itself.

It was a peculiar experience. Except for Bella Bella, we had not seen a single house on the whole flight. We flew over an eternity of forested islands spread out like pieces of a puzzle on a mirror. But on the spot where I had hoped to find some trace of a prehistoric settlement, there was a newly built house. A single man lived here and he was just as surprised as I was by our unexpected meeting. He was from Pitcairn in Polynesia, where all of the inhabitants are descendants of the mutineers on the *Bounty*. I had been there with my expedition ship after the Easter Island expedition. At that time I brought the whole male population of the island on a two-day trip to the uninhabited and forested island Henderson. The goal was to find lumber for wood-carving, which was their major source of income. This man here was house-sitting, temporarily. The house had been built for tourism, but because of the storms it was closed until the summer.

I was still feeling disappointed when I saw a giant tree that had toppled over just by the house wall. All of its roots were showing, and beneath the turf, which had opened like a lid on a treasure chest, something white appeared: a huge kitchen refuse heap filled with shells. The new house had been built on top of an ancient settlement, one the archaeologists had not discovered. With our three aging guests we climbed through underbrush, struggling over rocks, between gigantic trees, and finally through a forest opening to the sea. Here, we were confronted by a wide beach, the widest and most beautiful sandy beach I have ever seen in America. It was the outward face of the Hakai Strait.

We sat down on some enormous logs of Canadian driftwood. It was a powerful sight and a great moment. Here, the old people said, the 'First Nation' people from along the whole coastline had gathered annually for celebrations and mask dances in the olden days. One had heard from his grandmother that there had been so many people that when they arrived in their canoes from north and south they could hear the drums playing far out into the ocean. They told their stories in such vivid detail that they must have taken part in some of the celebrations themselves when they were young. We learned that beyond the mouth of the Strait the offshore wind and the south-west current were so strong sometimes that they even drew modern fishing boats off course and they had to be picked up by rescue vessels from Victoria.

We listened and listened, and as proof of the wealth of the ocean the two old seamen brought us over to a smoothly polished wall of rock that looked like a side curtain flanking one side of the beach. Vertical fissures in the cliff were filled with live starfish, colourful sea anemones and other live glittering creatures that belong beneath the sea and were hanging there decoratively while waiting for the tide to come in again. I felt as if I were in a gigantic theatre. Stepping out from the forest was like opening a curtain and suddenly finding oneself on a stage, blinded by the limelight and hearing the sound of the surf from the rows of waving benches in the great blue theatre of the ocean. And then my eyesight took over and all the rows of benches were nothing but empty waves. And we were only a small group of people sitting on drift logs feeling that this theatre was ours. But those of us from the outside world had arrived too late for the great show itself.

As we sat there, I thought I heard a small theatre prompter.

You feel more at home here, sitting and listening to the quiet or to three aging Kwakiutl Indians, than when you yourself are at the lectern, wearing a black cape and a cap with a tassel . . .

One learns more from listening than speaking, I thought. And both the wind and the people who continue to live close to nature still have much to tell us which we cannot hear within university walls.

A scientist has to distinguish between legends and myths, and make use of both. Up until the last generation, the legend about the bearer of culture, Kane Akwea, had been the most important one here on this coast. When he reappears with the same name as the ancestor of the royal family in Polynesia, the legend breathes a spirit into the archaeologists' skeletons and the ethnologists' stone axes. It does not become a myth just because Kane in his own time was looked upon as a deity in human form. The Pharaohs, the Incas, the Emperor of Japan and the wandering god Odin of the Vikings were also regarded that way.

That Kane went to heaven and ended on the sun is a myth. But when the myth is identical for the worshippers of Kane among the Kwakiutl people and also on the closest Hawaiian islands, then it is science to consider the myth as a cultural parallel in the grand puzzle of migration routes in the Pacific Ocean.

Home again in the old house on Tenerife, the aku-aku had become so familiar that it came straight into the living room as soon as I lay down to collect my thoughts after a day's work. Jacqueline had turned on the television, but instead of interesting news about the conflict in the Middle East bomb tests in Pakistan, it was showing the World Cup. I closed my eyes demonstratively, but suddenly Jacqueline jumped out of the chair and cheered. Norway had beaten Brazil 2–1.

People had become completely crazy at the end of the twentieth century. The whole world talked about soccer. Tens of thousands sat on rows of benches with painted faces and screamed while the ball was kicked back and forth by someone running around on the grass.

Soccer is not for you?

I've never been interested, but now I'm starting to wonder.

The tiny voice was persistent. I, who supported the UN and One World and everything that represented peaceful coexistence between nations, had I not seen that here people had finally made something happen that was not controlled by politicians? People from all nations met and played together for peaceful entertainment without a thought of politics or weapons. Here, in a healthy sporting conflict, a small nation from Africa could compete with the superpowers without the millions needed for an arms race or a race out into space.

I should have kept in touch with what was going on. I began to understand when I was in the centre of the arena at the Lillehammer Olympics, welcoming all the nations to the opening ceremony. It cannot be denied that ping-pong and soccer reach more people and can do more for the sake of peace than political slogans or a five-year agreement between the United States and Cuba about archaeological co-operation.

But it is the past that interests you the most.

No – the future. But it is too soon to study that. We must not mistake that for the present. The present is not real. Grab it and it's gone. It is a short yet eternal transformation from what has been to what will be. We can't build on it. We are all on explorations into the unknown, and by looking backward in the wake of our own trail we can see the course we are taking.

The most important thing we can learn from the past is that no earlier civilization has survived. And the larger the pyramids and temples and statues they build in honour of their god or themselves, the harder was the fall. Most of them have been so completely eradicated that it required archaeologists to bring them into the light again. Neither the sun god nor the creative power behind the Big Bang smiles upon the huge buildings or powerful armies of mankind. They smile at the civilizations who respect their own creation and who show appreciation for it.

Where people have constructed great buildings they have also fought the greatest wars. When the archaeologist excavates to the bottom of the ruins of an extinct civilization, more often than not he will find the remnants of an even older one beneath it. And we would be wise to note that the most advanced culture is rarely the one at the top layer.

While civilizations come and go, primitive people live on as before in the wilderness.

Yes, and shoot at one another with bows and arrows. They have lived on this planet just as long as we have, and deep within ourselves we have changed just as little. We who think we have made enormous strides forward, have, at best, done so periodically between world wars, by changing the environment, not ourselves. We who are building today's civilization are so advanced that we can see through walls and roofs with the aid of a metal pole, we can change everything from the ozone layer and weather and wind to the life that pulsed before us in the oceans and the forests. We also attempt to improve our physique with gymnastics and a healthy diet, and at best we manage to maintain the muscles and the health our first forefathers were given by what we call the wilderness.

As so often before, when the television was turned off and Jacqueline grabbed a book from the shelf, I remain on the sofa, thinking. For my whole life I have tried to wheedle the secret out of the groups of people who smile the most. The smile is a gift of the god that comes from within. And we people have something strange within us that science cannot dissect because it disappears before the autopsy occurs. Some sort of receiver and transmitter with different frequencies than the television but also able to pass through walls and roofs, and controlling things such as instinct and intuition and conscience.

We have inherited certain things from the animal kingdom. As long as the frequency of life is turned on, every species is instructed in how to use its sensory horns, its wings, legs or genitals. We call it instinct and intuition. But mankind is born with responsibility for his actions; we call this a conscience. And since the time of Adam we have had the possibility of two-way communication, and those who still master this art send our wishes for advice and help. Civilized people believe they have to build churches and temples in order to become closer and to be heard better by the creator of heaven and earth. But when I think of what I have learned from those we call heathens, I often get the feeling that their transmitters and receivers were in good working order long before we taught them to believe that the creator of nature preferred being indoors.

When we left the longhouse in Bella Bella, a Kwakiutl Indian pressed a small pamphlet about totem poles into my hand. The Kwakiutl chief Mum-Xiou, whose Christian name was James Sewid, wrote: 'Our ancestors have a deep philosophy of life, and it is with their faith and laws that we have been raised. They saw the beauty in the nature that surrounded them with all its wealth, and tried to capture some of all this beauty in their daily life, in their legends, dances and art. My people believed in an almighty power that created everything, and they were in awe and filled with reverence at the greatness of creation.'

Jacqueline had a private hideaway for her favourite literature and old Indian art that she had collected through her life and that bears witness to the fact that, in most respects, we all like the same things. I asked her to find one of her books that reveals much of our joint view on life: *Touch the Earth: A Self-Portrait of the Indians' Existence.*

In it, the plains Indian Tatanga Mani from the Stoney tribe in

North America wrote: 'Oh yes, I went to a white man's school, I learned to read school books, newspapers and the Bible. But as time went on, I discovered that this wasn't enough. Civilized people become too dependent on their own printed pages. I turn to the Great Spirit's book, which is his whole creation. You can read a lot from that book if you study nature. You know that if you put all your books out into the sun and let rain and snow and insects wear them down, there will be nothing left. But the Great Spirit has given you and me the possibility to study in the university of nature, the forests, rivers, mountains and animals, ourselves included.'

Our Lord was there before the Big Bang and before Buddha, Jesus and Mohammed were born, I thought. But civilized people see nothing but roofs and walls and indoor television screens and outdoor traffic jams. How can we believe that anyone has created us when all we see around us are things we have created ourselves?

The Sioux Indian Ohiyesa tried to teach us some of what took place deep within his people: 'In an Indian's life there was only one unavoidable duty – the duty of prayer – the daily recognition of the Invisible and Eternal. His daily time of prayer was more important to him than his daily food. He awakened at dawn, put on his moccasins and went down to the edge of the water. Here he either threw a few handfuls of clean, clear water into his face, or dove in. After the bath he stood facing the dawn, and stared toward the sun as it rose over the horizon while he prayed his prayer without a word. His wife could go and pray by herself, but never with him. Every soul had to meet the morning sun, new aroma of soil and the Great Silence alone.

'At any time during the course of the day, when the red hunter caught sight of something that was strikingly beautiful or captivating – a black thunder cloud with the rainbow arched in glowing colours over the mountain, a foaming waterfall in a green canyon, an endless prairie blushing in the sunset – he would stop for a moment and stand as if in prayer. He saw no reason to reserve the seventh day as a holy day, because to him all days belonged to God.'

I also think that the sun is a well-chosen symbol for everyone to fix their eyes upon in prayer to an invisible Creator – not the least to those who neither know, nor understand why the Christians pray to the cross. The Incas, for example, directed their prayers to the highest, invisible Viracocha, who was represented in the sky by the sun, *inti*, and on earth by the Inca peoples' own priestly king. What has made an impression on me is that the Incas only looked upon the sun as the highest forefather of all life here on earth, while they called the ocean Mama-Ocllo, Mother Ocean.

And that is what we have come back to even in modern research. The sun fertilized the ocean with its rays and created life in the ocean. Fertilized particles of salt and minerals that floated about without genes or chromosomes on the wavy surface of the ocean. The first child of the sun in the ocean became the ancestors of all life on earth. St Francis of Assisi touched upon the same acknowledgement in the European Middle Ages, but it was in the wake of Darwin that modern science finally admitted that animals and human beings had the same progenitors with a visible ancestor that still lights up the sky. The halo around the head of a saint is no more than a visible inheritance.

Does that mean that man's forefathers came down from the trees?

I don't think so. Personally I think they went back to the edge of the water. If they had first managed to find safety in the trees, they would never have gone down to the ground again voluntarily. All the wild animals were already in place on the ground. As biologists say, all the niches in the ecosystem were occupied. If we had come to the world on a branch up in the trees, we would have remained there and groomed our tails and our climbing feet, rather than exposing ourselves to everything that ran and jumped on the ground with horns and claws and sharp teeth. We would have been stampeded to death on the animal trails, and back in the bush we would have wished for fur coats. I know from my own experience that in the jungle, the treetops are where one finds fruit and nuts. Hardly anything grows on the ground because the sun's rays cannot break through.

We were born naked – except for hair – to be able to wade with our heads above water. We stood upright with totally free arm movements in order to be able to dive and swim away from enemy attacks on land. We let climbing monkeys and gorillas share the jungle with the wild animals of the forest, and kept to the beaches and rivers where we could jump in, and where there was an endless amount of food reserved for the last of nature's children. The table was set at the water's edge and waited for the fingers of the wading ape. Shells and shellfish of all sorts, cleverly hidden behind lids and locked doors and in endless amounts.

Do you believe in creation?

One cannot avoid that. One cannot avoid the conclusion that there must have been something almighty behind the Big Bang that managed to create everything from nothing. There had to have been something supernatural that made the universe natural for us who were placed on a sterile planet by the rays of the sun.

Even in *On the Origin of the Species* Darwin admitted that just thinking that something as complex as the eye could have its origins in natural development would have been totally absurd.

Do you believe in God?

I believe in the same god as Abraham, Jesus and Mohammed. The Indians' Great Spirit. I think it would be a tragedy for the civilized part of the world if churches, synagogues and mosques were to close their doors. Not everyone can manage two-way communication with his inner being in the noise of traffic jams and TV programmes in a modern urban society. We need something to remind us of another dimension in our existence.

Are you Christian?

I am a Christian if Christianity began with the living Jesus of Nazareth and not others who came after him. I am a Christian if it is enough to see him as the most important person in history and the greatest thinker. I believe he had more two-way contact with conscience, intelligence and intuition than anyone else since the possibility of such contact was infused into the human brain.

But do you believe in God, the Trinity?

I don't think that God can be counted. One cannot count anything other than the tangible – apostles, popes and Bibles. Abraham did not count his God, nor did Mohammed, and certainly not Jesus, who protested when someone reverently addressed him as Father. There is only one Father, he said, and that is our common father in Heaven. We are all brothers.

Do you believe in the Bible?

I have read it as an immensely interesting collection of well-preserved scriptures from ancient times, not all equally valuable today. I have been most attentive to the first chapters of both the New and the Old Testaments. The story of creation begins with the light and the ocean and it is chronologically correct as we see it today, from fish and fowl to animals on land and human beings at the end. This could not have been a coincidence, and must be a result of sound ingenuity or keen intuition.

Do you believe in the Holy Spirit?

I think it is the name the church chose for what I call conscience. I envision it as a form of two-way contact with one's own inner being. Science does not have a better word for something so strange and important, something we all have that no one can find.

Do you believe in the future?

We create the future ourselves, now, while we still have time. Science has advanced to the point where it can dissect nature and its atoms. It would be smart if we learned to put it all correctly back together again as well, before nature itself takes drastic steps to save itself and us. If there were something I could wish for in the future, it would be that there would be an end to all the conflicts between the different religions, and that everyone who believes in a creative force behind nature would use intelligence, conscience, intuition, the Holy Spirit and everything that is in our collective power to get advice and help to preserve nature before we completely disturb the great day of rest.

Do you believe in me?

He who does not believe in himself will get nowhere.

Appendix

The Red Thread

What a life! I am completely confused. Do you yourself understand what has driven you?

Others have also asked me that. I can only answer by referring to my expeditions. They have created a red thread throughout my unsettled life.

It started with the **Marquesas Islands** in 1937–8. The journey had two goals. As an experimental philosopher I wanted to try to return to mankind's original existence to look at civilization from the perspective of an outsider. As a cautious scientist I wanted to study the beginning of biological life on islands that once had risen lifeless from the bottom of the sea. The philosophical answer was that man cannot return to the natural state, but neither can he continue safely without planning the course of civilization. The scientific answer was that wind and sea currents were the key to the riddle of all life on the Polynesian islands.

I went to **British Columbia** in 1939 to search for traces left by seafarers who had sailed from South-East Asia in the early Stone Age and not reached Polynesia before the beginning of our own millennium. I found that the North-West American coastal Indians filled all the requirements for the missing link between Asia and Polynesia.

The ***Kon-Tiki*** expedition started in 1947 to refute the dogma that South American balsa rafts could not transport people and cultivated plants live over the ocean from Peru to Polynesia. I proved that the balsa raft could handle the voyage and was more seaworthy than any pre-European vessel, and that the Polynesians might be right in their claim that their ancestors found an earlier population on the islands.

I organized the **Galapagos** expedition in 1952–3 to bring professional archaeologists to a group of islands that no one believed had been visited by people before the arrival of the Europeans. We found shards of pots that specialists at the American Museum of Natural History identified as the remnants of at least 131 different pre-Incan jars from Ecuador and Peru.

I brought a team of archaeologists to **Easter Island** in 1955–6 to search for possible traces of raft voyagers from Peru who could have been there before the Polynesians. We found traces of older civilizations that were previously unknown, suggesting the possibility of a South American point of origin. Excavations and legends on the island also sparked my interest in the importance of the reed ship in the spreading of ancient culture.

I sailed from Morocco with the reed ship ***Ra I*** in 1969 to discount the dogma that papyrus reed could only be used on rivers because the reed would sink within two weeks. We found that papyrus ships could float for months if the reed bundles were only properly tied.

I sailed with ***Ra II*** in 1970 from Morocco to Barbados to show that if a papyrus ship was properly built, it could cross the Atlantic Ocean. We proved that the oldest known form of vessel in North Africa and the Mediterranean area could have reached America just as easily as a Viking ship or a caravel.

The *Tigris* expedition in 1977–8 was, like the Ra journeys, an experiment with both the crew and the vessel. I wanted to show that even with cramped space and stress, peaceful co-operation was possible between people of different colour, nationality and faith, and that Mesopotamian berdi reed was just as good for boat building as papyrus, and that when harvested in the right season berdi reed had a floating ability that would have given the Sumerian boat-builders the possibility of visiting both the Indus valley and the Red Sea on the same voyage.

The expeditions to the **Maldives** in 1983 and 1984 were organized to confirm a suspicion that ancient seafarers had been in contact with remote coral reefs in the middle of the Indian Ocean long before Vasco da Gama and the Arabs. Our excavations showed that before the Arabs discovered the group of islands in 1153 the Buddhists had built stupas on the ruins of earlier Hindu temples. From even earlier times we found stone sculptures of unknown seafarers with elegant moustaches and prolonged ears, like those on Easter Island.

The expeditions to **Easter Island** in 1986, 1987 and 1988 had two main goals. We wanted to experiment with the theory held by the Czechoslovakian engineer Pavel Pavel that the Easter Island statues were moved in an upright position, as the island dwellers claimed when they said that they 'walked'. In addition we wanted to reintroduce the Easter Island *toromiro* tree, a species that would have been extinct on our planet if I had not brought the last seeds from a dying tree on Easter Island in 1956 and had them planted in the botanical garden in Gothenburg. With the aid of a rope tied to the top and the bottom of a statue, a handful of Easter Island residents managed to wriggle a statue forward in an upright position. The first *toromiro* trees we planted did not survive, but the species was saved and later reintroduced by other seeds from Gothenburg.

The archaeological project in **Túcume** in Peru in 1988–93 was organized in co-operation with the Peruvian authorities and the Kon-Tiki Museum to search among the pyramids for possible proof that seafaring in Peru did not begin with the Spanish conquest. We found proof that the coastal population in Peru had based its subsistence on ocean fishing and ocean trade from the earliest settlements until Inca Yupanqi conquered the coast with his mountain Indians, three generations before the arrival of the Spanish. We also found clear links to Easter Island in the form of reed ships crewed by mythical men with bird heads, and symbolic motifs that otherwise have only been seen in religious art on Easter Island.

I arrived on the Canary Islands in 1990 and remained. I came to explore the step pyramids in **Guimar** on Tenerife, which people thought were piles of stones left by the first Spaniards to have cleared the ground. I found that they were astronomically oriented temple pyramids built of quarry stone from a dried flow of lava and with steps from the west toward the sunrise, which led up to a pebbled platform. They were in the valley where the last Guanche king surrendered to the Spanish after the first voyage by Columbus to America. He was the last of the white and bearded seafarers that were only kept alive in the legends in Mexico and Peru.

Index